DEAD FRIENDS
BY
JASON R. DAVIS

Published by
Jason R. Davis
Weston, WI 54476

Please visit us online at http://jasonrdavis.com

Author website
http://jasonrdavis.com

Edited by 360 Editing (a division of Uncomfortably Dark Horror). Editor: Candace Nola

Cover Illustration by Don Noble

Dedicated to my John Ennenbach
We miss you...

Special Thanks to:
My wife, Patty Davis and my brother Mike Ennenbach
Thank you for your encouragement and support.

Part 1

CHAPTER 1

"This place is a mess."

Lizzie felt her stomach flip as the smell of the room wafted over her. She looked around the front entryway to the cabin and agreed that her best friend was right. This place was a shithole. Sarah had never been one to mince words and was known for being extremely blunt. Which is why when she said this place was a mess, Lizzie had to wonder why she was being so nice.

"Yeah, it sure is."

"And what is that smell? It smells like.... Did your uncle have a cat?"

"I'm not sure. He might have."

"It smells like urine."

"Oh my God, he didn't piss all over the place, did he? If we find piss-stained furniture, I'm gone."

Lizzie took another step into the room, trying not to gag, as the smell was overwhelming. Did her uncle have a cat? The lawyer hadn't said anything, but there really hadn't been too many details. It had been a quick meeting. Her Uncle Tom had passed away and, as his next of kin, she inherited his house and money.

She was surprised when the lawyer had told her just how much money. She didn't know much about her uncle. He had stayed away from her family while she had grown up and her dad had only talked about him in passing here and there, but the stories were always tinged with sadness. She could tell her dad never liked to talk about him, and she had no clue where he had made all his money. From the little she knew of him, she guessed it didn't come from working. He hadn't had a job in over twenty years. So, without working, he had owned a house, a car that he had hardly driven in the past twenty years he had owned it, and nearly half a million dollars.

And now it was all hers. Lizzie still couldn't believe it. As she stepped into what was obviously the living room of the small house, she thought about how she had just gone from almost evicted, because she couldn't pay her rent two months in a row, to having a house and a small fortune. It had come to her as simply as taking that step into this room.

Though looking at the room around her, it was impossible to imagine that someone with all that money lived here. The couch and lounge chair both looked like they were as old as the house and there were clear indentations in the fabric from where he liked to sit. The floor was littered with garbage, wrappers, and discarded boxes, both from microwave dinners and pizza. There was a spot where the tv had once been, but there had been some kind of explosion, and the wall was blackened around the clear rectangle shape, a ghost of what had been there. She guessed that under the piles of newspapers there would be the coffee table, but she was afraid to touch any of it to find out.

"So, how much do you think to have someone come in here and just nuke all this stuff?" Sarah walked up behind her, having checked out the room directly opposite. Sarah was her roommate, though. If Lizzie moved into the house now that she owned it, *a house, she owned a house,* the thought still amazed her, she wasn't sure if Sarah would join her. It wasn't like they would still be living in the city. In fact, it was a forty-minute drive from the city.

It would be rough for her if Sarah didn't move with her. Sarah was like a sister, though she was the blonde opposite to Lizzie's dark auburn locks. Sarah was the beautiful one and Lizzie was the normal bookish one. The Yin to Lizzie's Yang. Lizzie didn't have too many people she could still count on, besides her brother, and it was near impossible to talk to him.

What was she going to do if Sarah stayed in Steven's Point?

"I have no idea." Lizzie said as Sarah stepped around her and over to the table buried in the far corner. Lizzie hadn't noticed it at first due to the mounds of books and papers covering, and nearly burying, the cheap wooden tabletop. How much stuff could her uncle really have? As she approached the far corner; she could tell these papers were different from the rest of the trash. Maybe that's what had caught Sarah's attention.

Sarah picked up the first of the loose, discolored pages and then looked back at her.

"What's all this stuff?"

"No clue." She reached down to another stack of pages and touched it. The paper felt coarse and brittle. She was afraid to pick it up, but it was hard to read even though the words were large. It was all handwritten, but as she scanned the different texts,

5

she could tell the penmanship was that of various authors. Some of it looked like it would be easier to read, pages covered with large block letters, but others were going to be a challenge, those filled with small cursive strokes. One thing the pages had in common: they all looked extremely old.

"Was your uncle into Satanism?"

Lizzie looked over at the page Sarah had in her hand. There was a large six-pointed star with each point touching a surrounding circle and beneath it was drawn a man. The print by the man was very large, making sure there was no doubt when it had been written. The man was meant to be 'the sacrifice.'

Lizzie saw Sarah visibly shudder as she dropped the page back onto the pile, and she shared her friend's disgust. The house alone was disgusting, but even though she had hardly known him, she couldn't imagine her uncle being into something so disturbing.

Just what else were they going to find in the house?

"Let's hope not. I don't want to find some hidden room in the basement where he did all his blood sacrifices," Lizzie said.

"Yuck! Maybe that's where that awful smell is coming from."

"Sarah! You got me worried we're going to find a closet full of dead animals or something."

"Hey, are you going to keep the house or just get rid of it? You have plenty of money now. Why not buy a condo in the city?"

Lizzie thought about that as she stepped around the large La-Z-Boy chair that was in the center of the room. The room was dark, and she hadn't noticed a spot where something had soiled the carpet until she stepped in it. She looked down and saw something dark smearing up around her shoe, and she grimaced. It was so dreary in there. Why did she think she was going to keep the house? Sarah was right, it would be so much easier just to sell the house and then she wouldn't have to worry about losing her roommate.

She made it to the window and pulled the curtains open, hoping that a little light would make the place less depressing. That was a mistake. One tug on the curtain and the curtain rod above split in half, both sides collapsing to the floor in a pile of tattered cloth and dust. She coughed, the dust attacking her lungs, and she had to step back.

The room stayed dark despite the bright sun outside. The windows she had tried to reach were painted black and, in some places, there were boards nailed to the sides.

"Why would your uncle do that?"

"Maybe he was a vampire."

"You think."

Lizzie laughed, "I have no idea. My dad had said he was crazy."

"I am starting to agree with him."

Lizzie went back to the short hallway in the entryway. She couldn't take the cramped room anymore and there was still more of the little cabin to explore. With any luck, the front room was the worst of it. It had to be, right? Since that was the room he had spent the most time in?

After a few deep breaths of clean air, enjoying that they had left the front door open, she went into the other room. It was what many would use for a dining room, though it had shelves built into the walls with fancy plates decorating them, though dust covered any designs. The rest of the room showed no trace of it having been used for dining purposes. The table was missing all the chairs. More papers littered this room, and the table was spilling over with piles of books. Many piles had given up, their contents having collapsed to the floor, covered in dust where they lay.

"Hey you, don't be doing that!" Sarah rushed to join her in the room. Sarah looked at the shelves. "Why did he have those?"

"What? Wait, what did I do?"

"You left me behind. I don't want to be in here alone." Sarah leaned down so she could get a closer look at the plates. "I never took your uncle for the sort to have nice stuff like this."

"He used to be married. Maybe those had been my aunt Cynthia's?"

"Really? Like he had been normal once?"

"I guess." She tried to recall some of the stories her dad had told her about him, but there hadn't been many. "Cynthia had passed away before I was born, and I know it was shortly after that they had gotten rich and stuff. Then he bought this house. I think he bought it for her because it was close to her family."

"So, like, her family lives around here?"

"No clue."

"Huh."

She owned this house now. It was so weird to think about. She had a house, and she had money. She could pay off her car and her student loans. She could even buy a new car; get rid of the cheap piece of junk she was driving... She could get a nice car, something really flashy. After all, she had the money. Why not spend it?

Of course, the lawyer had advised her that some of it would go to taxes and there was some kind of payment she would have to make for getting the inheritance. Still, with all that, she still had more money than she would have made working most of her life.

Now she could have some real fun. She could get rid of this house, or just keep it and buy more houses. Maybe that's what she would do, start buying houses and renting them out. She could become a real estate mogul like Donald Trump. No, not like him. She didn't want to be known for being a douche. Eventually, she'd probably have to kick people out or stuff.

But she could do stuff now. She could really do things! She no longer had to worry about paying her cell phone bill, waiting for it to get turned off before making a payment arrangement to give her a little bit more time to come up with the money. She didn't have to worry about all the bill collectors calling, trying to get the power bill paid. Her cable wouldn't keep getting turned off because she didn't have the money. Hell, she could probably buy the cable company and be done with it.

Okay, so she didn't have quite that much money, but she had a lot. What was she going to do with it all?

It was so odd. When her parents had passed away, they hadn't left her with much. Her dad had been sick for so long and most of their savings had been lost to paying doctor's bills. The house was in foreclosure when her parents died in a car crash, so the bank had taken it. Their life insurance policies had been bare minimum, leftovers from her mom's work, just enough to cover the funeral costs.

It was hard thinking about it. They had been gone a couple years and, as each day passed, she still thought of them. She wanted to call them, tell them about everything that happened in her life, the good and the bad. She craved the sound of her mother's voice, scolding her for spending too much on her latest trip to the bookstore. As much as it hurt when her mother would nag at her, she missed it, knowing that each time her mother came down on her, it was all because she loved her, and was just trying to take care of her the best way she knew how.

Then there was her dad. He had been such a gentle man, a good man who had always been there for her. Even when it would upset her mother, he always had her back. If he happened to visit her in the city and see the moldy, meager state of her fridge, he would sneak her a few hundred bucks. When her power had been cut off because she couldn't afford to pay the bill, he had gone behind her mother's back and paid it.

He had been her keeper, her confidant, her rock. She had always looked up to him. Now, they were both gone, and she was left with this damn house and her uncle's unexplainable money. At least with the money, she wouldn't have to worry about the power bill anymore, but what she really wanted was to have one last phone call with them.

"Hey, I thought Jessica and Dennis were coming? What happened? Dennis couldn't keep his pants on this morning?" Sarah asked on her way through a swinging door on the other side of the room.

"I don't know. They were supposed to show up to meet us, but then Jess called saying they weren't coming. I think Dennis' dad came up."

"Uh-oh, more lectures from Father Tony about the dangers of pre-marital sex." Sarah's voice was muffled as the door swung closed behind her. Sarah never seemed to understand that Lizzie couldn't hear her when she walked away from her. Lizzie could hear the muffled sound of Sarah continuing on as though she could still be heard. But Lizzie didn't need to hear her to know what she was saying. Dennis' father, Father Tony, as they liked to call him, was a pastor who always lectured them all on their choice of lifestyle. Thankfully, he lived hours away, so he didn't come up to visit too often, but when he did, they were all in for a sermon.

"I don't know why he is so hard on them. Everyone knows they are going to tie the knot. They've been together since before Roland and I broke up," Lizzie said. She made sure to talk loud enough for her friend to hear her. She focused on one of the plates; it was different than the others. It had a black tarnish to it, and the gold that ran down the edge seemed to be glowing red. It drew her in, and she couldn't help herself as she neared it and reached out to touch it. The dust hadn't settled on it like it had the others. He must have handled this one more often or actually spent time cleaning it. There was an image on the front, a woman dancing, and as Lizzie stared at it, she could have sworn that the woman was moving in the light, that she was turning.

11

A scream came suddenly from the other room, breaking her out of her reverie. She heard the scream and knew, logically, that it was her best friend. The scream sounded terrifying, but strangely, Lizzie couldn't react appropriately; she felt detached from herself.

It took her a moment to fully pull herself away from the scene on the plate. She shuddered as the world around her snapped back into focus. With a loud popping sound, she was sucked back to reality. The plate fell to the floor and shattered as she turned toward the sound of Sarah screaming.

Then she was running. Quickly, she burst through the swinging door and stopped immediately on the other side, her mind trapping her, unable to comprehend the horror of what she saw.

CHAPTER 2

There stood a skeleton of a man, his skin stretched tight over his bones, making him nearly transparent. He was naked, covered in dirt, and he stood there in the kitchen on the other side of the center island. He was fighting with Sarah. He was pulling at her clothes and when he saw exposed skin, he bit down. Already, her arms were red with blood from where he had taken chunks of her flesh.

Lizzie stood frozen just inside the doorway. She had no clue what she should do. This seemed impossible. They were there to check out the house she had just inherited. There was nothing in the lawyer's description of the place that implied there would be a crazy, naked man attacking them. The house was hidden back in the woods; the home of the reclusive hermit who had once been her uncle. Nowhere in the description was there mention of a crazy man who would want to eat them.

Her mind felt like it was going into overdrive while it detached itself from her body. Why couldn't she move? She stood helplessly watching Sarah's clothes being torn away. Tears streamed down her own face, but she was trapped in her own body, listening to Sarah scream. She couldn't breathe. Her lungs burned. She watched as her body struggled to betray her, as it desired nothing more than to turn around and flee.

Neither Sarah, nor the crazed man, saw her there as both were turned away. Lizzie could simply run right back out the door and leave this craziness behind her. It would be easy. She could run to her car, call the police, and drive away. The realtor and the crazy man could have this place. She would leave and never come back.

Something told her that even if she did leave, there would be no escape from whatever this was. Her mind would always be locked in this room, in this moment, and though she would be away from this place, she would always be there. Someday, she knew she would have to come back. There was no getting away...

Why, and why did it matter now?

It didn't. She had to do something. This man was tearing her friend apart. She had to...what? What could she do?

She looked around the kitchen for anything she could use to fend him off.

The man ripped a large chunk of Sarah's shoulder; the flesh pulling away, stretching before tearing, like paper being pulled apart. Then he turned toward Lizzie. He grinned at her; his teeth covered in blood and sinew, giving her a wide toothed smile that seemed too large for his mouth. He had too many teeth and all of them looked sharper than they should have been. Red drops dripped onto the countertop, and he bent over, licking it up. The gore smeared across the counter and continued to drip from his mouth.

Sarah must have felt the change in his attention and burst into action, attempting to escape. She took three steps before the man's thin arms wrapped around her and pulled her back toward him. He turned to her so that she was facing Lizzie andLizzie could see her friend's blood covered, tear-streaked face. Strands of hair were stuck to it, and there were patches from where he had pulled some out.

Almost as though he could read her thoughts, he reached up and grabbed another handful of hair, pulling back, until it ripped away from the scalp. He licked it as it came free, before stuffing it into his mouth.

"Just let her go," Lizzie squeaked, trying to find her voice.

Sarah cried harder. "Please, just please," she sobbed.

The naked man didn't speak as he kept his gaze on Lizzie, flashing her that large red toothed smile. He stood there, watching her. Sarah struggled to get away, but she couldn't break from his grip. He was stronger than he looked.

"I don't know what to do," Lizzie said as she looked at Sarah, pleading, "Please, let her go."

Sarah shook in his arms, trying to kick her foot back into his exposed testes. He held her tightly and, pulling her in closer to him, forced her off balance. Her knee hit the corner of the counter and before she could register the pain, the naked man pulled Sarah back hard by the hair. She let out an earth-shattering scream as more hair was pulled free and she slipped.

Lizzie watched as her friend started to fall, held by one arm around her chest and another in her long hair. The man grabbed more hair, sensing that she was getting away and both her arms were grabbing at him to push him away.

"Please, let her go," Lizzie said again, her voice trembling with fear. The man kept smiling at her, cackling as he pulled harder, then relaxing his grip as she pulled away. She didn't make it very far, as his grip would tighten and Sarah would get yanked back to him.

Those eyes. That laugh. Lizzie knew she would hear that sickly cackle for the rest of her life, the nightmares, she predicted, would never let her forget it.

The man didn't take his eyes off her, and Lizzie found herself pulled into them. Time slowed. His laugh grew louder and rang through her head like a bell, a church bell chime, with every dong, in time with her heartbeat. One naked man became two as her vision doubled. Yet somehow, she still watched him, the true him, and those hollow, dark recessed eyes.

Time passed, but it was lost on them. He had her as well, but it wasn't in some death grip. He was in her soul, and she could feel the darkness spreading. A chill ran through her as her insides grew cold. It was in her bones, her blood, and it was expanding, getting closer to her heart. It would freeze her completely if she let it.

Another scream rang out. She wasn't sure if it was from her or Sarah, but her vision came back into focus, and she saw them again. The naked man was nodding at her; that smile never disappearing, but he turned from her and looked at the prey in his arms. He licked the blood from his lips and momentarily closed his eyes in relish; his head lifting for a moment as he experienced pure bliss.

Then, in a flash, his eyes were open and alert, and he was studying Sarah.

Lizzie knew she had to do something. But what? What could she do? She could rush him. She realized she had to rush him. That naked, disgusting form had her friend. If she hit him and they toppled over, then she and Sarah could beat him up, or even just run away. They could get out of there.

On some level, that rational brain of hers was trying to convince her that she needed to do it. She needed to attack this man, or she was never going to get her friend back. If she didn't attack, her friend would be gone, probably dead or something worse.

What was worse than death?

She knew what worse was. There was living after life was taken from you. That half-life of existing after something like this defiled you. She knew that. She was studying psychology, after all. She knew what something like this did to the living corpse it left behind.

Why hadn't Sarah and Lizzie taken those rape prevention courses at the 'Y'? They had both talked about it, knowing that it was always a possibility, especially being young girls on a college campus. They lived where every woman needed to be on constant guard for potential sexual assault. Every year, multiple attacks would happen and go unreported. It was believed that colleges were a breeding ground for sexual predators, and Lizzie and Sarah were prime bait.

Why hadn't they gone?

Because there was always another study group to go to, or a drink with a friend to go for. There was always something on the go, and who had time to dedicate to some class at the 'Y.' They could always do it some other time. It wasn't like it was ever going to happen to them.

But now here it was. It was going to happen to them.

The man continued to study Sarah. He had pulled her close and was smelling the hair in his hand, then biting down on it. He noticed that Lizzie was studying him and spit it out to nuzzle up to Sarah's neck and lick the tears that were spilling down her cheeks.

Sarah, with her eyes closed, was whimpering in his grip. She would occasionally twitch, trying to pull away from him, but it was obvious the fight had gone out of her.

The laugh got louder. Lizzie wasn't convinced it even came from the man anymore. It felt like it was echoing inside her head. It seemed misplaced; he was across the room, but she heard his voice so clearly, cackling in her thoughts.

"Please," she whimpered, if only to hear her own voice to try to counteract the sound of his.

The laughing intensified and her forehead throbbed with its rhythm. Stars formed at the edge of her vision, and the pain sharpened as she tried to pull her focus from the naked man to look at her friend.

Sarah was covered in sweat and blood. It had melded together and was running from her scalp, where there were now visible patches of exposed tissue. Her shirt had been torn, and the naked man had exposed one of her breasts. He was grabbing at it violently. There were cuts from his nails where he had squeezed, and more blood smeared her flesh.

We're not going to get out of this alive.

Lizzie felt her legs give out. She lowered herself to the floor and kneeled there, raptured by sobs. She couldn't watch anymore and buried her face in her hands.

Sarah screamed and Lizzie heard her fall. She landed hard and Lizzie heard the 'plop' as flesh limply hit the tile floor. The bastard had probably thrown her down. Lizzie couldn't look to see. Sarah would be on the other side of the kitchen island.

What did it matter? They were both dead. Why did any of it matter anymore?

If she could turn into a puddle of tears and sink into the floor right there, she would. The tears just kept flowing, and she felt her shirt getting damp.

Before she had the chance to lie down and accept her fate, she noticed a shadow looming over her. It must be her turn. He was there for her.

She looked up and there he was. His member dangling between his legs, its thick purple shaft right in her face. She could see where there were cuts along it. Flesh had been torn away in some places, and the meat underneath was exposed. She was surprised that it was brown and ash gray underneath. It was so close to her face, and as disgusting as the torn piece of meat was, she couldn't get past the intense smell of decay that emanated from it.

She didn't want to look at it, but found it impossible to turn away. She finally pulled her eyes from his disgusting member to study the rest of him. She had been terrified by his blood-soaked mouth before, but looking at him from a different angle, having to look up at him, and with how close he stood, she saw more of his decomposed state.

He had scrapes all over his body, some of them still bled. She had originally mistaken the dark splotches all over his body for dirt, but now she could see they were under his skin. It was like some kind of bruising or infection, and they made what was his ash white skin take on an unearthly hue in patches. Maybe it was dirt, but somehow had gotten under his skin? It looked like scales with thin white lines that crisscrossed his skin.

That didn't make sense either...

When people say, 'What kind of rock have you been living under?' they were referring to him. He looked like he had crawled out from under that rock but, while he had been under there, he died, and they forgot to tell him he was dead.

He cackled and reached for her, grabbing her by the back of her head, and pulled her closer to him. She knew what he would want her to do and fought against him, pulling her head back. Again, she was surprised by his strength, this time feeling it for herself. She was unable to break free. The stench grew worse. Rotten meat. The reek of it twisted her stomach, and she could feel vomit inching up the back of her throat.

This couldn't really be happening. But it was. Why was this happening to them?

The tip of his penis twitched.

Oh God, don't let him get hard.

Then she watched as a small white object protruded from the head. It emerged, wiggling back and forth, almost like a finger beckoning her closer. She was already close enough that she could see lines around its body, circular lines, like segments. The part that had first emerged was larger, and she thought she could see an opening. Was that a mouth? *Oh, my Lord, is that...*

Is that a maggot?

She'd never been this close to one in real life, but she was sure it was a maggot. It wriggled its way free and fell onto her chin.

"NO!"

She felt the scream push through her until it exploded from her lungs in a rush. The scream was so powerful it slammed into the man, and the pure intensity made him step back, releasing her as he stumbled.

She snapped.

She didn't think, but went into action. She attacked. She pushed herself up, and in one motion, pushed out with her hands. They connected with his chest, and she felt his sudden shift as he lost his balance. He fell back, and she persisted. He hit the counter, which kept him upright, but he was dazed, stunned by her blow. She followed up with a knee to his groin, and he made an audible gasp as he bent over.

She didn't stop. She put her hands together and brought them down on his back. He fell to his knees, then collapsed to the floor.

Lizzie stood there, watching him. She was panting, not realizing how much effort went into beating someone up, but she had done it. She had stopped him.

She wasn't sure how long she stood there, feeling proud of herself. It was longer than she should have. She knew that much.

Sarah! She needed to check on her!

Lizzie hurried around the counter, hoping to find that her friend was okay. She saw the blood before she came upon her body. It had become a river, flowing through the cracks in the floor, toward the open back door, originating from her friend's head.

Lizzie was sure she would never forget how her hair was all wet and matted in the pool. She couldn't help but think how upset Sarah would be when she saw herself in the mirror. Sarah couldn't go a second without making certain her hair was perfect. There were lumps of it that were drenched with blood that had turned her sunlit rays of blond into dark red mush.

She needed to do Sarah's hair before she woke up. That's what she needed to do.

Lizzie had lowered herself down, keeping her legs together and staying poised like a lady when she looked into Sarah's eyes. They were open, looking off into the distance.

They didn't blink. Not even when a fly landed on one.

Then she noticed that some of the blood was coming out from the side of one of Sarah's eyes. Half her skull was caved in on that side, making her face uneven. It shouldn't be like that. And her mouth... her jaw was ripped away and there were teeth missing... her smile... she was going to be pissed. Sarah was relentless about using teeth whitener, so she had that super sweet, innocent as cherry pie smile that often lured guys in.

She had to get Sarah out of there. She wasn't going to be happy about her new looks, but maybe the doctors could do something to help return her to her perfect form.

Lizzie reached forward and pushed Sarah's shoulder.

"Hey, we gotta get out of here. I need you to get up."

Sarah didn't move. Lizzie thought about trying to nudge her friend again, but she didn't have time. Sarah needed help, but Lizzie didn't think she could carry her. Would she be able to drag her?

So much blood. It was going to get all over her, but what choice did she have?

She reached forward, trying to grab Sarah's shirt, adjusting her balance while also trying not to step in any blood. It was tricky, and she didn't realize, until she tasted the iron in her own mouth, that she was biting her lip.

Sarah's shirt was wet, but Lizzie got a good grip on it and pulled. Sarah's body slid across the floor, streaking through the blood, letting more of it soak into her blouse. As Lizzie moved her across the tile, there was a scraping sound and she tensed at how loud it sounded in the stillness that had descended upon the house, since she had knocked the naked man down.

She stopped. She was losing her balance and feared she would fall on her butt, and then her own jeans would be covered in red.

Damn. Why hadn't Dennis come out to meet them? Sure, Sarah and Lizzie were friends with Jessica, and Dennis was just her boyfriend, but he was useful. When Sarah had needed someone to carry her new mattress up four flights of stairs in her apartment complex, because the elevator was out of order, Dennis had done it. He had complained about the last two flights of stairs, and gotten irritated with their giggles and jibes, but he had done it.

Who else could she ask to help her move a dead body when she needed it?

No! Sarah wasn't dead. She couldn't think that way. She just needed to get her out of there and go for help. She had to get Sarah to the hospital and call the police before the man woke back up. He could regain consciousness at any time, any noise could do it.

She listened to her breathing. It sounded loud and raspy to her. It was deafening. She tried to control it and breathe easier, but her heart was racing. Her body was betraying her. She wanted to keep quiet, as still as the house around her, but every part of her seemed to cry out in betrayal. Her ankle popped as she reached forward to grab Sarah again, and she winced.

She pulled on Sarah again and the scraping sound on the tile screamed through the kitchen. Lizzie looked over at the man, worried he would wake up.

He was staring at her, and that smile had returned to his lips. He was lying there on the ground, watching her. There hadn't been any sign that he had regained consciousness. Had he been watching her this whole time?

"Come on, Sarah!" Lizzie reached forward and pawed for clothing. "I need you to help me here. Get Up!"

Her hands couldn't make purchase, throwing her off balance. She didn't fall back though and was able to push off, standing as she stumbled back until she hit the wall and regained her balance.

24

The man laughed at her; his cackle echoing off the linoleum. She didn't turn to look, to see that blood-red smile, but it didn't help because looking at her friend was almost worse.

Sarah's cold, dead eyes continued to stare at her. Lizzie had never seen a dead person's eyes before. She hadn't thought they would look any different, eyes would look the same whether someone was alive or dead, but she knew that wasn't true. No matter how still someone alive might lie, there was always some movement to their eyes, a twitch or a throb as blood circulated through the corneas.

Only the dead remained still. And Sarah wasn't moving.

Lizzie heard something sliding on the floor. She didn't turn to look. She knew the man was pulling himself towards her. The image of his blood-filled mouth, the maggot that had slithered from the tip of his penis, all of it was burned deep into her memory. Another look in his direction would only be more nightmare fuel.

Instead, she turned away from the man, away from her friend, and ran out the kitchen door.

CHAPTER 3

Lizzie rushed through the open door and burst into the daylight. The fresh air should have been a relief compared to the stench and horrors inside the little cottage, but the world fell away with her first step of freedom. She pitched forward and landed on the hard-packed earth of the backyard.

She hurt, and the fall had forced the breath from her lungs. She struggled to get turned over. Her hands burned, scraped on the way down, and now what the hell was all of this? Everywhere she turned, there was green. The grass was tall, surrounding her, and it was loud with...life.

Lizzie couldn't see anything, but she heard it. The ground around her was alive with motion. She listened as things moved through the grass. There was the bounce of harmless animals as they scurried away, but there were other things, things that she could hear slithering, and those noises... They sounded like creatures coming towards her.

Her heart beat loudly in her chest, pounding out a scream that told her to get up and get the hell out of there. She felt its pulse in her ears as it throbbed. She was trying to hold her breath to hear what was coming towards her, but it was impossible. Her lungs burned, and she breathed harder in her attempt to fight it.

The slithering stopped. It had to be a snake, right? Logically, it had to be, but what if it wasn't? What if it was the old man? Had he followed her? Was he slithering his way towards her, pulling himself on his stomach, scraping that exposed penis across the ground?

She needed to get up, to run away. Snakes were more afraid of her than she was of them, right? Or was that spiders?

She twisted herself around and pushed herself up. Her hand touched the ground when something long, with a lot of legs, crawled over it. Her hand shot back in the air as she recoiled, looking at the place she had touched.

What was that?

She felt the wetness return to the corner of her eyes.

No! No more tears. I just need to get out of here. I can't cry. Come on, we can do this.

She pushed herself up and started to stand. Pain shot up from her ankle. Damn, she must have twisted it on her way down, but at least the pain was bearable. She had to get out of there and then she could focus on any injuries. She needed to get to the road, find a phone, call for help.

She took a tentative step and her ankle threatened to give out. She took another step. She could walk. She had to walk, because if she didn't...

Behind her, that cackling laugh floated out into the woods, echoing into a cacophony of noise around her. Leaves fell and birds flew to escape. It reverberated through her head like firecrackers going off behind her eyes and stars flashed in her vision. She heard trees splintering, their bark falling, exposing the cracks beneath, and inside, her heart sank.

Before turning around, Lizzie knew what she would see. She wanted to stop herself, but couldn't. She turned and there he was, standing in the doorway, arms outstretched and grasping both sides of the door frame. He looked like he was preparing to launch himself at her.

Those long talon-like nails, each hand a claw, holding the door frame. The wood creaked under the pressure of his grasp. He was rocking back and forth, each motion preparing to expel him from the house towards her. Those black, soulless eyes were fixed on her, the smile permeated her brain. She refused to look at his smile. She wanted to close her eyes to avoid it, but she knew, in the pit of her stomach, that the moment she did, he would be on top of her.

It was no longer a question of if she could walk. Now she had to run, and she tried. Her first step, the snake that had been slithering near her, wheeled up and launched at her and she felt it before she saw it. Fire exploded in her leg and her body no longer supported her weight. The grass again rose up to meet her and it forced all the air out of her.

She was confused as the world swayed back and forth. No, wait, that was her. She shook her head back and forth. It hurt. All of her hurt, her leg especially. She felt the fire fade and part of her leg started to go numb. That was good.

Was she going into shock?

She wasn't hurt so that must be it, but how could she be going into shock?

She wasn't sure, but as the world around her swam, she had two reoccurring thoughts. The first was how all around her, nothing seemed real. It was like a picture show, and she was watching it through some kind of monitor. It couldn't be real. Her friends didn't die in real life. In real life, she wouldn't be in the woods lying on the ground after having been bitten by a snake.

I hope that snake wasn't poisonous. She had no idea what kind of snakes were in these woods, but even if she did, she hadn't seen enough of it to know what kind of snake it was. It had been a vicious bugger, that's for sure.

The other thought that kept fighting to press in on her was the need to escape. It wasn't safe for her to be lying on the ground like this.

Of course, it isn't safe. I've just been bitten by a snake and my friend is dead just inside the house. The thing that killed Sarah was right there, and if she didn't get moving, she would be next.

She knew she had to flee, but she couldn't gather the gumption to do anything about it. She just wanted to lie there and wait for whatever happened. Maybe some young, dashing prince charming would show up to rescue her.

She's seen way too many fairy tales. Which might be the case, but she couldn't shake the thought that someone would show up in the nick of time and save her. That was how the stories always went, wasn't it?

But this isn't a fairy tale, and you're not a princess. A voice rang in her head, telling her to get up, get out of there, find some semblance of survival instincts and run, you stupid, stupid girl. If she didn't run, someone would find her there, but they would find her dead. She would be a corpse to be buried and when they put her in her grave, her tombstone would read:

Elizabeth Rogers
She died because she was too damn
lazy to get up and save herself.

And it would be true, because she lay on the ground, feeling the numbness feeding on her as it pushed away all her senses.
What did any of it matter?
Her life mattered.
There was a loud crashing sound as something large hit the ground.
It was him. He was coming after her and wouldn't be far. He would be on top of her, and then what was he going to do?
Maggots. Maggots filling her, eating her from the inside out, that smiling face over her, those red teeth, sharp as they tore into her. She knew exactly what he was going to do with her.
Her mind hadn't fully grasped what she needed to do yet, but somewhere, something inside her woke up. Through some core survival instinct, she was pulling herself away from the house before she realized she had moved.
It was like her mind pulled her out of a dark haze, aware of the world again. She was on her elbows, walking herself backward. She kicked herself back, not sure where the snake had gone, and worried it would return.
She felt the fire return to her leg, throbbing, but the pain felt good. The pain helped push away some

of the cobwebs that kept threatening to reweave themselves through her thoughts.

Run, damn you! The thought screamed through her mind. She couldn't backpedal like this through the woods. She would never get anywhere. She had to get up and get the hell out of there. She needed to leave this house once and for all.

Something thrashed behind her, and she couldn't help herself; she looked up at the house. The naked man was no longer in the doorframe, but he wasn't running after her either. He had fallen out as she had and fought to get himself on all fours. He watched her. She couldn't see his whole face, his mouth was hidden by the tall grass, but those eyes tracked her movement.

She didn't need to see the mouth. She knew the smile was there.

Around her, the woods grew dark. A chill ran down her spine, and she couldn't stop the shiver that touched her soul. There was something else watching her. Something far worse than the naked man.

She looked into the woods. It stood just inside the tree line. It was the shape of a tall man, but she knew it was something else. It was evil, darkness, the absence of life, swirling inside the shadow of a man, leering at her from behind a large, gnarled tree.

She wasn't sure how she stood, but she found herself running away from the house and the thing in the woods. She ran to the woods across the clearing and fought through branches that reached out, grabbing at her. They slapped her face and arms. Occasionally, one would scrape across her leg, and she would bite down on her lip, pushing away the agonizing scream that threatened.

She wasn't sure how far she ran, or if the naked man, or the death shadow, still followed her. But as she got away from the clearing, the sky had lightened, and she could see the sun again. She was out of breath, her whole leg was ablaze, she had to pee, and tears rolled down her cheek. She cried from the pain, the death of her friend, everything rolled together in an unmeasurable mess of emotion.

She ran as far as she could until her legs couldn't hold her weight anymore and she collapsed against the closest tree. Her breath was coming in harsh rasping gasps, the air around her was thick with those white fluffy things she had chased as a kid, and they were getting in her lungs. So much life around her and it was killing her.

Cottonwood. They were seeds from a cottonwood tree. She didn't know how she knew that, but it was true. The seeds were drifting around her. It was almost picturesque; they were so white and light and seemed to glow in the shifting sunlight as they drifted around her.

There really were a lot of them.

The airborne fluff continued to fall. It grew thicker. All around her was a blanket of white cottonwood and had it not been late summer, she would have thought it was a thick winter snowfall.

She found it hard to focus. Her breathing came out in shorter gasps. Why was she trying to run? It was so nice out here, and it was the perfect place to just lie down and take a nap. It was peaceful. Why not enjoy it? *I could make a snow angel.* It was so beautiful.

The ground looked soft. It looked like snow, but she imagined how comfortable it would be to lie down in all that cotton.

Is this where cotton comes from?

No, it couldn't be, and that didn't seem right, but it was so soft. A piece landed on her hand, and she felt its delicate lightness. It danced in front of her as she watched it fluttering in the wind.

It was entrancing. She focused solely on the little flake on her hand. It flowed back and forth, moving to its own rhythm to music only it could hear.

She didn't blink.

She barely breathed.

Everything became that little fluff of cottonwood seed. The world around her at first became white from the falling seeds, then grew darker as so many of them fell that the sun was blanked out.

Nothing else mattered.

She barely breathed. The world around her swayed back and forth. No, that wasn't right. She swayed though the earth around her was still and inviting.

Laughter boomed through the surrounding trees, and the vibration rumbled through her entire body. It wasn't the cackle of the naked man. This was a laugh so rich and deep, that it felt to her as though it could crack open the earth and move mountains. This felt like the laugh of a god, and it pulled her from the trance she had fallen into.

She fell forward onto her hands and knees, gasping hard and coughing.

"tik-a-tok, tik-a-tee, you are dying, on your knees," a voice chimed around her, coming from everywhere and speaking in a singsong manner that swam

34

through Lizzie's head. She heard it but couldn't concentrate on it. Was it a man, a woman? She didn't know, but it was strong.

"tik-a-too, tik-a-tee, you are young, too young for me. tik-a-too, tik-a-tet, you will die, but not die yet."

Lizzie took in a deep gush of breath and then coughed one hard and final time. A large clump of the white fluff landed with a wet plop onto the ground, and she could breathe again. She didn't take her eyes from it as it wriggled, and she was reminded of the maggot that slithered out-

No, she didn't want to think about it, but she couldn't stop herself. That mental image would stay with her forever.

The woods around her faded, going dark. She looked up to see the trees had disappeared, and a man stood over her. As close as he was, she still couldn't make out any details. Even in this, absent of light, he stood in the shadows, yet she saw him clearly. It hurt her head to look at him.

"tik-a-tee, tik-a-too, devily dee, devily do. tik-a-too, tik-a-tay, your time will come, just not today. You have much to do, you have much to say," he spoke in that sing-song cadence, but it was far from song. The voice became rough like sandpaper, and it gritted as he spoke. He talked slowly, almost like a cowboy out of an old western, but that didn't fit with the accent. She could hear a trace of one, but wasn't sure from where she recognized it.

It was difficult to listen, and she didn't want to hear his words. That stupid rhyming made everything he said sound like kid speak, like garbled noise.

As she looked away, finding the fluff covered ground hard to look at as it glowed white in the darkness with its own light. It hurt her eyes, but she would gladly burn her eyes out to keep from looking back up at the man, who was not a man, the darkness that was not darkness, that hovered above her.

The thing must have sensed her discomfort, and it uttered a long, loud howl that dwindled into a laugh. She didn't have to look up to know he was gone. The fluff around her faded, and she felt the warmth of the sun on her skin. The hot suffocating wind was a welcome sensation as it moved around her, and the cotton fluff danced upon it once more.

She could breathe properly again, and she pulled in large gulps of air. She had escaped the house, escaped the naked man, and had survived some kind of woods demon she had no way of explaining. Now she was alone in the woods. She had to find the road and get help.

Then, that mad cackling echoed in the woods around her, booming off the trees surrounding her. She didn't have to turn to know the naked man was behind her. She was surprised to see that she had barely made it out of the clearing behind the house, and he stood there in the tall grass.

His appendage wagged between his legs, and that grin with those dark eyes locked on her. How could he stand there with his bare feet? She had crawled on her hands and knees, and she felt every cut and scrape. He stood there with no problem, no sign of any pain, just that tooth-filled grin.

The man ran towards her, and she stepped back, turning to run away, and she hit the tree she had been leaning on. She fell back, twisting awkwardly as she did and landed on her butt, but she didn't stop.

She continued to backpedal quickly, watching as the man neared her. He ran faster on his bare feet than she could move spider-crawling backwards.

He came to the edge of the clearing and stopped, not entering the woods. Lizzie didn't stop. She kept going; she needed to get away from that smile and those eyes.

A moment later, she was surprised to find herself on the road. It should have taken longer to reach it; something wasn't right. She must not have realized how long she had back peddled. She never looked away from the naked man as he stood stopped in the yard. *Oh no, never take your eyes off the devil or you become his,* her grandmother would say.

She barely heard the blast of horn as the man's cackle all but consumed her. So loud this time, she was sure her ears bled as it reverberated through her core, sending her into convulsions.

The last thing she remembered before she passed out was the feeling of hard, hot cement beneath her and a dark shape standing over her.

"Are you okay?" A woman's voice asked, but Lizzie couldn't answer, as she was already gone. She drifted off, the cackling laugh following her into unconsciousness.

CHAPTER 4

Beep...
Beep beep...
Beep...
Beep beep...
Tik...
Tik-a-too...
Tik...
Tik-a-tok...

Lizzie's eyes shot open; a scream caught in her chest that never made it past her lips. She wanted to scream forever into the darkness, but something was wrong. She held it in, and it burned her lungs like a fire storming inside her.

It was dark. Wherever she was, it was dark, but she wasn't completely blind. There was light coming from somewhere, and she was looking up at the ceiling tile. Her neck was stiff, her body sore. She didn't move, and her eyes struggled to stay open.

She felt a chill that went deep into her bones, and she shivered uncontrollably.

She tried to focus on the light, to keep her eyes open. It appeared to be coming from outside the room and illuminated just enough around her to allow her to see the walls.

Walls of a room that trapped her. They were white, and she was flooded with a sense of familiarity. She didn't know what time it was, though it felt like nighttime...

Wait...it was the house. She was back at the house. The naked man or the tik-tok man from the woods must have dragged her back here and now they were going to...

To what?

Was she tied up?

She wasn't sure. When she tried to move, the room spun around her. The ground seemed to shake. Was it an earthquake?

A loud laugh started somewhere deep in the darkness, then turned into cackling. The room echoed with it. She saw cracks forming across the ceiling and heard more racing along the tile on the floor. Dust started sprinkling down around her like snow...Snow... White fluff... Her chest grew tighter as a flash of the woods came back to her and the fluffy cottonwood seeds filled the room around her. Was this a nightmare? Or had she never escaped? She was going to die.

The tears came back to her, and she felt herself thrashing, fighting back, but it was as if she floated a million miles away, separated from her body.

She heard a woman's voice nearby. "Calm down. It's going to be okay." Lizzie tried to focus on the sound, to reach out to the voice. Was it an angel who came to rescue her? Finally, she was saved.

She focused on her heartbeat, shaking her chest. It was pounding so loudly that it throbbed in her ears. Still, she could hear the angelic voice and she felt wetness at the corner of her eyes, though she didn't know why she was crying.

"Just lie back down. Everything's okay. You're safe now. You're safe," the voice told her. And she felt safe. The voice reached her, relaxing her, pushing her back down on the bed. She hadn't realized she had arched her back up off the bed as she focused on the ceiling.

Light flooded the room, and she suddenly saw where she was. The beeping equipment, the wall mounted TV and a little wooden cabinet on the other side of the room made the hospital room unmistakable. She thought she smelled the faint odor of anesthetic, but it was hard to over her own stench. She stunk of old sweat.

How long had she been out? Had she been in a coma? Her muscles were sore, but she didn't feel weak. She wouldn't have energy if she'd been in a coma, right? That's what she thought, but she wasn't sure.

"Come on, girl, just breathe. Deep breaths."

Lizzie felt something touch her shoulder, and she jumped, her scared eyes shooting in the direction of the touch. There stood the owner of the voice, and Lizzie looked at her with eyes wide open. Another scream held at the tip of her tongue.

A large black woman looked at Lizzie with so much heartwarming compassion and sadness that Lizzie felt like she could trust her, but how could she trust anyone? She reacted in a panic, recoiling away from the kind-faced woman, trying to get as far away as possible. She felt the bed rock and thought it might tip. The need to escape flooded her again.

The nurse reached out and grabbed both of her shoulders, keeping her eyes locked on Lizzie. As she did, another woman rushed into the room and secured Lizzie's legs, rendering her helpless. She fell flat back onto the bed.

No, I am not going to be helpless! Not ever again! She thrashed.

"It's okay. You are okay. You are okay. We need you to relax. Everything is okay."

The woman's mouth was moving. Lizzie could hear the words, but they just didn't make sense. There was a wall inside her mind, and all she heard was that cackling. It had stayed in the room after the darkness left, and she could hear it echoing along the undercurrent. It reverberated around her. It was a part of her, inside her and it just made...her...want...to...*SCREAM!*

It finally erupted. The scream billowed out, shattering the glass. She didn't know where it came from, but she was now in a rainfall of tiny shards that glistened in the fluorescent light.

A man emerged from behind the curtain. A curtain? She hadn't noticed that before, but one whole wall of her room was just a curtain. Beyond that was a lighted hallway she could only catch a glimpse of before the curtain fell back into place.

"What's going on?" The man asked with an air of authority. She guessed he was a doctor. He entered the room fully. *Is it really a room if it only has three walls?*

"She woke up and immediately went into hysterics," said the short, stout woman wearing flowered scrubs. She wore glasses and her silver hair was pulled back into a tight ponytail. She didn't look old, though. Her face was young, ageless even, and Lizzie felt so confused as she studied the woman's rosy cheeks.

"This the woman they found in the woods?"

The silver-haired woman nodded.

"Okay, let her go," the doctor said as he stepped closer to the bed. He held his hands up, showing there was nothing in them. He was moving slowly and kept his eyes locked on hers. "You are going to be okay," he said soothingly as he approached.

The woman at the end of the bed let Lizzie's legs go and took a tentative step back. The two shared a skeptical glance, neither one trusting the other. Then Lizzie felt the pressure relax on her shoulders and turned to see the first woman straightening.

The kind nurse didn't step back. She stayed there, looking down at Lizzie with a deep sadness. Lizzie could see the winkles creasing her gentle face and felt a fond affection for the woman. Something about her was like that of a grandmother. It wasn't of her own grandma, but there was that quality all grandmothers had in how she looked at her. She pictured Mrs. Brady from that old TV show. The one with all the sisters and brothers. Mrs. Brady hadn't been a grandmother, but she should have been, as she had that same kindness. It made Lizzie want to reach up and give the woman a hug.

"Did we get any identification?" The doctor asked the nurse as he stood next to her, the pair looking down at Lizzie.

"No, she didn't have anything on her when they brought her in, and this is the first time she has regained consciousness."

"Hi, my name is Doctor Everson," he directed at Lizzie, as he eased closer to her, bending down. She was sure she could see he had something in his hand. It was long and she could see the glint of metal. "Can you tell me what your name is?"

His voice was smooth, and it calmed her frayed nerves. He was a doctor. He was a good guy, the white hat from westerns, or maybe her Prince Charming. No, doctors didn't do the saving. Well, she guessed they actually did do the saving, but they weren't the rescuers that pulled you from a burning building. This man was just going to look her over and make sure she was okay. She needed to trust him; she knew that.

He still had something metal hidden in his hand. What was he hiding from her?

And why were they asking for her name? Hadn't the nurse called her by name when she had first woken up?

Lizzie's head spun, and she struggled to concentrate. None of this made sense. She needed to talk, and realized the doctor was waiting for her to answer, hovering over her but not moving any closer. It was like the world was hanging, waiting for her response and everyone was watching her.

"Lizzie," she said, to break the stillness, and it proved harder than she would have thought. Her throat was dry, and it came out as a raspy breath. It sent her into a flurry of dry coughs, and she thought one of them would come to rub her back or offer her water. Instead, they stood there, statues afraid to come any closer.

"Okay, Lizzie. Is that short for something?"

She wanted to reply, but feared it would send her into another coughing fit. She wished she could write it down but didn't see a pen or paper.

"Elizabeth. Elizabeth Rogers."

"Okay Lizzie, is there any family I should call?"

"Rolan-" She didn't finish. She knew that wasn't right, and it took her a minute before she remembered that she had broken up with Roland. That had been over a month ago. Who could they call? Other than her brother, who did she have now?

She really didn't want to make Brian upset, and there was nothing he could do for her, so why bother calling him? She was pretty good at avoiding him and didn't want to change that now. Especially not for this.

Sarah would have been the one to call. Her friend until the end, the girl she had grown up with and was like a sister to her. The girl whose dead, glassy eyes kept looking back at her every time she closed her eyes.

The three others in the room were watching her and the doctor was saying something...

"Roland who? Can I get a last name?"

"Never mind him," she said as she tried to wiggle herself up in the bed. She wanted to sit up but didn't trust herself yet. The world still threatened to do some more spinning. "Can I get some water?"

"Sure. Nurse?" The doctor looked at the one who was standing at the foot of her bed. The nurse pursed her lips but nodded and turned to the first cabinet on the right. She scanned her ID card into a panel to the side and it popped open. Lizzie couldn't see what was inside of it, but she saw the large hospital cup the woman pulled out and then went to a sink to her left that Lizzie hadn't noticed before.

"Lizzie, is there anyone we can call tik-a-too?" She heard the doctor say and her head snapped towards him, her shoulders tensing.

"Where's Sarah?"

"Lizzie, I need you to stay calm," he said in that milk chocolate tone of voice that made her want to melt, but it was too late for melting. She had heard it. He must be one of them.

"Who's Sarah tik-a-too?" the black nurse asked. She had a notepad and was taking notes.

They were all with him, the tik tok man from the woods. What were they going to do to her? She thought again about that glint of metal. Oh *no, they were going to cut her throat. They're going to kill me!*

She tried to see what he had done with it, but he had positioned his hand so it was obscured from her view, hidden behind his body.

"Lizzie, come on Lizzie. I need you to focus and stay calm. Who can we call? Who should know that you're here in the hospital?"

I'm not in any hospital. It may look like a hospital, but these people want to cut me open. They're going to slice me up like they opened up Sarah. They want to know who they can call so I can give them more people to kill.

She shook her head. At first it was a simple back and forth, signaling her refusal, but as she again worked to pull herself up in the bed, it grew more furious.

"She's having a seizure!" someone called out. Lizzie clawed at the bed, trying to pull at anything that would give her leverage.

Arms pressed down on her shoulder, and someone grabbed her head. She closed her eyes, refusing to see the knife coming at her. That must have been what was in his hand. Though doctors didn't call them knives. They were scalpels, and they were even sharper than knives. They were razors that could slice through her flesh with barely any pressure. He was bringing it down on her; she knew it. It was coming for her eyes. It was always about the eyes. They were the windows to the soul, and they wanted to look inside of her.

No, they wanted her soul.

Here it comes.

Light blossomed around her. Everything turned pink as the light pushed in on her closed eyes. Then her eyes were forced open, and she saw the light that pointed straight at her, blinding her as it hovered there.

Then it turned off, and she saw through the circles of light that clouded her vision. The doctor straightened and said, "She might have hit her head harder than the EMTs thought."

"We don't know what she's been through. She was beaten up pretty bad when they brought her in. It looked like she'd been attacked," the nurse who had gone for the water said. She held the large jug in her hand and was standing across from the doctor on the other side of the bed.

"Attacked? Here, in the woods? That's unlikely."

"Maybe."

"Okay, well, get her name to Lowe. He'll want an update, and if she was attacked, he'll need to start an investigation, I guess." This the doctor said to the

47

black nurse, who took down the notes, then nodded and left.

This was getting really frustrating. They were talking about her like she wasn't even there. What was she, some lab animal, waiting to be dissected? *Don't worry about that right now.* She thought as she realized she needed to get away from them. They were with him. She was sure that as soon as she let her guard down, they were going to strike. So, she couldn't allow her guard to fall. No matter what, she had to stay alert to what they were up to.

"Drink this...it's poison." She heard the nurse say, though it sounded more like she had hissed out the last part. Lizzie turned to see that the woman's face had become that of a snake, its tongue flicking out as she held the large cup out to her. "Drinksssss."

"Get away from me," Lizzie said. She reached up and grabbed the cup from the thing's hand. It wasn't even a hand, not anymore. It had become a viscous claw, its talons extending around the cup, and Lizzie could see where they dug into the plastic. She grabbed the cup and, tearing off the top, flung its contents at the thing's face. The water hit the serpent nurse, and she stumbled back, sputtering from the sudden display.

The nurse took the hint and stayed back, but the hairs on the back of Lizzie's neck rose. She turned just in time to see the doctor moving towards her, presumably to push her back down. All he would have to do was get her down flat and then the other one would be back to strap her down.

"No! Get away!"

"Lizzie, calm down," the doctor was repeating, his smooth voice tinged with sternness. He was getting frustrated. Well, that was too bad. She was not going to make this easy for them. Her friend had died because she had made it too easy. She was done making it easy. If they wanted to hurt her, they were going to have to fight for it.

He reached out to push her down onto the bed, and she pushed his arms away. She didn't hold back. As she grabbed his arms, she dug in her nails into his flesh and twisted.

"Ugh," the doctor cried out, stumbling back in pain and confusion. "Lizzie, you have to let us help you."

The room started to shake around her. The cackling grew stronger inside her head and in the back of her mind, she heard the shadow man chanting. "tik-a-tak, tik-a-too, boo, boo, boo..." The cacophony of sound grew more persistent as it bounced around her brain. It brought tears to her eyes as it pushed its way through, and it hurt. When she fought against it, lightning bolts struck behind her eyes.

"Get...sedative...dy," she heard the doctor saying, but it was hard to hear him outside her mind, as the voice in her head grew stronger.

"Li...This wi...ck...you...lit...ile," the doctor said. She only caught pieces of it, but thought again about that metal object he had in his hand. She caught a glimpse of what he was holding. It was a long tube with a sharp point. A needle. They were going to try to poison her again. They were...

"Okay, it's inssss."

Lizzie spun her head to see the nurse standing near an IV drip. She had a needle inserted into a piece of plastic connected to it. She pulled out the needle and looked at her, a smile at the corner of her snake-like mouth. Its tongue flicked in and out. Then its mouth opened, and Lizzie watched as long fangs flicked out as the snake thing prepared to attack.

They were going to poison her with snake venom. It would look like a natural death, death by snake.

But why would that matter?

She had no clue. *What did any of it matter anymore? Who cared about any of it?*

She did... Wait, what was happening to her? This wasn't right. She was upset. She needed to fight back, but found that she couldn't move.

They had done it. They had poisoned her, after all. The needle, the IV.

She looked down at her hands. On her left hand, she saw the IV was running into her. They had slipped it to her that way. She hadn't needed to watch out for the doctor.

Damn, how could I have been so stupid?

She felt herself slipping away. It would be the last time. She was going to die. Damn, she was too young for this. She hadn't traveled enough. She should have traveled more. Gone to England and gotten laid by some hot Englishman or checked out China and visited the great wall.

She wouldn't be doing any of that now.

The sedative did its job, and Lizzie faded off to sleep. As she drifted off, she could barely make out what the two were saying.

"...she be okay?"

"...been through a lot, b...be okay."

Then the darkness took her, and she slipped away...

CHAPTER 5

The next time she woke up, her head felt heavy, her mouth felt like it was full of cotton and her wrists... She could feel there was something soft but tight fastened around them. Restraints. She pulled on them.

Why was she tied down?

Her head hurt. She tried to think, but everything was blurry and slow, and... dark.

She tried looking around the room, blinking away the fog from her eyes. She could vaguely make out shapes. A round object on the wall, a rectangle that glowed in front of her with fuzzy things moving around in it.

She looked away from it. Trying to focus on the glowing box only made her head hurt more. She turned towards the window and realized she hadn't fully looked at the room before. The memories of her last stint with consciousness were becoming less hazy. She vaguely remembered being awake with people that had stood over her, snake people that had been trying to poison her, to eat her. That didn't seem right, but she couldn't shake the image of large fangs coming at her, a mouth with a forked tongue flicking from between its lips.

She focused, trying to remember what really happened, but couldn't shake the image of those large fangs, of feeling them stabbing into her shoulder. She wanted to remember more, but it wasn't coming to her. Something was blocking her memory. It probably had to do with whatever the IV drip was running into her arm, but she felt like she would never fully remember everything from before. It was too much like a dream, and dreams only faded over time.

Slowly, she scanned more of the room, making sure not to move too quickly. Her brain felt detached from her skull and any sudden movement, she was sure, would result in one of her migraines. She was obviously in a hospital room, and in a bed that kept her head elevated. She thought they were called gurneys, but not sure if that was just something out of a Tv show, or if they were actually called that. To her left, there was a C-shaped stand that was positioned on wheels and stretched over the top so that she could eat when served. Currently, it was positioned behind the tall metal IV stand. Next to that was some kind of machine that had scraggly lines and numbers that changed every so often. It was past these machines that she could look out the window.

She couldn't see the ground outside, but she did see the top of a streetlight. It shone bright in the dark sky, and past it she could just make out the lightly clouded sky and the stars. They shined brightly, and she took comfort in seeing them because if the stars were out, then it wasn't a sun hidden day.

Had she really been afraid of that? To her surprise, she actually had been. Though if the sun was gone, wouldn't she still be able to see the stars during the day? She'd seen a solar eclipse once, and when the sun was covered, the stars were able to be seen, so it was possible.

She pushed the thought down and took her time to study the cabinet that was in the corner, to the side of the window and next to the little bench that was on the far wall. Why was she so drawn to it? It was a standard wooden cabinet, though taller than anything she had ever seen before. This one was tall enough to stand from floor to ceiling, and she couldn't help but wonder how they got it into the room. It looked like it extended into the panel tiles. What was in it? What did they need to hide that was so large?

Above the bench and suspended from the wall, was the large tv. She debated turning up the volume, not really sure what she would watch in the middle of the night, but it would be noise in the too quiet room. Since she'd been up, she'd not even heard any signs of life from outside the room, or much else for that matter. The only thing she heard was the occasional rhythmic beep from the machine. The television stayed muted. She saw the remote on the desk across the room, and she wasn't sure if she could reach it with the IV still attached to her arm.

Not like you could if you wanted to. You know you're still restrained. You won't be going anywhere until the doctor comes back and you can get your hands freed. She thought to herself, that inner voice speaking to her, and it was right. There was no way she could do anything.

To the right of the desk was another cabinet. This one wasn't as high, but it was wider. Past it, to her right, was a light blue curtain that looked like it ran on a track around her bed. It must be there for her privacy when she needed to change, though she would have preferred just to have a door on her room.

Which was what truly frustrated her about the room, or more adequately described, her large cubby hole put off to the side. She had no door. She had no fourth wall. Where the wall on her right side should be was one long curtain. It ran the length of where the fourth wall should be. It didn't stretch fully to the floor, so under it, she could see the slight glow from the hallway beyond.

Behind the bed, to her right, were more gadgets hooked up to her. *I mean, Christ, with how much crap was connected to me, you would think they needed to jumpstart me like a car. I'm not on life support, so what the hell is all this garbage?*

Her head was clearing. She hadn't realized it at first, but it felt like forever since she could properly focus. Her memories were coming back, but they were distorted and none of them made sense. It was like a dream that wasn't a dream, or something that was real that should have been a dream. That just about summed up her whole day (*had it been more than a day?*) but in that sense, it was a nightmare, one that wouldn't end.

Had there been something about one of her nurses being a snake that was going to poison her? Oh god, she hoped she hadn't actually hit her doctor, though it did explain the restraints.

She slammed her head back into her pillow, trying to hide from the empty room, so embarrassed that she never wanted to see another living soul. She had, hadn't she? She had hit her doctor and who knows who else. She was pretty sure she had been thrashing around for a while. Anyone could have been caught with a loose fist.

Someone should have gone ahead and hit me back. I deserved it. But of course, none of them had hit her back, not physically. She wasn't sure what kind of sedative they had given her, but it had done its job.

They had been asking her questions, though, before she had freaked out. She was pretty sure she had mentioned Roland, but what else had she said? Another wave of embarrassment hit her. Had they called him? Great, what would he be thinking? He already thought of her as an emotional flake who found any reason to go nuts. What would he think if the doctor mentioned something about her episode? Of course, he would never come visit her, but the story would be spread amongst their friends by the time she got home. It would be years before she would ever live it down.

What if she had told them about her brother? That... Now, that would be worse. There would be no way he could get there to visit her, he would be trapped in Madison worrying about her. She would need to call him and let him know she was okay.

She should call him, just in case they had called... But it was the middle of the night. Even if they had called him and he had stayed up late fretting about her, he would be asleep now. Worry only lasted so long before exhaustion took its toll.

Where was her phone?

She looked around the little room and didn't see it. Maybe it was with her clothes, wherever those were... She wasn't sure. Maybe that was the purpose of one of the cabinets across the room. Probably...though she wished they would have left her phone close by so she could use it.

She lay back in bed.

What was she going to do? She was up now and didn't feel tired at all. The bed was getting uncomfortable, and she wished she could at least lower the back portion and turn on her side. The restraints made any movement impossible. She was going to lie on her back, whether she liked it or not.

"Hello," she said into the dark room. Her voice was timid and cracked. She hadn't realized just how thirsty she was, her cotton mouth more noticeable as she spoke. She swallowed saliva a few times, though there was not much to work with, before she tried again, this time a little louder into the quiet.

"Hello? Anyone out there?"

She waited. She didn't hear any kind of a response and she had a sudden, scary thought. What if she was alone? What if no one was out there manning the nurses' station? What if she wasn't even near a nurse's station? Would she just have to lie there until someone finally checked on her?

The thought of spending the next few hours lying in the bed, waiting for someone to finally pull back the curtain and slip into her little space, was torturous. Could she really last that long? No tv, no internet, no phone.

She continued to listen. The only sound she heard was her own breathing, which grew louder the more anxious she became, and the machine that kept a constant beep next to her.

How did they ever expect anyone to sleep in here with that damn machine beeping all night? *Yeah, well, people didn't go to hospitals to sleep, they went there to get better.* If she wanted to sleep, she should dig herself a grave. Wasn't that the old adage? She didn't think she had it right, but her mind was still working through the haze of the meds.

The sedatives.

The drugs. They had drugged her. How could they drug her and knock her out like that?

Wasn't there supposed to be one of those call buttons at the ready? Something she could use to page the nurses. There was something on the side of her bed. It was a small box connected by a cord that ran below the bed. It had a few buttons on it, but she couldn't say for sure what any of them were, as the pictures on each button had been worn off by use.

She could just start pressing buttons at random if she could reach it. She tried to grab at it, but the restraint was just tight enough that she couldn't grasp the dangling box.

"Ugh!" the cry escaped her in frustration as she slammed herself back onto the bed. "Hello!"

"Hello!" she called again; this time louder as she grew more confident in her voice. She was still so thirsty, but her throat didn't feel as restricted as before.

Being awake must be helping, she thought as she lifted her head again, cocking it to hear better. She thought she heard the sound of a chair creaking out in the hallway. Was she by a nursing station, after all? Could they hear her? Maybe that last time had been loud enough.

There it was again, another creak. Then the definite sound of someone shifting their weight to stand. *There was someone out there and they were getting up.*

Lizzie listened intently as she heard the release of the chair, recognizing it as the sound of the chair rising to its unseated state. Then came the soft steps and slight squeak of a person wearing well-worn tennis shoes, but the person was walking away from her. The footsteps grew quieter. They were leaving her. Were they going to go tell someone she was awake? Why wouldn't they just call someone, and then come in to check on her?

"Heeellooo!" she said again, this time exaggerating as she spoke, trying to put as much strength as she could, expelling the air from her lungs in force as it formed the word. She reminded herself of Josh Gad when he sang "Hello" in his opening number for the Book of Mormon. She had never seen the musical, but the soundtrack was in heavy rotation on her phone.

Then the sound of footsteps returned. She could hear them getting closer, and then saw as the light under the curtains showed them. They reached the edge, and just as Lizzie was expecting a huge 'pulling back of curtains' reveal, a short woman slipped in and disappeared as the curtain closed again behind her.

"Hello Lizzie, how are you feeling?" The nurse asked, as she was illuminated by a faint light. She was standing by a switch on the wall and what must have been a dimmer as she brought up the light gradually. Lizzie recognized the woman as one of the nurses from earlier, the one who...had Lizzie really thought this woman had turned into a snake?

"I'm okay," she said, not really sure if she actually was. She didn't feel like she was hurting too much. Other than a slight headache and the fuzziness around her thoughts, she felt fine. She didn't even feel the soreness she would have expected for all the falling she had gone through, and all the scrapes she had gotten running through the woods.

"That's good. I'm Elisabeth. I'll be your nurse tonight. Can I get you anything?"

"Water?"

"Sure. I'll refill your cup." she spoke softly and if there was any resentment from before, it didn't show. The woman moved gently and smoothly as she glided over to the little table next to the bed. Lizzie hadn't noticed the water bottle next to her, but watched as the nurse grabbed it and took it to the sink across the room. She filled it, then turned back towards Lizzie. "I bet you'd like some ice."

"Just the water is fine."

Elisabeth had already started towards the hallway but stopped and turned to the bed. She was quick to bring the water, tilting the cup so Lizzie could drink from the straw.

Lizzie looked at that approaching straw protruding from the water cup and was filled with a strong sense of dread. A déjà vu washed over her, and a rasping voice whispered in her ear. *It's poison*. That was impossible, but she couldn't shake the feeling as it mixed with the hazy memory of this woman with a serpent's face. She closed her eyes to push away the memory and allowed herself to drink.

The water may not have been ice cold, but it was still chilled, soothing her throat as it made its way to her empty stomach. She felt it move inside her, the touch of it on her insides filling her with a cooling, relaxing sensation. It seemed to flow through and back up, and she felt her head become lighter, her brain waking up a little more as some of the haziness chipped away.

"No, no, not too much," Elisabeth said softly as she pulled the cup back. She eased it away and Lizzie felt the little drips that leaked from the corners of her mouth, running down her chin.

She was alive. Why was it that with everything that had happened, it wasn't until that drink of water that she truly felt like she had survived? She was safe now; she was in a hospital, and everything was going to be okay.

"Thank you," and she was grateful. Water had never tasted so good.

"That's good. You seem to be feeling better."

"I guess so."

"Good. Do you know where you are?"

"No, not really."

"That makes sense. From your chart, you were unconscious when the EMTs brought you in and you've only been awake a few times."

"I have? I don't remember too much. It feels more like it was all a dream."

"Yeah, the sedatives can do that."

"So where am I?"

"You're at Atlas Healthcare in Wautoma, the Christmas tree capital of the world."

"Okay, why am I here? And why am I in these handcuff thingies?"

"Um, well, you were brought in earlier today sometime in the afternoon. They were originally going to keep you in the ER, but they brought you up here to intensive care when you weren't waking up. Hope you have good insurance, eh?" The woman said that last part, with the strong "eh" that mixed many northern Wisconsin accents with Canadian. It was interesting how the accent wasn't always there when the nurse talked, but it occasionally slipped in depending on what she was saying. Most of the time, Lizzie would have guessed she was from farther south but still in the Midwest. It was hard to tell, as culture became more centered around televisions, accents seemed to fade.

"No, not really. College student."

"Oh crap. Yeah, well, at least staying in intensive care won't be as bad as those student loan payments. And if you don't like your major, you can always take up boxing."

"Sure. So, did I really attack the doctor...and you? I had hoped I'd dreamed that."

"You swung, but it was a swing and a miss."

"I'm sorry."

"Part of the job. Is there something I can get for you? There's no one else on the ward, so you have it all to yourself, but I still need to keep watch in case an emergency comes in."

"Can you open the curtain and let some light in? I don't want to be in the dark right now."

"Sure."

The nurse went to one side and grabbed the edge and worked the curtain. She had it halfway when curiosity got the better of her and she turned to look back at Lizzie, "Do you mind me asking, what happened to you?"

"I'm not sure. My best friend and I were at a house, my uncle's house...that I inherited...which I guess makes it my house."

"I guess so," Elisabeth said as she finished pulling back the curtain.

Lizzie could see the nurse station across the little hallway, though all she saw of it from her angle was the counter and on that, a rack holder with a single file in it. That must be her file. Had they pulled her whole history? Was there information in there about the broken arm she had at fifteen, or the tonsils she had removed when she was ten?

Elisabeth walked back over to her and, to Lizzie's surprise, pulled up the reclining chair that was next to her bed.

"We went there, and then there was this strange naked man in the kitchen. He attacked us...well, he attacked Sarah."

"Wow, did she get away, okay?"

"No, I think he killed her. I barely got away. I don't know how, but I ended up here."

"Yeah, you need to talk to the cops."

"I know," though she had forgotten about needing the police and why. How could she have forgotten Sarah?

Those dead eyes looking at her, watching her as she ran away to leave her there...

"I can call the sheriff's office. I'm not sure anyone's there this time of night, but I'd think someone would be available."

"Thank you. Do you know if they called my brother?"

"I don't think so. Do you want me to call him?"

Lizzie hadn't realized how much that had been worrying her until the sudden release of tears, glad that they hadn't. The nurse quickly scrambled for the Kleenex.

Lizzie tried to wipe them away herself, but was stopped by the wrist restraints. She laughed as she looked at them. It was the tired laugh of the frustrated and it brought more tears. She was laughing and crying, and, in her head, there rolled a hurricane of emotions. Her parents were dead, her best friend was dead, her other friends were miles away and busy back in Stevens Point and Madison, leaving only her brother.

There was no way she could unload all this on him. It would only make him worry about something he could do nothing about. It wouldn't even do to talk to him over the phone and hear that robotic voice of his machine talking back to her. Was there anything less helpful than to hear a computer-generated voice even if it was her brother's words typed by stylus on his keypad?

Elisabeth dabbed at Lizzie's cheeks and Lizzie looked into her kind eyes. This woman who barely even knew her seemed genuinely concerned for her. How could Lizzie have ever thought of this woman as a snake?

"Thank you."

"No problem. I take it you don't want to talk to your brother?"

"It's not that. I do, it's just...it's complicated." Lizzie didn't know what else to say, and the nurse seemed to understand. She stood there, and they both looked at each other, one knowing the other wanted to say more, and that when she was ready, the nurse would listen.

Lizzie let out a long sigh, and looked down, catching sight again of the ungodly large clasps around her wrists.

"Do you think you can do something about this?" Lizzie asked, looking up again and catching Elisabeth's eye.

"You promise you're not going to slug me again?"

"No, but I'll dance a jig if you do."

The nurse didn't know what to make of it, and Lizzie wasn't sure what she had meant by it. She ended up cocking an unsure eyebrow at the nurse in what had to look like a mix between a puppy dog pleading for forgiveness and an older sister who was ready to drag you into something naughty that would definitely get you in trouble. The look would have probably been more convincing had Lizzie not had the streaks of fresh tears and the red, puffy eyes of the recent crying.

"Yeah, forget I said that," she said. "But I'd still appreciate it if you'd take these off me."

"Just, please, no hitting. I'd have to do more paperwork."

Elisabeth was quick with the straps and Lizzie was free, lifting her arms into the air, happy to be loose.

She stretched, then yawned. The early morning was starting to catch up to her, and she was beginning to think she might actually be able to get some rest.

"Here," the nurse said, bringing over the plastic cup, and Lizzie was grateful to hold it herself as she brought the straw to her mouth. She took a long drink, felt the cool water hit her stomach, and then realized something else. She was hungry. Very hungry. Which was announced to Elisabeth by the roar that erupted from Lizzie's stomach. It could have scared a bear to run for safety.

"You know, the cafeteria is closed, but we keep some light stuff in the fridge. I think we may have some crackers and some jello, but there's not much else in there."

"Yeah," Lizzie nodded in relief.

"And then I'll call the sheriff, okay?"

Lizzie nodded as she lay back on the bed. She was spent. By the time Elisabeth had left the room and pulled the curtain closed behind her, Lizzie was already caught in the first nightmare.

The cackling voice surrounded her as maggots swarmed over her. She twisted and turned in her sleep, violently shaking the bed, but there was no waking. Not until the nightmares were ready to let her slip back into reality. It would be a while. They enjoyed playing with their new toy. The maggots grew in size, their mouths exposing long vampire like fangs. She wanted to scream. She wanted to wake up, but she was trapped. She wanted it all to end.

End it, end it now, she pleaded in her mind.

But she could barely hear her own thoughts over the cackling voice.

"tik-a-tee, tik-a-tet... your death does not come yet..."

She slipped further into the darkness.

CHAPTER 6

Is there ever a true release from the darkness? Does it not always have some hold on our souls? Even in following Christ, there is always some sliver of doubt nestled away in the corners of the mind. These slivers often go ignored and are allowed to remain. Those who are blind to them are often the ones with the largest nooks and crannies for those thoughts to hide in. It leads people down paths of corruption. They find ways to justify actions that are unethical and morally disturbing. They allow these dark thoughts to influence them in ways they are unaware of.

No one is ever truly free of the dark, only blind to it.

Even as Lizzie woke up in a brightly lit room, she found her gaze drawn to the shadows that collected in the corners of the room. She tried to wipe away the sleep from her eyes, but found herself once again restrained.

She glanced at her hands, noticing the tray by her bed and the Jello sitting there on a little plate. Then she noticed the woman sitting in the soft chair reserved for guests. The woman had obviously been sleeping, still wearing the nursing scrubs she had worn all night. She was awake now, and already leaning forward to stand.

"I'll take care of those," she said as she rose, nodding to Lizzie's restrained wrists. "I put them back on when you started flailing in your sleep. You had some nasty nightmares, and I was afraid you might hurt yourself."

Lizzie nodded and watched as she undid the straps. Elisabeth finished with them and then, without waiting for Lizzie to ask, she brought the cup over from the tray and handed it to her. Lizzie sipped at it, grateful for the refreshing liquid. She noticed that inside the cup were the remnants of ice, so at some point in the morning Elisabeth had refilled it with ice water long before Lizzie had woken.

The water tasted and felt great, and Lizzie had to wonder if the woman was psychic with how she had known just what Lizzie had needed before she herself even had.

That was when she truly saw the woman. She had silver hair just as Lizzie had noticed the night before, and maybe that's why Lizzie been confused about her age. Her face was of someone Lizzie's age and on second look, and in the bright morning sun, it was obvious the silver hair was a dye, and a really good one.

"Who does your hair? It's amazing!"

Elisabeth sparkled, a smile warming her face. She took a second to look down, embarrassed, probably not used to taking compliments and especially about her hair, before she looked up again.

"A girl my mom knows. Her name's Rachel and she works out of her living room, but she really knows her stuff. She does some wicked coloring."

"It looks great," Lizzie said, and meant it. The silver just caught the light and somehow transformed it, so it brightened the room. And it was so different. Who dyes their hair silver? Everyone always wants to be blond or the redhead, but no one does silver. It was amazing.

Though seeing it in the morning light reminded her and Lizzie had to ask, "Why are you still here? Shouldn't you be off by now?"

"I am. I kinda stuck around. Long story, but yeah, I ended up falling asleep in your chair and then you woke me up."

"You should go home, get some sleep."

"I will. I wanted you to know I called the Sheriff's department. They said they'll send a deputy here around ten, which should be in an hour or so, so you got some time for breakfast and the kitchen is still open so all you have to do is call down to them."

"Okay."

"I did get the Jello for you earlier," Elisabeth motioned to the glob of gelatin on a plate. "It was a while ago; not sure I'd eat it."

"Yeah... so how's the cafeteria food?"

"Decent. Better when you're sick."

"What?" Lizzie said, not able to suppress the giggle that escaped her. She couldn't believe she was giggling. She had just lost her best friend yesterday, a friend she had known for most of her life. There wasn't much she and Sarah didn't do together. How would she ever go shopping without her?

But now she was laughing with this stranger. Something about being around this woman helped her to forget some of the pain and the grief. She still

69

felt it hiding on the fringes, keeping to the corner of her thoughts, but it stayed there, not pulling her in while Elisabeth was around. And the woman had stayed when she hadn't needed to. Maybe that unabashed kindness was part of what allowed her to keep those stashes of grief secure, or at least at bay.

"You know... 'better when you're sick,'" she was saying with her hands lifted in air quotes. "Such as being so sick you can't taste it," Elisabeth said, trying unsuccessfully to hide the giggle.

"That bad, huh?"

"Yeah."

They were interrupted when another nurse entered the room and walked over to the chart.

"Hey Lizzie, good morning. I'm Annie and I'll be your RN this morning. Elisabeth is keeping you company, I see. So, how are you doing?" This new nurse seemed much more 'matter of fact' as she entered the room with her painted-on smile. She was short, thin, and had short multicolored hair, but didn't seem as warm or friendly as Elisabeth was. Lizzie looked at Elisabeth and saw that she was not happy with this newcomer.

"I'm fine," Lizzie said as Annie picked up her chart and started to finger through it, occasionally jotting down notes before putting it back in the rack by the door. Then she scanned a card she had unclipped from her waste on a pad on the wall before she proceeded to the patient of the room.

"Okay, so I'm just going to take some vitals and get you checked out." Annie was already pulling a stethoscope from behind the bed and motioning for her to hold out her arm. "Would you like Beth to stay or for her to go?"

Lizzie had no problem with 'Beth' staying, though she could tell this new nurse would like her gone. Looking back at Elisabeth, she could tell the feeling was mutual. Though Annie must be the senior, as Elisabeth lowered her glare first and could barely be heard when she mumbled, "I should be getting home, anyway."

Before Lizzie could call out to stop her, she was already out of the room and hurrying down the hallway.

"I got some good news for you. Looks like you'll probably be released today now that you're up. The doctor will be in soon for a final checkup and Janice from accounting will be in for your insurance and payment information."

"Wait, what?" Lizzie's head was already spinning, and she lost focus on what the nurse was saying. Her vision had blurred when the nurse said something about "home" and "insurance." Did she have homeowner's insurance? What was the woman talking about?

The room swirled around her, colors elongating as they stretched into odd distortions of their former existence. She couldn't breathe. What was going on? Money? All this was about money. Who did that? She wasn't out of the hospital yet. Hadn't even seen the light of day after seeing her best friend brutally killed and they were already there to take from her? Couldn't they just bill her, send her something in the mail?

"It's not a big deal. Janice will just take down your information, and if you want to make a payment, you can. It's not required. No one is asking you to pay it all off or anything today." The nurse said. Lizzie wasn't even sure if the woman had seen her reaction.

The realization hit her. She was all alone to deal with things like this now.

No, she'd been alone before, just as alone as she had been since her parents were gone. She couldn't rely on her brother, and her uncle had never been there for her. It was always her and her alone. That was the way of the world she lived in.

Lizzie found herself nodding in agreement with whatever the nurse was saying. She had stopped listening. It didn't matter. She was getting out later today, so who cared about anything in this place?

Elisabeth had been nice. Why did all the nice ones have to go? She wished she could have talked to her more, but was that her trying to replace the friend she lost? Could she be so callous to move on from caring about Sarah, who she had known most of her life?

No, but it had been nice to talk to someone. It got her to stop thinking about Sarah, and even if it was only for a short while, it had helped. The pain would be there. Who knew for how long, though she didn't think it was going away anytime soon. She knew it would be there whenever she had a moment alone or when she did something benign, like looking at a piece of lemon cake, the kind Sarah loved so much. It would be there whenever Lizzie went to Penny's, the store they had gone to countless times just wandering the aisles, talking amongst themselves, and trying on whatever they liked.

Sarah would be with her for a long time.

"Okay, well, your vitals are looking good. BP is up, but with what you've been through, that is understandable. You'll need to follow up though in a week or two with your regular doctor, but I'm not thinking anything of it."

Lizzie just nodded. Insurance. Her friend was lost, and they wanted to talk about insurance. Something about that made it all now seem so real. It had been real before, all through the night, but the drugs or the dream of it all had made her find a way to ignore the reality.

Annie must have taken her nodding as if she understood, as she was already heading to the chart by the curtain. She grabbed it and was making quick notations when something occurred to her and looked back up at Lizzie.

"I almost forgot. There was a notation about the sheriff's department. They called earlier, and I let them know you weren't awake yet. I'm assuming they'll be stopping by. I don't need to restrain you until they get here, do I?"

"Why would I?"

"Oh, some types of people hear police and run."

Annie never saw the open-mouthed stare she got from Lizzie as she finished her notations and was quick to leave down the hallway. Really? Did she look like a person who regularly hid from the police?

Actually, she had no idea what she looked like. She hadn't seen a mirror since she had left her apartment in Steven's Point yesterday. Then they had only been going to the lawyer's office as he had things he had wanted to discuss. When he had told her about the money and the house, the two of them hadn't been able to help themselves and had to go check it out.

73

Sarah had started making calls immediately and invited all her friends. They hadn't even gotten their coffee from the barista at Starbucks when they'd heard back that a few of them had said they'd be there.

Had any of them actually been there, Sarah may have still been alive. That or someone else might have died, and she'd still have her best friend hanging around.

"Damn, what a bitch." Sarah said.

At first Lizzie thought she was losing her mind, that the voice had been internal, loud in her head. Though it was so much louder than her other thought voices that were trapped in there.

Then Sarah appeared, walking out from behind the elevated bed. She looked just like Lizzie had last seen her, the large open area on her neck where the naked man had bitten into her, ripping away her flesh. That perky pink shirt she had been wearing now drenched in blood that had blossomed out from the large hole in her neck. Her head had that large gash in it that Lizzie hadn't noticed before but probably came from when she had crashed to the floor... Then there were Sarah's eyes. Her dead, lifeless eyes still were pale as they fixed on her.

"I thought they were never going to leave, but that last one... Did you see that condescending look? She thought you were trailer park; I could see it in her eyes."

Lizzie felt paralyzed, her eyes open wide, her mouth suddenly dry as she struggled to find words. She wanted to scream, but it was caught in her throat. Her mind was racing faster than her mouth as the onslaught of thoughts attacked her in silence. *I can't do that. I can't scream. Screaming would just bring that nurse back in here, as well as anyone else nearby, and then I would definitely get restrained again. On top of that, they would find a nice, white padded room and put my name on it. My name. It would be saved just for me, as here is Lizzie in the looney bin as she has finally lost it. Her and her books, all those crazy thoughts, finally drove her nuts, and it would be true, I would be crazy, and everyone would be right. And maybe, just maybe, I am crazy. After all, here's my best friend back from the dead and talking to me just like I was.*

Her tongue felt like a layer of dust was settling, but she couldn't close her mouth. She tried, but the best she could do was just sit there, mouth mostly closed, drool starting to wet the corners, and still not saying anything. What do you say to your dead best friend when she shows up in your hospital room? *'Hey, how you doing? How's death? Have you met Elvis?'*

Okay, maybe the Elvis question was a little off. Though she might have run into David Bowie. He'd been hot in Labyrinth. Maybe she'd seen him somewhere there in the afterlife and they've had a few go-arounds. That'd be just Sarah's way of doing things. She always got the hot guys.

I really am losing it.

"Lizzie. Earth to Lizzie. Anyone home?"

"This isn't happening." Lizzie said as she tossed off the thin sheet like blanket and threw her feet off the bed to touch the cold linoleum floor. She hadn't noticed that the IVs were gone, but had they still been attached they wouldn't have stopped her from dashing to the bathroom.

She made it with her stomach already lurching, trying to expel contents that were not there. Her bladder had been screaming at her, but she'd been ignoring it. Now as she lowered herself over the bowl of the toilet, it was done holding back. She heaved into the toilet, only stomach juices emerging from her, but she could feel the warmth between her legs and smell the putrid scent of urine. The floor grew wet and warm. Tears streaked her face, but she couldn't stop dry heaving into the open bowl. Maybe it was disgust with what she now sat in, or with how she abandoned her friend, but it sure as shit couldn't be disgust with how her friend looked because she wasn't real. It hadn't really been her standing there in Lizzie's hospital room. That was just impossible, and Lizzie refused to believe it.

"Lizzie, it's going to be okay. I'm here."

Lizzie turned to see that Sarah stood in the doorway. She looked pained at seeing Lizzie this way.

No! This isn't real. This can't be happening!

Lizzie kicked out, though as she tried to reach with her foot to close the door, it slipped on shit and urine that coated the floor. Her feet gave out from supporting her and she fell the short distance to the hard tile floor.

"Get out!" Lizzie yelled it, not sure if she was furious that her friend was back from the dead or at herself for the mess she had made. She kept kicking out her feet, trying to get purchase on the door that remained just out of reach. She started to push herself towards it, not taking her eyes off Sarah, who held her hands up and backed away. "Get out! Get out! Get out!"

Lizzie was finally able to reach the door with her foot and pulled on it. The door swung and slammed into its frame with an audible thud that reverberated along the tile. Her stomach was still tight, threatening more heaving in the future, but for now it was done. Her breath came in quick heavy gasps, and she could feel the energy her flight had given her dissipate. Exhaustion was fighting its way in, but she wasn't ready for it. She'd slept enough. She was tired, but also tired of this place. She wanted out of there, away from snake nurses and dead friends that came to visit her.

There was a light rapping on the door. Lizzie didn't look up, her chin stayed resting on her chest. Spittle ran down her cheek, and she felt like she was on the verge of sleep, no matter how hard she fought against it.

"Elizabeth? Are you okay in there?" Lizzie recognized the nurse's voice. The nurse was persistent as she was already turning the knob as she spoke.

"Go away." The fight gone from her voice.

"I just want to-" Annie didn't get to finish as she saw the mess Lizzie was in, the pile of shit, urine, and teenager all together in one large mess on the floor. Lizzie tried to kick the door closed, but couldn't find the strength to put any force into it. She was a flailing turtle of a person on the floor, acting like she had one too many beers at the fraternity kegger.

"We need to get you cleaned up. Sheriff's department is here." Annie said as she moved around behind Lizzie. Then Lizzie felt the woman's hands under her arms and Lizzie was being lifted.

"Get your hands off of me."

She tried to wiggle free, but the woman had a really strong grip. The more Lizzie tried to twist out of it, the tighter those hands clamped onto her underarm and it was really beginning to hurt. She tried to push herself up, thinking a change in direction would break her free from the nurse or that the push against her would send both of them backward. Instead, her feet slipped out from under her, putting her more into the control of the surprisingly strong woman.

She was defeated. This woman had her.

"It's going to be okay." Sarah said. Lizzie's head shot up, and she looked to see Sarah standing in the doorway. She looked like she was about to cry, worrying about her friend. Behind her stood a large burly man wearing a dark-colored police uniform. He was watching her without any kind of compassion, his face showing the frustration of being called there for someone who was obviously crazy. Lizzie couldn't give two shits if the man thought she was crazy, but her friend, *her friend,* was dead. She shouldn't be watching her with those eyes, wearing that same expression she had when she told her she'd dumped Roland because the bastard had cheated on her.

Annie saw where she was looking and called out to the police officer.

"Do you mind? She's been through a lot. Give me a minute to clean her up and I'll have her out to you."

"Sure." The man said, but he made no movement to leave the room. He just stayed there watching them, that bored, impatient look pasted on his face.

"Do you mind going out into the hallway?" Nurse Annie said as she helped Lizzie into the chair positioned in the shower. Lizzie hadn't noticed that she had stopped fighting the nurse and had helped her. She was vaguely aware of anything other than her friend. Annie and the officer didn't seem to see her. They just talked around her like she wasn't there. Did they not see this hideously disfigured woman standing between them? You would think the nurse would be rushing to her, calling for her a doctor, or that the police officer would be asking her questions. Such as 'With you being dead, how did you manage to get to the hospital,' and 'do you know who killed you?'

Lizzie's head was really beginning to hurt as too many thoughts kept trying to come to the forefront and people talking around her. It was all too much. She just wanted to collapse and pass out. *Wait, I'm already sitting... I could pass out right here...* But she couldn't. She still felt too much weight on her.

Lizzie felt the nurse's hands leave her, and she immediately wanted to slump forward and fall to the floor. Why did she need to stay sitting up, anyway? She was already covered in yuck, let her just fall over and die in it.

She watched through the haze of her closed eyes as Annie closed the door so that Sarah and the officer were trapped outside. Then the nurse turned back to Lizzie. Lizzie looked up at her, but her face was gone. The snake's face had returned. Who had she last seen with a snake face? She vaguely remembered who it was, but it had been a nurse. Were they all snake people?

"Lizzie!" She heard a voice trying to reach her and knew it was Sarah. Was it a ghost Sarah or dead girl in the hallway Sarah? She didn't know, and she didn't care. She didn't care that the nurse was a snake anymore. She just wanted to sleep. *Here, the floor looks nice. I'm just going to lie here for a bit.*

"Lizzie, wake up!"

CHAPTER 7

Lizzie didn't want to go back there. She didn't want to go back into the house that her friend had died in. She didn't want to go back inside the small, wooden, decrepit place that some random stranger, old and naked, had come at her; tried to eat her and God only knows what else to her. She didn't want to go near the place of that shadow man, but even more so, she didn't want to go near the maggots.

Why was that troubling her? She wasn't sure. Since she'd last been there, she had plenty of nightmares. She'd dreamed about the shadow man and his ticky-tat way of talking. She'd dreamed of the old man as she stared up at him with his member dangling in her face, but the ones she truly feared, the ones that woke her up in a sweat were the ones when she dreamed she was in a bathtub covered in maggots, all of them with their hungry mouths. They were eating her alive, tearing her apart and laying their eggs inside of her, more maggots bursting out of her.

As she stepped out of the back seat of the car, bringing her back there, the image of that single white wormlike creature as it fell on her from the man's penis kept leaping into her thoughts. Though unlike how it happened, she kept remembering it wrong. In her thoughts, it fell into her open mouth, made its way into her stomach and was eating her while laying its eggs. With the butterflies she felt in her stomach, she couldn't help but think there was some truth to nagging sense.

"Lizzie? You okay?"

Lizzie looked over at her friend, who had brought her back there. She didn't want to be back there, but they needed to get her keys and somewhere in there she had dropped them. The police, when they went there, hadn't found them. They'd found her phone, but that had been it... Well, the phone, and the bodies. They had found Sarah and the corpse of the old man. He was also dead, though how she had no clue. The cops knew. They already knew who he was. In fact, the sheriff had been to the old man's funeral a week before he had killed Sarah in the cabin. The guy was dead. He had been a rotting corpse, buried three miles away, but somehow had found himself in her cabin to terrorize her and kill her best friend in the world.

It had been when the cops had found the corpse of the old man, lying there in what was now her kitchen, that their questioning of her had shifted. She was no longer being looked at as a victim. They no longer trusted her, or the story she was telling them. No matter how much she pleaded with them that it was the truth, she could see the doubt in their eyes.

She had been in the hospital for three days and was questioned by the police for the last two days.

"Are you sure you're okay?" Elisabeth asked. Lizzie looked over at her and her boyfriend. She was thankful they had brought her out there, but tepid, as she was only beginning to know these people. Lizzie felt like she had started to lean on Elisabeth and was using her to fill the void that Sarah had left. Elisabeth's boyfriend, though, was just as nice as Elisabeth was, and he had suggested they come out there. Well, he'd suggested coming by himself so he could get Lizzie's car and look for her keys...

What had possessed me to say I wanted to come back here? Sure, he'd need someone to come with him as they'd have two vehicles, but anyone could have ridden with him. She doubted Elisabeth would have come. The girl barely left Lizzie's side, becoming her protector the more the sheriff dug into her with questions.

The old man...how could he have attacked her and killed her friend? He'd been dead for a week. The sheriff knew the man and had been at his funeral when they put him in the ground. He'd died of bone cancer, barely able to lift his own arm, not able to walk for the last three months when the cancer got bad. There was no way he could have attacked them, or so the sheriff said.

Lizzie didn't know. She had no answers of her own other than what she saw.

Maybe she really was crazy?

"Liz?" Elisabeth said, the concern heavy in her voice, pulling Lizzie from her thoughts.

Lizzie looked over at her, trying to not be a zombie as she walked around to the front of the car. Her thoughts kept pulling her deep into her own mind. She just had to not get lost in them. Don't focus on them, right? That was easier said than done.

"Yeah, I'm fine. Just trying not to remember the last time I was here."

"I get that," Elisabeth's boyfriend said. Lizzie struggled to remember his name and felt she should really remember it by now, as they've hung out for more than a day.

"Chuck, you mind going in first. I'll stay out here with Lizzie while you check it out."

"Sure, let me get killed in the spooky old death house."

"Chuck!"

The color drained from his face as he realized what he had just said. Elisabeth was making jerking motions with her head towards Lizzie.

"Oh my God, I can't believe I just said that."

It was alright. Lizzie barely even noticed as she had slipped back into her thoughts. She found her gaze drifting over Elisabeth and Chuck to settle on the old cabin. Her first time there, she hadn't really looked at it. Sarah had been talking, but Lizzie had been on the phone with Brian, her brother. He had been having another meltdown because his caregiver had a family emergency. Samuel, her brother's normal caregiver, had called her and told her what was going on. Samuel had called their service and Jerome, the backup, was on his way. None of this mattered to Brian, and he had called her in a frenzy. She had to listen to him rant in that computerized voice as he typed it from his end of the call.

"It's still a dump." Sarah said, as though she could read Lizzie's thoughts. Lizzie looked over, across the car to the other side, and there she stood. Of course, her dead friend was still with her. No matter where she went, Sarah followed now, though she did have the decency not to follow her into the bathroom.

Lizzie tried to pretend she wasn't there, but it was hard. Closing her eyes never helped. Wishing the nightmare away didn't do anything. Sarah was there, whether she liked it or not.

Sarah was right, though; the house was a dump. It looked like it had once been painted a drab yellow, though not that much of the paint was still visible, having peeled away long ago. The remnants of the paint lay in a bed of debris around the base of the house, having been torn away after years of neglect and vicious winters tearing at it.

Outside, you couldn't really see that the windows were blacked out. With the sun coming down and the boards that looked hastily placed to cover them, the house just looked dark inside. Her uncle really didn't want anyone seeing in, or maybe he didn't want to see what was out there? Had her uncle seen the shadow man? Had he been hiding from him?

Maybe there were answers inside? She hadn't thought about that before, but there could be something in there that explained that thing.

Now you're just reaching. You know that. You just don't want to go back in there and are trying to give yourself reason to go in, never mind that you've come all the way back out here, you need to go in or else you'll be running the rest of your life afraid to face anything.

And somewhere inside her, she was okay with that. Why not just run away from everything?

"Okay, well, I guess I'll go in then. It's unlocked, right?" Chuck said as he neared the door. It was obvious he didn't relish the idea of going in alone.

"Should be. I doubt the sheriff's department locked up after themselves and I'm not sure where my keys are," Lizzie said as she finally moved, taking tentative steps towards the house. The dried leaves crackled beneath her, fallen from the trees overhead. There were a lot of them. She was surrounded by trees. The whole area was nothing but trees, and then a clearing with an old house. It was like the house was hiding from the modern world, and the only connection to it was that small driveway barely wide enough for one car. "Be careful. The woods all rotted on the stairs."

She had stopped him just before he had stepped onto the first step. There were only three of them to reach the small landing and the front door overhang. It was odd how it was set up. The overhang was blocked off, walled on three sides so that it didn't allow for those inside to look out past the person directly at the door. Visitors had to walk up the stairs next to the house. It didn't allow someone inside to look out, but outside, no one could see in.

Why would he be so worried about someone looking in? It was obvious the overhang was not a part of the original design, as the metal was unpainted, and it didn't fit in with the architecture. It looked like it had been hastily done, with ribbed sheet metal quickly bolted together to add another layer to hide her uncle away from the outside world. He had to have built it himself.

"Your uncle was nuts." She didn't know who had said it. It was getting hard, as Lizzie could no longer tell if it had been Sarah or Elisabeth. Both of them were behind her, and it had been just a whisper.

"I see what you mean. One of the boards collapsed, probably one of the deputies that'd been trampling around out here. I should be okay using the sides."

"You be careful." Elisabeth called after him. He disappeared and then there was a door slamming shut, what must have been the screen door as he entered the house.

"I don't like him going in there alone," Lizzie said.

"This house is a dump. Why did your uncle live out here? It's in the middle of nowhere, hidden in trees. I've heard of getting off the grid, but this is going too far." Elisabeth said, Lizzie sure it was her this time.

"And you live here because?" Lizzie said, looking back at her.

"Hey, I live in town." Elisabeth held her hand up, motioning towards the house and the surrounding clearing. "This wanting to know no one. He was hiding from someone."

"Well, he did leave me a lot of money." Lizzie said quietly, biting back what she wanted to say. That dread turning in her stomach. Her gut told her that he wasn't out there to hide from someone, he was hiding from something and that eventually it got him.

"Yeah, I'd be careful with that money. You got no idea where it came from?"

"None." Though it was becoming nice having it. The lawyer had somehow found out she was in the hospital and had let her know he had the money already put into her account as of yesterday, a full week sooner than anyone had expected. That allowed her to get ahold of someone, a person that one of the nicer deputies had suggested, that would come out and clean the mess of the kitchen so she wouldn't have to see the blood.

Once Lizzie had told the lawyer about it, he had taken care of all the details. Lizzie didn't have to worry about any of it. She guessed with money, none of that stuff was important anymore, though the revelation was still mind-boggling.

Lizzie started towards the side of the house. She had to see it, to see where it happened, but she wasn't sure she could go in the house. Not yet, but if she went around back...

"Hey! where ya going?" She heard Elisabeth rushing to catch up.

"You can see into the kitchen from the back clearing."

"I thought you didn't want to go in there."

"I don't. I just want to see in, see where it-"

She didn't finish saying it as she went around the corner. As she walked along the side of the house, she could see more of the backyard, and it was different from what she remembered. When she had left the kitchen through the back door, it had been a small clearing, no buildings, just woods, but now she could clearly see a large shed. It was unpainted and old but used. She saw a well-trampled path that ran from the house.

What had her uncle been doing in there? It was large enough to fit three cars and something she'd more often find on farms for those large tractors. Back there in all the woods, she couldn't see a way for them to bring in any large vehicles. So why was it there?

She had to pull her attention away from the shed. It wasn't why she was back there. She came around the corner and stepped into the backyard and turned back towards the cabin.

The kitchen door was open, the screen door twisted at the bottom hinge, the top broken so that the door hung off to the side. The wooden interior door was still open as it had been and now as she walked up, she could see where the small metal stairs that were supposed to lead up to the door had been pulled away; set to the side where there was nothing but the kitchen wall. They were out of place there, almost belonging more in line with a photo out of Alice in Wonderland, a staircase to nowhere. It would have been funny if she wasn't where her friend had been killed. It did make her wonder about the sickness of the mind that drove her uncle to move them over there, never wanting whoever climbed them to get in.

Maybe he was dealing with zombies? Lizzie shook away the thought as she heard Elisabeth calling out to her.

"Lizzie! Wait up." Elisabeth called. Lizzie wasn't sure why she was supposed to wait. She was standing there by the back door. She hadn't run around the house, so why would it take Elisabeth so long to catch up?

"Hey, what are you doing back here?" Chuck said, looking at her from where he had been standing in the kitchen.

Lizzie barely noticed either of them, her eyes transfixed on the last place she had last seen Sarah alive. The tile floor was spotless. The cleaners weren't supposed to clean up more than the mess the bodies had made, but as she looked in, the kitchen was clean. All of it. She was sure the kitchen hadn't been that clean in over ten years, as it actually now looked like a room that food could be prepared in.

It truly was amazing what mountains money could move. Whoever had come out there had gone the extra mile, that was for sure, and to have been out there on their own? Lizzie didn't think she'd ever be able to stay out there by herself. It was all just too creepy. Too much nature, all the bugs and animals. Never mind that the last time she'd been out there, there had been a homicidal dead man out to massacre them. How had her uncle been able to do it?

"Lizzie, we should get away from here." Elisabeth said. She came up to her, gently wrapping an arm around her shoulders. It was soothing, and Lizzie wanted to melt back into the woman as she guided her away. Lizzie didn't want to go though, pushing away from those comforting thoughts as she twisted out of Elisabeth's grip and looked back at where her friend fell.

"I did... I died there."

Lizzie didn't have to turn to know that Sarah was also behind her. She could hear the tears in the dead woman's voice and knew those tears were for her own death. Lizzie wanted to turn to her, but to say what? How do you comfort the dead?

Maybe that was what she needed to do. Maybe Sarah was a ghost and until she came to deal with it, she'd always be there to haunt Lizzie?

As much as it hurt Lizzie to have her there with her, she wasn't ready to let Sarah go. She couldn't help Sarah with her grief when she was barely holding on dealing with her own.

"...nothing..." Chuck was saying, though Lizzie hadn't heard anything else. They were talking around her about her, and she tried to shake free from the thoughts that kept tying her down so she could once again focus. There'd just been so many thoughts and memories in such a short time it kept drowning her in randomness.

"What?"

"I'd been through the house. I found your keys, but that was it. You sure you lost your purse in here?"

"I thought I had. I don't know."

"Well, here's this," he said as he held out to her keys.

"Thanks." she said, her voice flat as she flipped over the keys in her hand.

"Was there anything else we need out here, or should we go?" Chuck said as he jumped down the short distance to the ground.

She wanted to say yes, let's get out of there, but found herself climbing into the little kitchen. She didn't know why. She didn't want to go in, but something inside called to her. She could feel a thrumming course through the wood as she touched it. The air was different, cooler, and she knew if it was winter and cold outside, that air would be warmer. It wanted her in there and would accommodate her. She just had to finish going in.

"Woah." Chuck said as both he and Elisabeth reached out, grabbing her and pulling her back. She didn't fight them. They were right, but as much as she knew it, she still wanted to go in there.

"Lizzie?" Elisabeth moved to face her and look into her eyes.

"I'm fine. We can get out of here."

"You sure?"

"Yeah, let's just go. I don't ever want to come back here."

"Yeah, the place is a dump." Chuck said as he led them back to their cars.

"You know you love it out here." Elisabeth was teasing him, wrapping her arms around him.

"In the woods, yes. This house, no way. I saw inside there. There's voodoo, or witchcraft shit all over in there. I think I'm cursed for just walking through it."

"You're kidding."

"He's not. Sarah and I saw some of it when we'd gone through. It's disgusting and creepy in there. I'd never want to stay the night."

Elisabeth studied the two of them as they stood to look back at the house. In the woods, something rushed through the underbrush, and it was loud in the silence around them. There were no birds chirping, and Lizzie didn't hear any flies buzzing around her. The slight breeze pushed back strands of her hair, but the leaves surrounding her remained still and silent.

Where were the mosquitoes? It was fall; they should be eating them alive. There had been plenty in town and had even been some really big nasty ones larger than she'd ever seen back home. She was here, out in the woods, where they should be attacking and feeding on her like a pack of vampires at a feast.

By the house, it was silent, dead, and that silence grew, pressing in more as she had realized and listened for it. The open clearing and the space around her was closing in, suddenly feeling much smaller, almost on top of her.

"Okay, well, I'm thinking we get out of here unless there was something else you need," Elisabeth said. Chuck nodded, and she turned to Lizzie.

"Sure."

"Okay, so we're probably going to head back to my house. You can meet us there if you'd like. You remember the way, right?"

"I don't know. I might just head back home. I should check on my brother, see that he's okay, and see how Jess and Dennis are doing. Sarah was their friend, too."

"Yeah, you don't have to follow us. I didn't know if you wanted to drive this late or not."

"I'm not sure."

"Okay." Elisabeth said, but Lizzie could feel the worry in her voice.

Lizzie looked back at the house. The sun was lowering on the far side, casting shadows towards them. She just didn't know how she felt or what she wanted to do. Where should she go? She didn't know and if left alone, would she just sit in her car in some parking lot crying? Was that a bad thing? It probably was, but still just felt right. She didn't want to be around people right now, no matter how nice they've been to her.

"So, what are you going to do with the house? Sell it?"

"I don't know." But she did know. She wasn't going to do anything with it. She'd be back there again. She didn't know why, but there was something in there she needed. She should go in and look. Her back muscles wouldn't relax until she did. That little nestling of a panic attack she'd had all morning, that shortness of breath she felt would never go away until she did.

She watched as her friends climbed into their car and she walked over to her own driver's side door. As they pulled away, she opened her door and got in. The world around her felt like a dream that was fading, but for now, it was time to leave. She wasn't going to go back in, not alone.

Sarah was waiting in the car's passenger seat. She was still crying.

"I'm dead."

Lizzie nodded.

"I'm dead, and I'm still here. What am I, a ghost?"

Lizzie shrugged. What did she say to her dead friend? Lizzie sure as hell didn't have any of the answers.

"Can we get out of here, please?"

Lizzie nodded again, starting the car, and turning around to drive down the driveway. They got to the end of the drive and saw that Elisabeth and Chuck had stopped at the end, waiting to turn on the main road.

Lizzie didn't feel like she was really there. Everything around her was slipping into this unreal dream and she just sat there watching. She saw the brake lights dim on the car in front of her as it eased forward into the road. Then the truck felt like it came out of nowhere as it struck. The car had been a small compact. The semi was a large behemoth of a vehicle in comparison and had been going way too fast. The little car was hit broadside.

Lizzie was unsure how long she sat there, trying to comprehend what she had just seen. It had been

Sarah tugging at her arm, screaming for her to call 911, and telling her she needed to rush to help them.

Help who? It couldn't be. No, not again. But yes, it was all happening again, and more of her friends were probably dead.

Slowly, Lizzie pulled herself out of her seat, getting back out of the car. She knew what she would see but walked to where the car was positioned against a tree, both sides smashed in by the multiple impacts. There was no rush. Why? She knew what she would find...

CHAPTER 8

It should've been raining. Funerals should always be cold and miserable. They should be drab affairs with the weather as an echo for the emotional storm raging inside the attendees. Otherwise, it just felt wrong that the emotions being felt were somehow hollow in the sun. It was like the whole day was false and would plague her memories as being false. None of this was real. The sun, her emotions, all of it was just a movie playing out around her and she was just a background player watching as people cried.

Lizzie felt that way. Something had twisted inside her and now she was a shell. There had to be a living person somewhere deep inside, but she didn't recognize it. That person was no longer home to her. The ghost that remained was unrecognizable.

The outside world was no better. When she had finally returned to her apartment in the city, it felt foreign, the objects inside no longer having any meaning to what was left of her life. The moving shapes of cars and buses no longer gave her that sense of security as she watched them drive by and imagined them crashing into cars her friends were driving. Each touch made her jump. The coffee shop's hissing of froth sounded like screams. All of it was strange, and she had never before felt so alone. She now saw the world for the darkness that it was. The torment that existed in the shadows that danced around her. They were swarming around her, just waiting for their chance to take her.

The hardest part was that she wanted to join them. Already, she'd lost three friends in the span of a week. Why couldn't she have been with them? Everyone around her seemed to be dying and here they left her to survive in this world.

No, they hadn't left her. Maybe it would be easier if they had, but they were all three with her as an ever-present reminder that they were dead, and she was not.

She looked at the priest, who was reciting some prayer. Around her, many had their heads bowed, shedding tears for Sarah. Next to the priest stood Sarah's mom, an arm around her from Sarah's dad. They had both been like second parents to Lizzie while growing up, and now they barely acknowledged her.

They blame you. She didn't know why, and it wasn't fair. She had called them shortly after returning to the apartment, and they had come over to get some of Sarah's things. When they had arrived, Sarah's mom had gone into her room while her dad stayed with Lizzie. He'd tried to talk to her but wouldn't look her in the eye. Joann, Sarah's mom, would, but there was hate there, and neither of them pretended to be polite. They came, took what they wanted, and left. John barely mentioned anything about the funeral until they were out the door. Even then, it was clear they didn't want her there.

She came anyway, and they had yet to say anything to her, openly avoiding getting near her. She had to talk to them to make them understand that none of this was her fault.

"And now we lay this blessed soul to rest. She was taken too soon, but we are comforted with knowing that she has joined you, Lord, up in the gentle pastors of your heavenly grace."

The priest was finishing his prayer, and Lizzie felt the hand in her chest tighten. Soon they would ask for people to come up there and speak. Sarah's parents were sure to say something, and Lizzie had been dreading that they would openly blame her. The accusing finger would point at her, and they would cry out, "Murderer!"

"I can't believe Rick came." Sarah said from behind Lizzie.

"Who's Rick?" Elisabeth said, standing next to her. The side of her face was crushed in, and when she spoke, it was hard for her to say it without a lisp, adding a 'th' sound. Who's came out as Who'sth. Next to Elisabeth was Chuck. Since he died, he hadn't said much to Lizzie or to any of them. He mostly glared at them, blaming them for his death. He would sit and mope when Lizzie went anywhere to eat and at night, he would scream out the window, trying to get someone to wake him up from his nightmare.

"He's my old boyfriend. I dumped him six months ago, but he never took the hint and has been stalking me. I thought he was going to go psycho on me, and they'd find me sliced up out in the woods somewhere. Go figure."

Lizzie fought against the tears. They wanted to burst from her, but she bit down hard on her lip. She was not about to cry. Not now, not with all the people surrounding her. She felt the wetness touching the corner of her eyes, but she was sure as hell not about to give in.

Why did she fight it? She lost her friend. Sarah had died right in front of her. She had every damned reason to be bawling her eyes out. It was logical.

Yeah, but was it logical for my best friend who was dead to be standing there at her own funeral, making jokes about boys she'd dated? Lizzie had a hard time keeping it all together just because she lost her friend. Having her ghost still there was driving her crazy. They were all three, always there. They stayed with her, going wherever she went. She had to find a way to get rid of them.

And then there was the tickety-tac man. Her shadow man still came to her, though he was often a thing that tortured her nightmares. She wasn't sure if he was real anymore or just something that was a part of her dreams. She thought she had seen him out in the woods, but he might have just been the first crack in her sanity.

"Thank you all for coming. There's a gathering at the house. Most of you are welcome to stop by and offer your condolences." Sarah's dad was saying. As he did, he looked directly at Lizzie, and she knew who the 'most' being welcome referred to and she wasn't one of them. It was written on his face.

How could she explain it to them? She had a flower basket in her car. She figured after the memorial, she would give it to them, offer her words, and wrap her arms around them. The Jones had been like family to her. She had grown up there just as much as in her own home and with Sarah, and vice versa.

"Um, I don't like how my dad keeps giving you the stink-eye. Maybe we shouldn't have come?" Sarah said, looking at her dad as he finished his remarks. For a brief moment Lizzie thought he was going to come to her, but he turned away, taking his wife in his arms as they walked towards the line of cars parked along the narrow service road.

"I don't know about Lizzie, but I remember you were saying how much you thought it would be cool to see your own funeral." Elisabeth said, fighting to talk through the lisp.

"Hey, this isn't easy for me being dead."

"You're not the only one. Hello." Chuck made a sound behind Elisabeth as they both stared at the other dead woman. "At least you get to go to your funeral. I doubt Lizzie will go to ours, and we don't even know when it is."

It wasn't easy to ignore her dead followers. They were always there now, no one else able to see them and always fraying at the edge of what Lizzie believed was her sanity.

As the progression of mourners left to their cars parked along the path, Lizzie turned to go the other way. It wasn't that she didn't want to see the others. She did, even though she knew they didn't want to see her. There were at least a few she would have liked to talk to, Jess especially, but Lizzie's parents were buried nearby. Lizzie needed to say hello. It'd been a while since she had visited them. Being there amongst the dead that stayed buried, she realized that it had been longer than she had ever intended.

101

It took her a few missed attempts to find their gravestone, but she finally found it. The large slab of marble was more than they should have had on the grave, and she hadn't thought about it before as he never came to the funeral, but it had to have been bought by her uncle.

She wondered just how much he had been in her life without her ever knowing it. What did he even know about her? Why did he leave most of his money to her and not split it evenly with her brother? It was a raw deal that just because her brother was disabled, he'd get less. Did her uncle think he wouldn't need it, or did he just not care?

Though it didn't matter now. She looked down at the beautiful tombstone, the nice plot that had her parents next to each other, as it topped a hill. It was elegant, and of course, had their names and lifespans etched on the front. Below it was stated simply, "Loved by son and daughter."

She didn't stop the tears this time as they rolled down her face, looking at the graves.

"Who's this?" Elisabeth said.

"Oh, Lizzie..."

Elisabeth and Sarah came up behind her, and she could feel them standing there without turning. She often tried not to look at them anymore. They were all bloody messes. Sarah understood, but Chuck and Elisabeth had both just shown up hours after their deaths. Lizzie had just finished talking to the EMTs and the police when they had finally given her the okay to leave. She was driving down the road, Sarah hanging out in the passenger seat, riding shotgun like she had so often done while alive, when Elisabeth and Chuck both just showed up in the back seat.

They had been as surprised as she had been.

They were just there, both of them screaming and causing Lizzie to drive off the road, barely able to keep control of the car.

"I'm sure they're in heaven. They won't be stuck down here like whatever we are." Sarah said, putting her arm around Lizzie's shoulder. She wasn't sure if she really felt it, but thought there was a chill to where the dead friend touched her. They had already discovered that the dead couldn't walk through objects for some reason, but if Lizzie tried to close a door on them to keep them from following her, they just appeared next to her. She had no control over it and, according to them, neither did they.

Though, since they were probably figments of her imagination and she was slowing driving the crazy train on a short trip to hell, did it really have to make any logical sense about what the dead could and could not do? She didn't think so. Soon they would be the only ones she talked to as they locked her away in some white room with padded walls. The day was coming. She just didn't know how much longer until it did.

Lizzie sat down. It wasn't planned and was more of a fall than a chosen action of sitting, but the earth was soft, and she landed without hurting herself too much. If she wasn't sore from being chased by a murderer who the cops say was already dead, she might not have hurt at all from the fall. As it was, the bruises still hadn't faded completely and caused her to wince.

Behind her, she heard the two dead girls whispering. She could barely hear more than snippets of what they were saying.

"...parents...killed..." was enough for her to know that Sarah was filling Elisabeth in on the whole parents being killed in a car wreck much like their own. Lizzie was sure that Elisabeth was noting the similarities as well because it was true, death was all around Lizzie. It was like a black cloud that hung over her, following her wherever she went.

Maybe that was why she stayed away from her brother so much? She knew it wasn't true, but she had no better explanation for it. It wasn't his fault he was sick, but just because he was, didn't mean she always had to be around. He had doctors and caregivers who took care of him. She wasn't needed. Something more she told herself, an excuse just to justify keeping him so distant.

But who are you really kidding?

She crawled across the ground and sat on her parents' graves, leaning back against the tombstone. The tears continued, the sobs coming in waves as she allowed herself to think of more things she had done wrong in her life, more people she felt responsible for ruining their lives. *You know, when you want to, you can make yourself responsible for anything when you try hard enough*, and she was trying incredibly hard to make herself the destroyer of the universe.

Lizzie had stopped paying attention to her dead friends, so she didn't see when Chuck had been walking around the graves. She hadn't seen when he had bent down on the back side of her parents' graves and then had stood up to motion the rest of them over. They left her alone to cry there as they went around, and she cried even harder now she even chasing away her dead friends. Everyone was leaving her, and it was all her fault.

"Liz, you should see this."

Lizzie ignored them, wiping away one set of tears only to feel that another wave, this one accompanying a headache, was coming.

"Who would have done that?" Elisabeth was asking.

"I don't know, but they really scratched the hell out of it. This is marble. They'd have to have some serious tools to etch that in," Chuck said.

"Really?"

"I mean, I'm not an expert, but that's hard rock. Have you ever taken a knife to anything solid? It might scratch it, but nothing like how deep that is."

"So, you're saying someone came out here with power tools?"

"No, just someone put a lot of work into it. I'm surprised no one noticed it or hadn't said anything."

Lizzie glanced up as Sarah came around from behind her, having just saw what the other two had been talking about. She lowered herself to Lizzie, her eyes sorrowful. Lizzie forced herself to hold back the next round of tears, trying to wipe and hide them away now that someone had noticed her.

"I think you should see this."

"What is it?" She tried to say, unsure of what her friend actually heard. Sarah nodded, though, and acted as she understood. That's what lifelong friendship was, being able to know what someone meant, even if the words came out unclear.

"You should see it."

"Okay."

It took her a little bit of effort to get up. The soft earth made her limbs unsteady, and her soreness fought against her. She wasn't sure of her legs and had to use the solid tombstone to help her stand. Even then, her knees wobbled and more than once she saw Sarah reach out to try to help her, only to pull her hands back.

Lizzie understood why. While her dead friends weren't substantial enough to move objects, there was something else entirely that happened when they touched one another. Sarah had reached out for her once before and they had both had a sudden sickness overtake them, their stomachs threatening to relieve themselves and their heads exploding in pain. Lizzie wasn't exactly sure what it meant or what it was, but they had learned that they weren't meant to touch.

So, Sarah could only watch as Lizzie struggled to get strength back in her legs as she eased her way to what they were looking at.

On the back of the tombstone was etched deep in the marble the words, "I'm Sorry Johnny Boy." and underneath, probably was meant to be a signature, the initials of her uncle. He had at some point come to visit her parents and had felt the need to forcefully etch in the stone his apology. What was he sorry for? Lizzie would never know.

Lizzie's knees gave out, her legs collapsing under her, and she barely missed the headstone as she fell to the ground.

"Lizzie!" she heard from a familiar voice, but not from the dead friends around her. This was one she hadn't heard without the hiss of a cell static in over a week, and she couldn't help but wonder how she was hearing it.

Did it matter? She had just fallen. She was on the ground, lying next to this marble altar of her parent's death.

"Lizzie!" the voice called again.

"Ah shit, it's Jess. I love her and all, but she really does have the worst timing."

"Who's Jess." Elisabeth asked, looking from Sarah to Chuck and then back.

"A friend of ours. She was supposed to be out there with us. If she had, maybe I'd still be alive, though I'm not bitter or anything." By her tone, it was hard not to notice that Sarah was indeed still bitter and had she been able to touch the woman who was quickly approaching, she would probably try choke her.

Lizzie didn't look up as they talked. She had noticed something on the marble. It was something else scratched there, but this wasn't as deep and hidden lower on the base where the grass nearly covered it. She eased closer and pushed aside the blades of grass.

Her uncle had etched this without the care or the tools and somehow, she had known that it had been there just for her. She didn't know how she knew, but could see him. She watched as he had tossed aside his etching tools, took a long pull from some bottle. He was wavering back and forth, so he must have been drunk as he pulled out the screwdriver and dropped down to the ground, lying there just as she was. He reached out and painstakingly scratched the stone to read, "Beware the dead" and below it, "stay in the house."

CHAPTER 9

"Oh my God! Liz, are you okay?"

Lizzie turned and looked up, having to shield her eyes from the sun that the short woman only barely blocked. She had recognized the voice when she heard it calling out, but even now, she wasn't sure she could believe Jessica had been there. Though it did make sense, as Jess was just as much one of Sarah's friends as she was.

"Here, let me help you up. Did you hit your head when you fell? I'm so sorry I haven't been by to check in on you. Dennis and I were out of town, but we hurried back as soon as we heard. Why didn't you call us to tell us? Patty was the one who called. I don't even know how she heard." Jessica said as she was pulling Lizzie up. Jessica was known for speaking like that. When she was excited, she would release a torrent of words that often had everyone around her struggling to keep up and no one could get a word in.

Not that Lizzie had anything she wanted to say. Her mind was still reeling from the gravestone. Had it really said to 'beware the dead?' Why would it say that? How could her uncle have known?

Lizzie looked at the three dead things that were gathered around her. Elisabeth and Sarah looked concerned, but Chuck was glaring again. She was to beware of them. Why? What could they do? They were dead. They were annoying, but they couldn't touch her or anything else solid. Why did she need to beware?

"Hello? Earth to Lizzie? Did you hit your head? I can-"

"I'm fine. Did you talk to Sarah's parents? How are they doing?"

"Well, not good. I really didn't get a chance to talk to them much. I saw you walking off and wanted to catch up."

"Thanks."

"Yeah, no problem. Dennis stayed over there. Why didn't you talk to them? They're like your second family."

"They blame me."

"You're kidding? Why?"

"Because she fucking got their daughter killed, you dumbass," Chuck screamed in her ear. Lizzie winced, not realizing he had rushed to catch up to them as they were walking back to Sarah's grave. Jessica hadn't noticed the brutally deformed man right next to her. Lizzie could barely keep from looking at him. It seemed the more he was there, the angrier he became. He blamed her. She hadn't caused his death, but that didn't matter. He was there, and he had died when she had not.

"I lived," Lizzie said, lowering her eyes so she didn't have to look into the hatred that burned in his eyes as he continued to glare at her.

110

"Oh, girl," and before Lizzie could protest, she was pulled into the shorter woman and had to fight to keep herself from falling farther forward into her. "It's not your fault. You gotta know that, don't ya? It's not your fault."

"Sure."

"Oh no, you're not getting away from me that easily. I'm not letting you go until you say it."

"I'm okay."

"Say it."

"I'm okay."

"You know that's not what I mean."

"Come on, admit to it. You killed us," Chuck whispered into her ear.

"Chuck!" Elisabeth yelled, and Lizzie looked up to see that she was working with Sarah to pull him away from Jessica.

"Liz," Jessica released her from the hug to hold her out at arm's length, studying her. Lizzie was sure her friend could see the tears, both the ones that had fallen and the ones that were threatening the horizon.

"Say it with me. Its...not...your...fault." She waited each time, watching and making sure Lizzie repeated it back to her. "Good."

It brought more tears, and somehow, even though the larger woman was shorter than her, Lizzie found herself burying her face in Jessica's shoulder.

"It's going to be okay." Sarah was saying behind her.

"We're here for you." Now it was Elisabeth near her as well.

"You're all pathetic." She could hear the disdain in Chuck's voice. She wasn't sure if she preferred him not to be talking to her. The silence had been filled with his hatred, but at least he had stayed quiet. She wasn't sure if this new development was for the better.

"Come on, I don't know who's all still around, but Dennis will be waiting for us at the car. I know you probably don't want to go back to the house, so...I don't know. How have you been? You able to sleep? You know you could stay with us for a while. It'd be like it used to be when we were roommates."

It had only been four months since Jessica had moved in with Dennis, but she made this sound like it had been a time long ago and that staying with her would be some trip down nostalgia lane. It wasn't that long ago, and they hadn't stopped hanging out together. They had just gone shoe shopping two weeks ago and Lizzie had found herself some really nice flats that she'd been wearing. Jessica had talked about Dennis the whole time, and Sarah had kept trying to bring up Roland, knowing that Lizzie had just separated. Sarah was hungry for all the juicy details and was hoping Jess would help her get her friend to spill the beans.

They had laughed and talked and had spent the whole day together. Why couldn't things just return to that? That one moment in time, possibly the last one that she had been so completely lost in her friends and happiness. She hadn't been worrying about school... Who cared if she changed majors again? If she did, it would be her third major in two years, and she hadn't been worried about pleasing anyone else. She had just enjoyed being with people she cared about and was glad to be alive. She had been happy that her friends were alive and were there with her.

"I'm not sure. I don't want to trouble you and Dennis."

"Liz, it's no trouble. You know that."

"I know."

"Do you really want to sleep in that apartment alone with what happened?"

She wouldn't be alone. She had all her dead hanger-on's who didn't go away. She would never be alone. She had Chuck to scream all night while Sarah and Elisabeth fought with him to shut up. Lizzie had her crying and, of course, there were all the nightmares when she could get to sleep. The shadow man that followed her inside the dreamworld and then lingered into her waking life.

Lizzie was never alone. She would never be alone again. They would never allow it. She would always have someone there to make her life miserable. If she went to the bathroom, Sarah or Elisabeth would be there with her. Chuck would be there, and he would torture her, watch her even when taking a shower. He had tried that morning, but Sarah prevented it. Eventually, she'd get tired of stopping him.

"I'll be fine."

"No, you won't. You can either sleep at our place or I'm staying there. You're not getting rid of me."

"I'm fine. I said I was fine."

"Hey, I'm only trying to help and be here for you."

"But you act like I need someone to save me, like I can't handle this or do things on my own. You're not my mother. Dennis isn't my father, and I don't need to be babied."

113

They were getting closer to the cars and Lizzie could see Dennis was giving Sarah's mom a hug before she got in their car. She didn't know if they could hear them, but she feared the worst. As the car drove off and Dennis looked at them with a pained look, Lizzie was pretty sure she was right. They'd heard it. She didn't know how much, but they did.

Dennis walked toward them. He was Jessica's matching set. They were both larger, but shorter and if you only looked at body dimensions, looked like they could be brother and sister. However, where Jessica had dark hair, his was a brilliant red. He kept a well-manicured beard that somehow brought out his smile rather than hid it in the hair. As he approached, she saw the smile, but could tell it was for her benefit, while not genuine to how he felt. There was a deep sadness in his eyes as they wore lines at the corners.

Before saying anything, he stepped to Lizzie and wrapped his arms around her in a hug. "We're here for you."

As Lizzie pulled back from him, she couldn't suppress the slight smile and the fresh wave of tears. "Thank you."

"So, where we off to?" He looked at them both. He was trying so hard not to act upset, and it was odd, but Lizzie felt herself relaxing as he hid his own grief from them.

"What did she say?" Jessica asked, nodding to the car that was leaving the driveway at the edge of the cemetery.

"That she would be okay. She loves us, but that all of us may not be welcomed at their house for drinks. She's worried it would cause undo drama."

"That woman was like a second mother to Liz and now they're blaming her like she killed her. That's not right."

"Yeah, it's bullshit, but it'll take a while. They just need to deal with it in their own way."

"Hey, I'm right here," Lizzie said, her voice tinged with the frustration of having them both talk about her as though she wasn't there.

"Oh, there you are. Thought we'd lost ya," Dennis said with his smirk, his sarcasm heavy on his tongue. "So, who's up for lunch?"

"Don't know. Haven't really thought about food much the last couple of days." Lizzie looked over her shoulder. The others followed the disfigured trio that walked behind them. Lizzie had no way of telling them, her two living friends, about the dead ones. How every time she tried to eat, they were there, and she found her appetite slip away.

"We don't need food. We need Belts." Jessica said with a giggle, pushing Lizzie softly towards their car.

"You just think ice cream is the solution to all." Dennis laughed.

"And you agree. Remember when we took your dad there? I thought his eyes were going to explode out of his head when he saw the size of the cone. It was bigger than his head."

Lizzie allowed herself to drift back as they started to tease each other. Her car wasn't parked too far away, but she'd have to leave them soon to walk to it. She wasn't sure she was ready to do that. Not yet.

She figured she'd follow them there. She didn't like the idea of leaving her car in the cemetery and she knew where Belt's Soft Serve was.

The last time she followed someone, they ended up dead. She saw the crash, watching as the truck plowed into the car, the sound of crushing metal and breaking glass, shouting through her memories.

"So, you just going to follow us there?" Jessica asked, "I mean, you could ride with us. It's up to you. Dennis has to move his trombone out from the passenger seat. Don't ask why he brought it, I'm not really sure, and he just laughs when I ask him."

The car. The crashing. The screeching metal.

"I can make it work. I don't really want to drive myself right now."

"Well, sure. Climb in." Dennis said with a shrug.

* * * *

"Are you sure we shouldn't go somewhere with, you know," Dennis playfully added, "actual food?"

They were along the highway and halfway to Belts, but as Lizzie sat in the back seat, she was beginning to sense that while Jessica had suggested it, she wasn't really in the mood for a massive ice cream cone.

"I'm fine with whatever. I'm not really all that hungry."

She watched as they shared a glance back and forth. She knew they were talking in ways she couldn't see. Part of it was probably eye contact, but they were also probably texting each other back and forth even while Dennis was driving. Lizzie noticed that his cell phone was not mounted on the vent magnetic holder where he normally kept it. They were talking, scheming, and it had something to do with her.

"Hey, how's this? We go back to our place and grill up some brats. Dennis can go to the meat market, and I can soak up some wood chips while he's gone. It'll give us a chance to girl talk, and he can do whatever he needs to do."

Yep, they were planning something. They were manipulating her, but did it really matter? They were in a car, and there were no dead people in there with her. It was such a relief that the only other occupant in the back seat was a dinged up old trombone that Dennis played when he performed with his jazz band. It was heaven, and she hadn't thought about just how nice it would be to not have them there.

"Sure."

"It'll be okay." Dennis said, looking at her through the rearview. "We're here for you."

They're there for her. Everyone was there for her. At least, that was what they said. She wanted to ask them just how much they would be there for her if they knew she had been talking to the dead for the last week.

"Hey Dennis?" Dennis had turned back to watch the road but turned to look at her, nodding for her to continue. "You have a buddy who gives lessons in self-defense, right?"

"Kinda." He turned back to watch the road as they neared a stop. He turned on the signal and she saw that they were taking a right turn. When they stopped, he looked back at her. "Ben teaches Karate at a dojo over on Wildwood drive. It's not really a self-defense class, but, well..."

She nodded to him, and he made his turn.

"So, you want to learn karate?" Jessica asked. She played with the word karate, stretching it out, toying with each syllable, making her sound like an eighty's schoolgirl. Lizzie winced. She'd already been making fun of the idea to herself, let alone hearing it from her friend.

"I don't know. It was just a thought."

"Well, Ben's a good guy. He doesn't own or run the place, but the guy who does is supposed to be some world-renowned champion, I guess. I think the first class is free, so you can check it out."

"Look, Liz, I shouldn't kid. I know you've been through some shit." Jessica said. Lizzie didn't know what she looked like, but Jessica had stopped joking with her and looked concerned. "If you want, I'll take a class or two with you. Check it out."

"I'll be fine. It was just a thought."

"Okay, well, the offer stands."

"Thanks."

CHAPTER 10

The room was bright. So bright that it hurt her eyes. Light spilled out from everywhere. The wall panels were white with radiance and hiding the ceiling high above her as it was lost to the glow. It was like she was standing in nothing as the white light cascaded everything away. There was so much of it and the brightness was turned up to such a degree that it hurt her eyes. She couldn't see anything because it blinded her. Tears rolled down her cheeks and even when she closed her eyes, that glow surrounding her was still there. She couldn't escape it.

It was another white room. She was in a padded room. It was her room; she knew it. She had told her friends, and they thought she was crazy and now she would be locked away forever.

She would never see her brother again...

Maybe he would come and visit, *just like you visit him,* her inner voice said sarcastically. She knew she was right. He would never come. How often did she ever visit him, even when he was having another form of treatment?

"Hey! Help me! Someone help me!" She screamed, but no one responded. She was left alone in the silence of the maddening hum of electric lights.

She rushed to the wall and slammed her hand into it. She had tried to watch it hit home, but her hand disappeared into the light a second before it made that dull thud. When she pulled her hand back, there was a light trail as she tried to blink away the brilliant light shadows.

Where was the door? If she was in this room, someone had to have put her there. There had to be a door. She just had to find it.

"Let me out!"

She pounded against the wall. Then she pounded again. Inside her, she felt something shifting. A change was going on inside of her. She was scared. Who wouldn't be? She woke up in a padded room, with no memory of how she had gotten there. She had been thrown off by how bright it was, but that didn't change that someone had taken her. That fear was quickly turning into an anger, and she pounded harder, faster, forcing through the nothingness of her first few hits until she was hitting the padded walls.

She started moving along with her hands, pounding more and more. Each time she moved, she hit harder and harder. Her fists felt like hammers, and they were destroying layers beneath the ones that were lit. But as she moved along, she never found the corner or even the door. The wall just continued with no end.

Her heart was racing, and she felt her blood burning with intensity. Each blow to the wall, she found a deeper strength reserve and kept pushing herself to break through.

"Come on, you bastards! Let me out! Show yourselves and let me out!"

Her fist slammed down, and she heard something. It didn't sound like the padding this time. What was that? Could it be...? She didn't want to get her hopes up, but now, instead of moving further down the wall, she stayed and brought her fist down again.

Sure enough, that had been a cracking sound she'd heard. It was like glass breaking, but not the regular stuff. Regular glass shatters when it breaks. This sounded like tempered glass, and she could hear it as the glass cracked. She brought her fist down again and more glass crackled under the force of her hammer headed fist. Again and again, the blows rained down.

The white light flickered and turned red as blood splashed across its surface. It never darkened enough to see the wall, but the flashes grew longer and spread around her. The whole room was flickering, not all at once, but different parts at different times, as though a strobe light had started to rotate around her. It was moving around her, sudden pockets of darkness shifting furiously in the light.

Then all light was gone, the remnants of it still creating exploding stars in her vision and her mind playing tricks on her between the world of light and dark. As she watched the darkness beyond, her vision swam with light that swallowed the dark just to have the dark again swallowed by the light. It was an ever-changing void that she wasn't sure if she saw it or imagined it taking over her vision.

It's like when you were a girl and closed your eyes. You remember seeing it then, how the black consumes the white just to then again be lost to the white. Remember all those sleepless nights filled with the insomnia game? You're right back there again, a lost, scared little girl, waiting to hear how you were losing your brother to a disease that you knew they couldn't stop...

It was an endless game as the light and dark danced around her, the walls uncertain as all traces of them gone. She could be in an endless void for as far as she knew.

She had to stop it or succumb to it. She already felt her consciousness slipping into the void cascading around her. She needed to focus, but on what?

Inside, she felt that fire that had been burning, dwindling, and she knew she could not let it fade to embers. She had to fuel the flame. Her anger needed to burn.

She closed her eyes, pushing away the thoughts of the light/dark show that continued. Instead, she let her mind wander until it fell upon her father.

"Dad," she whispered. "How could you?"

How could he... How could he leave her to take care of her brother or to finish growing up on her own? How could he not be there to help guide her through figuring out what it was she wanted to do with her life? How could he not be here for her when she lost her best friend, or to be here as she thought she was going crazy? He wasn't here when she needed him most. How could he leave her alone?

Both of them. She missed them both, but it had been her father driving the car, so she could blame him. Blame was a hard thing, but when it came to fanning the flames of anger, it was gasoline to a spark.

She felt it rising inside of her, rising, and intertwining with anguish and hurt to form a deep rage at her father for abandoning her.

"Ahhh!" she bellowed out a primordial roar and started slamming out her fists. She hadn't moved away from where the wall had been, and tried to bring her fists back down to again hammer into its surface, but with all her might she only hit air.

"Tik-a-tat, tik-a-tee, oh, what a oh, what shall we be?"

She recognized the voice behind her. Her chest clenched, and she had to fight from losing that burning anger as she spun. Around her it remained dark, and she didn't see anyone. He was there, though. Now that he spoke, she was listening more intently, trying to focus on the raspy breathing she heard. Though it somehow always managed to stay behind her no matter how fast she turned, she could hear those deep intakes of breath.

Fear will not win. Fear will not win. I will not let it take me. So where are you, you son of a bitch?

"Come on, you bastard!" She yelled into the darkness, billowing out with it, pushing back again the cloud of fear that had tried to overtake her.

"Tik-a-tee, tik-a-tet, we're not done yet." She heard the voice and felt the hot breath on her shoulder. She turned, swinging wide so as to make sure not to miss in the darkness. Her fist felt the heat of warm air, but where she had hoped to hit him, there was nothing.

"Show yourself!"

She was determined to hold on to her anger. She kept punching the air, hoping to have her fist drive home and hear the man call out in pain. *But it isn't a man, and you can't hit air,* that voice said inside her head.

Come on! Hit him! You're better than this.

Was she? She had never been much of a fighter. She had never gotten into a fight, not even with Natalie, when Lizzie had heard the rumor that she was screwing around with Roland. She had seen her flirting with him, and Lizzie had wanted to hit her, to beat the ever-living shit out of her.

Though her not doing it had more to do with Sarah calming her down than Lizzie chickening out. Still, she had never hit anyone. She wasn't sure she even knew how. Sure, just ball up your fist and swing, but wasn't there also a way of breaking your own thumb if you did it wrong? That's what she'd seen in the movies.

None of it mattered, as she felt the anger fading. The shadow man was there. How was she ever supposed to handle him? He couldn't be hit, or hurt. She should have known that.

Though in truth, she didn't know what to believe because if he could touch her and breath on her, then she should be able to hit him. It was the Freddy Krueger theory, that if he could hurt and kill, then he can be hurt. Though if Lizzie remembered right, that didn't work out for 'what's her name' in that movie.

Lizzie wasn't a huge fan of horror movies, but Roland had been and had subjected her to a number of vintage 80s films that he termed as 'classics.' She thought they were old and cheesy, but that never stopped him. He did get annoyed with her occasional jabs at their corniness, but mostly they were gross with many people being sliced and diced in increasingly gory ways.

In that first Freddy movie, she remembered that one. It was when the girl tried to bring Freddy to the real world so she could kill him; the idea being that if she could bring articles of his clothing across, she could bring him across.

Though, as she continued to strike at the air, her arms flailing more uselessly as she kept trying, she realized the fault. She didn't have anywhere to bring the shadow man. He was here with her, and just because he could touch her, that didn't mean she could touch him. It was a false argument. There was no guarantee that if she hit him, she could hurt him.

Around her, the room grew bright. She was back in the well-lit padded room, staring at the walls. There was no longer any sign of her blood on the wall in front of her or any of the surrounding walls. It was like she was somehow transported to a new room, everything she had done before completely wiped away.

"tik-a-tat…" The voice had become low, almost like a growl. It was behind her, and something told her she shouldn't turn around to look, that if she stayed there, she would be safe. He wouldn't attack her back. Of course not…

None of that was true. He'd attack her back, her front, her side. It didn't matter if she turned or not.

That didn't make it any easier, and she found herself turning to face him slowly, not wanting to see him again.

He stood in the far corner some distance from her. He was darkness, even in the light, and she struggled to remember him. She knew he had nearly been on her before, so much that she had smelled his sour breath, yet she still didn't know what he looked like.

Even now, when she looked at him, she couldn't tell what he looked like. She was close enough to make out something about him, but other than his black clothes, there was nothing. It was like his face was hidden in shadows even as light shined on him. Then there was his general shape. She swore that it kept changing as she watched him. There was some kind of thick, dark haze that shifted with him. Perpetual fog that kept her from ever making out any details.

It was like he was smoke in the shape of a man, but how was that possible?

That laugh of his filled the room, vibrating off the walls around her. Then he took a step towards her, and the room shook. Another step and then another, each time the room crashed down around her. Inside, that fire she had was gone. If she wasn't so terrified, she might have run towards him and slammed a slurry of blows into him. Now, with each step, she felt her heart skip a beat. Her breath came in quick gasps, and she had to fight to keep herself from collapsing in an emotional shutdown.

He neared her and she could smell that familiar musty smell of wet earth that permeated around him. He took another step towards her, and a piece of the ceiling crashed near her. She couldn't stop herself from taking a step back. It didn't help as he was nearly on top of her; she could see two glowing orbs that must have been his eyes.

"Tik-a-tat, tik-a-tor, for now there is one more."
The thing said. Then it was gone, its laugh lingering in a loud torrent that violently fumbled around her. More of the ceiling was falling. The whole room was tearing itself apart around her.

She felt the tears sting her cheeks as the lights went out, leaving her in complete darkness. But now, the darkness was left with that laugh that just kept on growing as it came from all around her. She felt herself vibrating. Then she was shaking, and she thought she was going to vomit as every part of her was twisting and rocketing back and forth. She'd never felt something push her around so violently.

Then she felt the floor beneath her give away, and the last thing she remembered was that she was falling helplessly to her death.

CHAPTER 11

It took Lizzie longer than it should have to realize that she was waking up from the nightmare. The world around her still shook and the laughter, his laughter, followed her even when she opened her eyes and saw she was back in her bedroom.

Had all that only been a dream?

"Lizzie, wake up!" Sarah was yelling at her and the shaking? It was Sarah and Elisabeth somehow. Lizzie wasn't sure just how they were doing it, shaking her bed.

They hadn't been able to move things before. How were they doing this? She didn't have time to think about it too much as she saw their worried faces as they were looking down at her. They were scared, but they were dead. *What could scare them?*

"What?" she said. Her voice was little more than a whisper, her throat dry and raspy, as she was still not fully awake.

The laughing wasn't going away, but it changed. It didn't sound like it had in her dream. It wasn't that growing cackle that had shaken the room, but a deep, raucous sound that was exploding out of the other room. It was coming from Sarah's room.

Lizzie's face went pale, and she turned to her best friend, then to Elisabeth.

"Where's Chuck?"

They both turned to the open door. Across the hallway was Sarah's old room, the door wide open.

She hadn't stayed with Jessica and Dennis. They had been kind enough to offer and had pushed, saying that they had plenty of room for her, but she still said no. She understood their concern. They didn't want her sleeping alone, not there in that apartment she had once shared with Sarah. What they didn't realize was that she still shared the apartment with her.

The first night she had slept in the apartment she had done just like she always had. When she had gone to bed, she had made sure the door was locked and the inside doors were all closed.

It had driven her three guests nuts. Well, one dead roommate and two guests. The apartment had been Sarah's too, and when she'd been woken up around two a.m. because they were all bored, she had been reminded of that. It seems that dead people don't sleep, and without friends to torment, they get bored.

Since then, she'd gotten in the habit of keeping open all the doors in the apartment and the television on. That is, all the doors but her own. Not her room. Her door always stayed closed. Last night was the exception.

Coming home after the funeral and being with Jessica and Dennis had left her in an awful state, and she couldn't stand to be alone. Sarah and Elisabeth had been happy to stay with her and it had almost felt like a slumber party until she, mid-party, crashed.

That had left her leaving all the doors open, even her bedroom. Oh no, that meant that Chuck could have been in there watching her sleep at any time. Who knows what he might have tried to do?

She knew this was a childish thought. It wasn't like guys hadn't seen her naked, though never when she hadn't wanted them to. Him checking her out while she was sleeping was not cool.

She looked at Sarah, who was still looking at the other room, scared. The thought returned. What could spook a dead woman? She was already dead.

"Sarah? What is it?"

Sarah slowly turned to look at her, her remaining wide-eyed. "He's in there," she whispered.

"Who, Chuck? What's he doing in your-" Lizzie was going to say room, but before she could, she saw that Sarah was shaking her head.

Lizzie looked back at the open door. If it wasn't Chuck, then who was in that room?

She couldn't stop it. The memories of that naked man as the maggot slid from his scrotum to land on her chin twisted her stomach. The laugh wasn't right. She was pretty sure of that, but could she be certain? She remembered the penis lurking over her and later looking into Sarah's eyes, but other than that, most of that day had become a hazy blur. Could she say for sure that wasn't his laugh? She didn't think she could.

But how could he have found her? The police had said he had been dead. It couldn't be him.

He could find me. He had already been dead when he attacked Sarah and I, so what was possible didn't make sense anymore...

Yet she was surrounded by dead people. They were becoming a part of her everyday life. She was beginning to think that the dead just don't stay dead anymore.

No, that had not been his laugh. It had stopped, of course, the other room now eerily quiet. The whole apartment was. The two people hovering over her weren't making a sound. All of them were watching that open door and the other room.

"What's going on? Sarah?" Lizzie tried to whisper as quietly as she could.

"Some guy showed up. He went in there."

"Should I call 911?" As soon as she said it, she realized just how stupid the question was, but it was too late. The words had already escaped her. To her surprise, Sarah shook her head.

"I think he's dead."

"If not, he's got a terminal case of missing-the-back-of-your-head disease," Elisabeth whispered, and Lizzie had to struggle to take her eyes off the woman. Of course, if it was another dead person now joining her undead entourage, they would be able to see how the person died. All of them had telltale signs like gory tattoos, each identifying their deaths. They were bleeding but not bleeding wounds, as blood sometimes seemed to trickle, but no messes were ever found beneath these walking corpses that followed her.

"Who's dead?" Lizzie whispered as she tossed away the tangled covers and pushed herself out of bed.

"No clue." Sarah said as she looked over at Elisabeth, who shared her ignorance and was shaking her head.

Who the hell was in the other bedroom? She didn't want to go in there, but she had to find out. Besides, they couldn't hurt her, right? Both she and the dead person would get intensely sick, so it wasn't even possible.

The wood panel floor was cold to her bare feet as she stepped into the hallway. The air in the apartment had a chill as well, and she wondered what it was like outside. Had the temperature finally dropped? Should she be turning on the furnace? The little fog of her breath escaping as she breathed made her think it was time.

Behind her, Elisabeth and Sarah both hung back in her room. Of course, the two dead people were hanging back, afraid. After all, what did Lizzie have to lose? Only her life, so you know, no big deal.

She gave them both dirty looks before turning back and taking another step towards the room.

A crash came from inside the room and Lizzie quickly was beginning to realize that everything she had thought she had known or had learned about the dead was wrong.

Fearing the worst, she held her breath and took the last step, entering the room.

* * * *

There was another crash as she entered and this time she saw the glass from the picture frame gliding across the room, stopping just inches of her foot. She looked at it and then where it came from to see two dead men entangled and fighting each other. One she recognized. The other was a stranger to her.

Chuck was underneath, but the new guy was on top and had Chuck pinned down. Chuck was flailing back and forth, fighting. The two of them were kicking out, thrashing the bed, Sarah's dresser, her clothes hamper... and the furniture was moving as they did. That wasn't possible, but it was happening. The picture that had fallen had been on Sarah's dresser. These two had knocked it down. The hamper was swaying back and forth, ready to topple over at any time. Then, with one swift kick, it fell out over and a week's worth of forgotten dirty clothes spilled out.

Lizzie's jaw hung open as she watched the fight, but then she heard the gasp come out behind her.

"Stop it!"

The first yell didn't come from Lizzie, but from behind her. "I said stop it!" Sarah bellowed, and the stranger turned to them in surprise. Chuck took the opportunity to push him off, and the stranger rolled with the push and used the momentum.

"Yeah, and who the hell are you?" The stranger's voice was a raspy gurgle and Lizzie watched as exposed muscle tissue from under his jaw waved with the motion of what was left of his mouth. Half the bottom row of teeth was missing, one dangled there, and the flesh from his neck hung strung down in what seemed to only be held together by hair from his overgrown beard. She could almost see through the long hair, the large hole through his chin. It was hard to look away, but she had to, as she thought she was going to puke. She had started to get used to the disfiguration of her friends. They weren't looking good themselves, their own deaths all gruesome, leaving them horrified remnants to follow her around. This stranger who was obviously dead was much worse.

"Doesn't matter. You're in my fucking room." Sarah said, quickly passing Lizzie to loom over him.

"Like hell it doesn't. What the hell's going on here? Wait." He was confused. Lizzie watched as he struggled to fight with himself when it came to forming words. "Why can't I talk right? What's wrong with my mouth?"

"Half of it's missing, dumb ass. That's what happens when you blow your brains out." Chuck grumbled as he pushed himself up from the floor. He glared at Lizzie and then turned that hate at the rest of them standing by the door.

"Missing? Blown Brains." The man was confused but getting angrier as he tried to speak.

"Can you tell us who you are? Because we don't know you. Right?" Lizzie looked at Elisabeth and she nodded. None of them knew who the hell he was, so why was he here? So far, Lizzie kind of understood why her friends were coming to her. They all had at least some connection. She didn't know why they were back from the dead, but she knew why they came to her. She'd been the last one with them, each of them before they died. Unless this man died in the same apartment, it didn't make sense for this stranger to be there.

"I..." He looked at them strangely, his hostility shifting, transforming as Lizzie could see his eyes getting wet. He looked around the room at them, his gaze lingering on Elisabeth, his brow raised in curiosity. Then that look was gone, and he turned back to study Chuck. His hostility returned and with a fire he turned that blazing stare back to Lizzie.

"Josh. My name's Josh."

"Any idea what you're doing here?" Lizzie asked, but Sarah was quick to snap herself back into the discussion, and more importantly, what she wanted to know.

"And what the hell are you doing in my bedroom?" You would think Sarah had found them going through her underwear drawer and had pulled out one of her panties.

Josh ignored them, continuing to glower at Chuck. If they were dogs, they'd be growling at each other, both with their macho egos on full display. Lizzie was getting sick of it.

And then she noticed the glass on the floor. She hadn't thought too much of it before, but there was something odd about that. She couldn't place her finger on why it bothered her, but it did.

"So, are we done here? No more fighting?" Lizzie said.

"Who the hell are you people?" He barked. Lizzie didn't know how she understood him, his speech was garbled by the missing parts of his mouth, but she still did. She let it go, but still ignored him, her glare lingering on Chuck.

Chuck shrugged his shoulders, looking at Josh and then back to Elisabeth. A weak smile flashed as he stepped over to her and hugged her. It felt right to see them hold each other, and Lizzie realized that since they had died, she hadn't seen them touch one another. It had been like they had been avoiding it. Now they did, and the hug grew stronger, and she barely heard him whisper to her, "It'll be okay."

Lizzie hoped so, and she turned to Sarah.

"You guys figure all this out. I'm going back to bed."

Sarah nodded and then to everyone, "Okay everyone, now let's get out of my room. Out, out, out!"

"I want to know just what the hell is going on! Who are you people, and how did I get here?"

"Josh. You're dead. Face it and live with it. We don't know who the hell you are or why you're here, but there it is. Next time, don't blow your brains out."

Lizzie heard her friend giving Josh the low down, but she didn't wait to watch her get them out of her room. She was too tired and felt like she was going to have a lot of bullshit to deal with in the morning. She walked across the room, closed the door, and crashed down onto her bed.

She knew she'd been tired and after the initial surge of energy from being forcefully awakened waned, she was ready to sleep.

Questions haunted her. There were many of them. Why had people she had known, some friends but Chuck she had barely met, come back from the dead? Why were they hovering around her? What was the connection to the new guy, the one no one knew anything about? Though he did seem like he recognized them. She might be wrong, but she thought she had seen it, just a hint of it when he looked at Chuck. And why had they been fighting?

And there was something about the glass, how it had shattered and slid across the floor. There was something odd about that and she couldn't place what it was? Maybe in the morning she'd figure it out.

A long yawn escaped her, and by the time she'd stretched and settled back into bed, she was drifting off to sleep. This time, the nightmares left her alone.

CHAPTER 12

The phone was ringing. She understood that it was ringing. She had that sensation of being ripped from some shared collective deep in the bowels of sleep to open her eyes to the revelation, and yes, there it was, her phone on the nightstand. The screen was lit up, and she saw the unfamiliar number on her lock screen.

"Probably a telemarketer," she mumbled under her breath as she crashed back into her pillow. The room was bright. It was obviously sometime in the morning, but she wasn't ready to get up yet... and really, what was the point anymore? She had no job, no classes, no life... Why the hell not sleep in until noon? The idea sure as hell appealed to her.

She grabbed a spare pillow and turned it over, snuggling into it like it was someone lying there with her. It took some work, a little wriggling back and forth, but finally she had found that spot when everything felt comfortable and soft, perfect to go back to sleep and ignore the rest of the world.

Someone was knocking at the door. She didn't want to answer it, and the pillow she was snuggling into became earmuffs as she pulled it down over her head.

"Hey Lizzie! Lizzie! Someone's at the door."

Sarah was her best friend. She had been since childhood and now after death, but right then Lizzie wanted to scream at her. Didn't she know that Lizzie just wanted to hide and get back to sleep? It just wasn't fair. All she wanted to do was go back to sleep. Wouldn't anyone just let her? The world seemed hellbent on preventing it.

"Lizzie?"

Lizzie felt the groan escape her and it surprised her to find that she was getting up. The long stretch came and then she was reaching out to her cell phone, glancing at the time but more at the displayed list of missed calls. The majority of the missed calls came from a number she vaguely recognized, but her sleep deprived mind couldn't place it.

She tossed the phone on the bed as she stood and went to the closet, only to realize that she hadn't checked the time. Sure, she'd looked at it, but had completely blanked.

"Lizzie, they're still knocking."

"So, let them knock. It's probably just more Jehovah's Witnesses or something."

"I don't think so. They'd have given up by now."

That was probably true, she thought as she finished pulling on her pants and tossed on a t-shirt that had hung in her closet. She didn't pay attention to what it said. She didn't really care yet. It was still too early for her to deal with people. Whoever was at the door was about to get her at her worst.

"You know, sometimes I wish you were a ghost rather than whatever you are," Lizzie said as she straightened the shirt and looked at herself in the mirror. She was never going to win any beauty pageants, that was for sure. She grimaced, wishing she had Sarah's body.

Someone was still knocking on the front door, but Lizzie noticed that outside her room it had quieted enough that she could make out the faint sound of someone sobbing.

Lizzie opened the door to her room to see Sarah sitting on the floor, her knees pulled up to her chest.

"You know, I was just kidding. It was like, so you could float through the door and see who it was. Ya know?" Lizzie said, and Sarah launched into a new torrent of tears.

"How would you like to be dead, or told you should be a ghost because it makes your best friends' life better? You'd just love that, wouldn't you?"

"Sarah, you know it's not like that."

"You know it's like that. You just said it."

The knocking on the front door stopped. *Thank God for small miracles* as whoever it was must have gone away.

Lizzie's cell phone started ringing again.

"Oh, for fuck's sake." She spun and dashed into her room and grabbed the buzzing rectangle. Without looking at the caller ID, she tapped the screen, ready to release the full pulsating rage burning through her.

"Tik-a-tat, tik-a-tuk, I smell a good fuck," came the familiar raspy voice. Even through the electronics of the phone, she could feel his hot breath on her, and her cell dropped from her hand.

"Hello! Lizzie, you there?" She heard coming from the phone as it fell. She looked at it, not wanting to touch it when it landed. She recognized the voice, but that hadn't been there before. No, the shadow man had called her. What was going on?

Slowly, she bent and reached for it, afraid it was somehow going to reach up and bite her. That was crazy, though, right?

"Hey, Lizzie, I heard you answer."

She picked up the phone, though she refused to bring it to her ear.

"Hey."

"Liz, hey, I'm at your door. You mind letting me in?"

That voice. It wasn't the shadow man, but another voice that made her recoil. She'd heard it enough through the last few years, and one she thought she was done with a month ago when she had dumped his cheating ass.

"Roland, why the hell are you here?"

"Liz, come on, let's talk?"

Ugh, she thought all this was over. Sure, she hadn't caught him with Natalie, but those hadn't been her panties she had found in his place. When she'd confronted him about it, he stuttered like a floundering fool, then had the gall to tell her that she must have left them there. Did he really think she wouldn't recognize her own panties?

Such a creep...

Yet she found herself lowering her phone, hitting disconnect as she tossed in on the bed and going to the front door. There was no knocking, but she knew he was on the other side, like she could feel his presence there. She imagined she could hear his breathing, then felt it when his breath held, waiting for her to open the door. Her hand lingered on the knob. Maybe she imagined he was holding his breath because she was holding her own.

"Lizzie, we need to talk," Chuck said. He had come up behind her, and she hadn't even realized he had been following her to the door.

"Not now," she hissed back at him.

"It's important."

"You're dead. I don't think anything's going to change in the next five minutes."

"Liz-"

"It can wait," she said just before she opened the door and saw the tall, lanky man in the hallway outside her apartment. He was standing there, a bouquet of roses in his hands.

"What are you doing here?" She didn't reach for the flowers, but he continued to hold them out for her. It felt like a long minute, stretching into eternity as she held his eyes with her glare. Then he gave in, lowering both his arms and his eyes.

"I heard about Sarah. Guess I just wanted to check in and make sure you're doing okay."

"I'm fine. You can go now." She didn't step into the hall, and she didn't get out of the door frame to let him in. Her arms crossed, her body language screaming 'pissed off woman who'd been cheated on and was now ready to get payback' as she stood there.

"Liz, I know that's bullshit."

"Yeah, and how do you know that?"

"I know you and I knew Sarah. You two were inseparable."

Lizzie fought to keep her breathing calm and her anger in check, but her chest burned while she bit back the curses she wanted to spew at him. This piece of bile actually felt like he could console her, that he knew something about her. If he knew anything about her, he'd have known not to cheat on her. Where does he get off at implying that he knew her?

"Liz, can I come in? Maybe you could put these in water?"

"Just toss them in the dumpster."

"If that's what you want. I guess I can just toss these away too."

She hadn't noticed the envelope that had been in his other hand. She looked at it and had to think about it. What was the date today... Could those be...

He brought up the envelope, jostling the flowers as he needed the other hand to open and pull out the contents. He got frustrated and handed the envelope to her. She opened it and there they ...were... tickets to see Ed Sheeran tonight. The event was in Milwaukee, so they'd have a three-hour drive.

She remembered when they bought the tickets, how they had laughed and made plans to make a weekend of it, getting a hotel and maybe while they were in town checking it out and maybe going to a Brewers game. It seemed like forever ago, and in a way, it was a lifetime ago, as so much in her life had changed now. For one, she was no longer with Roland. Why would he show up now and still want to go? She would have thought he would have sold the tickets or taken whoever he was screwing.

He couldn't be dumb enough to think she'd go with him, right? She had always thought he'd been smarter than that. He was a sure-fire geek and computer nerd. He should have something in that head of his telling him that the idea of them going together would be idiotic.

He kept looking at the floor, occasionally sneaking a peek up at her. He was probably gauging how she was reacting as she let him fidget.

"What do you think you are doing? What do you expect to happen here?" She returned the tickets to the envelope.

"I'm not expecting anything to happen. I came to say that I'm sorry. I messed up. In addition to that, I'm worried about you, and I wanted to see if you were okay. As to that," he raised his eyes and nodded to the envelope she was now playing with in her hand, hitting the corner of it into her palms as she continued to study him. "We'd already bought the tickets. I never felt right about selling them, and I had no one else to take. I thought maybe we could go. Not as a couple, but just as two people. No strings."

"You know how stupid that is, right? There's no way I'm going with you."

"You don't have to. You could take yourself. Hell, you can have my ticket. I just thought you could use it as a distraction from, well…"

If she was honest with herself, she really did want to go. She loved Ed Sheeran, and the tickets were really good. Roland had spent more than he should have on them. He'd spent all that money just to go and do something so stupid. Maybe he really was dumb under all that smart exterior.

Lizzie was wavering. She knew she shouldn't be.

"Shut the door, Liz. He's not a good guy, and we really need to talk to you," Sarah said into her ear. Of course, Sarah was listening. Hell, they were probably all behind her, watching and listening. She never had moments alone anymore...

Maybe she could use that to her benefit. If she did go to the show with him, it wouldn't be like she'd be alone with him. Oh, how odd of chaperones they were, but they'd keep her from doing something stupid.

Was she really thinking of doing it, though? She thought she was done with this loser. She should shut the door and never see him again. Let that be the end of it.

But she wasn't shutting the door.

She could go, but they both go in their own vehicles... No, that wouldn't work. Milwaukee was what, two hours away, three? She'd never actually been there, so she wasn't sure. Either way, it was too far and made no sense to take separate vehicles. Even if he was a creep that she didn't want to be around, she still couldn't bring herself to be that wasteful.

Dammit, she was going to do this. She knew it was a bad idea, stupid really, but she had already said 'yes' to herself. It was just a matter of telling the asshole.

Her stomach twisted at the thought of spending at least four hours in the car alone with him. Then she was reminded that she had just gotten up, was standing on the threshold of the hallway, and still hadn't gone to the bathroom. Her bladder was reminding her that it was not going to be patient for much longer.

Then her phone started chirping again from the bedroom and she realized she really needed to get out of the hallway.

"Fine, I'll go. Give me a call later and we'll get it figured out when to leave." She started to close the door but then opened it again, ignoring his outstretched hand as he tried to hand her the roses. "Better yet, just text me."

She closed the door and rushed to her room. The bathroom was calling, but going in there without her phone just wasn't happening. She grabbed it and glanced at the recent missed call. That same number again.

"Liz, I can't believe-" Sarah started, but Elisabeth was talking over her.

"Lizzie, we really need to-" Elisabeth was saying. In the background, she could hear Chuck.

"For crying out loud."

"-you're going out with him."

"-talk to you."

She rushed into her bathroom, ignoring the cacophony of voices trying to get her attention. She slammed the door behind her.

* * * *

The voicemail had been from the lawyer and had taken away any joy she had about the concert. His words, a nervous stutter as he bumbled through leaving the message, repeatedly saying there wasn't much he could say over the phone.

"Ms. Rogers, I'm calling to say that there has been a mistake in the, in the reading of the will. You see, your uncle, well, there's not much I can, I can say over the phone. You see, he changed his will right before he died, and it had been so recent that our filing records hadn't recorded it yet. If you can call to

147

set up an appointment, I really need to go over it with you. I'm, I'm sorry for all of this."

She'd lost all that money. She knew it, and that was why he was so nervous. He had to tell her that she wasn't getting it. She was going to go back to being broke. All the good fortune of having that money was going to evaporate, and she'd never get to know how it felt to be that rich.

"Liz?"

Lizzie looked up to see Sarah looking at her, concern etched on her face. Any signs of the tears from earlier gone, leaving only the gory remains of Sarah's death. It was yet another reminder that her friend was dead, and any tears were shallow to the tragedy she had already endured.

"Yeah, I'm fine."

"Yeah, you don't look it."

Her phone buzzed, and she took a quick look at it. It was Roland. She lowered the phone, realizing just how late in the morning it really was. It was past ten. She slept in for most of the morning. Five minutes ago, that wasn't a problem, but now with the prospect of finding a new job looming, sleeping in this late felt like such a waste.

What was she going to do? Go back to school? It'd be too late to register for this semester, and she hadn't decided on a new major, having given up on her last one shortly before deciding not to go back.

What the hell!? She thought her life would be getting so much easier, and now she was getting nothing but all these problems.

"Lizzie, we need to talk," Elisabeth said. Then a crash came from the other room and Lizzie rushed to see what was going on.

Lizzie's apartment was not that large, and, like most, she guessed. There was the front door that opened into a split between the nook that was the kitchen and the open area for a living room. The little space between what she had guessed would be a dining area and the hallway then led back to the two bedrooms and the tiny bathroom. It was just like nearly any other apartment she had ever seen, and she looked forward to one day not living there.

Though with her currently not having a paycheck and no income in the near future, it was a bit above what she could afford. Even working, it had been tough for her.

She hurried into the living room to find Chuck and the stranger standing nose to nose squaring off again, but the picture that was on the floor was on the other side of the room. It had been a picture of her and Roland that had been sitting on the corner shelf between the curbside find of a couch and the lazy boy that had been a goodwill special.

Sarah was standing near the picture, staring at it in horror.

"What's going on here?" Lizzie scanned the room. Sarah looked at her apologetically, but the other two didn't turn away from one another.

"Just don't like being told what I can and can't do," the large man said, then sat in the Lazy-boy.

"I get that." Lizzie said.

"Lizzie, something weirds going on," Elisabeth said, moving to stand next to Sarah. Chuck continued to glare.

"I know... I know you two from somewhere. And that ain't good." Josh said to Chuck, then pointed to Elisabeth.

"Really? You do?" Elisabeth said, the shock evident.

"Let's start simple. What's your name?" Lizzie said.

"I told you last night." The man said.

"Yeah well, middle of the night. I just remember you were fighting with Chuck and another picture got broken. So yeah, I wasn't really focused, or really even awake."

"Name's Josh."

"Okay Josh, and you know you're dead, right?"

"Yeah. Just because I blew my brains out doesn't mean I don't have any."

"Nice. Really funny." Chuck said.

"Give 'em a break. It's not like you were much better when you first got here. Until he came, you were Mr. Grumps." Lizzie turned back to Josh, sitting in the chair. "Now the big question. Do you know how you got here?"

"Nope. I shot myself in the morning after my wife went off to work and woke up here last night."

"Really? So, you didn't show up here right after you died?"

"Nope. Not even sure if it's the same day. What day is it?"

"Lizzie, something else is going on."

"What?" Lizzie asked, turning slowly, lingering her gaze on Josh.

"Broken pictures," Sarah said.

"Yeah, all our frames are getting ruined. I'm going to have to go to the dollar store later and buy some more."

"I'm not talking about that." Sarah went to the next picture on the shelf and then, with an intense look of concentration, she reached out and pushed it. "Remember when I first came back, and I couldn't interact with anything? Well, we can't grab anything as far as I know, but look at this."

"I know I recognize you two," Josh grumbled as Lizzie watched Sarah push the picture frame until it fell from the shelf and crashed to the floor.

"Sorry."

Lizzie's phone rang, the chirping sound making her jump. Lizzie didn't look to see who it was. She clicked "answer" as she brought it up.

"Hello?"

"Ms. Rogers."

"Yes?"

"Hello, I know I've called a few times this morning, but I really need you to come to my office. I'll be able to meet you any time. I'll reschedule whatever I must, but it really is rather urgent." The lawyer sounded frazzled. That wasn't good.

"Is everything okay?" She felt the dread creeping up into her voice.

"Yes, just there's a new will we found with some new details we need to go over."

She remembered the text she had gotten earlier and pulled the phone away from her face so that she could swipe and see it.

"How about we leave at 2?" Roland's text read.

"I can get there in half an hour."

She could have Roland pick her up from the office. Maybe she'd get lunch while she waited for him after meeting with the lawyer. That was if she still had any money.

Damn! She couldn't believe she had allowed herself to get talked into going with him. *Eddie, I hope you know how much I love you to put up with his cheating ass.*

"I got it!" Josh exclaimed, and he stood quickly. "It's you two! You're the idiots that pulled out in front of my truck! You fucking idiots ruined my life, I'm going to kill you, you son-of-" and with that Josh was leaping across the coffee table, which was surprising with his large mass, and slammed into Chuck who had stood there frozen with shock. They both fell to the ground, everything on the table clattering out of their way, remotes, books, and magazines flung to the floor.

"Fuck this, I'm out." Lizzie said, grabbing her keys and purse, then storming out the front door.

CHAPTER 13

She wasn't surprised when she got into the car to find Sarah in the passenger seat, with Chuck and Elisabeth sitting in the back.

"Where's Josh?"

"Who cares? I don't," Chuck said, obviously still upset that he had been attacked by the larger man.

"Okay, I meant to ask you guys this last night because I gotta know, what happens when you're not with me, in the car or whatever?"

Lizzie turns to Sarah, who shrugs, "I'm not really sure. It's like yesterday when you left with Jess. We were with you in the cemetery, but once you got in the car, you were gone, and then we were back with you when you got out. It's like ... well, I don't know how to describe it."

"It's like we don't exist and then we do." Chuck said, obviously frustrated.

"It scares me sometimes. You'll leave and we just disappear, and well, I don't know what this is. I mean, we're dead, right, but we're linked somehow to you, and when you leave, we just are gone and then come back wherever you are. Well, what if we don't come back sometime? What happens then? Do we move on? Are we lost in limbo? The darkness scares me," Elisabeth was holding herself, struggling to hold in tears. "I don't know why, but it does."

"And what happens when you are in the car? Why did Josh not come with me? I mean, I know there's not enough room for him. You really need a bigger car, Liz, but who chose that he would be the one in the darkness?" Sarah added.

"It's scary." Elisabeth said.

"I hate not having any kind of control." Chuck continued as he turned to look out the window.

"I don't know what to do. I don't know what happened, why you're here. I've googled it and such, but I don't know. I wish there was something I could do to help." Lizzie said as she started the car.

"We know that. Liz, you're like a sister. I know you'll be here for us. And we're here for you, anytime you need us," Sarah said as she reached out for a hug but stopped herself, remembering that they couldn't touch.

"Love you, sis," Lizzie said as she put the car into gear, wiping away tears of her own.

* * * *

Lizzie hadn't been surprised that once she parked the car and got out, Josh was standing there waiting for them. He was disoriented, looking around at the parking structure, and now she understood why.

The rest of them soon appeared around him, not having to get out of the car, but just at one moment sitting there and the next to be standing outside. None of it made any sense, but did she really want the answers?

Josh immediately turned to Chuck and Elisabeth, his fist already clenching.

"Stop it!" Lizzie said forcefully. Something must have shifted in her voice, because all of them had stopped moving and looked at her. She quickly glanced around to see if she saw anyone in the structure before continuing. "We'll talk about this later. Josh, I get that you're pissed. Not sure what your situation is as we don't know you, right?"

She turned to Elisabeth and Chuck to confirm that they didn't know him. They both shook their heads.

"So we'll talk later and work this out. Right now, I gotta find out what's going on with this lawyer and why he needs to see me so bad. I can't have you guys fighting while I'm trying to talk to him. You guys make it hard sometimes when I'm talking to living people that I've been lucky no one's sought to have me committed. Please, not in front of the lawyer who actually could and probably would have me locked up. I don't know if I trust this guy. He's a lawyer."

"The only good lawyer is a dead lawyer." Josh quipped, and Lizzie nodded.

"So please, no getting upset," she turned and looked at Sarah, "with whatever news he has for us. We need to remain focused."

Josh was seething. She could tell he didn't want to do what she was asking. His fists opening and closing were signs he was ready to throw another punch.

"Josh, I don't know what you've been through-"

"I was losing everything. All of it was going to slip away. My lawyer said I'd never see my family again. All because of these two idiots."

"Josh. Listen to me," she moved so that she could get him to see her, then her eyes locked on his. It was hard with his disfigured face to look at him, but she fought to keep her disgust in check. "We don't know what's going on and I'll be honest, we should have tried to figure this out. We really should have, but Sarah… I was being selfish, and I don't know how I'd been able to handle her being dead. So, her and these two… I've been selfish. You being here now, that changes things and we'll figure this out. I don't know what's happening or why you're here, but trust me. Okay."

Josh wasn't saying anything, but just watched her. Maybe she was getting through to him. She'd like to think that maybe some of those psych classes were paying off, but in truth, she just said what felt right. Those psych classes had just taught her about Pavlov and Id and superegos. She hoped that speaking from the heart would help him.

"I don't know you."

"I know that. We don't know you either, which is-"

"I don't know you, so I have no way of knowing if I can trust you. Why should I?"

A car door slammed shut nearby and Lizzie turned, scanning to see if she saw anyone. In the distance, the sound of another vehicle making its turns in the garage as it circled through the layers, trying to find a parking spot. It was getting closer.

"I know you don't know me. I'm just asking you work with me for a little while and go from there."

Josh continued to stare at her, and she felt like the scene was going to continue until someone saw them. It would become awkward, her standing there glaring at nothing. Then her phone rang, and she was relieved for a break in the growing tension.

"Yeah?" she said as soon as she tapped the green button that was just below the glowing picture of her friend Jessica.

"How ya holding up?"

"I'm doing okay, Jess," she said. The group of the dead started to walk around her, growing uncomfortable with just standing around in the parking structure.

"Really? It's okay. You know you can talk to me."

"Who is it?" Sarah mouthed even though she had to know Jessica couldn't hear her.

"Jess," Lizzie mouthed back, and then into the receiver, "Yeah. While I was in the hospital, I had met with a nurse and she's helping me through it."

"A grief counselor? That's good." Lizzie wasn't going to correct her, but it helped if her friends thought she had already been talking to someone. She knew that if she'd said anything else, it would be the beginning of phone calls from a variety of friends and acquaintances, all offering their ears and their advice on professional help. This way, Jess would get the word out she already had someone helping.

That was much easier than explaining that she wasn't grieving because she hadn't really lost her best friend. She was right there and continued to be with her.

"Fine, I'll trust you for now, but can we just get going? This parking garage makes me uneasy. Don't know why, but it makes me feel like I'm in my own grave." Josh said as he leaned against her car.

"You know, I'm also here to talk and hey, I wanted to ask," she said. "Dennis is working today, but I'm off with nothing to do. You want to get together later?"

"I have plans this evening."

"How about lunch?"

"Sure. I'm at the lawyer's office now, but can meet up when we're done."

"Okay, when and where?"

"I'm thinking sushi."

"Hmm, well," Jessica said, and Lizzie could picture her as she closed her eyes, thinking about her favorite places downtown. "We could go to Little Joe's."

"That works. Meet you there?" She said as Josh started pounding against the car. She turned away from him and started walking towards the stairs.

"Is that really necessary?" Elisabeth hissed at him just before he quit and followed Lizzie.

"I don't know what's worse between the two of you." Sarah said. Lizzie wasn't paying any of them attention and missed the look Sarah gave the two men. "You two keep acting like a bunch of children. We're dead. Get over it."

"What the hell did I do?" Chuck asked, running a little to catch up.

"Both of you have acted like children. You're no better than him, yelling all night long."

"I get bored."

Lizzie didn't wait for them as she entered the stairwell, the fire door slamming shut behind her. The silence enclosed around her, and she embraced its briefness as she and Jess finalized their lunch plans, and she disconnected the call.

She took a long, deep breath, letting it out in a sigh. She was alone, and it felt great.

"So, what floor is this lawyer on?" Sarah asked. Lizzie opened her eyes to see that they were all gathered around her. Her solitude was gone, she hoped that it would not be forever lost.

* * * *

The entryway for the lawyer's office wasn't much better for privacy, and Lizzie felt cramped in the little amount of space that was used for a waiting area. She had been surprised her first time there, and it hadn't changed in the last two weeks. It was nothing like she'd ever seen when she watched them lawyer shows. Where was all the glass and the polished metal? There was none of it.

Instead, what she found was that the office was in a complex, on the third floor and over a bank. The front office area when she walked in had a younger man sitting behind a desk, an older computer and a monitor littered with post-it notes. The desk was covered in folders, and in fact, folders of paper were everywhere. The walls were lined with filed cabinets and even these had files on top of them. The whole room was a graveyard of dead trees, as there was enough paper to fill a forest.

Quickly after introducing herself to the man, his name was Adam, and he had a slight lisp, she sat in one of the two chairs. Both were old leather chairs, dark brown and not fashionable to the light decor of the room. Though the room itself didn't have much of a theme going for it. The walls were off white, and Adam's desk was gray with dark accents. Someone really needed to fire the interior designer, but that wasn't her place. At least it didn't smell bad in there.

Her first time there, she had thought she was in the wrong office. It was only after confirming she wasn't that she thought the phone call and letter had all been some sort of scam. After all, who would leave her anything? She had forgotten about her uncle, her parents had long since passed away, and the little family on her mother's side was nonexistent. She never knew why, but her mom wouldn't talk about it.

Now she was there again, and her dead entourage took up the extra room around her. She had to wonder about whatever force kept them with her and how it worked? Especially with the size of the small room, it would be nice if one or two of them had vanished into that in between nothing Sarah had told her about.

Immediately Josh had taken the other chair and was quickly becoming bored with waiting. She was starting to get the sense that he was a highly impatient person. Maybe that had something to do with how he had barreled into Chuck and Elisabeth.

"Thank you, Mrs. Robbins. I'll talk to you again next week." Adam said into the phone. He had been taking a payment and now lowered the receiver as he looked over at her. "I can check to see if he's ready."

"Thank you."

He rose and stepped through the door behind him. Other than the entrance, it was the only other door in the room.

"Hurry up and wait. Just as bad as being in the military." Josh said as he slumped down in the chair.

"You have some big date?" Elisabeth gave him a frustrated glare and Lizzie suspected that the truck driver was getting on many of their nerves.

"Hey Charles, tell me, you like a good joke?" Josh said, not even looking at him, keeping his eyes returning Elisabeth's stare.

"Sure."

"You can come in," Adam said as he quickly emerged from the office. Lizzie was quick to stand, already feeling crowded by the bickering dead people scrambling around her. The dead could be so annoying, even if they couldn't physically interact with her.

"So, this man was working on his roof, and it was hot and all that. He was putting down some new shingles with his friend, helping him. His friend was getting frustrated and asks him, 'Hey, what time is it?'" She heard Josh as he told them the joke when she left the room. Sarah was following, and Lizzie wished the rest of them would stay in the outer office.

If she'd been unimpressed with the piles of files in the outer office, she was equally unimpressed with the lack of files and the dingy furniture in the inner room. Even the computer looked like it had been out of date five years ago. The desk looked like one of those back-to-school specials on sale for fifty bucks at any office supply store and the chair was a thrifty high back rolling chair with its faux leather torn along the back side. She sat in the chair across from the lawyer.

The man behind the desk looked tired and old. When she'd seen him before, he had been an older man, yes, with a complete matching set of silver hair and beard, but it had been perfectly in place. In fact, despite all the chaos his office represented, his appearance had been perfect.

What has happened to this man? He looked so haggard now, his hair on end and skin was an ashen pale. His eyes were dark, deep shadows under them, as though he hadn't slept since she'd seen him. His suit could have been the same one he'd worn then and has since never been removed. It was wrinkled and fit him poorly. Had he lost weight since she'd seen him?

Oh no, he'd better not be dying. If he did, would he become one of her ghosts? Something about this unkempt old man following her around sent a twinge of disgust through her. It just seemed wrong.

"Hello Miss Rogers," he said as he looked up from his computer screen. "Do you like music?"

She was surprised by the question, and he must have noticed as he smiled at her, and his pale face colored with embarrassment. She could see red stains on his teeth in that smile and she barely suppressed a shudder as she thought of the naked man as he crushed Sarah's skull.

"I'm sorry. I just, sometimes in rough times, get lost in a good melody. I didn't mean to keep you waiting but had been listening to Dylan and was lost in that soulful way he releases his pain."

"The man saw as his watch slipped off, but he couldn't stop it. It was going to go off the side of the roof." Josh said, watching Chuck for any kind of reaction as they entered the room. Chuck lingered in the doorway, not entering the quickly filling space.

Lizzie briefly glanced up at them, annoyed. "I listen to mainly Imagine Dragons and stuff like that. I love Ed Sheeran."

"He has some good stuff. Nothing as intense as Dylan, but it's great to just disappear into the rhythm and let your thoughts fade."

"Stop it!" Elisabeth hissed at Josh who didn't care as he kept telling his joke.

"So, the man ran across the roof, slid down the ladder and was running back around to the other side of the house, back over to where he had been when his watch had slipped off. All of this while his son-"

"Thought you said it had been a friend helping him on the roof?"

The lawyer seemed to have drifted away, looking blankly out his window, studying the view of the neighboring rooftop. Lizzie was relieved as she glared at the men that only she could see and hear and who had no regard that she was trying to have a conversation. Neither of them paid her notice, and she briefly caught Elisabeth's eye as she shrugged apologetically back at her.

"You're right, his friend-"

"I'm sorry. Where was I? Oh yes, sorry about that. I haven't been sleeping well since my partner passed away last month. I don't know if you remember me telling you that, but he did, and this was his case. He'd been managing much of your uncle's dealings for the last ten, fifteen years." The lawyer said. She tried to pay attention to him, but the lawyer spoke softly while Josh was loud, his voice boisterous.

"But the man ran around to the side of the house. He was huffing, of course, by this point and the friend watched him, wondering why he was hurrying so much just to pick up his watch that by this point would have fallen to the ground."

Lizzie was shaking her head, getting frustrated with all the noise and confusion floating around her. It was all too much, and she found herself closing her eyes to help herself focus. At the funeral it hadn't even been this bad, but with both talking, Josh and the lawyer, it was like she had struggled to listen to two fighting, squabbling kids as they talked over one another. She just couldn't do it.

"-Are you okay?" The lawyer cut off whatever story he was just about to tell her when he'd seen her shaking her head, noticing the first in the latest set of tears.

"-Yeah" she gasped.

She could feel more tears welling up, and she had no clue why. *Why now? Why here?* She could feel her chest tightening and knew she was on the verge of letting loose.

Come on, girl, get it together.

"Liz?" Sarah asked. Lizzie heard the lawyer getting up from behind his desk. She tried to push them all away, but found that the harder she tried, the more she thought of Sarah lying there on the floor.

That had been her fault. All of it was her fault. Sarah wouldn't have been there if it hadn't been for Lizzie asking her. Sarah would still be alive with her today and really be there for her.

"Are you okay? Can I get you something or call someone? I mean-"

He was hovering over her, and she wanted to listen to him and get this over with, but she just couldn't tune it out. Josh was telling that hideous joke and with all the surrounding chaos, she just kept hearing him.

"The man reached out and grabbed it. The friend had watched and couldn't believe it. He called down and asked, 'how'd you do that?' and the man replied, 'well, the watch always was a bit slow.'"

Lizzie couldn't help it. The joke wasn't even funny, but she found herself giving in and letting the laughter take her. It brought on more tears, and she truly thought she had snapped; her last thread of sanity, gone.

"Lizzie, come on. It's going to be okay." Sarah was saying. Lizzie held her head in her hands, the laughter shaking through her, but she could feel her friend close to her.

"I'll be fine." Lizzie said, trying to rein in the fluttering of all the different emotions.

"Are you sure? I can get you a glass of water."

"I'm fine, really." And if she just kept repeating that long enough, she might start to believe it herself.

"You sure Lizzie?"

"Yes, I'm fine." Lizzie said, looking briefly at her best friend before looking back at the lawyer. She knew eventually she'd remember his name. It was something to do with food. She remembered that much.

The lawyer was going to the door anyway, and she had no doubt he would return with a cup, probably filled from the fountain in the hallway. So then, she had been surprised when a figure emerged in the door handing the surprised lawyer a bottle of water.

"Thought she could use some water," Adam was saying to the much older gentleman, who nodded his appreciation. Though as Adam went back into the outer room and the lawyer was turning away from the door, she noticed that he was closing it behind him.

Josh had quickly ducked into the room, pushing up against Elisabeth, leaving Chuck to sit it out in the waiting room.

"So, you want to hear another one?" Josh said as soon as the door was closed and the lawyer returned to his seat behind the desk, passingly handing her the water as he had gone by.

"I hadn't realized you and your uncle were so close," he said as he started sorting through his piles of folders, looking for one he eventually found near his computer. He pulled it out and perused the contents, occasionally looking at her. It took a few seconds to realize that he was purposely avoiding eye contact.

She glared at Josh for a moment longer, long enough to see the little smirk and his quick glance at her. The smug bastard was enjoying this, and he was doing it on purpose. He was doing it, and she was sure it was because he knew she couldn't do a damn thing about it. She couldn't just walk right over there and knock that damn smirk right off his mouth.

She would have too. She'd never hit another person in her life, but she felt the anger, the violence rising inside of her. She had never wanted to hit someone so hard in her life.

"We weren't. I don't know if I've ever met him. He had a huge fight with my dad, and they'd never talked until just over a year ago, shortly before my parents passed away."

"Oh, my misunderstanding."

"My best friend just died last week." She turned to look back at the lawyer, who was now looking up from his folder and studying her. She could feel those judgmental eyes on her, and she hoped she was about to wipe that right off him. "She had been murdered in my uncle's house while we were checking it out."

She watched the color drain from his face and his jaw was ready to hit the floor. *Win! Score one for the crazy person. We'll see if he still wants to judge her for breaking down in his office.* Though she didn't feel like a winner. Far from it.

"I...I'm sorry for your loss. This happened at your uncle's house?"

"Yeah."

"You got a key?"

"Yeah, Adam had given it to me when I had stopped by to sign the paperwork you left for me."

"Right, right. Hmm," he studied the piece of paper again that he had pulled from the folder. Then he pulled out an envelope that she hadn't noticed before.

"Is there a problem?"

"What? For you, no, probably not. For me, maybe. It all depends on how you would like to proceed and if you decide to come after us, I completely understand. I just want to start by saying I'm sorry about all of this."

"What's going on?" She looked at Josh, surprised that he was staying quiet. He was still smiling at her, but didn't say a word. He just made that childish motion of zipping his mouth and then flicking over his shoulder as though throwing away a key. She turned back to the lawyer, who was again looking her over. *My God, he thinks I'm crazy.*

"I'm sorry, but we misread the will. That is to say-" cutting her off as he could see she was obviously about to say something. "We left something out."

167

"You see, your uncle changed his will a few days before he passed, and we hadn't logged the new will into our system, so we went off what we had recorded in our latest file." He handed over the envelope. "This was left to you by your uncle."

She gingerly took the envelope. It was yellow with age, probably having sat around that dirty old house for years before he finally used it. Then she looked at the front to see her name delicately printed in that messy handwriting of his. Each letter of her name was printed large and readable, and he had spelled out her whole name, not the nickname everyone else called her. "Elizabeth" plainly visible as she took it.

She immediately noticed the hum that emanated from it the moment it touched her fingers and there was something inside it. There was a lump of something larger and irregular and she felt a piece of a sharp edge that was ready to bite her.

"Okay, so what is so important that I needed to rush down here?"

"Well, that's it. The new will stated that you were not to take possession of the house or have any of the money until you took possession of that envelope. We couldn't transfer the money or move ahead with anything else until you had it."

"Really? So, what's inside it?"

"No clue. It arrived sealed."

"Okay then, well, that's odd, but so was my uncle."

"Never met him. All his business was normally through my partner. This thing with the new will, it's all strange. Doesn't make sense to me, but-" The lawyer doesn't finish what he was saying and instead looks out his office window. "Tik-tok."

"What?" She looked around to see that everyone else had heard it too. They were all studying the lawyer. Even Josh, who probably had no clue who the shadow man was had caught on and turned to watch the lawyer.

"Tik-tok." The lawyer seemed to break out of whatever trance he had gone into and turned to look at her, though she didn't feel like he had fully returned. His eyes were glazed over, and he had this dreamy quality to his voice as he spoke. "Tick tock, it's getting close to lunch, and I have a meeting. Was there anything else I can help you with?"

Lizzie shook her head and got up slowly, not taking her eyes off the man. He had already dismissed her and had gone back to shuffling the paperwork on his desk. She watched and wasn't sure if he even realized he did it, as he slipped her folder as far away from himself as he could on the desk and then, as if that wasn't good enough, buried it under all the other files.

She left the office, catching him turning back to the window and gazing out. The sounds of Johnny Cash followed her out. She hadn't even seen him press play or turn to his computer. As she waved to Adam, who returned it politely, she could hear the soulful chorus of "When the man comes around."

In the elevator, she realized she was still holding the envelope. Why hadn't she opened it in his office or even now as she was in the elevator?

She turned it over and studied the writing. It was her name, written in large letters. Whoever wrote it had taken great care to get it right and there were indentations from the pressure from the pen.

"You gonna open it or just stare at it all day?"

"Shut up Josh." Sarah hissed at the larger man.

"What you gonna do to me, sweetheart? Kill me again?"

"Calm down." Chuck said. Lizzie ignored them, something that when no one else was trying to talk to her, she was getting quite good at.

"Go ahead, playboy, take another shot. If not, then just stand there in your corner and let the adults here have a conversation."

"What the hell is your problem?" Chuck was getting closer to Josh, his fists clenched.

"My problem? Really? You're going to ask me what the fuck my problem is." The door to the elevator opened and Lizzie was quick to exit into the parking structure. "My problem is I'm fucking dead. I'm dead because my life was ruined when you two dipshits pulled out in front me. I was facing vehicular manslaughter charges, and my scum bag of a lawyer said the best he could get me was six years in jail. I was going to jail, no way to support my wife and kids, all because of you two dumbasses.

"Then it gets better because I just don't die, I'm stuck in some kind of limbo purgatory hell with you two shits, that glaring bitch, and some kid who we follow around with no fucking control, always just whisked away to wherever she is.

"This is bullshit, and she's got an envelope, something in her hand, right there, and she's not rushing to open it. Fuck this. Fuck you! I want this shit to end, and she's not doing a damned thing about it."

Lizzie hadn't really thought much about it, but noticed it struck her as if there was something different. It was how she heard him talking so crisply.

She looked at her friend Sarah and noticed that, yes, her face was different. Like part of it had healed a little and wasn't so disgusting to look at and that she'd been able to speak clearly the longer she was dead.

"Lizzie?" Sarah was looking at her. Those soft blue eyes that had melted away many hearts still had the ring of bloodshot, but it had clearly faded since she had first come back from the dead.

"Don't trust the dead." Isn't that what someone had written on her parents' tombstone? Something close to it. What did that mean? Had someone else been surrounded by them?

"Just open the fucking envelope."

"You think all this has something to do with her uncle?" Elisabeth said, looking back and forth from Lizzie to Josh and then back.

"And you don't? Are you that fucking dense?"

They were all looking at her. She could feel their dead eyes collectively drilling into her.

"What about all that creepy shit we saw there? It was like, like he worshiped the devil or, I don't know."

Lizzie had forgotten about the carvings on the floor, the drawings, what had looked like blood, the burned candles. All of it was pushed away, and she hadn't realized just how hard she had tried to forget it. It was like how she kept forgetting that her best friend was dead, which was so easy to do because there she was, standing and talking to her. But that wasn't her, not truly. That dead thing was not the girl who had slept over at her house.

She turned the envelope over in her hand and then grabbed a corner to rip it open.

Her phone chirped, breaking her focus. Then another chirp. She pulled it out and looked at the screen. There were nearly ten messages, all from Jess, the last one saying, "There you are! I see you. Walking over."

That was when Lizzie heard the screeching of tires, a horn blaring, and amongst all of it, she heard the screaming.

CHAPTER 14

Lizzie ran. She wasn't sure if she should be running away. That was her instinct. Run and get away from whatever was going on. The screaming wasn't good, and she'd heard enough of it in the last month...

But she thought she had recognized that screamed and '*oh god*,' she knew it was Jess. Deep in her gut, Lizzie just knew it and there was no way she could run away and leave her friend to die. She'd done too much of that lately. She was not going to let down another one of her friends.

And if she had run away, she knew what was coming. She knew that soon she would see her friend. That Jess would be joining her for lunch and every other lunch soon thereafter. She would be with her eternally as one of the dead that surrounded her.

That sinking feeling in her stomach had already stolen any thoughts of an appetite. That couldn't stop her, and she didn't let it.

So Lizzie was running again, but against all her desire, she ran towards the screaming. It didn't take her long. Within fifty feet she rounded the corner, and at the lower edge of the ramp she saw where there was a car stopped, its hazards flashing and the driver's side door open.

Lizzie had somehow known what she would see. She knew there would be a car stopped, the driver out to examine a body, shock already clutching their rational mind as they stood over the dead or dying while they were immobile as they watched.

She was so sure of it that she already had tears wetting her cheek when she rounded the corner and saw the stopped vehicle in the middle of the car path. The driver stood outside of his car; the door open. It was almost just how she had imagined it... but it wasn't. What Lizzie hadn't expected was Jess, standing there yelling at the driver and occasionally punctuating words while slamming her large, oversized purse down on the man's hood.

"-you need to get your eyes checked. How do you pull out here and not see me? Pay attention." She was yelling at the man. The man stood there and as Lizzie approached, she could see his mouth opening and closing, never allowed to get a word in. He looked like a fish as he would just open and close, open and close, never given that moment to speak out and defend himself.

Jess was a professional talker. At least she should be. She could talk forever and not let anyone else get a word in. Lizzie had learned never to argue with her, as it was impossible to win. The woman would just browbeat you into submission.

Lizzie almost felt sorry for the man. He towered over Jess, but as Lizzie approached, she could tell that Jess was dominating him. He was already backpedaling to his car, occasionally looking over his shoulder to assure himself the door was still open, and he'd be able to make his getaway.

"Watch it, watch it, watch it." Jess continued to slam her purse down. Already there was a dent from previous purse attacks.

"Leave the poor man alone." Lizzie felt her heart relaxing, and she took a deep breath as she slowed her walk up to her. Her friend was still alive, and she was A-okay with that.

"I didn't see you; you came out of nowhere." The man insisted, taking the chance to finally speak when Jess had turned her head away.

"And you still think you don't need glasses? I mean really, how can you not see this?" She ran her hands up and down her bright orange dress as though presenting it to him, though her face you could tell this was no offer. She was still red, her face burning with anger as Lizzie came up to her.

"So, who's your new friend?" Lizzie asked.

"Some blind man who somehow convinced the DMV to give him a license. I should get your plate number and report you. You were driving like a maniac through here."

"Hey!" He tried to get more out, but Jess had turned back to him and was bringing her full attention down on him.

"What's your name again? Bobby what? I want your license number and your address. Who's your insurance provider?"

"Jess, let him go. You hungry? I'm ready for lunch." Lizzie said. Behind her, she heard Josh whispering to someone.

"Who the hell is this girl?"

"That's Jess. We've all been friends since freshman year. Trust me, you do not want to get on her bad side. She can use that tongue like a green beret can use a knife," Sarah said.

"This little...jerk... almost killed me. He came speeding around this corner, and I just barely got out of the way. He'd have gotten me if I hadn't jumped, so yeah, I feel he needs to be ... I don't know, something." Jess threw her hands up in frustration and let out a long sigh before turning back to the bewildered man.

"I didn't see you; you just came out of nowhere. I came around the corner and there was nothing, then a big flash of light and I saw you there jumping to the side. I jerked the wheel, or I still would have clipped you. I stopped and there you were." He was talking in a rush. He probably never noticed Lizzie's open mouth as she turned to look at her friend. There, just barely reflecting from the light above, was the cross Jess always worn around her neck.

Lizzie didn't have time to think about it, as Jess was already approaching the man. He was rushing to get into his car. He must have seen it too, the fire burning in her eyes.

"Jess, come on." Lizzie said, reaching for her.

"Damn, this is getting good. Cat fight!" Josh yelled from behind her.

"Cat fighting is two women going at it. She's going to tear that man apart." Chuck said quietly.

"Nah, that man's enough of a pussy to qualify."

"I'd like to see you try to go up against her." Sarah said, rushing to keep up with Lizzie. The man had made it back into his car, closed the door and, to his credit, had locked himself in.

Jess, however, wasn't letting him get away that easily. When she had pulled on the door handle and found it wasn't going to open, she started kicking the door. Though there wasn't much to the kick as she was wearing open-toed heels and after one kick, had pulled her foot back, howling. Which only fueled her anger as she started hitting the window.

Lizzie felt sorry for the man. He looked so scared in his car.

"I'm calling the police," he said, holding up his phone to show Jess the screen. '911' was already keyed in and all he would need to do is click the round red button to initiate the call.

"I'm hoping he calls them. Can you imagine the cop when he shows up? I mean, he knows that's only for emergencies, right?" Josh said. Lizzie looked over and saw him leaning against a Ford pickup parked a stall down.

She was surprised that they were being good, so to speak. Maybe they were all just enjoying the show, but not Sarah. She was right there with her, and that made sense. Sarah was Jess' friend, too. There had been many times Sarah had to hold Jess back. She was small, talked a lot, and came off as being nice, but Jess had one hell of a temper once you set her off.

"Get out of there, you little twat."

"Jess, when did you eat this morning? Jess..." She wasn't listening and gingerly Lizzie touched her shoulder. Jess turned and looked at her in surprise, and Lizzie's next words stuck to her tongue.

Jess didn't look right. Her eyes were open wide to where Lizzie could see red forming around them. It wasn't like her eyes were bloodshot, but a ring of dark red circled the rim, and when they stared at her, it didn't feel like Jess saw her.

"Jess?"

She was breathing heavily. Her whole upper body was quivering. Lizzie thought she was having a seizure as her body was spasming. The eyes rolled up into her head and only the whites remained. Drool dripped down the side of her mouth. She was convulsing and Lizzie was left standing there, not sure what to do or how to help.

Then Jess closed her eyes and Lizzie had just enough time to see her body go limp to reach out and catch her. She couldn't keep her up. Lizzie was nowhere near strong enough, but she could hold her and ease her down to the cold, hard cement.

"Is she going to be okay?" Lizzie heard the man ask. She turned to look at him. He hadn't gotten out of his car but had rolled down the window.

"I'm sure she'll be fine."

He nodded, then looked to the lowering slope of the parking garage and then into his rearview mirror. No one was there. They were alone. "Look, I didn't see her. She just came out of nowhere."

Lizzie nodded and then looked around, noticing for the first time that she hadn't seen Jessica's car, which was odd if she had just parked there and was coming towards Lizzie. How did she know where exactly to find her? That was some dumb luck on Jessica's part, as Lizzie had only told her the name of the lawyer and where his office was located. She hadn't told her anything about what parking garage or where she had parked.

"You should get out of here." Lizzie said, and she didn't have to look at Sarah to know she was drilling her eyes into her. "She'll be fine."

"Here." he opened his door and handed her a business card. She didn't look at it as she slipped it into her jeans pocket. "If you need to contact me."

She didn't watch him, but heard the door close. Moments later, the car was pulling away.

"Did you see her eyes?" Lizzie said to Sarah, as she sat there with her friend.

"No, why?"

"There was something wrong. They were red. I mean, like, well, part of them were. It was weird."

"Really?"

"Yeah."

"Hey, what's going on?" Josh said, pushing himself off the truck to walk over to them.

"You ever seen anything like that?" Lizzie turned to Elisabeth who had been standing back. Chuck had his arm around her, and they were keeping a distance from everyone. Had she been crying? Something was up with those two, but Lizzie didn't think now was the time to pressure them.

"I didn't see. What happened?"

"Her eyes were red." Lizzie said.

"Like blood shot?"

"No, like she had a ring of red around her normal blue eyes."

"Shit, who cares? What does any of this have to do with us? Nothing, unlike that envelope you conveniently forgot and slid into your back pocket." Josh said, already losing interest.

"That's odd. No, I've never heard of a red ring. Bloodshot or red eyes are burst blood vessels that can look and turn the pupils red. Just a red ring, that's just very... well, odd." Elisabeth raised her arms in frustration and Lizzie turned back to Sarah. Jess sighed, and her head rolled back and forth as she vaguely started to come around.

"Lizzie? Sarah?" Jess whispered; her eyes were still shut. Lizzie's eyes shot straight to Sarah, whose own eyes had gone wide. Around them, everyone else grew still, and it felt like all the air had been sucked out of the parking garage, everyone afraid to breathe.

"We're here. I'm here, Jess." Lizzie said, holding her hand. Jessica's eyes fluttered then open and at first, she just stared at the cement ceiling. *Thank God*, her eyes were normal. The red ring was gone. Then those eyes fell on Lizzie and focused on her.

"*We're* here?" She said, "Who else is with you?"

CHAPTER 15

"I must really be losing it. I could have sworn I heard you talking to Sarah."

Lizzie looked over Jessica's shoulder to where Sarah was hovering. She had a pang of guilt. She really wanted to tell Jess just how right she was. She wanted to confess to her that their best friend was there and standing right behind her.

They were both sitting outside. The day had warmed up to where it wasn't uncomfortable and many of the cafes and pubs had opened their front areas to outside seating. Someone from colder states might have felt it a bit chilly, but Jessica and Lizzie were born Wisconsinites, and the chill was refreshing.

It hadn't taken them long to get to the cafe as it had been just around the corner, and they been able to quickly walk there. It went unsaid that neither of them wanted to ride in a car.

"Oh, come on, can we just get some food for takeout?" Josh groaned. He had made his opinion clear that he didn't want to sit around while a bunch of damned women jibber-jabbered, his words. He wanted out of there. He didn't want to be there or anywhere.

He was coming to terms with the fact that he killed himself. He'd been high, drunk, and stupid and had gotten the gun from his security case. So, he deserved to be... somewhere. He didn't know if that meant hell or just an eternity of nothing. It didn't matter. What did matter was that he wanted it all to be over with. He wanted to slip into the dark and let the world around him go away. His family was gone. What did he have to exist for?

"Lizzie, earth to Lizzie." Jessica said, snapping her fingers. As she did, the waitress was lowering their salads in front of them. Lizzie looked briefly at it, thanking the server before looking back at her friend. She'd gotten so used to dead friends around her always talking amongst themselves, it was getting easier to just zone out when someone living was talking to her. She knew that wasn't a good thing. She'd have to work on getting better about that.

"Sorry about that?"

"About what?"

"Drifting off there. My mind keeps doing that lately."

"I'm sure. It's been hard on all of us, and well, we're worried about you."

"Who's we?"

"Some of the sisters. I know you didn't get into the sorority, but my sisters still care. And Dennis, as well as Tammy and Cynthia. You have friends, you know. We're all here for you."

Funny, Lizzie couldn't remember the last time she'd talked to half of the people on Jessica's list and the sorority had made it clear that she had not been good enough stock to be one of their sisters. Though Lizzie wouldn't say anything about that to

Jessica, she couldn't do anything about the comebacks and the thoughts that festered.

"I know," was all she said, keeping her eyes downcast, studying her salad. It was what she'd ordered and normally she loved the Mediterranean salad with grilled chicken, but she was losing her appetite. Hearing Jessica talk about all these artificial friends as though they were people who cared about her made her wonder just how much Jessica cared. After all, it's been nearly two weeks before they had even seen each other and even now something was off. It was like there was this rift between them, and Lizzie wasn't sure what to say anymore.

They sat in silence for a minute that stretched into another.

"Come on, this is bullshit. Let's just get out of here." Josh said. He kicked at a chair, and it fell over. Sarah looked at it, shocked, but Lizzie didn't notice it. Elisabeth and Josh were gone again, walking somewhere nearby. More and more, they seemed to go off to be on their own.

Lizzie looked up and saw that Jessica was looking at something. She turned and saw that Jessica was looking at the chair toppled over. She didn't see Josh standing there, but Lizzie saw as he squatted near it. He looked puzzled, like he wanted to reach out and touch it, but kept pulling his hand back, not daring.

"That was odd," Jessica said, and Lizzie looked back at her. She had a faraway look, like she was thinking about something. "You know, it's weird, but sometimes I feel like Sarah hasn't moved on. It's almost like I can feel her and know she's here with us."

Lizzie felt another stab of guilt and looked at her dead friend. Should she tell Jess? Lizzie highly doubted that Jessica would believe her. She knew she wouldn't have if positions had been reversed. Just how would she take it? She knew she wouldn't get Jessica committed, so that was off the table. She didn't think she'd think her friend was messing with her, but she also didn't think she'd believe her.

No, she knew what she would do, and her passive aggressive nature was probably to blame. She'd listen to her friend, tell her it would all be okay, and over the course of the next few days or weeks, stop calling and asking to hang out. She'd distance herself until months down the line they would find themselves getting together and she would casually ask, "So hey, you still seeing dead people?" and if she said yes, would drop her out of her life completely.

She looked at her friend, who was reading something off her phone in one hand, holding the fork in the other, and munching on some of the salad. She was completely oblivious to Lizzie across from her and her inner turmoil.

"I know what you mean," Lizzie said as she pushed around a radish until it fell out of the salad bowl.

"I think we need to get out of here." Josh said quietly into Lizzie's ear. She recoiled from it as he had never been that close to her before. It was kinda freaky.

"Liz, I think he's right. Did you see what he did? That shouldn't be possible," Sarah said.

"I keep saying we need to get out of here and read that letter. Something's gotta be in there about all this."

She felt something pinch her butt and looked at Josh, who was on the other side, both hands in view.

What the hell? She reached back and found the letter, that bump in the envelope right where she had been pinched.

"Dennis just texted, wondering what you're doing tonight."

"Got plans."

"Really?" Jessica looked up from her phone, setting down the fork. "With who?"

Great. Open mouth and insert foot. Lizzie did not want to tell Jessica that she was going with Roland to a show in Milwaukee. She should lie. It was the only way. She should just up and lie.

"Roland. We've had tickets to see Ed Sheeran."
Dammit. What is wrong with you?

"For fuck's sake, will you just open the damned envelope?" Josh screamed. She tried to ignore him.

"Wait, what!? You're going with Roland? I thought you dumped him because he was fooling around with that Natalie tramp."

"Yeah, ...well..." Lizzie fidgeted more with her salad. Now it was starting to feel like old times. These were the conversations she remembered having with her BFFs. Though she did wish she wasn't the one to be on the hot seat discussing how she was going out with the ex-boyfriend she had just broken up with a short time ago. She did deserve it. She was the idiot who had said yes to going.

"Yeah, well what? I mean, come on. He turned you into a wreck. You're still trying to get over him and now you guys are going back on a date. He already cheated on you once."

"It isn't a date."

"He's picking you up?"

Lizzie nodded, not trusting her mouth anymore. It seemed to have become too honest for her own good.

"And you're going to a show together. How is this not a date?"

"I don't want it to be. I can't stand the asshole. We just... We got the tickets and I really want to go to the show."

"So go by yourself or hell, take me."

"It's not that easy. He showed up at the apartment and he's-" her phone started buzzing and she flipped it over from how she had put it on the table to see that Roland was calling. "Shit."

Jessica stood so she could look down at the caller ID from the other side of the table. "Here, let me talk to the son-of-a-bitch."

Lizzie clicked on the side of the phone, silencing it until it went to voicemail.

"We'd bought the tickets when they went on sale. He's held on to them. And God, I just want to see my Eddie. They're really good tickets."

"You're Eddie, huh?"

"Yes, my Eddie. He's going to look down at me from that stage and realize how much he needs me in his life and going to take me off to tour with him."

"You are a dreamer."

Lizzie threw a carrot at her.

"Someone kill me. Again. And again," Josh said as he started slamming his fist into his head. "This is hell. There is no big mystery. I'm just in hell."

Lizzie's phone buzzed again, and she looked down, this time to see the text message Roland had sent.

"Rdy to pick u up." She saw on the screen, and she quickly mentally translated to 'I'm ready to pick you up." She shook her head and turned back over the phone. She wasn't ready to deal with him again. Not yet.

And you still have to survive a three-hour car trip with him.

Ugh.

"So, tell me, how is this a good idea?"

Lizzie winced, shrugging in acknowledgment that her friend was right. "I get to see Ed Sheeran and try to have him run away with me so I can have wonderful, beautiful babies with him."

Jessica lowered her head, shaking it. They were both giggling.

"You dumb bitch!"

Lizzie was getting so used to Josh cursing and yelling at her that it took a moment before she realized that wasn't Josh yelling. For Jessica, it hadn't taken so long, and she had quickly looked up and past Lizzie to the screaming behind her. By the time Lizzie did turn, she had been just in time to see the man a few buildings down as he slapped the girl he was with. Lizzie assumed he was with. He had his other arm wrapped around her possessively and was pulling her along.

That was all it took for Jessica, as she was already up and rushing to the two strangers. She had looked at Lizzie as she rushed past. Had those red rings returned to her eyes? Lizzie wasn't sure, but she remembered them and thought about how close Jessica had nearly come to getting killed.

What if...? What if something was killing her friends or those close around her? It was crazy, but just what if? It was killing them and leaving their spirits with her. It was targeting those she cared about. Jessica was someone she cared about. What if that red ring was some kind of marker...? Then Jessica could be in danger.

That's a lot of 'what ifs's'. There's also the what if that she could be crazy and imagining all of this?

As Lizzie stood, she noticed that the few others that had been dining outside had looked, but were now focusing intently on their food. Everyone seemed to be actively ignoring what was going on.

"Now get in the car and let's get home." The man was yelling. Lizzie was paying more attention to him as they were getting closer. He was taller than them both and muscular. Lizzie didn't find it attractive, but she could see other girls fawning over him, though he had that Magic Mike vibe and damn, that was such a turnoff. He stood hovering over the shorter, dark-skinned woman. He was leading her to his car, the door open for her.

"What does she think she's doing?" Sarah yelled. It sounded like she wasn't that much farther than Lizzie, hurrying behind her.

"This woman's crazy." Josh said, and Lizzie could swear she heard him laughing. This was her friend they were dealing with, and that asshole was laughing. Lizzie would have to talk to him later.

"Read what's in that envelope and he won't be so ornery. It's all he's asking for," her inner voice told her. It was far calmer than she thought it should be as she was running on full alert chasing her friend.

"Hey asshole." Jessica said. Lizzie cringed. She had no idea what her friend was going to do. He was a beast. Jessica was a fly when it came to him. A fly on the wall and Lizzie sensed she was about to get swat.

It didn't take Lizzie long to realize, though, that her friend wasn't a fly. She was a full-on hornet. She ran right at the man and, as he turned, she slammed her fist straight into his jaw.

Lizzie stopped and felt a force and a crushing instant headache as Sarah slammed in behind her, but it couldn't be helped. She was left awestruck, watching the blow and the cascading effect of the shock registering on the large man's face.

"What the fuck?" The man spit out blood from his newly busted lip. "You fucking hit me. What the fuck, you dumb bitch, you fucking hit me!"

That was all the man was able to say. While he had staggered back, spitting out the words with blood punctuating the curses, Jessica had moved with the momentum. In the distance she had moved to rush the guy, she had kicked off her heels and moved with the grace of a dancer as she sidestepped the guy, lifted her knee high, and brought her foot crashing down, hard, into the side of the man's knee. The large man crashed to the ground, first with a crunch on his ass, and then Lizzie watched as his head smacked the pavement with a loud crack.

She held her breath as Jessica stood. Did they just kill the man? He wasn't moving. What kind of trouble would they be in? They had attacked this random man on the street, surrounded by witnesses. Jessica murdered him. She could go to prison. They'd send her away with the death penalty. What was the law in Wisconsin? Was it life or injection?

Then the other thought hit her like a fist in the gut and she quickly looked around at the surrounding crowd. What if he did die... and came back like the others?

She didn't see him in the crowd. Yeah, she didn't see him, but all the others had come back in the middle of the night. He might not come until she was asleep.

"You okay?" She heard Jessica saying. She looked at her, about to reply, when she saw that Jess wasn't talking to her. She'd walked over to the other girl and was looking at her. The girl was crying, but she still nodded.

"It was my fault. You shouldn't have hit him; he'll only be upset when he gets up. It was my fault. I had forgotten to pay the cell bill and his phone was turned off. I shouldn't have forgotten." The woman was in tears, backing away from Jessica as Lizzie approached. She was shaking her head vigorously back and forth. It was obvious that Jess wasn't going to get anywhere with her.

"Fuck!" the man screamed from the ground. He started rolling back and forth, grabbing at his head. Tears were streaming down his cheeks.

Well, at least he wasn't dead.

Lizzie moved to help the girl, moving slowly as the girl backed against the wall of a corner grocery store. She saw inside how people were gathered near the window, watching the commotion outside. *Sure, and none of them were willing to come outside and help. Assholes.*

"It's going to be okay." Lizzie said. Jess must have realized she was not being any help, as she turned away from the woman and walked back to the man on the ground. Lizzie didn't turn around, but it didn't take long before she heard him screaming.

"She shouldn't be doing that. It was my fault." The woman said, almost in a whisper as she hugged herself and backed away from Jessica.

"I know. She's a mean person. It's going to be okay." Lizzie said to her. She reached out to the woman to gently touch her arm, but the woman quickly recoiled, moving a few steps away from Lizzie.

The woman wouldn't look up and Lizzie again tried to ease herself close to her. The woman kept her eyes locked on her boyfriend. She was a mess, but Lizzie could see that when her makeup wasn't smeared and she wasn't hiding herself in this pity, she was beautiful enough to be a model. Maybe she was. She was rail thin, had that long brunette's hair that was perfect even with all the craziness going on around them.

Lizzie almost admired her. But then, how could someone this beautiful be with such a jerk? Did she not see how amazing she looked? She could go out and find anyone better than this piece of shit with no problem, but here she was.

Lizzie was finally close enough to touch her again, and gently lay her hand on her shoulder. The woman's eyes focused on her for the first time and shot wide open with a look of sheer terror. It was like the touch electrified her. Her mouth moved wordlessly, and she pushed herself away. She was desperate to get away, pulling her shoulder back from Lizzie's hand, and nearly falling in the sudden jerky motion.

Finally, she found her voice as she whispered, "moun ki gen madichon."

"What?"

"Madichon. Madichon!" The woman hissed it at her, then spit to the ground. Before Lizzie fully realized what was happening, the woman turned around and ran. She didn't just jog away; she ran at full speed like she was running for her life to get away from Lizzie.

"What the hell was that?" Jessica asked. She stepped up next to Lizzie as they watched the woman running across the street, nearly getting hit by a car.

Lizzie looked over at her friend. Behind her, she could see the man getting up. He was staring at them with venom, but he was also holding his side and could barely stand. She didn't think he was going to start anything, and he didn't as he stumbled and climbed into his car.

"Don't know," Lizzie said, and then cocked her head back in the direction of the man. "So, where you learn all that?"

"Remember that guy Dennis told you about? Well, he's one hell of a self-defense teacher... and he teaches a little boxing on the side," Jessica said with a wry smile.

"Excuse me. Excuse me. Are either of you going to pay, or do I need to call the police?"

They both looked over at the waiter who was standing next to their table, their checks in hand.

Both broke out in laughter and walked back to the table.

Sarah and Josh were already there, sitting in their abandoned chairs. Where the hell were Elisabeth and Chuck and how had they missed all the action? Lizzie was going to have to ask them if they ever returned.

CHAPTER 16

"So why didn't you sell the tickets?" Lizzie was sitting in the passenger seat of Roland's car, not sure how she had let herself be talked into letting him drive. She wasn't even sure how she had let him talk her into going. Sure, she loved Ed Sheeran and, up until their breakup, had been looking forward to this getaway weekend they had planned. That had been a month ago. She had completely forgotten about the concert and with everything going on, it just hadn't seemed like something she'd have to worry about.

This was a terrible idea. What was she doing here?

"I don't know. I just didn't."

"And you couldn't take someone else?"

"Didn't seem right. Ya know? These were our tickets."

"You could have just paid me back my half and taken anyone you'd like." She was watching what she said. It was too early in the night, and she didn't want to start it off with a fight. Still, she knew the edge was there, and he had to take the meaning of what she was implying...After all, she had dumped him because he had been cheating on her. If he wanted to be with the other girl so badly, why didn't he just take her? Now there was nothing to stop them from being together. She had done him the favor of letting him go so he could go off and cheat on another woman.

She could feel the anger starting to well up in her again, a rising tide that nudged her to start up the old fights. It wanted the war of words again, as the fire hadn't faded as much as she thought it had. The wounds were still too fresh.

Get your mind off of it.

She looked in the back seat, noticing again how empty it was, and took a long, deep breath. Her dead friends weren't with them. She took another breath and looked down at the bump under her sweater where the talisman rested on her chest. It felt cool to her skin, and it was weird, but she swore she could feel a faint hum thrumming through her.

She had found the talisman when she had finally opened the letter from her uncle. Jessica had left shortly after chasing away the dick who'd hit his girlfriend. She'd said that she wasn't feeling too well, and Lizzie agreed with her. Jess had grown extremely pale and dark bags had formed beneath her eyes.

Lizzie had been left in the parking garage, Josh once again hounding her to open the damned envelope. She'd been annoyed at first, but had stood there, looking at it, feeling the bulging contents. She wasn't sure how long she had stood there looking at it. The garage had felt distant. Her dead stalkers were silenced. She had just stood there, caressing that lump in the envelope. Then she had finally opened it, ripping away the yellowed envelope.

It came with a cryptic note, telling her only that she should put on the necklace right away and then go to his house. There, she would find a letter explaining everything in his bedroom. There would be a box she was to go through with pertinent information about the legacy he had left her.

The sane part of her had chuckled in her mind at this and thought, "Money isn't really a legacy, but if he was referring to his own special kind of lunacy, then maybe that was the legacy he had left for her."

But she hadn't been able to take comfort in that thought. There was too much of the crazy. It surrounded her, making her feel that money was not the legacy he was referring to. *Yeah, your legacy is the dead people, and they were throwing a party all around her.*

Josh had burst out laughing when he read the note over her shoulder. He wailed, screamed, and shouted into the air. When that had not been enough, his emotions running him through the gamut, he started crying as he fell back into a nearby car. His legs had given out, and he worked himself onto the cold cement.

Lizzie had watched him and had almost felt sorry for him. She had known he was hoping for an answer in the note, something that would tell him why he was there; why they all were. Instead, there was some crappy necklace and instructions to go to his house. What, had the guy been so paranoid that he didn't trust his own lawyers with whatever his 'legacy' was?

She had looked at the odd-looking thing as she pulled it from the envelope. The object was on a strand of cowhide that had been tied into a large loop. She'd seen the type of work before, often when visiting Native American tourist traps and in Indian gift shops. Hanging on it, though, looked like something a medicine man might have made. It was a large round ring with string crisscrossing on the inside. Inside the ring and tied to the strings were animal teeth. It was impossible to tell what the teeth were from; it was vicious as the teeth were long, fang-like, and sharp.

She had held it up to the light, dreading wearing the thing.

"What the hell is that?" Josh asked.

"Liz, the man was nuts. Are you sure you can trust...that?" Sarah asked as she pointed to the necklace. She looked disgusted by it and was glaring at it like a snake getting ready to strike her.

Sarah was right, though. Her uncle had obviously been nuts, but what had made him that way?

What the hell?

Lizzie put on the necklace, and Josh and Sarah both disappeared. She wasn't sure, but she assumed that Chuck and Elisabeth were also gone. She was free. They were free. Now maybe she could return to some kind of sanity.

"Earth to Liz. Lizzie, anyone home?"

Lizzie blinked, bringing her back to the car she was in and the man who sat behind the wheel.

She looked over at him. Roland was watching the road but stealing looks when he could spare them to study her with those bright blue eyes.

"Yeah."

"Really? So, what do you say?"

"About what?"

"You weren't listening."

"What were you asking?" Lizzie said, getting increasingly annoyed. He used to do this to her all the time. He would talk and drone on about boring crap until she got to the point that she couldn't take anymore and would zone out. Then he would start asking her about it, like there would be some great quiz on whatever useless nonsense he had told her.

She thought she had become an expert at tuning him out. How had she put up with his useless rambles while they had been dating? Oh yeah, she'd talk over him, not allowing him to get rolling into what conversation he'd started. When she'd talked long enough, he'd shut up.

She hadn't done it this time because she hadn't felt like talking to him. It wasn't that she had nothing to say, as so much was happening in her life. No, she didn't like to talk because she was afraid of what she would say and who she would say it to. The last thing she needed was for people thinking she was crazy. If she started talking to people who weren't there, that would be the end of it. She'd be in the padded room and hitting the walls.

It was an effort, but she tried to bring herself back into the conversation.

"I asked a few things." She said, trying to cover up, but realized she had no clue what he had been talking about? Probably some old cheesy horror franchise that was getting a reboot.

"Huh? No, you didn't. You've sat there for the last half hour, stealing glances at the back seat like you're expecting to see someone back there. What I had been talking about was me asking you if you were okay."

"Yeah, I'm fine." Lizzie said, pulling herself around so she sat straight in her seat. She didn't know if she was really doing it, but she felt small, like she was making herself disappear into the seat... She made them disappear. Why couldn't she make herself disappear like that?

"Really?" He stole another quick glance at her.

She didn't look back, keeping her eyes on the road. She guessed they were nearing Madison as she saw the sign for the Cascade Mountain resort that was near Portage. She hoped that wasn't the case, as if it was. They'd only shared the car ride for under an hour. She was already getting antsy and wanted to pull out her hair.

"Because I see a mess. I can tell you haven't been sleeping. You look tired as all get out and your skin is getting pale. I mean, you're always white, but this is ghost white. I don't think you've seen the sun in weeks." He stole another glance over. Lizzie wasn't sure how she looked and didn't think it was any of his business. Inside, though, she felt a heat in her chest and knew there was wetness forming in the corner of her eyes. Who the hell was this bastard, to think he could tell her she looked like a wreck? "Have you? What have you been doing since Sarah died? We share friends. I know none of them have seen you. We're all worried about you."

He finished, and they sat in the car in silence for a mile with her mind racing. They were driving to a concert hours away, so he would have her alone in the car. Jessica asked her out to lunch all in the same day. Jess had acted shocked about them going, but had she faked it? Lizzie wasn't sure and, as she thought about it, she was beginning to feel like she was set up. They all planned this.

But who in hell thought it would be a good idea for Roland to be the one to get her alone? She was going to kill them. Really, who in the hell thought she was going to bare her soul to Roland?

"Who were you originally going to give my ticket to?"

"I told you-"

"No, you told me some excuse to get me to go with you. Was it Natalie?"

"I don't want to go into that again. I was never with Natalie. Please, let's not fight."

"But who were you going to take?"

The car grew to the unsteady quiet again as they drove miles down the interstate, listening to only the hum from the road and the occasional car that passed them.

"Sarah said she'd buy your ticket. She was going to buy both tickets and I think she planned to take you. She knew how much you wanted to go."

Lizzie felt the anger that had been ballooning up inside her deflate, and a single tear found its way to rolling down her cheek. Sarah. Sarah wasn't with her anymore. With the necklace on, her friend was no longer there and now Lizzie was going to have to start grieving. Her best friend was dead, and one of the last things she had planned was to take her to see her favorite singer.

Lizzie wasn't sure what to say. This time the silence that stretched until they made it past Madison was broken only by the sniffles as she fought to hold back the floodgate of tears. She couldn't stop herself from looking into the back seat, this time hoping to see Sarah sitting back there, smiling at her. It would have been a relief just to have her tell her how stupid she was going to this concert with *him*. Her friend would scold her, call her out on this bullshit. Her friend who would be there for her.

She felt the pinching between her breasts when she shifted in the seat, the rings of pain from the teeth causing her to wince briefly. She had put the necklace on. She had sent her friend away, releasing her. Now Lizzie would be alone.

She couldn't remember a time when she didn't have any friends. Sarah had been her bestie since...since... well, long enough that she couldn't remember a time without her.

Now she had no one.

She felt utterly alone, stuck in hell with the lying sack of shit she had allowed herself to listen to, too. It was fitting, really. It suited her, didn't it? They deserved each other. His lying and her betraying her friend, getting her killed and now sending her away.

You didn't send her away. You released her. Now she'll be wherever dead people go. With any luck, it was a better place, and Sarah was up in heaven somewhere.

Though as often as she tried to convince herself of that, she didn't truly believe it.

"So, what's your favorite Sheeran song?" Roland said. The silence must have stretched to a point that he couldn't help himself and tried again at the dangerous art of talking.

"Huh?"

"What's your favorite Ed Sheeran song?"

"I like all of them."

"Sure, but you gotta have a favorite."

"I do."

"What is it?"

"It changes. For like, the last month I've been listening to 'Happier.'"

"Really?"

"Yeah, why?"

"Just not sure I know that one."

"You do. It goes 'Only one month we've been apart, you look happier...'" Lizzie screeched out. Roland started laughing as he shook his head.

"Please, please stop."

"Hey now, I can sing," she said.

"Remember, I heard you karaoke. No, you can't."

"Fine, like you can do any better."

"You're right, but I know my limitations."

"Oh, your karaoke is just as bad as the rest of us."

"I'm not going to argue. Just I know to wait until I've had enough to drink that I don't realize how bad I am."

Now it was Lizzie who was shaking her head, and an honest laugh that welled from so deep within her that the painful memories from earlier were momentarily slipping away from her. With any luck, they would stay away for a little. The wetness that still hovered in the corner of her eyes threatened that they weren't going to be gone for long.

"So, oh wise one, what's your favorite song?"

"The A-Team," he said and in such a way that made it sound like he was announcing it proudly, which was odd. She couldn't imagine him liking any of Eddie's music that way.

"Really? Why is that your favorite?"

"Because."

"Oh no, give." Lizzie was having a hard time repressing the smile she had somehow slipped into her voice. They were doing it, for better or worse, that old patter of returning barbs to one another and everything was mentally hidden under the fog of the last month.

She wasn't sure she liked that, but it was hard. They'd been dating for a year and much of it had been a lot of fun.

"How can I not love the A-Team?"

"You're stalling."

"No, just don't see why I need to explain it. I didn't make you explain yours."

"Yeah, you do."

"Why?"

"Because I want to know why the A-Team?"

"Well... it's the A-Team. How can't you love a song referring to an old school 80s show?"

Lizzie sat there, staring at him, not sure if he was serious or just playing with her. She knew her mouth hung open, and she was looking at him dumbfounded, but really, how could anyone blame her? There was just no way he could be this ignorant. Either that or he'd never even listened to the song.

He hadn't. She should have seen it. Eddie wasn't his normal stuff. She had known that since she had first started dating him. He liked all that heavy devil music with squealing vocals and where the singer, if you could call them that, was grunting indiscriminately throughout the song.

"What?" He asked, glancing over at her, registering her look of utter amazement at him as she realized something else. He would never have bought these tickets if not for how much she had wanted to go. How had she never seen it before?

"That's not what the song is about."

"What do you mean?"

"Eddie's A-Team. It's not about some obscure-"

"The A-Team was not an obscure show. It was huge."

"Whatever. So. The song is not about some show trapped back in the 80s."

"There's also a movie."

"So?"

"The movie had Bradley Cooper and Liam, what's his name in it. That 'Taken' guy, he played Hannibal. It was awesome."

Lizzie had never before wanted to smack her head into the dashboard as much as she wanted to right then. The pain had to be less than listening to Roland as he tried to explain the song has something to do with whatever show he was talking about. She had never been able to understand his love for ancient television. She knew he also loved to watch old black and white twilight zone episodes on holidays. How lame was that?

"The song... it has nothing to do with the movie... the show, any of it." She said. She had a hard time not yelling words at him. He was an idiot. How did she ever put up with him? "It's about angels. The song is about drug addiction and angels. A young woman who drifts away and because she's too blind to the path her life is taking, she overdosed and dies. The angel's die. Get it."

They sat in silence for a while as the miles passed by, marked by the white lines and green signs. Finally, he glances over at her. "Na, I still say it's about the A-team."

Her mouth dropped open, and he saw it, returning her stunned expression with a smile of his own. If he wasn't driving, she would have hit him right there, putting all her strength and weight into it, because right then, the only thing she wanted to do was to knock that smile right off his lips.

"I'm just kidding with you. Loosen up. Try to have some fun tonight, okay?"

CHAPTER 17

Okay, Lizzie knew she'd enjoy the concert. That much had been a given even with the moment of doubt beforehand, by the complete and utter ignorance of her companion. She just hadn't realized how much she would enjoy the concert.

Their tickets were amazing, right up near the stage. The music had been loud but phenomenal, and Eddie... Eddie had been to die for.

She had watched him as he soulfully sung to the crowd of adoring fans, but she could swear it felt like he was singing directly to her. He would look at her and she thought he was looking directly into her eyes. She had nearly melted to the ground, leaving a drooling puddle. Roland had caught her, and she was sure she saw a smile as he pulled her back up.

It was after the music had died away and they were filing out of the amphitheater that she noticed how close she was to Roland. She could feel her back occasionally brushing against his chest and thought she felt his warm breath on her neck. Their hands occasionally brushed against one another and what was this? No, her heart could not be skipping a beat. Not again, and not for him.

Yet here they were, walking. They had made it outside the theater and were making their way down the street. The night was cool, and somehow, she had allowed him to take her hand. They weren't going towards the parking lot, and all she could think about was how natural his hand felt in hers and how wonderful the show had been.

They turned a corner, and it was well lit, the streetlights on both sides were decorated with dangling orange lights as the area was prepared for the upcoming holiday. The streetlights themselves were lower than many of the other nearby streets and done in that faux style of classic candle lit elegance. Then she noticed they weren't walking down a street. It was brick, a fake street not wide enough to be real but perfect for late night walks. She was sure there were kids who would ride their bikes or skateboards down it, but she saw no evidence of it. Maybe it was heavily patrolled to keep them away.

It was nice and peaceful and when had her hand snuck into his? She looked down at it and then felt helpless as her gaze climbed up his arm, up his chest until they fell on his eyes. He smiled at her, and neither of them said anything. They just walked.

Eventually they found themselves walking along the water, as Lake Michigan stretched out before them. The night had drifted into a surreal dream and if they took a step off into the water; she was sure they could walk on it, following the path of the moon that led the way into some far-off land.

"You enjoying yourself?" Roland asked as they stopped beneath one of the streetlights.

"I am."

"Good." He gave her hand a gentle squeeze and flashed her a slight smile as he kept his eyes locked on hers.

"I hate to do this-"

"Oh?"

"I need to go to the bathroom. You going to be okay here for a couple minutes." He said. She could see his embarrassment as his face turned red.

"Yes, go, I'm a big girl." She giggled, smiling at him, and she could see how relieved he was.

"Okay. Good, I'll be right back." He said, and then without thinking, both temporarily lost in the moment and forgetting the last month and half, he bent down and kissed her. She returned the kiss until he pulled away and they were both standing there looking at each other, questioning one another with their eyes.

"I'll be right back."

"Okay."

He backed away; his eyes locked on hers until he was a few feet. Then he turned, rushing off to one of the open bars along the strip. She watched him go, then sat on a bench. She hadn't noticed it before, but since he was not there now, clouding her mind, she could sit and take stock of her situation.

No, this is the last thing I should be doing. I don't want to be with him. That ship had already sailed. He had sunk it. HE had sunk it...

Then why was she still thinking of him, or why return that kiss? A better question was how he had talked her into going. Obviously, she still had feelings for him.

No, she had to get her mind off him. She was not doing this again. She knew how it would end.

End...

Something about that thought seemed wrong. Did she know how it would end? Sure, he'd cheat. She'd be heartbroken all over again, this time without Sarah to help her get through it.

Something about that was nagging at her. There was a thought just out of reach, but if she could grab it, maybe some of what had happened today, maybe even the last few weeks, would start to make sense to her.

If it was a word, it would be right there at the tip of her tongue. She knew it was there. Dammit!

She opened her purse and pulled out her phone. It had been off since the concert and figured now would be as good a time as any to check her messages. Maybe there'd be one from Jess that would explain it all, or even better, one from her uncle. At least he seemed to know something would be wrong with her...

Of course, he had known she would have things going on in her life, strange things that made no sense. He had written her a letter warning her. He had even left a note on the back of her father's grave, trying to give her a clue. Of course, he had known. How had the letter started, not with a greeting, but with two apologetic words... "I'm sorry."

Her uncle had known her friends would come back from the grave. It had been happening to him, too. It seemed so obvious once she took time to think about it. How else would he have known to leave the talisman for her? He knew she would need it.

He knew, but how did he know? How would he know that right away her best friend would die?

210

Because... Because her dying, the shadow man, they were a part of it. It took her friends.

Her phone came to life as messages rolled in. The first came from Jessica, but then a barrage of messages came from an unknown number. What the hell was going on?

Jessica... The shadow man...

Earlier that day, she had seen something. Her friend had that red ring around her irises. She was sure of it and had been acting so weird. She was going to get into a fight with that guy. What would have happened if Lizzie hadn't hurried up?

Mentally, Lizzie could see what would have happened. The man had rushed to get back into his car, afraid of the small woman who was coming at him viciously. He would first back away, putting his car in reverse, but he couldn't back all the way down the parking garage ramp. He'd have to go forward. Jessica would get back in front of the car to get him to stop. He would try to slow down, but somehow his foot would slip, and he would careen into Jessica. She would roll under his car or slam into his windshield. Either way, her head would get smashed and there would be no way she survived. Her friend would have been dead.

She knew it was true. Lizzie had saved her, unlike Sarah, where she hadn't been able to get to her in time. But tonight, Lizzie wasn't in Stevens Point to protect her friend, and somehow, from deep in her gut, she sensed that the shadow man was on the prowl seeking his next victim. If she was right, it would be someone she knew and cared for. It would be the one he tried and failed on earlier that day.

Lizzie only glanced at a few of the messages, but she found it impossible to focus on any of them. Her head hurt and tears were bubbling up inside her. They hadn't burst through the dam yet, but painfully waited just behind her eyes.

Screw this, she needed to know.

She called her friend's number.

CHAPTER 18

"Hey girl," came the familiar voice Lizzie had hoped to hear. Immediately, she released a breath she hadn't realized she'd been holding. That was, until the next part of the message played. "Leave a message."

Jessica probably had forgotten that her voicemail introduction was old and tacky. Lizzie had forgotten about it. She hadn't paid it much attention as she usually texted and when she did call, if no one answered, she just hung up.

For that one heartbeat of a second, though, she had allowed herself the chance to take a breath and relax. That was shattered with thoughts of the different ways Jessica might have been killed danced in her head. The shadow man was merciless. Lizzie had learned that when Sarah was killed, but since then, he had continued to take those close to her or having anything to do with her.

That explained Josh. It was strange to think he had only awakened her that morning, having arrived in the middle of the night. So much had happened today that it was easy to forget, but now that she concentrated on it, why was Josh there? She had never met him before, but he had been the one who killed Elisabeth and Chuck. They were connected.

"Jessica. Call me. Please." She could hear the desperation in her own voice.

What if she'd been hit by a car? Sure, the shadow man had already tried that today, but it was one of the easier ways to kill someone. Though when she thought about it, there were so many other possibilities. She could imagine the elevator in Jessica's building, the cable snapping or the doors allowing for her to step into an empty shaft. Either way would leave her friend to pummel to her death.

Jessica could be just as easily mugged as she walked to her car. Though admittedly Lizzie would have to highly doubt that was possible. After seeing her in action earlier today, Lizzie wasn't sure how many muggers it would take to put her down. Just one desperate soul out to devour off the weak wasn't going to do it. Where had that fighter emerged from? She had never seen Jessica do that before. It was amazing.

Dennis had said something about the training Jess was doing. Maybe Lizzie should look into it? Why though? Lizzie's problems all seemed to come from the supernatural, so how would throwing a punch help?

Though, if there were multiple attackers...

Lizzie knew lingering on the thought wasn't helping her as she disconnected the call, but she couldn't help but picturing her friend lying in her own blood as she was dying. Her keys were in her hand. She was right next to her car. Jessica had almost made it before the three had jumped out at her. The first one she had taken down, but the next two both had knives.

It would have been just like Sarah, but this time Lizzie wasn't there to watch the light slowly fade from her friend's eyes.

She started reading through the messages on her phone. The oldest ones were from Jess, all of them worried about her. Lizzie knew Jess would have hated her being out with Roland, and Liz didn't blame her for it. She was just about to get into the newer messages, the ones from the number she didn't recognize when her phone rang, that same unfamiliar number calling her.

"Hello?"

"Hey Liz, everything going okay?" Jessica asked. Lizzie let out a long breath at hearing her friend's voice.

"Yeah, hey who's number is this?"

"Dennis's work phone. The idiot left his cell at home but had this. Thank God I remembered your number." There was a joking tone to her voice as she spoke and it tried to set Lizzie's mind at ease, but there were a lot of messages still. She was having a hard time reconciling that it was just because she was checking up on her friend. Especially since Jess had texted more times today and had spoken to her more than she had in the entire last month of their friendship. Still, Lizzie wondered if it was best to let it go and just talk to her friend. Maybe she was wrong. Maybe her gut was wrong.

"That explains it. So, what's up?"

"Well, you tell me. Is Roland being a bastard?"

"He's being civil." Her mind raced to the kiss they had just shared, her memory clinging to his smell, his

215

taste. He tasted like peppermints, like the candy he always kept with him, and the essence of pineapple she knew came from the deodorant that he used.

"He's not being an ass. He's still not claiming he never slept with that Natalie, is he?"

"It hasn't come up. Hey, so what's wrong with your cell?"

"Battery's dead. Been busy today, forgot to charge it. Then Dennis whisked me away for some camping trip getaway. God only knows where we are right now. He ran in to get some ice for the cooler and I wanted to give you a call. I've been worried about you."

"I'm fine."

"You didn't look fine, and what was that with that woman? You went pale just by her talking to you."

"I was just spooked, but come on, Ms. Bruce Lee."

"I told you; I've been taking self-defense classes."

"Yeah, well, that was pretty impressive."

"He shouldn't have been pushing her around." Lizzie noticed the chance in Jess's voice. A sadness had creeped into her tone and Lizzie wondered if something was hidden there in her past. Sarah, she had grown up with, but Jess was a new friend. There was still much Lizzie didn't know about her.

"Okay, I gotta go. He's taking me up to some cabin his parents have on timeshare or whatever."

"Thought you said you were going camping."

"We're in the woods and there's no internet. I don't care if we're in a cabin or a tent. It's all camping to me."

Lizzie barely stifled the giggle as her friend said her goodbyes and the phone disconnected. Jessica was okay. She was alive and Lizzie had been worrying for nothing.

Maybe she was being crazy or had been crazy and was now pulling herself out of it. All this silliness with some shadowy figure and a dead man who killed her best friend. She didn't know what the hell happened; she should just admit that to herself.

"Hey, miss, you got a light?" Lizzie heard from behind her, and instinctively her neck hair rose. She realized just how alone it was on the street and, for the first time, wondered how long Roland had been away. He should be back by now. Where the hell was he?

She turned to look at the owner of the voice. It had been raspy, near whisper and impossible to know if it had been a man or woman.

When she first looked back, her heart skipped. It was him. He had found her. Hundreds of miles away, and here he was. The shadow man was there, his face obscured by darkness.

But the image of the shadow man faded as another man stood tall and was just barely able to be seen in the dim light. He wasn't even close to her, and she could smell his breath, the alcohol emanating from him like he was a distillery. His large coat hid his slender frame but did nothing to conceal his gaunt, dirt-covered face.

The man was imposing enough, but as he bent over to lower himself to her, the streetlight caught his eyes. Lizzie could just barely see it, but she had already known. She knew that if the sun shone bright, she would see those red rings around his irises. The shadow man was there, after all. She didn't have to see him to feel his presence.

"Come on, give me a light." He said as he reached out for her. She had seen him coming, fearing it, and was quick to push herself forward and twist into a spin while rising from the bench. She moved just in time, his hand only brushing against the back of her sweater, leaving traces of dirt from his fingers.

His hands were covered in it, and she couldn't help but remember what the sheriff had said about the old man. A dead man had killed her friend. Was this guy dead, too? He wreaked enough to call it in question, but she didn't have time to think about it. He was already lunging over the bench, reaching those dirty hands out to grab her.

"What the hell?" She quickly stepped back. He came down hard to the cement, and he slammed his fist into the pavement in frustration. She wasn't waiting for his next move as she dashed around behind the bench where the man had just been. A cackling escaped him, and he twisted himself up to look at her.

"What's the matter, little girl? Don't want to wet the noodle?" His face was covered in the blood that was running from his nose. He didn't pay it any attention and continued to howl louder with laughter as he pulled himself forward.

His legs came down from the bench, limp behind him, and she would have expected him to stand up and come at her again. He was aggressive in his attack, continuing to come after her, not allowing her to catch her breath.

Just run away, she screamed internally to herself, but she didn't. She got away from him so far, she just had to keep out of reach. Then what? Eventually, he would catch her.

Jessica wouldn't run away. She had stood up to it earlier today. She had fought against people, taken down that man. She had really kicked some ass. *So come on Lizzie, are you going to run away for the rest of your life? Hell no!*

She started to plan her attack. He was going to get up and lunge back over the bench and she would grab his arm, pull him off balance, and then slam her fist into his face, knocking him out. *That's right, it seemed simple enough.* She just had to do it once he came at her.

Wait, don't you hurt yourself more if you ball your fist the wrong way? She thought she'd heard that somewhere.

It didn't matter, as she never got the chance to test it. The guy didn't stand. Instead, he quickly crawled under the bench and grabbed her legs. She had just seen that he was under the bench and hadn't registered the change fast enough. Her mind had still been on formulating the plan of him coming over.

He caught her off guard. By the time it clicked, and her mental gears started moving, he was close. She only had time to take a step back, but then he had her, grabbing the leg nearest him. She was still trying to pull it away when he lurched forward and wrapped his arms around her, pulling his weight into her leg it threw her off balance.

She fell back, twisting as she did so to work her way free. It seemed impossible. His grip tight on her. She would have questioned his strength, but it didn't matter. She'd been through this before, and she recognized the sensation of having the shadow man nearby. She could almost imagine his singsong chant and feel his damp breath. He was there; it was him possessing the man, and once again, he had her.

The cement was hard, and she crashed into it without any way of catching herself. Her air escaped her lungs even as she fought to keep it. The lungs that betrayed her felt pained and were angry with her as they tried to pull in on themselves. Her whole body hated her. It recognized the pain and knew it was her fault. She had the chance to get away, and she hadn't.

As she fought to pull air into her recovering lungs, she could feel his hands moving up her legs. He would grab higher and higher then pull his body a few inches at a time.

"Tik-a-tat, tik-a-tat, tik-a-tat" in that old raspy voice kept screaming through her mind.

Stars danced around her. She was still having a hard time, but she was able to gasp short gulps of air. Her vision was getting cloudy, and she felt her eyes watering.

His hand left her leg, and she felt it come down on her waist, reaching and grabbing the gap between her pants and the flesh hidden beneath. She tried to wiggle away, but his grip was firm on her jeans. She shook harder, coughing with the exertion as she was finally pulling in air.

"Come here, honey, light my fire." The voice rasped, coughing spastically as it spoke.

She kicked out with her legs and reached with her arms, trying to pull herself away.

"Help! Get away from me! Someone, help me." She screamed, finally finding her voice now that she had air. Her throat burned with the effort.

"No one." He hissed, "No one to hear you." She felt him slither over her legs like a snake as he was working his way up. Her legs were trapped, her efforts to kick him away useless. Instead, she fought to twist herself away. Maybe she could somehow push him off her so she could get up, but it was useless.

"Get off me!" She stopped, slamming her fists down and twisted her body again, reaching down and pushing the man away. He was so much stronger than her, but she fought with everything she had.

Her arms gave out, and she tried again to twist and pull herself free. His hands let go and she found herself able to move. She landed on her chest, and something crunched against her. It bit into her breast, but she couldn't stop to think about it. She had to...

His arm reached up and grabbed part of her shirt. His nails were long and dug into her flesh even through the fabric of her sweater.

Why had she thought she could fight him? She should have just run away. He never would have caught her. She wouldn't be under him now, and none of this would be happening. Why did this always happen to her?

He was going to rape her. As sure as she knew she was going to die tonight, and that it would be by his hands, she knew he was going to violate her first.

And she had no way of stopping him...

Fresh tears rolled down her cheek and she let her arms fall to the side. It was going to happen whether she fought him or not. What did it matter? It was all over.

"What the hell! Get off her!" She heard the familiar voice, but it sounded like it was miles away at the end of a very long tunnel. She couldn't concentrate on it, barely hearing the words but not grasping the meaning of what was being said.

Around her, the world was blurry, and she could feel the darkness closing in, surrounding her and pulling her into unconsciousness. She didn't care. The coolness of the sidewalk beneath her was comforting and so inviting. Maybe they could all just leave her there and let her become a statue.

She felt the weight on top of her rip away and she couldn't help but release a giggle. Floating man going away, she thought, floating man returning to the shadows, light as a feather. Another tear rolled down her cheek. She felt it as it slid down its path.

There was shuffling around her, but it was a world away. Why should any of that concern her? She heard more shouting and knew who was yelling. It was Roland, but why was he at the end of the tunnel? He should be here with her. Why had they been so far apart?

Her head hurt as she tried to think of the reason, but nothing came.

"Lizzie! Lizzie, are you okay? Do I need to get an ambulance?" He was getting closer until she finally opened her eyes. She had slipped off, not realizing she had closed them. Now her eyes were wide open, and she saw him hovering over her.

He looked so concerned. Was that really for her?

"Hey big boy. Where have you been?" She said, and the words sounded strange to her.

The tears flooded out from her as reality crashed into her like a freight train. She could stop it, but didn't feel like she had to. Roland understood and pulled her up and into his chest. She reached out and pulled him closer, clinging to him so he wouldn't disappear on her again. Never again. He needed to always be with her. She needed him.

"It's okay. The bad man is gone away. I chased him." He said to her gently.

But he was wrong, and she knew it. The bad man hadn't gone away, just the vessel it had possessed.

CHAPTER 19

"I think I'm losing my mind. They're always there, or they were. So much death... and these things keep happening. I don't know how much more I can take." Lizzie said, holding back the fresh wave of tears that lingered on the horizon. If it wasn't for the hot cup warming her cold hands, she would probably have slipped back into the balling mess Roland had helped off that sidewalk.

It wasn't much. They were only at the late-night coffee shop near the hotel they were about to check into. Since she didn't let him call the cops on the bum he had chased off, something he still felt was a mistake. She had allowed him to lead her there.

Her hands still shook when they weren't clutching the hot cup, so she held it tight. The tea still steamed, though they had been talking for a few minutes. She didn't know why she should trust him enough to tell him everything, but she had.

This was the guy who cheated on her. That anger still flowed hot and heavy inside her, but he was also the guy she had spent so much time with. Talking to him was easy. She had started telling him some of the story and then all of it just rolled off her tongue.

His hand rested gently on her wrist, and she looked up from the steam of the cup to meet his eyes.

"It going to be okay. We'll get through this. You said they were always with you, but they're not now?"

"Not since I put on this." She pulled the talisman out from under her shirt. In the dim light of the coffee shop, it had a menacing quality to it as the lights overhead seemed to flow around it, bathing it in shadow. Roland reached for it, but then pulled his hand back. She could see the hesitation. He was unsure of what to think or do. His hand shifted to rest on her hand.

"Okay. We'll get through this."

She wanted to ask about Natalie and where she was in his plans for helping her. Instead, she bit back the words and let the anger ebb out of her.

"I'm worried about Jessica. I just have this feeling that it's after her right now. It's just a gut feeling, bu-"

"Do you even know what 'it' is?"

"No, but I'm sure it has something to do with my uncle."

"Sounds like it."

Damn, he was taking this better than she had, though she did suppose she'd had more information to tell him, more for him to go on than when all of this started happening to her. She had the pieces thrown at her and now he could see the whole puzzle. At least as much of the puzzle as she already knew.

"I don't know. It seems like it's killing my friends or anyone who has anything to do with me. Jessica's my next closest friend. I don't know what I'd do if I lost her."

"Liz, we'll get through this." He said to her. Behind them, the door jingled, and a blast of cool night air brushed against them, raising the hairs on her arm. She turned to see two college aged girls entering. They were giggling, talking about someone named Michael. One was dressed nicer than the other and Liz guessed she had just finished what had to have been a bad date if they were together and the girl was not with the boy.

They looked happy. She had been like them once. The weight on her chest made her doubt she would ever be like that again.

"I think that might be why he stopped talking to everyone?"

"Who?"

"My uncle. I mean, he just cut himself off, hid himself alone in that cabin. My dad never knew why. He thought it had something to do with a big fight they had and the loss of my aunt. What if there was all this going on?"

"Well, how long was he out there?"

"Eighteen years, I think. It started after I was born, but long enough that I don't remember any of it."

"That's a long time to be out there alone."

"What if he had to be? What If it was the only way people would stop dying?"

"But he made you that talisman thingy."

"Yeah, but it sounded like in the letter that it doesn't work for too long. I don't know how any of this works."

Roland let out a long breath, looking at their hands for a long minute before looking back into her eyes. When he did, she saw the hint of a tear tucked away on the edge, just ready to slip away down his cheek.

"It'll be okay. Okay. You hear me? It'll all be okay." He said it solemnly and she could feel the amount of will he put into his words, like repeating them would somehow make them all true.

"I know." She looked at her tea, the steam having gone and the lukewarm cup still untouched on the table. "I gotta use the bathroom, then maybe we can get out of here?"

"Sure."

She found the bathroom in the corner of the small coffee shop, down a narrow dark hallway. The woman's bathroom was at the end just before the steel door marked "Exit" and right below it a sign proclaiming, "Keep Door Closed, Alarm Will Sound."

The bathroom was just like others she'd been in. It was a large chain and while she hadn't been all over the country, the ones in Wisconsin seemed to all follow the same layout. She was quick to pee and felt comfortable doing so in the large clean room.

It was a large room. Larger than it needed to be and larger than bathrooms in other coffee shops, retail stores and restaurants. It offered more privacy, as only one person could be in the room at a time. It gave her plenty of space. It was warm and comfortable...reassuring. It helped bite back the unease she had been feeling that everything was wrong.

She washed her hands, looked in the mirror, and the room was no longer so large. In fact, it had suddenly become quite crowded.

They were all there, standing behind her. Josh, Elisabeth, Chuck, and Sarah all stood behind her. And they looked angry. The hatred that burned in Sarah's eyes was foreign, as Lizzie had never seen anything like it. Her eyes, all their eyes, were black, and they all bared their teeth in snarls. Nothing of the friendly camaraderie they had shared the past weeks was there. They all looked so rageful and all that anger was focused on her.

She turned to look at them directly, but they weren't there. She couldn't see them without seeing their reflections in the mirror.

She didn't have time to think anything more of it as she felt something wrap around her. Then she was spun around and pushed so that her head slammed against the mirror.

"Look at us!" An echo of voices, yelling in concert at her. She could hear them as it vibrated through her skull, the sound loud enough to push through any of her thoughts.

"I... I thought you were gone."

"Where would we go?" Elisabeth's voice asked, her voice empty.

The force that had pushed her against the mirror released her and she pulled back to see that it had been Sarah's hand that had her.

"Yeah, whatever that thing is, it doesn't release us." Josh said. Strangely enough, he was at the back of the group and looked at her with less hostility than the rest of them. In fact, was he... he looked like he felt sad for her, or was that guilt?

"You sent us to hell," Sarah snarled at her and then thrust Lizzie's head back into the mirror. It slammed with an audible crack, and she was sure she would find shards of glass wedges in her skin and hair. She tried to close her eyes to protect them, but the pressure on the back of her head let up as

Sarah quickly reached around to hold open her eyelids.

"Oh, no! Keep those peepers open. You wouldn't want to make me have to cut those off, would you?" Sarah hissed as she leaned in close to Lizzie's ear. She got close, her lips near enough to kiss Lizzie's ear if she chose to, and Lizzie couldn't help but flash back to remembering the smiling man that had killed her. Sarah was looking at her in the eye through the reflection as she whispered, "Look at me. See what you did. You did this to us. I should have known it was about you. It is always about you. You did this."

Lizzie tried to breathe and hold back the tears that were streaming as she stared at what had been her best friend. She was different now. Her skin was ashen, which made the red lips vibrant, and as bright as the blood seeping from her eyes and dripping from her scalp. There were patches of her hair missing, and what was left was clumped together.

She looked so...fresh. If Lizzie hadn't already seen her friend post death, or how she'd been healing in death, she would have thought Sarah had just died and was still in that pool of blood back in her uncle's kitchen. Well, her kitchen now, but it didn't matter. Her friend, dead friend, mattered. Before Lizzie had put on the talisman, each of her dead companions had looked better. She wouldn't say their dead conditions were healing, but they had faded, the image of death not as strong around them. Sarah had almost looked like she had before they had entered the cabin.

Now death permeated from them, their stench filling her nostrils when there was no way she should be able to smell anything. She never had before.

They were… more real, but how when she couldn't even see them if not looking through the mirror?

"Say something, bitch." Sarah snapped at her as she slammed Lizzie back into the mirror. This time it was hard enough that darkness swam around her on a river of stars. She felt her body go limp as she crashed to the floor.

Someone knocked on the door.

"Are you alright in there?" A woman's voice called out from the other side of the door. Lizzie wanted to respond to her. She opened her mouth to yell, but her air was cut off. Something hard was wrapped around her throat.

She tried to open her eyes, but some invisible fabric was wedged against her face. It smelled like dirt and decay. She didn't want to imagine what it was, but it kept light from forming in the world around her.

She tried again to call out, but she opened her mouth in vain as she felt something forced into it. She couldn't keep away the horrific thought of the old man's penis, the one who had killed Sarah. She remembered the maggot that fell on her and gagged at the fear that it had somehow been forced into her. *No… he wasn't there with them, but Chuck and Josh were.*

"Miss, I'm going to get the manager. If you're having a seizure, don't worry, as we will be calling 911. Are you sure you're not okay?"

"Oh no, you are definitely not okay. How stupid does this bitch have to be? 'Are you sure you're not okay?'" Sarah hissed into her ear. "Like if you are having a seizure, can you please take it somewhere else to die?"

On the last word, Lizzie felt her head being lifted and then slammed back to the floor.

"Sarah," she tried to gasp out the name around whatever had been forced into her mouth. The attempt pulled the cloth further in and she spasmodically shook against being restrained. Her body shook more vehemently without her having any control. She felt like a blind passenger in her own body as it continued to writhe around on the floor, and she couldn't stop herself or see what was happening around her.

There was the cloth, and she felt it touching the back of her throat. She couldn't breathe.

"You're going to die. I'm going to kill you. You sent us to that place. You put us there and you know what?"

"Miss?" A new voice spoke from the other side of the door, the concern evident in his soft-spoken tone. Strangers outside the door were worried about her while her best friend was trying to pound her head through the tile.

"We know why we're here. Yes, we know."

Lizzie heard keys jingling on the other side of the door as the pressure on top of her intensified.

"Lizzie!" Roland called out from the other side. "We're coming in, okay?"

Cold struck against her ear in an arctic blast as Sarah hissed the words, "We're here because of you. You killed us."

The door to the hall swung open and the pressure on Lizzie disappeared, as well as the gagging sensation down her throat. Whatever had been in her mouth and on top of her was gone. She was left only the aftereffects. Small tremors ran through her as she gasped in mouthfuls of air.

She felt arms around her and saw a shape forming above her as the darkness faded.

"Sir, I don't think you should be lifting her up like that." The barista, probably the manager, said from behind him. She could feel the smile creasing her lips and she wasn't sure why, but God, it felt so good to be held in his arms.

"Lizzie, are you okay?"

"Cindy, call an ambulance." The manager said to the scared-looking woman who stood behind him.

Lizzie shook her head, though it hurt. Marbles seemed to be rattling around in there as the grey matter didn't quite feel right. She bared it as she pushed herself up to lie back on her elbows.

"No, I'm fine." She said to them, her voice a bare whisper. Though she knew she wasn't, she was not going to another hospital. She had had enough of them and had no intention of going back to one tonight, even if it was only for a couple of hours.

After all, who knew when her friends would return?

CHAPTER 20

Anthropophobia is the fear of people. Often it is a social fear, or something thought of as intense shyness. It can manifest itself in being afraid of meeting new people, or even looking them in the eye. It can be an intense awkwardness around a group. There are many ways that people can experience this intense fear.

Lizzie had always been timid and hated being around people. She hadn't started being comfortable around people until she had met Sarah. Sarah had made it okay. Without Sarah, she never went up to people... It was too much work, and she would often stay in her room, devouring books and Netflix. If she didn't need to speak or hang out with someone, she simply wouldn't. She had never been afraid of people; she just didn't know what to say.

So, when the crowd had swarmed in around her, so many people asking her if she was alright, the anvil hit her like a hammer blow. She couldn't breathe, her eyes were dry, but tears tried to flood them anyway, her skin crawled with the sensation that things were crawling all over her, and the slightest touch made her jump. Her eyes tried to look everywhere at once and that just made the feeling of the world collapsing around her even worse.

"I need to get out of here." She heard herself gasping but didn't recognize her voice. It sounded strangled and alien to her own ears.

"We should call an ambulance."

"What's wrong with her?"

"She looks like she's on drugs."

"I have a cousin who does heroin. She looks like that sometimes.

"What's wrong with her?"

"We really should call someone. We can't have people collapsing in our bathrooms and not-"

The voices just kept assaulting her. The lights were too bright. Everything was too much.

What was this? Why was this happening to her? Why were these things always happening to her?

The weight intensified on her chest, her breath coming out in shorter gasps. She thought she was going to collapse again as she tried to make her way to the door.

A voice spoke to her softly in her ear. It broke through the noise, tearing through the cacophony and releasing some of the pain in her chest. A different kind of tear, that of relief, escaped her as she heard it.

"It's going to be okay. Just breathe. I've got you. It's all going to be okay. Let's just get out of here." Roland said, and now she did collapse. She fell into his arms and let him guide her to the exit.

Roland... Sarah and Jessica had helped her find him, and back when they were together, he had been her comfort. She hadn't realized just how much she had relied on him to be her shield in the ocean of people. Roland, her protector, her gunslinger, taking on the dark forces outside.

Roland, whom she now clung to, to save her.

* * * *

Outside, the cool night air struck her like a physical blow, a hammer that slammed into her and forcing away the fog of what had just happened. Her strength returned and before they had reached the end of the block, she could walk on her own, though she found herself staying in the warmth of his arms.

"We still have that hotel room we paid for. I didn't want to bring it up earlier, but I don't think we should be driving back this late," he said. She felt his words rumble through him, the vibration a comfort to her, continuing to calm her frayed nerves.

"Sure."

"Yeah?"

She pulled her head away long enough that he looked down at her and they were locked in each other's eyes. It had been so long since she had lost herself in those eyes. They were the ocean on a clear day, and she could always sink into them when he did this.

Then she pulled his head down to meet hers and her aching lips found his. They kissed, and as she felt the warmth flood through her, emanating from her, she kissed him harder.

From there, she didn't remember getting to the hotel room; the memories lost in a haze of continual lustful kisses. She needed him. He was warmth, and he was her comfort. She needed to wrap herself up in him and allow him to get inside her. She desired to feel every part of him and for them to become one.

They were in the room. He had his arms around her and pulled her into him. She kissed him again while running her hands under his shirt, down his back. She let her fingernails drag on his skin, knowing how it drove him wild. The reaction was immediate, the lump in his pants expanding. She ran her fingers gently over it and could feel the rock-hard member itching to bust loose from its constraints.

She ran her fingers along him, following the curvature. Roland tensed against her touch, and she looked into his eyes to see them closed, himself lost in a moan of pleasure. It brought a smile to her and awoke a hunger deep inside.

How long had it been since she'd felt him? *Too long.*

Thoughts of death, the crowd at the coffee shop, all of it faded as she gave in to the desire. Her hands shook with anticipation. She needed him. She needed *this.*

She carefully eased the zipper down, easing out his member. Then she broke free from their latest kiss, another entanglement of tongues, and lowered herself to her knees. He was shaking with excitement, and she had the brief worry she was going to give him a heart attack if she waited too long. He wanted and needed her just as badly as she needed him.

She took him in, tasting the sweat of excitement that trickled from him. The moment she wrapped her lips around it, his body shuddered. She continued, playing with his shaft, running her tongue up and down the different parts, many times lingering on the enlarged head and eye. Then she would take it all in again and viciously stroke with her hands while taking him in and out. He let out another moan, this one much deeper, and she could feel his legs shake.

She had to wonder if it had been as long for him as it had been for her. But then what about Natalie? No, she wasn't going to think about-

"Ah!" He let out a small gasp, and she knew she had allowed herself to get distracted. Her teeth... He tried to pull away just a little from her, but she wasn't going to let him get away that easily. She needed this too badly.

As he was still unsteady, she pushed on him, and he fell back, the bed waiting for him. He thumped down on it and was already backpedaling to the head, his smile growing as he watched her climb him.

That's it, those pants are coming off. She reached forward and undid the button and then the belt. Then she viciously tore at pulling off the blue jeans, shaking them back and forth like a dog playing with a toy until they came free. The pants flew across the room as she focused on the next target, his boxer shorts.

It didn't take long and then she was again working on his shaft, stroking it, sucking on it, sending waves of passion through Roland as he arched his back. He was lost to the passion, concern for her lost in the moment.

With one last flick of her tongue across the eye of his member, she looked up at him. Then, like a stalking cat, purring as she moved, she swayed back and forth, and worked her way up the bed. She kept her body low, letting the small swells of her breast rub across his already excited erection. Small kisses ran along his stomach and then to his erect nipples. She took a short moment to suck on each one, giving each a little nibble before moving to his chest and then finally her lips high enough to reach his own.

"Are you sure?" He gasped, breaking away from her kiss. His body trembling with excitement and anticipation. His eyes were questioning, and it fought with every other part of his body that demanded he have her then and now.

She nodded, hunger in her eyes, demanding that she have him. Every other thought of the last few weeks was gone from her mind, and all she was focused on was this moment.

"Then I think you're overdressed."

The corner of her mouth went up as she pulled back until she was sitting on his exposed member, though she tried not to put all her weight down. Then she rocked back and forth, gently gyrating as she crossed her arms and pulled her shirt over her head.

The totem hung there between her exposed breasts, and she tried to ignore it as she reached behind her, thrusting out her breasts as she undid the clasps of her bra. As soon as they were released, his hands immediately had them, kneading them, and rubbing her nipples and the flesh beneath. She inhaled deeply, waves of her own pleasure flooding her senses. And what had she been thinking about before? His fingers flicked at her nipple and then she felt his fingers rubbing them between. Her breath caught and her back arched.

Something had been happening over the course of the last few weeks, but as she felt his hands and the moisture between her legs intensifying. It was there, nagging at her, but she didn't even have to try to push it out of her mind.

She quickly reached down to fumble with the button on her pants. It released and another pair of hands assisted her in getting the zipper down. Then she moved herself off him, pushing down her pants as she did and then kicking them off as she lay there on the bed. As she had done her part, Roland had done his, moving with her, first out of her way and then guiding on top of her. It was like a dance that had been performed, each working in time with the other and moving in a rhythm. They moved in time to music of their own making, and they were well rehearsed to make these actions look like a well-choreographed sequence.

The dance ended, and he was on top of her, his mouth on her breasts, his tongue sending new sensations of pleasure while his fingers searched below. They found their target, and she couldn't restrain the gasp of pleasure that escaped her. He worked magic, both hands and tongue, creating their own orchestra of ecstasy.

Then his hands pulled away, and his lips found hers. A second later, he found his way inside of her. The rest of the night fell away. She needed this. Oh God, how she needed this.

CHAPTER 21

The wind had turned cold. There had been a chill earlier, but it hadn't bothered her, so when she left, she hadn't grabbed her jacket from the counter. It wasn't winter yet, and the nights had been mild. She was a big girl. She'd grown up there and had lived there all her life. She could handle a little October chill.

And it hadn't been that cold when she left. *Come on Jess, you're tougher than this*, she thought as she tripped over another root. She'd been walking through the woods for a while , stumbling through the dark forest, trying to find her damned boyfriend. Dennis had gone out there earlier and at this point in her search for him, she was sure she was going to kill him if she did find him.

Damn! Another root she hadn't seen, and nearly tripped over. She caught herself. She always had been graced with amazing balance, but after the years of boxing and martial arts training, her balance only improved. Now she was not only a fighting machine that people often overlooked due to her smaller stature, but she was also as graceful as a butterfly on a spring morning. Dance like a butterfly, sting like a bee.

She scanned around her with her flashlight. She was still on the path Dennis had taken. He had told her it was the path to the lake, though she thought they were much closer to the lake than this. She'd been walking for twenty minutes and still had no trace of it.

Had he lied to her? If so, his ass was grass when she got her hands on him.

She had just left to hang out with Lizzie earlier when Dennis had called and said he had planned for them to go to his dad's cabin for the weekend. They'd never been up there, and Lizzie had never heard of his dad owning a cabin, which she had thought was strange for how long they'd been together. She would have thought he'd have said something in all that time. He knew how much she loved rustic cabins. They brought back some of her best memories with her grandpa and fishing trips as a little girl.

He knew that. She had told him stories about it.

Then, when he picked her up, he had explained that his dad had just bought the cabin. He hadn't discussed it with any of them, even his mom. So now both his parents were fighting. The big D word, divorce, has been thrown around a few times, though Jessica couldn't imagine it coming to that. Those two were such an amazing couple who normally did everything together.

This trip had been as much as a romantic getaway for them as it was an escape from his parents' fighting. Though Jessica didn't know how much his dad paid for it, she thought that whenever his mom did come to give it a chance, she would like it.

The cabin was clean, much cleaner than she expected after hearing the story of his dad buying it on a whim. She had assumed his dad had gotten it especially cheap, which led her to believe it would have been a small shack covered in dust and filled with animal bones. She had expected to walk into a horror film, much like Lizzie had, and was surprised when she had found a well cleaned, nicely furnished rustic cabin home out in the woods.

Dennis had immediately put their bags in the upper bedroom and then had gone outside to start up the wood stove. Okay, maybe it was a charcoal grill... she hadn't looked it over too closely but knew he had to work to get the fire started and once it warmed up, he had thrown on steaks he had brought with him.

He had done it up, that was sure. He had cooked steaks on the grill and lit the fireplace in the main room of the cabin. Then somehow, he had placed and lit half a dozen candles throughout so that when he brought in dinner; they had cozy firelight, that romantic flicker washing over them as they ate.

If there wasn't the air hanging over them about his parents fighting, she would have thought he was going to propose to her. He had already asked her to marry him once before, but that had been a shamefully bad attempt and had gone terribly. She knew he felt bad about that and wondered if he was going to do it again now that he had gone all out and created this wonderful setting.

She felt a tingle inside her. No, that tingle was on her arm. She felt something dancing along the skin, and found herself back in the woods, ripped out of her memory from earlier to look at her arm, shaking it and quickly stepping away from where she had been.

She flashed the flashlight in that direction and couldn't see anything, and she still felt that tingling. She looked. It was getting closer to her body, moving up her arm. She moved the light beam to her arm and...

There was nothing there. She ran her hand along her fingers along her arm, accidentally flashing the light into her own eyes, but couldn't feel anything where she had felt the tingle. There was nothing there.

Damn, she was really starting to hate the woods. What had ever allowed her to think she would like it out there?

This wasn't anything like when she had gone camping with her parents as a kid. Those places had woods, but it was like a controlled wooded area. Small patches of trees that were easy to walk through and you never got the sense that you were getting lost. No matter which way she walked, she would have found a campsite within ten to fifteen minutes. Now, she had no clue which way she was going. She wasn't where she had been coming from. Both ways looked the same. It was all the same, and it was so dark out there.

On their drive up, she had marveled at how beautiful the moon had been. It had been large in the sky and so bright she was sure that if Dennis had turned off his lights, they'd be able to find their way in that dark brightness.

Yeah, well, where was that moon now because she couldn't see a thing? The trees reached so high and all of them joined together to blot out any chance of her seeing the sky above her.

She was lost. She should call out, yell, and maybe Dennis could hear her. She didn't want him to know she was freaking out, but she was out there looking for him. Why not call out his name?

"Dennis!" she yelled, not quite at the top of her lungs, not yet, but she still had a booming voice and in the silence of the woods around her, it was loud to her own ears. "Dennis!"

Why had he even left the cabin? He had set the scene. It was perfect. She thought he was going to come around the table and get down on one knee. They had been sharing a moment, just looking deeply into one another's eyes.

Then he stood up and said he needed to take a walk down to the lake and that he'd be right back and that was it. A half hour later and he still hadn't returned. It had gotten dark, and he had left without a flashlight. Jessica didn't know what to do, afraid that if she left to look for him, he would return to find her missing.

She had started looking through drawers in the kitchen, not even realizing she was doing it. She just needed to do something while she waited. It was when she found the flashlight that it occurred to her that she had been searching for it.

What was up with him? This wasn't like him, and it made those knots forming in her stomach twist to think about what it meant. What if he hadn't brought her up there to propose again? What if he brought her up there to break it off? Could she have done something wrong? Something that might have upset him. She couldn't think of anything. Nothing. They had been happy, or so she thought.

But he had walked away from her. No real explanation. He just got up and left.

What the hell!? The path ended abruptly in thorn bushes. She hadn't been paying attention and walked right into them, and they were tearing into her flesh. As she pulled herself back, she could see the scrapes on her hands as well as something else. There was something white and stringy. It stretched out from the bushes and was all over her arms, clinging to her sweater and hands.

It took her far longer than it should have to recognize the strands of the spider web. It probably had something to do with all the shifting black things that had kept her from fully comprehending what she had stepped into.

"Oh God, what the fuck." She exclaimed as she took another step back, stumbling as she did. *Damn another root, they're frickin' everywhere*, she thought as she bit back another curse.

She lifted her foot higher and took another step backwards, this time slow so as to not put all her weight down when she wasn't sure of the ground. Her arms still had so much of the white crap on them, and she kept shaking them, trying to get it off her. Those couldn't be spiders. She had to keep telling herself that, but she could feel the tickling sensation moving across her arms. Then she felt them getting under her shirt. They were getting everywhere.

Her foot came down on something raised, but it was also soft. She shifted her balance; glad she had kept her calm and had moved slowly. It wasn't easy as she felt the dancing devils getting everywhere.

She turned as she moved and shone the flashlight down; glad she hadn't dropped it.

Dennis was on the ground. A shape just behind it looked like a person hovering over him. If Jessica had continued back, she would have fallen over the person. The person was looking down, close to Dennis, as though she were kissing on his chest and neck. She was moving viciously, and it almost looked like they were making out if it wasn't for how still Dennis was with his eyes open and lifeless.

Then the face looked up at her, blood dripping from her mouth and Jessica recognized her, though it wasn't easy. The woman's face was mangled, her skull looking like it had been crushed, one eye having exploded out of its socket and had dripped, now dried, on her cheek. Her teeth were white beneath the blood splatter and caught in a haunting smile as she spoke.

"Hey Jess, missed me?" Sarah said, her voice on the verge of a cackling laugh as she spoke.

"...Sarah..." The name escaped her own lips, though Jessica didn't know this alien weak sound.

In the woods behind Sarah, others emerged, all mangled, blood dripping from wounds. None of these people she recognized, and she found herself looking back at what was her former friend as she stood up from where she had been devouring Jess's fiancé.

Jessica wanted to back away and run. She could feel the tingle all over her body. It was electricity in the air and sent sparks to every part of her, telling her to run. The dead were there for her, and she needed to escape.

Spiders. That was what made her tingle. *Come on Jess, they're covering your body. You were trying to shake them off when you stumbled upon the dead.*

She shone the light back into the bushes behind her, but they were gone. Behind her was a wide-open clearing, inside of which stood the shadow of a man. She flashed the light to where she saw the shadow, but the light went through him. She had to blink, wondering if she actually saw it, but then a twig snapped, and it brought her spinning back to face the oncoming horror.

Jess, if you want to run, now you can. You saw where the path went. Through the clearing, the path went on. You can get out of here, escape.

She looked down at her boyfriend. The mangled mess of his neck was exposed, his trachea stretched out to the side. She could see that his eyes were gone, their sockets rough from where someone must have fought to scoop them out.

They had done this. Sarah had done this. Sarah.

Inside her, the flame burned, and she knew she wasn't going to run. She knew it from the moment she had seen Dennis on the ground. She wasn't a runner. She was a fighter.

As Sarah came into range, Jessica took a brief step back and then launched forward, using her full weight and all her training to bring the blow to a perfect slam into her jaw. It connected and, with a satisfying crunch, it drove Sarah's face back. Then she realized too late that her fist had broken through Sarah's jaw, sinking through the brittle bone into her face. It threw Jessica's balance off. She had made a beginner's error for any fight. She had over committed her weight, and, with that mistake, she found herself falling forward.

Within a heartbeat, she could feel hands on her. Sarah twisted around, and as Jessica fell, she could feel the woman falling with her. Jessica fought to soften her landing, but she could feel Sarah's hands as they pulled at her. She was trapped. All of them were around her and she knew it. Soon they would all be tearing into her.

She briefly wondered how Sarah would be munching on her with her mouth a crunched, smashed in, pulp of bone and dead flesh. As she hit the ground, Jess twisted herself and realized her hand was still buried in Sarah's face. Her hand being stuck prevented her from being able to turn with the fall, allowing the blunt force of the drop slam into her shoulder. The air left her. She winced in pain.

She rolled naturally from the fall, but her hand held fast. She could feel something soft and wet sucking on it, like a muscle contracting around her hand. She tried to pull away, but the feeling intensified, nearly crushing her fingers together.

Jess turned to look, not being able to see too well and not sure where she had dropped the flashlight. What she saw in the dark was what was left of Sarah's face around Jessica's hand. What had been her mouth was wrapped around Jessica's hand, and she was trying to gnaw on it, using the fractured pieces of her jaw to bite down with teeth that were no longer there.

"Ugh," escaped her, and she pulled harder on her hand. As she did, the spiders that had been crawling on her moved along her arms and up her legs. They danced in her hair and along her skin. She wanted to brush them away, but already Sarah was reaching out, frantically clawing at her, pulling at her clothes.

Then there were the other dead people. They had surrounded her and were dropping to their knees, reaching out their hands at her. She didn't know when, but she had somehow become a victim in some zombie film as the dead surrounded her, grunting and reaching to tear at her flesh. When did zombies become real? Had she missed the email on that one?

"Get the fuck off me, you mother fucking fuckers!" She wasn't just talking about spiders or zombie things; she was talking about all of it. She kicked out and thrashed, trying to keep them from getting a good grip on her. When she thought she had worked herself into having room to move, she quickly reached down to push herself up.

Jess was hoping to check the closest zombie and get it out of her way so she could run back to the cabin. She stopped when she felt her hand slip in a puddle of something wet and sticky under her.

Blood.

Dennis's Blood

Don't think about it, don't think about it, don't think about it.

She didn't have time to think about it, just work with it. Maybe it was why these things were having a hard time grabbing hold of her. Now that she realized just how much of it had spread on the ground around her, she noticed how much she was covered in it.

The others had also fallen into it. His blood was keeping her alive, as their hands were just as slick as hers. Even in the dark, she had balance and her inner perception; she relied on her fighter instinct now. As she moved, she looked inside to find that center and pushed in to find that calm that came to her when the outer rage burned.

She found her balance, twisted, and turned, spinning as she stood so they couldn't grab her, and then she was standing. There was a large man on his knees in front of her. She didn't even slow her momentum as she shifted her weight, accounting for the slippery ground, and brought her knee up to connect with his face. It found its home and its head rocked back. The force of the blow propelled him out of her way.

Then she was running past him. She was on the path; she knew it was the right one and if she continued to run, she would find herself back at the cabin, safe and able to call for help. All she had to do was keep running. The flashlight was gone, but the moon had re-emerged. The path was lit by the moonlight bright enough for her to see, and she knew if she went back, she wouldn't trip on a single root.

Yet she stopped in the path and turned back around to face the dead.

Jessica was not a runner. She hadn't run since she was a child and had run away that first time. That time when he had hurt her mom. She ran then, and her mom was put into the hospital. Jessica had run and run, and run until she found a place to run, too.

She had only been a teenager when she had found the gym, the small one that was almost hidden in its neighborhood. It was an old building and looked like it had been there for a long time, though Jessica hadn't remembered ever seeing it before.

She had stepped into the building crying, unsure of why she was going in. She hadn't ever been in any gym other than the one at her school and that was for P.E. and cheerleading practice.

Inside it wreaked of sweat, old and new, and while the building seemed abandoned on the outside, inside was a bustle of activity. Upon walking through the door, she was attacked by the noise of clattering weights as they crashed down, and the loud thump from the back of the room as people dropped barbells. To her left was a line of treadmills currently being used by a couple of old women as they walked, focused on some far destination as though they would ever get there.

She didn't know what to do; she hadn't known why she had gone in there. She just stood there in the doorway, unsure of herself. She just kept watching in her mind as her dad struck her mom, throwing her against the wall.

"Can I help you?"

She blinked herself out of her trance and turned to see an older man stand behind the counter. He wasn't old, old, but she'd guess he was easily over 50. A woman who came in behind her and walked past tossed down a card on the counter as she addressed the man as "Stone."

"Hey Rachel," Stone said to the passerby, keeping his eyes on this crying teenager who had just appeared from outside. "You competing in Strongman this weekend?"

"Not sure. Might have to work."

"Okay, just let me know and I'll need your entry fee by Friday."

Jessica watched as the woman strode across the gym to where there stood a boxing ring in the back corner. A man already stood in the ring, stretching.

Without pausing, the woman tossed her gym bag aside and climbed into the ring.

"You ready to get your ass kicked?" She asked.

The man in headgear and boxing gloves nodded. She gave him a clap on the back and then jumped down to where her bag had landed and started taking out her own boxing equipment.

"Hey kid! Can I help you?"

With a sniff and a swipe at drying tears, Jessica turned from the spectacle in the back.

"Do you teach people how to fight?"

"We do. We offer classes. Boxing, Tai Kwan Do, and other forms of self-defense. You should have your parents come sign you up."

"What if it's my dad I need to defend myself from?"

She saw something cross the man's face; a cracking of stone, she thought, as the man had looked as hard as nails. Then he looked down to study the floor and then up to look outside the window. He looked anywhere except to look back at the kid crying before him.

Jessica knew when she wasn't wanted. It came from growing up and knowing that you were never wanted around. Stone might have felt this way but was being better than her dad would have been. He would have flat out yelled at her, telling her to get her lazy, ugly ass out of there.

She went to leave. Stone called out to her before she could do more than put her hand on the door.

"Are you a runner or a fighter?"

Jessica turned back to look at him.

"I don't want him hitting her."

"Are you a runner or a fighter?"

"I don't know." Her tears returned.

"Go out that door and you're a runner. You'll what, run away in a year or so, end up on the streets. Maybe end up in foster care when they find you if you're lucky. If you're not lucky, you'll actually get away, maybe make it to some big city and end up doing what to survive? Have you thought about that?"

Her hand dropped away from the door. She felt sick to her stomach. He couldn't be right, could he? She wasn't going to abandon her mom, was she?

She turned back to him, finding a resolve forming inside her that she never knew was there.

"I'm a fighter."

"Are you sure? Because it looks like you ran here."

"He hurts my mom. I want him to stop."

"Then call the police." Stone locked eyes with her and Jessica stepped closer to his counter.

"Cops don't care. They've come and never do anything."

"I can call them. I've got friends."

Jessica looked past him as Rachel was climbing back into the ring. She was in full fighting gear now and she had a dangerous air around her. She was electrified with grace and moved with confidence.

"There's other ways to fight."

"Yeah, yeah, there are." Stone looked back at the ring. "Wait until she's done with her lesson, then talk to her. Tell her I'll pay for your lessons."

"What do you mean?"

"I mean, you're going to become a fighter."

And she had. Years of boxing, followed by various forms of kickboxing and karate, turned her into one hell of a fighter.

It took time, but eventually her dad stopped hitting her mom.

She was a fighter. She had made that decision. She was done running. The initial fear had edged off her thoughts as she stood on the path and watched as the dead things worked themselves to where they were standing. Jessica wasn't sure what they were, if they were zombies or ghouls or whatever the correct term was. She knew they could be fast. They had been lashing at her, viciously grabbing at her before.

She had to be faster. They had to be stopped. *They killed Dennis; they could kill others*. She chanted that, repeating it in her head. Then she came at them.

The big one was closest. She struck him first with a roundhouse kick that was timed to keep her moving. Her foot had connected with his already broken face, and it crumpled more of his skull. The momentum of the blow sent him into a nearby tree with a satisfying 'crack.'

Two more had been behind him. These two were smaller and looked like they had been much younger when they died. They seemed different from Sarah and the larger man. They weren't moving fast to get to her, and they looked more at each other than at her. Their hands held each other's. Had these two been lovers?

Jessica wasn't going to waste time thinking about it. They were dead. Their feelings didn't matter. They were killers, and she was going to put them down.

Her fist flew forward, her weight behind the blow as it slammed into his face. He staggered back and, like she expected, the girl reached out for her. Jessica grabbed her and twisted, launching the girl over her back, sending her to the ground. Jessica followed it up with a kick, slamming the girl hard in the chest. Jessica didn't hold back and brought down her weight. She heard the satisfying crunch as ribs broke.

She spun around in time to see the man and Sarah both coming for her. Sarah's face was a mess, nearly unrecognizable, but Jessica knew those eyes, though the fury in them was foreign.

In most fights, Jessica would have considered the man to be the bigger threat and would have attacked him while blocking Sarah. Something screamed at her that if she did that, she was dead. The man had no life left in his eyes. This wasn't a fight of passion with him, but Sarah was a beast who had gone rabid. Turning away from her would be a costly mistake.

Her adrenaline was flowing. She could see herself as she moved, and it made her think of an action movie. She wasn't quite like Jackie Chan, and fights were always choreographed with chairs and ladders all around him so he could use them as weapons. No, this was bare knuckles. This was a classic Van Damme film. She was a master, a brawler, and she saw it all as she was on the attack for her remaining opponents.

Jessica approached them almost with a strut of confidence, and when Sarah reached forward, Jessica grabbed her arm. She pulled and used the force to twist and spin her into the man. The blow knocked him off his feet and freed Jessica to continue to spin; She drove a powerful blow into Sarah's already weakened head. There was more crunching as the blow connected and the center of Sarah's face caved in.

If she had been in an action film before, she had just crossed over into the absurd cheesiness of a bad horror film. One of those films that went over the top with gore, because as she hit Sarah, her fist sunk deeper into her face than Jessica thought it should. Her fist kept going until she felt the back of Sarah's skull.

What had been Sarah's brain, the grey matter that had made her a walking corpse, was all over Jessica's hand and it was like a jello mold around her fist. It suctioned around her hand as she tried to pull it back. Sarah wasn't fighting her, and her body had gone limp, but the skull wouldn't release her. As the body fell to the ground, Jessica was trapped and going with it. She fell and only had a moment to realize she was going to land next to Dennis.

I'm going to marry him... She had come out there to find her fiancé because he had been acting so weird, but they were supposed to be planning the best day of their lives for a future together. There was still a lot to do. They hadn't even been able to lock down a date yet, but she still could see it in her mind.

It was going to be in the church she had gone to while growing up. It was a beautiful church that loomed grandly in her memories. The cathedral rose high, the bell tower rising higher and ringing those wedding bells, announcing that it was her day. Their day, really, as they were joining their lives together.

She would have a purple dress, having already decided that she would never be satisfied with traditional white. Tradition was for those who invited her family, a mother, and a father. Her mother would be there, she would be giving Jessica away, but her father...

He would never be allowed within a hundred feet of the ceremony. Jessica had the restraining order and had taught him more than once what happened when he broke it. He broke it; she broke bones. Not just one, but multiple. She enjoyed hearing him scream.

So, no father to ruin the day. It was going to be filled with only things that would make her happy. Dennis. He made her happiest of all, and as her mother walked her down the aisle, he would be there, standing in front of Father Abraham. Dennis would be in a suit, his friends behind him, his older brother standing as his best man behind him. Tony Jr., the brother, would have the rings hidden away, his irresponsible self, doing something right this time.

She would walk the aisle and once next to him, he would take her hand, and hold that hand until they were married. She would never let him go.

And as she fell, she thought of him, how she loved him, and was never going to let him go. Not in her heart...

She landed hard, no hands available to steady or catch herself. Her balance was off by her hand being stuck, so she had no way to prepare, to tuck and roll with the motion. No, all her weight and the momentum of her punch came down on her and she crashed into the unforgiving earth with the air expelling in a rush from her lungs.

The thing that was Sarah landed on top of her and she immediately felt hands pulling at her. She knew it wouldn't be long before the things around her pulled themselves close and were biting into her. And really, what did it matter anymore?

She was looking into the dead eyes of Dennis, as he was less than a foot away from her. Those dead eyes that killed her soul and twisted the knife buried in her chest. She wanted tears to flow, but the cold had already dried them away.

She felt a stabbing pain as teeth ripped into her leg. Then more as something landed on top of her and tore a chunk out of her back. More hands grabbed at her; they were pulling in all different directions. If she wanted, she could turn over, or try to. She wasn't sure she could do it and use her hands to fight at them as they made their way onto her. She had done it once; she could probably do it again.

But she didn't. Instead, she reached out her hand, extending to where Dennis was. His was covered in blood, as was hers. Still, hers slipped into his like they were meant to always be holding each other.

Blood was filling her lungs. The pain shooting through her thoughts made everything around her impossible to focus on, but she fought it. As she gasped, wheezing towards her last breath, she coughed out, "I love you."

His hand slipped out of hers. She felt it, but had to blink away the tears to see why. The pain had dulled as the world grew colder. Through her blurry vision, she watched as Dennis was moving. He was a shape coming towards her.

She couldn't help herself, but she smiled as she coughed up another lung full of blood.

"Den-" she couldn't get it out as her chest spasmed. It didn't matter. She used her outstretched arm to pull herself towards him, though she could see he was nearly to her. She thought that maybe they would get their one last kiss. She hadn't realized just how much she yearned to feel those lips again.

His lips neared her own and she could see the blood splattering them. He had a large toothy smile, and she tried to force herself to return it through the pain. His mouth opened wide, and she had a brief second to mentally question why he was opening his mouth so wide when he was going to kiss her and why did it look like his mouth was full of spiders.

Then his mouth closed over her own, and her scream was cut short as he bit off her lips. The little bit that had remained of her mind, that had stayed focused on Dennis, was ripped away as insanity took her final moments before she was lost to eternal night.

CHAPTER 22

The first thing Lizzie felt when she woke up was an immense pain in her temple and that sense of being pulled out from some other world. The one she was in now was still rich in haze from the fog of slumber and remnants were fresh in her thoughts of the one she left behind.

Had it been real? Had any of that just happened? It had been so real to her. It felt more like memories than dream fragments, but if that was the case, why had she been Jessica? She had known her thoughts, her past, things that Jessica had never told her about herself. About her friend. She couldn't have made all that up, could she? She was unsure, but it unsettled her, because if it was real, then her friend was dead.

The rock formed in her stomach. She had wanted to warn her earlier. She had tried to warn Jessica that something was coming after her. She had known they were next, but maybe it was because of that premonition that she had dreamed about it.

The dream had been so real. Too real. She still felt the bone deep cold inside her, and as she opened her eyes and exhaled, a puff of mist formed from her lips. Lips that had just hours before been kissed by Roland. How could she have slept with him after everything that had happened between them? She would never have been that stupid, but she had.

The heart wants what the heart wants.

"But honey, that hadn't been your heart talking. That had been something else. That was your pussy talking, and it was hungry for the 'D'." A voice said to her in her head. She recognized it as a voice from long ago, though who it belonged to, she couldn't recall. It was a voice from out of time, floating in from some forgotten past.

As she tried to focus on it, more of the dream faded away, yet the cold remained. It was very cold, too cold even. A shiver ran through her. And that shouldn't be right. She shouldn't be shivering from a dream, should she?

Something tapped her back, and she remembered she was still in the hotel room. He was there too, asleep behind her in the bed.

How could she have been so stupid?

She wanted desperately to get out of there. She didn't know how long she had been asleep, but the little she had was enough to clear her mind. God! What had she been thinking?

Didn't matter. The deed was done and tomorrow he would wake up and remind her of it, maybe even try for a repeat, as if everything was forgotten and forgiven. *Men.*

She wished she had driven herself. Then she could sneak out into the night and disappear, letting the miles between them build until maybe this would become another ungodly nightmare.

First, she needed to call Jessica, make sure she was okay. It was the middle of the night. The outside light filtering through the hotel's curtains confirmed that suspicion, and she would probably wake her friend.

I just need to make sure she's okay.

But you know she's not.

I don't know that, just the dream had been so real.

The conversation played out in her mind, and she continued to lie there in indecision. She should wake up Roland and tell him about it. He would calm her down, tell her she was being silly, but 'hey, here's my cell phone if you want to call her.' He'd do all those things, as he was a good guy who cared for her. So why did he also have to be such a lying, cheating bastard?

Last night, she had believed all his bullshit. Why couldn't she believe him now? Because she had come to her senses, that's why. What had she been thinking?

She could feel him shift in the bed behind her and let out a soft moan.

He probably sensed that she was awake and was waking up, too. He had always been good about waking up with her whenever she couldn't sleep. He was usually a heavy sleeper, but the moment she had a bad dream, he was up and held her in his arms. Even when she had the nightmares return and she relived her parents death, he had cuddled her as she found herself crying on his chest.

She didn't want him to know she was awake. *Damn.* Maybe if she was still and stayed on her side, he wouldn't know, but she wanted to call Jess. *Damn.* What if she fell back to sleep waiting for him to fall back to sleep? *Damn, damn, damn.*

She pulled the blankets tighter around her. It was so cold in the room. They must have forgotten to turn on the heat when they came in. Considering how they had been with each other, she wasn't surprised. They had been generating their own heat.

Now the room was an icebox. She could use the temperature of the room as a refrigerator. Their bottled water would be nicely chilled for drinking where it sat on the little table across the room. The temp must have dropped lower than forecasted if the room was this cold. She hadn't brought enough clothes.

Roland moaned louder. Then he moaned even louder. This wasn't him waking up.

Then he screamed, and she turned over to see that she had gone from dreaming one nightmare to living in another.

"Tik-a-too, tik-a-ted. There's a dead man in your bed." The hideous voice cackled. She could see the dark shape that was sitting on Roland. It was hovering over him but watching her and smiling at her. Even in the dimly lit room, and his obscured form, she saw the bright whites of a chilling smile as he laughed at her. He was so close. Too close, she couldn't do anything but get away. Immediately, she jumped out of the bed and twisted, never taking her eyes off him. She didn't stop backing away until she hit the wall, then she pressed herself against it as hard as she could. She would have melted into it if she could find a way.

Run. She should just run away, get herself out of there and make her escape, but it had Roland. It had turned away from her, ignoring her because, for now, it had what it wanted.

Roland. She looked at him, and she could see that the shadow thing had one of its hands deep in

Roland's chest. It hadn't broken the skin; it was like the shadow man was only part way into this world and because of that, his hand didn't have any substance. He was in Roland's chest, but it had gone through the skin, not breaking it.

That wasn't true. As Lizzie watched Roland shake violently, the shadow man laughing as he squeezed inside. The shadow was killing him. It was suffocating him from the inside or squeezing his heart. She didn't know, but it didn't matter. This was how it really enjoyed taking lives.

She wasn't sure how she knew, but as soon as the thought occurred to her, she was certain she was right. It liked death and took it in any way that it could. When Sarah had been killed, it had no way of killing her directly. Same way with Josh and Elisabeth. It couldn't touch them directly. She didn't know why, and there was much of it that didn't make sense. There must be some set of rules this shadow had to play by, and killing directly was a no-no. It used surrogates and manipulation to take most of the lives, so it was less accustomed to the joy of taking life within its own dark grasp.

So, what had changed the rules? Why was it there now, killing Roland? Was it getting stronger? She vaguely recalled something Josh and Sarah had been arguing about. There had been many things, but something Sarah had wanted Lizzie to notice.

There had been the picture. Last night, *oh God, had it really just been last night* that Josh had appeared to them? It had, and this had easily become one of the longest days in human history, or at least she'd ever had, because it seemed like so much shit just kept rolling her way.

267

But the picture. It fell. The two fighting had been able to move it and the picture fell and then it broke. How had she not noticed that before?

She thought back to the hospital room and how Sarah, by herself, hadn't been able to move anything, no matter how hard she tried. Oh, and then there was touching each other. They had both made each other sick trying to do it, but at the coffee shop, Sarah had no issues with choking her.

You still don't know if Sarah was even there. It hadn't been like before. That could have been just you. You know you're losing your mind, right?

She wished she could silence her own thoughts, especially with some of the newer thought voices that kept giving her their opinions.

It had been Sarah, and she had been choking her. They were getting stronger. He was getting stronger. She was feeding it somehow.

It was all the people around her doing it. They kept dying. It fed off the death. It wanted her friends to die, her loved ones. It was killing them, all of them, and was going to keep doing it until she stopped it.

If she could stop it. Her uncle hadn't been able to.

Her uncle hadn't been able to. How did she know he had fought it? Because it all made sense. He had hidden himself back in the woods, away from everyone, cutting himself off from the outside world because anyone he cared about was killed.

She couldn't think about it right now, but it all was rushing at her. This thing had killed her parents. It killed her aunt. It had been after all of them and when her uncle couldn't handle it anymore; he had killed himself and it was killing everyone she loved.

Tears rolled down her cheek, but she paid them no mind. Instead, she looked around the room for something, anything, she could use. She heard Roland's wheezing breath and knew she had to be quick.

But why even try? Her uncle had years to fight this thing, and it had never done any good. How are you going to stop it?

She didn't know and the thought voice was becoming increasingly annoying. She wished it would just shut up. Shut up and let her think, dammit!

In the dim light, she could see Roland. His face was turning grey, dark lines stretching along his cheeks and bulging from around his eyes. She feared those were his veins. His blood was being replaced by the shadows' darkness and his veins were visible through his skin by their black hue.

She wasn't sure what possessed her to throw it, but she had unplugged the coffee maker by ripping it from the desk. The cable struck her, and she grabbed it, quickly wrapping it around the little gadget and then flung it across the room. She didn't wait to see the thing react as she grabbed more from the desk. She used the tray the coffee maker had been on, a local phone book, and a folder that must have contained local delivery options or the TV guide directory. It didn't matter because if she could lift it; she threw it. She didn't stop until she tried to lift the large lamp at the end of the desk, only to find that it was mounted in place. She was pulling at it, trying to shake it back and forth, wrestling it free, when she heard the laugh coming from behind her.

She couldn't get the lamp free, and she had nothing else to throw. Slumping her shoulders, she turned to look back at the bed, wrestling with another idea, one that was crazy and not like her at all...

She stopped thinking when she saw the thing was looking at her. Its eyes burned red with some internal flame, and they burned into her. Its smile was wide, and somehow the light that flickered from its eyes never touched his teeth, as they were white to the point that they seemed to glow and they were sharp, each tooth ending in a narrow point.

"Hello." It said, speaking to her for the first time without that sing-song cadence. Now it was fixated on her, and she was hypnotized as the unseen lips moved, only noticeable for how they blocked the glow of its teeth when it spoke.

"Get away from him," she said. She could hear the tears in her voice, but was surprised at the anger. Where had that come from? She wasn't sure but as she stood there, clenching and unclenching her fists, remembering what this thing has taken from her, her friends that it has killed. She knew the anger, and she embraced it. She wanted to be done with allowing this creature to come into her life and steal everywhere cared for from her.

"Why should I? What is he to you? A lover? A friend? You care about him that much?" The voice grated on her nerves. It was rough, a gravelly voice that echoed in her ears, as though many voices tried to speak as one.

Lizzie took a deep breath and let it out through her mouth. Her fists unclenched and she shook out her hands before she clenched them again. She could feel her nails digging in, the uneven edges from how she chewed at them threatening to break her skin.

"He's nobody to me." She tried to sound convincing. Yesterday she wasn't sure if she would even have stopped the shadow thing from taking Roland, though she liked to think that deep down she was a good person. Even a good person wouldn't let a lying, cheating son-of-a-bitch to die when she could stop it.

Today, she found that she still did care about him. Her feelings were still there, and that is why she had hated him so much. Because, under all that anger, she did love him.

She couldn't tell this thing that. It had some kind of connection to her. It killed those close to her. So, she had to find that anger and hate she had for Roland if she was ever going to save him.

She had to find a way to kill the shadow man.

It had been watching her as she stood there and the longer; she didn't say anything more, a sound grew from him. It wasn't until it developed into a sound; she recognized that she realized it was laughing at her.

"You sleep with him. He fucks you, and you say he is nobody to you." And as it said that Roland writhed in agony below it.

"Fuck you," the anger boiling up inside her. She had noticed something. She had just caught the slight glint of metal on the floor and had taken a moment to realize just what it was. The keys to the car had fallen to the floor, probably having dropped out of Roland's pockets as she had pulled his pants off him.

"Those you wish about and those you love,

271

From the wings of a morning dove,
All those in which you cherish.
Will slowly die in agony and perish.
They will be mine, these dreary few.
And once they are gone, I will come for you."

She didn't want to hear any more of his creepy words. Each one made her skin tingle and her back tense. She tuned him out the best she could as she made her plan. It wasn't a good one, and she knew it wouldn't work, but it was her doing something. She was so tired of not doing anything. She had to try something to stop him.

She rushed forward, grabbing the keys as she moved. Her arm rose high, she had her sights set, aimed for where she wanted to strike while fumbling in her hand to have one key out between her fingers. She was unsure of herself, having never been a fighter, but did all she could to put everything she had when she brought her hand down.

It struck just below the eyes. Or it would have, had the shadow man been anything more than a shadow. Her hand slipped through him, and then she was slipping through him, her momentum carrying her into him and landing on top of Roland.

This had been a mistake. She had realized it the moment she didn't make contact, but as she was flung over the bed, she realized just how much of a mistake it had been.

Her skin had turned near ice, as he was just so cold. She couldn't breathe. Her breath was frozen in her lungs. All of her was frozen. She was trapped and, even worse; she was in his essence and there she could see... something.

She didn't know what it was. Around her there was so much darkness. It was an ether. She knew she wasn't on earth. It was an 'other' place, one where there was no light to cast the shadows. Shadows were not made, they were things, and hid other things.

She could feel that hate that emanated from that place, from all the creatures that surrounded her there. She couldn't see them, only felt them, sensing that they were reaching out for her. They wanted to take her, torture her how they had been tortured. She was a creature of the light, and they hated her for it.

How did she know that?

Because she was inside of him. He was from this place, and he felt that way towards her. But that didn't make sense. If he hated her, all of them so much, then why not just kill her? Why kill her friends?

Because the shadow man-thing didn't hate her, it hated man. She was a person, one who lived in night and day. The shadow-man wanted all light to be perished from the world.

She was the lock that kept them at bay. She didn't know how that worked.

Now she was there in the dark place. Things were moving around her. They had noticed her. She could feel them moving towards her. A wave of fear ran through her, but it wasn't her fear. The shadow man was afraid of these things. It was afraid... of them. It didn't want it to get her.

She was not sure what to make of that and she didn't have the time to find out as she found herself ripped out of him, back in her own world and being hurled across the hotel room. She had the briefest of sensations of no control, weightlessness as she flew, and then pain. She hit the wall, and it forced the air out of her lungs. She fell to the floor, and everything hurt. Her insides felt like they had been squished, her arms and legs were sore. She wasn't sure if she broke anything. It felt like if she hadn't, then she had definitely sprained something, everything.

Across the room, cutting through the cold and dark, was a blood-curdling scream that was quickly cut short.

The room grew deathly still. The only thing Lizzie heard was the repetitive sound of her breathing. Even the hum from the electronics in the room were silent. The darkness felt out of time. She was all alone. She feared what she would find when she stood and looked at the bed.

She pulled herself up. Each movement took a concerted effort as she fought against the pain.

When she stood, she turned and saw Roland on the bed. The shadow man was gone. Roland wasn't breathing. His skin was ash grey, and she knew he wasn't coming back. She was alone in the room with her dead ex-boyfriend. A man she had made many public threats against his life and bodily harm.

She was quick putting on her clothes, finding her phone and wallet before grabbing the car keys and getting out of there.

Outside, the world was dark; the streetlights having burned out in the last half hour. She worked her way through the void as best she could and got into Roland's car. She felt a tinge of guilt as she drove away. She knew she should call the police. There would be plenty of questions and they would wonder why she just left. She wasn't sure if she had any answers for them.

She was empty. Empty of answers, empty of emotions, empty of everything. She was a shell, and even the tears weren't coming.

She made her way to the interstate. Within a half hour, she was speeding down the road, on her way, unsure of where she was going.

Part 2

CHAPTER 23

Her hands wouldn't stop shaking as she tried to wrap them around the coffee cup. She couldn't control her breathing. Like the rest of her, it was erratic and didn't want to be controlled. She couldn't calm down and why the hell should she want to? She had seen her ex-boyfriend with whom she had just had sex with, killed by some shadow creature from another plain of existence.

It reminded her of that movie Roland had once made her watch. It was the one with the guy who cut off his hand and replaced it with a chainsaw. He was looking at himself in the mirror, telling himself that everything was fine when his reflection grabbed him, looked at him with those wild and crazy eyes and said to him, "you just chopped up your girlfriend with a chainsaw, does that sound 'fine' to you?"

Well, she had just seen her friend die. In the last few weeks, she had seen most of her friends die, many of them coming back, and they had been nice to her until she put on the damn necklace. Why had she ever put it on? It didn't matter. Because as she tried to calm herself, she couldn't help but think of all that stuff. She closed her eyes to let a single tear fall and whispered, "does that sound fine to you?"

No, it sure as hell didn't. She wasn't fine and knew it, but what was she going to do about it? She had no one to talk to, and it seemed like anyone she did talk to ended up dead.

Her phone sat on the counter. Jessica still hadn't called her back. Lizzie had already left her four voicemails since she'd left the room. She had only made it forty-five minutes down the interstate before she was starting to drift off behind the wheel, and in that time, she had kept trying to get ahold of her friend, fearing she, too, was dead. That dream had been so vivid. It had to be more than just a dream.

She eased the coffee cup to her lips again, holding it tightly to keep it from shaking. It took an effort, but she sipped the bitter brew. She wasn't a plain coffee drinker, but hadn't been able to process the ingredients on the counter to sweeten her drink.

"Figured out what you want, or do you still need a few minutes?"

Lizzie jumped in her seat and looked up at the woman standing over her. The woman was smiling at her, her teeth yellow from years of coffee and cigarettes. Her eyes were dark, sunken in from what Lizzie guessed was lack of sleep. Her nose had a ring in it and Lizzie realized she couldn't guess the woman's age. She looked old, her skin wrinkled and ashen, but Lizzie wasn't sure. This woman looked life hardened, and that made her age irrelevant. She was ancient in the ways of life, and that was all that mattered.

"I'm sorry, you just startled me." Lizzie noticed, glancing at her coffee, thankful none of it had spilled. Had she really drunk three quarters of a cup already?

"It's okay." The waitress said as she brought over a fresh pot of the dark liquid. Steam rose from it as she poured. "Is everything okay?"

Lizzie internally chuckled at the question, not able to get that damn movie out of her head.

"Not really."

"Do I need to call someone for you? Or are you hiding from someone? I can call the sheriff. Pete's a decent guy. If your boyfriends doing something he shouldn't, Pete'll set him straight."

"No, but thank you. I just-" she cut off mid-sentence. What did she need? She wasn't sure of a lot of things. None of this, nothing in her life over the course of the last three weeks, made any sense.

So, if she needed anything, it was that. To make it all make sense. She needed to think.

No, she needed to figure out where to go. The cops would be looking for her, and the last thing she wanted was to explain why she had been with her cheating ex-boyfriend when he had died.

"I guess I just need a piece of paper and a pen if you have one?"

"Sure thing." The waitress said as she ripped off a piece of paper from her order pad and set it on the counter as well as a pen. "Did you want to eat anything?"

Lizzie thought about it. Her stomach was in knots and the coffee was only going to make it worse unless she ate something. She just wasn't sure what. She needed something to soak up all that acid that was burning her insides.

"I'll just have a waffle with wheat toast on the side."

There was a ding from the bell over the door to the diner, and the waitress looked up. Lizzie followed her gaze to see the two men, both looking tired. One of them smelled of diesel, though she wasn't sure which one. As it was an all-night truck stop, they were probably both truck drivers coming in for some middle of the night nourishment.

"Sure thing."

"World's going to hell in a handbasket. Come on, you hear some of the crazy shit they say been going on out there?" One of the truck drivers was saying. His voice billowed out from him, and it was obvious the man had no concept of an 'inside voice.'

"I'll be right with you, gentlemen." The waitress said, looking at them as they sat a couple stools down from her. They nodded, but she had already turned her attention back to Lizzie. "And like I said, need anything else. Just let me know."

The woman held her gaze, and Lizzie was transfixed by her. She couldn't turn away. Those eyes, the compassion emanating from this stranger as she briefly let her hand rest on Lizzie's own, kept her locked in this woman's control.

"Thank you." Lizzie felt herself say the words, but it didn't feel like it came from just her lips. Somewhere deep within her, she felt a weight lift and, for a short time, felt like it would be okay. Maybe she could think about everything that had happened, and she could make some sense of it.

There was a release and Lizzie found herself blinking her eyes, fighting back the tears that threatened. When she looked up again, the waitress was already talking to the two men, pouring them steaming coffee.

Okay, so Lizzie had to figure out what was going on.

She looked at the slip of order sheet the woman had given her and flipped it over to the blank back side. There she scribbled at the top, "What I know?"

So, what did she know? Well, her friends were dying and then sometime during the night, they came back to haunt her. Now with the necklace on, they only attacked her in mirrors and somehow had the strength to attack her and nearly kill her.

This wasn't working. She had to focus. She needed to figure out the timeline and keep it in order. If she just started writing down random thoughts, she would be all over the place.

Sarah had been killed by a dead man that Lizzie hadn't known. That was strange as it was the only time the shadow man had used someone not associated with her and had somehow dug up the thing from the nearby graveyard. Had the sheriff said the graveyard was nearby? No, he had said it was on the other side of town. The dead man had to have dug himself up to work his way across the small community to end up there for when they arrived. That seemed farfetched. So Lizzie had to wonder if someone was working with the shadow man or controlled by him like he controlled the dead man?

Something else about that didn't add up. Her uncle's note said she would be safe from the dead in his house, but somehow the dead man was able to get in. Sarah hadn't been able to get in. There had to be something different about the dead man.

"You know that was horseshit, right? Another government cover up."

"Yeah, like you know what happened."

283

"Hell yeah, I know. I know one of the survivors. He's a trucker. He said that the dead were attacking people."

Lizzie's head spun as she turned to look at the two men. They were completely focused on each other and their coffees. Neither seemed to notice her as she watched them intently.

"That's bullshit."

"You know, I'd agree. But I know the guy. He's not the kind of guy who makes this type of shit up."

"So, what, there were zombies and the government just up and nuked the town? Because the idea of home-grown terrorists blowing themselves up is more farfetched."

Lizzie vaguely recalled what the men were talking about. Something about terrorists blowing up a small town. She only remembered it from Sarah talking about the dumb flatlanders blowing themselves and everyone around them up. It had only been a blip on her radar as her parents had died and she was still reeling with it. The president could have been killed, and she'd barely have known, as she was lost in her own bubble and nothing else mattered.

Kind of like what she was doing now.

She wanted to break into their conversation and ask about the dead killing people, but didn't get a chance when Alice came by to refill their cups. They both stopped watching her, but she had looked at Lizzie with an inquiring raise of her eyebrow.

"You need something, honey?"

It seemed like all the world was trained on her, as everyone was watching her now. The two guys had turned to look, and Alice kept her gaze.

"No, I'm fine."

"Hey ya' cutie. What's got you out so late?" The taller of the two men said to her. He was the one whose friend told him about the dead. The other man shook his head, turning away from them both as he took another drink from his coffee.

"Nothing." She said as she focused on her own cup.

"We weren't disturbing you, were we?"

"It's okay."

"Just ignore my friend here. He seems to have zombies on the brain." The shorter man said, looking around his friend so he could look at her.

"Its....it's okay. I just hadn't heard anything abou-"

"He's talking about the town that somehow managed to blow itself up. Hayward, or something like that."

"Hammond." The taller man cut in. The waitress seemed bored with the conversation and stepped back, probably to place the men's orders with the cook.

"Hammond, that's right. You remember that, right?"

"Not really. My parents had just died. I don't think I really..." her voice trailed off and she saw the sympathy in their eyes.

"Sorry about your loss."

"It's okay."

"No, but I get what y'r saying. Anyways, Hammond had some kind of home-grown terrorist living there. No one ever said who, just that there had been a small cell, and they had built a dirty nuke. Fools had screwed up and blew themselves as well as the whole town right off the map."

"Which doesn't make no sense. If had been a dirty bomb, there would still be radiation all around there. There's not."

"How would you know? Military's had the area locked down since it happened."

"Not farther out. There'd still be traces."

"So, but your friend said there were zombies? Reanimated corpses?" She cut in.

"Yeah, this guy Bruce. He'd been my trainer, and we stay in touch. Ran into him a few months back shortly after it happened. He was pretty shaken up about it. Frustrated too, as they had him quarantined so long afterwards that he nearly lost his wife."

"Just why in the hell would he be in quarantine?"

"Because they don't know what caused the shit. He said there was something to do with spiders, but he didn't understand it all. Just said it had been some freaky shit and didn't know how he survived. Said if it got out that he was talking about it, that he'd be a dead man, or locked up for life."

"Then why'd he tell you?"

"Because he was stressed about it and needed to talk to someone. I was someone."

"Reeks like bullshit to me." The shorter man said and looked over to Lizzie, giving her a knowing wink. Though what he thought she knew, she wasn't sure. She had already drifted from the conversation, thinking about that day in the house. Had there been any spiders? She hadn't recalled seeing any. Each time she'd been there, she hadn't noticed any bugs. When was the last time she'd ever been in the woods and there had been none of the blood-sucking bastards?

"Order up," called the chef from the kitchen, and Lizzie turned to see her food in the elongated window. Alice appeared and made her way to it.

"It may-as-well-be. I'm just telling you what he told me. Something strange about what happened, though I'll admit it sounds crazy. But you think about it, there's some crazy shit in nature."

"Like what?"

Lizzie was only partially following their conversation, no longer participating as she watched Alice pull her food from the window, butter the waffle, then create a small plate of fixings to go with the food. Once done, Alice was able to magically hold it all as she brought it to Lizzie.

"You ever hear of zombie ants?"

"You're full of it."

"No, no. I saw it there on Facebook."

"It's on Facebook, so it's gotta be true, huh?"

"Hey asshole, there's good stuff on there. Saw some guy post about some article in one of them science magazines."

"Uh huh."

"Here ya go. You need anything else with these?" Alice, the waitress, asked as she set the plate down with all the condiments. She thanked Alice and tried to pay attention to the two men. It seemed interesting, but she wasn't sure it had anything to do with her situation.

"It's how this fungus controls these ants, you see, and has them doing what they want them to do. The ants are dead, and this fungus controls them."

"No, thank you," Lizzie said, and Alice nodded, giving the men a frustrated look before turning back to Lizzie with a wink and a nod.

"Think I heard about a movie like that? Something about kids being special zombies."

"What the hell are you talking about? No, this is about this fungus controlling ants."

"Enjoy. Hopefully, these dingleberries will talk about something a little less disgusting and allow you to eat in peace." Alice said, walking past them on her way into the back area.

"Sorry about that. Derek, shut the hell up." The shorter man said, looking at the other one.

"Sure thing. Sorry about that. You go ahead and eat up, honey. We'll talk about something more frustrating."

"Like how much longer the Bears coach has before he's run out of the city with his head on a...umm, I mean, how much longer until he's fired?"

Lizzie wasn't paying them too much attention. She looked over and acknowledged them, even nodding as they started into some new argument. She tried to act interested, but her mind was already whirling somewhere else. She couldn't stop herself from thinking about what the man had said.

The old man hadn't been the first time that dead things had come back, though she didn't think of them as zombies. That made her think of too many bad horror films and there was no room in her thoughts as she tried to focus on the new reality shaping itself around her for those. She had enough nightmares to worry about.

The old man had dug himself out of his own grave to find its way to her uncle's house. *Why? How?* Something was different there. It was like the shadow creature needed some way of starting... *this*, whatever *this* was.

She wrote on the paper.

Dead man
- how did he come back to life?
- why did he come back?

Friends
How is he killing them?
Why?
What does he get from it? He feeds off it somehow.

He's feeding from her... She had gotten a sense of that when she had merged with him earlier, but she wasn't sure how that worked. It was like, somehow, with how he tormented her, it fed him. That didn't make sense though, as he would eventually deplete whatever he got from her, and they would be done. Also, if he had been feeding off her uncle, then her uncle would probably not have survived as long, or the thing would have starved if her uncle hadn't been nourishing it.

Damn, why didn't the thing try to find someone else? What was so special about her family?

She wasn't sure if she did have any answers to any of it, and sitting in the diner wasn't going to do anything. She came in there for coffee. Was she really going to try to eat too? Her stomach twisted, and she knew its opinion was she would never eat again.

"It ain't no skin off my back."

"Hell, you'd never give anyone the shirt off your back, either."

"Asshole."

"Well, what do you expect? You only roll through here every couple of weeks. It'd be nice if I got to see my brother more often."

She looked at her piece of paper to avoid looking at the squabbling brothers. There wasn't anything new written there, but she saw what wasn't written there and began to realize what she needed to do. She had been right to not call her brother. If she had, it might have gotten him. Everyone she loved was in danger.

She had nowhere else to go. The cabin was it. It was far away from everyone hidden out in the woods. That would keep everyone else from dying, and with all the junk her uncle had, maybe there were some answers to be found.

It wasn't like she would be like her uncle. She wouldn't go there and stay hidden. She was just hiding for a little while as she got everything sorted out.

"Not hungry?" Alice, the waitress said as she seemed to appear out of nowhere.

"Not really." Lizzie said, quickly flipping over the piece of paper she had been writing on.

"Yeah, well, least your hands aren't shaking as much. Get some things figured out?"

"Maybe."

"Sometimes to find answers, we just need a respite along the way."

"Thank you."

"No problem."

Lizzie put the piece of paper in her little purse and pulled out her wallet. She didn't look at the bill but dropped forty dollars on the counter. She knew it was more than enough to cover it, but money wasn't her concern anymore. She almost relished the time a few weeks ago when it had been.

Lizzie was almost to the door when Alice called after her.

"Remember these dark times you're going through; you will find a path to the light. 'For He rescued us from the domain of darkness and transferred us to the kingdom of His beloved Son.'"

Lizzie gave her a weak smile. She respected the older woman, but never had appreciated when people quoted the Bible to her. She had enough of that growing up, and what did that faith ever do for her parents, her brother, or her? The woman had been nice, so she nodded a thanks and then turned to look at the two men sitting there.

"Hey, you guys, just so you know, I've seen it. Sometimes the dead do come back, and if there were enough of them, then I believe they would have nuked a town."

She left them there looking at each other, jaws dropped. She had to chuckle a little to herself as she walked to the car. If she ever had a mic drop moment, that would have been it.

CHAPTER 24

She hadn't intentionally timed her arrival at the cabin for dawn, but as she pulled into the long driveway with the sun peaking over the horizon, she was grateful for the sight. The place didn't look any less intimidating than the other times she had been there, but the thought of actually going through the front door in the dark hadn't been a pleasant one. Still, the sun cast long shadows that stretched from its small frame as though they were ready to grab her and take her into its dark confines.

If the shadow man was there, she would demand that he take her with him. She didn't want to die, but she'd had enough. She was done playing his games. She was there now in the cabin, where all this shit started. Maybe she was there for answers, but she knew that she could just as easily die and let it all end.

You know you can't do that. If you die, then this will go after your brother, and he can't live alone. He wouldn't be able to survive without his caregivers.

And she did know that. As much as she wanted to give up, it was always that thought that came back to her to keep her alive.

Damn, she was tired and sick of thinking about all this crap. It had been three hours and a couple different pit stops along the way for more coffee before she had found her way there. The long night had stretched and as it had, different shadow creatures had followed her along the road. Was she losing her mind with hallucinations or were the monsters she imagined real and chasing her? She wasn't sure.

Yet here she was, returning to the scene of the nightmare and stalling to get out of the car.

She reached over to the passenger seat and grabbed the plastic bags full of supplies she had bought at a convenience store near town. There were food items, enough to get her through a couple of days, she hoped, but she had also taken out a few hundred dollars in cash and had bought a prepaid cell phone. She wasn't sure if the police would be after her, but she wasn't ready to talk to them. Then she took a deep breath, glancing quickly at the place between her breasts where the talisman was nestled, and got out of the car.

Why are you doing this? You shouldn't be going in there. Not alone... Call someone, have them meet us here.

Her inner voice was screaming at her to turn around and run. She didn't blame it. She wanted to. If not to call a friend, then to get away from there. It wasn't just that her friend had died there. There was something else, a wrongness that she felt deep in her gut, that yelled at her to run.

She had to do this. There were answers in there. Her uncle had told her he had left her something here, something that might explain things. Then there was the shadow man. He had started following her after her first visit here. Maybe there was information about him? There were those occult symbols in the house, probably books, too. Maybe something she could find that would stop it.

She neared the front door, that voice screaming for her to call one of her friends, get them there to help her, to be there for her...

But they were all dead. She still hadn't been able to reach Jess, and that dream had felt so real. She knew it had to be more. She had probably watched her best friend as she was killed, and it had been because of her. Not only that, but it had been Sarah and the rest of her dead entourage that had somehow done it.

The talisman she had worn had darkened them, twisting them so that they turned against her. She wished she had never put it on, as it seemed like wherever it sent them was a place that equaled what she imagined hell to be like. Maybe it even was hell.

What kind of taint would forever darken her soul as she had condemned her friends, those she cared for most in this world, to an eternity of agony and torture?

She opened the door but stayed in the threshold. There was a cool breeze trickling out from the house and on it was carried the stench of death. Her nose wrinkled and her already twisted stomach wrenched harder into a knot. Goosebumps formed along her arm, and the wrongness of the house screamed at her. Every part of her told her not to go in there, yet she still heard that distant call, somewhere in the back of her thoughts, that told her she needed to go inside.

She was stalling again. The door was open. Nothing was baring her from entering except for her own thoughts. Her worried mind was on overdrive, thinking of her brother, remembering her friends that were killed, and what she was going to do once she did go inside. Everything, all trying to consume her at once, her brain spinning in a thousand directions, but none of them grappling on to her attention for long enough to focus.

A tear ran down her cheek, the motives behind it unclear. She had so many things she could cry over, but wasn't concentrating on any of them. Her chest hurt as she heaved in a large breath. That cold breeze from inside was turning her colder, and she felt the shiver run through her. It felt alien to her. Her body shook with the motion, but she didn't really feel like it was her that was shivering. No, it was something deep inside of her and it didn't want to go in there.

This is foolish. Just do it. Get your ass in there and start looking for that letter. He said he wrote you one. Maybe there were some answers. Maybe all the answers were in there.

Though she knew that couldn't be true. If her uncle had the answers, then none of this would be happening to her now. No, there might be answers inside the cabin, but it would not answer everything. Maybe there were some things that never had an answer.

She stepped over the threshold into the cabin and felt the breeze die away. Inside was actually warmer than it had been outside. It was comfortable in there, like the heat had been running and had kept the place at a decent temperature, as the weather had steadily gotten colder over the last couple of weeks.

That was impossible. There was no way the cabin was warmer inside, as it wasn't hooked to any city grid. The place had to run off its own system. She hadn't seen any power lines running to the place, so there couldn't be any power to the furnace. It had to be on generator power.

There was a distant clicking sound. A few seconds later, she heard the whooshing of air and saw a couple of pages far away on the other side of the room flicker as a tiny breeze sent warm air through the tiny place.

Of course, the place had power. She had seen her uncle's television and knew he also had a landline phone there as well, though where it was in all the piles of junk, she had no idea. She had no clue where anything was; the place was still a huge mess just like her previous visit.

Just because the place was hidden out in the boonies didn't mean it was cut off from the world, and it wasn't her uncle's cabin anymore. It was her cabin, and as she was hiding away from the world, it was her home.

This... this was her new home. She looked around it, looking at the endless piles of paper and what looked like trash littered about. There was a lot of it, and she didn't know where to start looking for that letter. To her left was the dining room and the door that led into the kitchen, and to her right was the living room and two doors. One must lead into the bathroom and the other, the bedroom. Neither of them was open, nor had they been in them when they were there last. Well, she guessed it was time to see the rest of the place.

She went to the farthest door first, figuring that one was the most likely to lead into the bedroom. Inside was a small room, her uncle's... no, her new bedroom inside. The bed was a small twin and to the left of it, with barely enough room to open any of the drawers, was a short but long dresser. On top of it was empty except for an envelope with her name on it.

She stepped into the tiny room, looking at the bare walls around her, and noticed there were no pictures hanging up. She glanced quickly into the living room and then back to the bedroom. There were no pictures anywhere, none of her family, nothing. There were no intimate details about anyone her uncle loved anywhere inside the house.

Except in the display case in the dining room. He had my aunt's decorative plates in there. Of course, she's been dead for a while, so there was no harm in keeping something that reminded him of her.

He lived without any visual memories of anyone he loved. He had been out there all alone and couldn't keep a picture of anyone. He must have been terrified that any visual representation would bring them harm. Did he have a rational fear that it would cause someone to die? Had he seen it happen, had he experienced it and so hid or destroyed all the pictures? Lizzie knew her dad sent him a picture every year of all of them together. Had he just thrown them out, or had he hidden them?

She grabbed the envelope, her hands shaking as she tried to rip it open. They seemed to have a mind of their own, not working with her to open and reveal the contents. She was surprised to find that she didn't want to read it. Somehow, not knowing what was going on, suddenly felt better than knowing. What if it was something worse? What if there was more to this and suddenly zombies were going to be breaking down her door?

She looked in the living room. The rest of the house was still. It was very quiet out there. Even the hiss of the heating vents had silenced, leaving the house eerily quiet with only the slight buzz of power that was hidden in the background of stillness.

"If there's someone else here, another dead man in the kitchen, I'd hear it, right?" She said to herself. The sound of her voice did nothing to calm her nerves, as she was no longer sure she was alone. She couldn't hear anyone else but couldn't shake the nagging feeling that they were there.

She kept the letter in her hand and walked quietly back through the house, making her way as silent as she could in the already deafening stillness. Each step she took she was worried it would shatter the peace with a creaking floorboard, but she was able to make it to the kitchen door. She stopped there, breathing as silently as she could, and listened.

She couldn't hear anything outside the normal sounds of an empty house. The refrigerator clicked and there was that ever-present buzz, but nothing that would betray a stranger waiting for her.

She let out the breath she had been holding, still standing there for a moment longer, not wanting to step into the kitchen. That was the room. It was where it had happened. That was where Sarah had died. She didn't think she could ever go into that room and not think of her best friend.

But she knew she had to go in there.

She gently pushed on the swinging door and entered the other room. It was empty. She was alone.

As she approached the back door leading out of the kitchen, only barely noticing that the door had had been fixed from her first time there, she realized that she had known the kitchen would be empty. It wasn't like before. She didn't know how she had known, but she had. She hadn't been afraid when she came to the kitchen, worried, yes, but not afraid.

The more she took time to think about it, the more she hadn't been afraid of the house ever since she stepped inside. That wrongness that had perpetually plagued her since she had first come to the house had vanished the moment she had crossed the threshold. Strangely, she felt more at peace there now... It was like she had come home somehow and now this place was hers and she didn't ever need to leave this place. It was hers and she was its protector.

That didn't make any sense. Still, comfortable in this new house or not, she locked the back door and went into the living room. There weren't many places to sit, as papers were everywhere. She figured she would have to fix that, maybe as soon as even today, as she didn't have much else on her agenda.

Yeah, you are going to clean off all the chairs and get ready for all the guests you're going to have over.

She realized the futility of it, but ignored it. She wasn't a neat freak, but the level of mess and clutter this place was in would eventually nag at her to the point of near insanity.

You think you're sane? Your dead friends, the creature you call the shadow man, a dead man killing your friend in this house that you decided to come back and hide in after watching your ex-boyfriend with whom you had just had sex with, killed right in front of you. You really think you are the picture of perfect sanity right now?

She sat in the well-worn brown lazy boy. The padding on the arms was flat and there were dark spots on the middle padding. The chair looked second hand and well used. Considering the condition of the place, her uncle had probably spent the majority of his time there.

She looked again at the interior of the house. There was just so much stuff. So many piles of books and old papers. Where would she start going through any of this? How much of it was garbage she could throw out? When did the garbage man come? Where did the mail get delivered and when were the power and utility bills due? There were so many things about the house she needed to find out and no clue as to how to go about doing so.

This really was her place now...

She looked at the envelope. Her name had been hastily scrawled on the front and had been held roughly in the past as it was crinkled as though it had been balled up once or twice. She could see spots where there was a change in texture and additional wrinkles in the paper. She recognized the signs of tears that had fallen as he had held it or maybe just rain drops.

But here it was... She had come there to find answers, and this envelope... inside was the letter that would have some. He had known that this would be happening to her. Obviously, this had been going on with him. Why else would he live in such a cabin so far from everyone, keeping them, his parents, her, her brother all at a distance? He had to have known.

Was their family cursed? It passed from one to the next, but that wasn't possible. Curses weren't real things, just something you read about in cheesy horror novels, but how else could she explain it? There was no other explanation.

This envelope held the key, the answers, and she suddenly found herself not wanting to open it.

Instead, she set it down on the arm of the chair and looked at the blacked-out window. Her chest was sore from the talisman, its sharp claws always scraping on her flesh when she moved. He had said in his other note that she only needed to wear it until she got to the house. Could she take it off now? She wouldn't know for sure until she read this other letter. Still, she found herself looking down, lifting the front of her shirt so she could see where it rested among her tiny breasts. It was an ugly thing, so small and yet seemed so powerful.

She lifted the strand that held up over her head and pulled it off. She let it slip through her fingers and fall to the floor; resting back in the chair. She closed her eyes as she felt a single tear free itself from her pained insides.

Outside, she heard the screaming. Her eyes shot back open, and she stood straight as she recognized the voices. They were back.

"Come out here, you bitch!"

Lizzie looked at the envelope, trying to ignore them. She ripped open the top.

"What the hell is this? What is happening?" That was Roland.

"I'm going to kill you, you fucking whore!" Chuck screamed. Then she heard the crying. The other voices were farther away, like they were screaming at the house but keeping their distance. The crying one was closer, like she was right at the blacked-out window. It was Elisabeth, and Lizzie felt her heart twist as she listened to the woman. She spoke just above a whisper, but somehow her voice carried, and Lizzie heard what she said.

"You did this to us. I was pregnant. I died, and it is still inside me. You killed us, this is all you fault. You killed all of us...and we are going to torture you and kill you. We must. It's the only way for this to end. You... you have to die."

CHAPTER 25

Elizabeth,

...I...I... I really don't know how to write this or even what to tell you. There's so much. I've written this letter so many times over the years, though not always addressed to you. I figured the curse would fall on to others before you. Then, when Tommy died, I knew you would be next.

I'm sure none of this makes any sense. It doesn't. It never has made any sense to me as well, and I've lived with it for nearly fifteen years. I think it's been fifteen. Time is a little hazy when you are isolated and it feels much longer, but when I try to do the math, that's what I come up with.

All this, I'm sure I sound like a crazy old hermit and I'm sure that's how I seem to you. I don't know what you've been through. I know a little about your life, and I have no clue how your life has been since my death to you reading this letter. I was hoping to make everything...

Shit. I'm losing myself and getting ahead of things. I'm sorry. I just don't know how to get this started. Tell you what you need to know and catch you up on the little that I know. I want you to be more prepared than I was.

I know you don't know too much about me. You think that your dad and I had a huge fight and then I chose to live out here in the woods? Bet you think I'm a really big weirdo, huh? Well, part of that is true. Your dad and I got into a fight, but it wasn't what kept me away. I had already moved out here to the cabin after Cynthia died and your dad was worried about me. The fight was about him wanting me to come stay with you guys and I wouldn't leave the cabin. He was afraid for me, how I could just leave behind my successful job and all my friends to live alone out here. How could I tell him I was doing it to keep him and everyone I cared about safe?

Cynthia was dead. It is my fault. That's not survivor's guilt, but a fact. You have to understand this curse that is your true inheritance, and I am so sorry that this burden has fallen on your shoulders. I still remember the day you were born. I was at the hospital with your dad. I held you in my arms. Your eyes were closed, and boy, could you scream. You came out with such a set of lungs on you.

You were also the most amazing thing I'd seen, and I couldn't wait for Cynthia and me to have one of our own. We were trying. In retrospect, it was a good thing that our wishes had never come true, as I think that would have broken me when this fell on me. Then this would have been your dad's burden, and we would have lost all of you. Well, I would already have been gone, but it would have been your dad's turn to lose everyone he loved.

Maybe that would have been a good thing. The blood line would have ended. Yeah, hate me for saying it. I hate myself for writing it, and I really don't think it was smart. I don't even think that would have ended it. It might have just made it worse.

I'm still getting ahead of myself. Let me start over.

I don't know what it is or what it wants. I don't know if it is a curse on our bloodline or something to do with this house and where it stands. I have a bunch of theories, but none of them matter. What does matter is that all those close to you, friends to you, anyone you keep in regular contact with, will die. I wish I could say that was the end of it, but they will die, and then come back and haunt you. (Though I don't think that haunting is the right word. Most of those who have come back have been very nice. They know I loved them, and they have never truly left me.)

Not all who come back, though, are people you know. I don't know why, but those connected with those who die around you, those who are killed by the curse and are affected by it. Damn, I don't think I'm explaining this well.

Say a man died. He had a girlfriend. She gets depressed because her boyfriend was killed and kills herself. Well, now not only is the boyfriend haunting you, but so is his girlfriend.

I don't know how or why this works this way. I've spent years trying to figure all this out and still, it doesn't make sense. As soon as I think I know all the rules and what they are, things change, and I have to learn everything new again.

Sometimes I think she does it just to mess with me, but I'm not ready to touch on that yet, so hey, what else do you need to know? Dead come back and haunt you. Check. Anyone you care about and keep in contact with is going to die. Check. Oh yes, even if you get too familiar with someone on a regular basis, guess what? They're going to die.

You'll end up never wanting to leave this cabin or talk to anyone from the outside world. I almost never left and my only contact with the outside was pretty much through phone and internet. Yes, there is internet here and WiFi. Sorry, but I destroyed my computer tonight. Well, shortly before writing this letter to you. You'll have to buy your own laptop, I guess, or bring your own if you thought to do so. Password for the WiFi is a set of numbers on the box in the corner. All the utility bills are paid for in advance for the next ten years.

Yeah, you don't have to worry about much financially. I bet you're wondering where all the money came from. I sure as hell didn't inherit it myself. All I had to start out was this cabin and the curse. I didn't even get a letter to explain any of it, just stories of my crazy uncle who lived by himself out in the woods.

What I found was a niche market that I could use my technical knowledge and craft things to make old objects of immense value work again. Essentially, I fixed old antique clocks. These clocks are each handcrafted so there are no set parts for them, so to fix them, I had to handcraft the replacement part to get them running again. On some clocks I made nearly a hundred grand and, being the poor boy, I was growing up, this blew me away.

The back barn is my tool shop and work area. It's less cluttered and safe as well. The same incantations that are placed around the house are placed around the barn as well. However, the path between the two can be dangerous. It partly has to do with the talisman, which I guess I should explain how that works. Well, I'll get to that in just a minute. I need to tell you one last bit about the clocks.

I have one that is finished for a Mr. Douglas. I had called and told him the work was complete and should be sending an employee to pick it up. It will probably be Mr. Ketchum. Ketchum is an older man, and he's grown surly in his old age. You won't like him. No one does. He's rude and pushy and will criticize everything. Just make sure you get the fifty grand they still owe for the work.

Oh, money. Yes, you got a lot in the inheritance, but there's more throughout the house. I didn't do much banking, so who knows how much is hidden away in this house? It's not like I got much of a chance to spend any of it. People came from all over the world for me to work on their clocks and I loved to work on them.

There's another clock that is partially done. That is Mr. Barlow's. His information will be in the barn. You'll have to look for it and let him know it won't be done. Be careful. He's a dangerous man. Very dark. I was always afraid of him. Something about him always felt, I don't know, they just felt wrong. I don't know how to say it. It's like, he could feel her

308

presence and that he enjoyed coming here. Maybe it's why I never dealt with any middlemen, and he came himself. He seemed to relish it and he always had more clocks for me to fix. It was like he was seeking them out. Be careful with him.

So, what else to pass on? I'm not really sure. When I started writing this, I wanted to pass on what I could. Now that I have started it, I don't want to quit. I don't have much interaction with people. Writing this letter, telling you what I have truly passed down to you and get it off my chest is refreshing, though I am so sorry what it means for you and the rest of my life.

When it was passed down to me, I wasn't given anything. Our uncle passed away, and I was told that I had inherited his estate, which was essentially this cabin. There was no money to live off of, no note, and I had no clue he had even existed. Our parents had died young, and Dan and I had grown up not even knowing about him.

Cynthia and I came to the cabin. It wasn't in any better condition then. It had no interior plumbing, and the kitchen was in what is the dining room now with an old wood stove. It was very different from, but in some ways, very much the same. I mean, the layout has changed, and I've done a lot of work to it. I'm not an architect so much of it I was teaching myself as I went, but I worked my way through it. It gets lonely and boring out here all alone. The only people you can talk to are ghosts from your past.

Cynthia died in the middle of the night. We had gone back to our apartment and were unsure what we were going to do with the cabin. I woke up in the morning with her cold body lying there; her face turned to me and those scared haunted eyes looking at me sleeping as the last thing she saw.

I can't tell you about that morning, of finding her, who I called, or really anything that happened for the next day, as it was all a blur. I had turned over to give her a kiss and had done so without even really looking at her, my eyes still only slits.

Then, it was the next day and I'm being woken up mid-way through the night by the sounds of screaming that quickly fell away to crying. I got out of bed, and saw her there sitting in the corner, her arms wrapped around her legs that she had pulled in. She had her head down and she was crying. It was obviously her; I knew it the moment I had heard the scream. She used to scream at mice many times over the years, and I knew the scream's owner.

I had called out her name before I approached. She had started when she had heard it. Then she looked up.

I'm not going to go into any details. It's hard to remember and so much of that time is confused, but she hadn't known she was dead. Something had happened, she was sure of that, but where I thought she had died of natural causes, she shook her head vehemently, 'no.'

That was when she told me about the shadow thing. At the time, I thought it was death and that all people who died had some grim reaper that came for them. I can not say how happy I was that your dad was out of town on business at the time and was only working as hard as he could to get home to us, that instead it was my best friend who came to me that day to try to console me through the grief and help me plan the funeral. Otherwise, it may have been your dad hit by the bus as he left my apartment instead of Eric.

The next morning, Eric's dead presence was in my apartment to join Cynthia. The day after that, my sister Sarah joined my dead friends. The city bus had crashed, and it hadn't been just her that was there. My apartment was starting to not feel big enough, as there were just too many of them. Now, not only were there the people who had been on the bus, but I now had the family that was in the car that the bus had hit.

310

All of them were confused. So was I, but I couldn't help but think how odd it was that my uncle had lived so far away from people. I've never been a superstitious person, but I had never heard of anyone having the dead, anyone connected with a person, any of it, coming back like this. It was a fair assessment to say that this was all connected, and I was freaking out. I needed to get away from people, and the cabin seemed like the best place.

Damn, I'm running out of paper. I tore these pages out of my last diary. I knew this day was coming; I hadn't thought of buying more. You might find past notes in the trash. Hell, maybe there's a note or two I've left for others in the past. I've outlived most the people I thought I would pass this curse onto.

For the last five years, I have been keeping diaries. There will be much of the information in there.

I'm sorry that I've left this for you. I wish I could have lived longer. If you're reading this, then something happened. I don't know what, but I've felt like something was coming for me these last few days. If I'm right... If not, there's also them. Maybe the dead finally got strong enough to kill me. There's been an odd thing of late, or maybe I'm just imagining things. I could be wrong, but I think in the last year or so, they've been getting stronger. They started as only mere shadows. I could see through them, there wasn't any substance. Now, I can see them as plain as day, like they were really there.

I wish I had more for you, but this is the best I can do. I want you to know that I have always loved your family and you. Your dad was my best friend, and I hated keeping him at a distance.

Damn. Okay, then. I'm sorry.

CHAPTER 26

Lizzie looked at the piece of paper in her hand. It had multiple spots across it from dried tears and she realized there were a few spots that were fresh. Her own tears that she hadn't realized had fallen as she had read the note. She wished there was more written, but as it was, the page was filled front and back with the words spread to the edges. Some were even hard to read as they came so close to where it had been ripped from a spiral notebook and still held the remnants of the binding.

She folded it back the way it had been, tri-folded as though it was a letter getting ready to be sent and put the paper back in the envelope addressed to her. Her uncle had never been around, but she scrambled for memories and barely caught them, thinking of times when he had been there. There was something she barely remembered, but as she struggled, she thought it was there. A few memories. She thought she had one of him and his wife as they had come to dinner and Lizzie had run between his legs, laughing, only to have him chase her through their house.

There was another memory, one of her as a baby. She often had this one, but so many times thought it was more of a dream than a memory. Maybe it was, but it was still a fun dream. She was crawling, still a baby. She was in her grandmother's house and crawling as though newly discovering some mythical ancient land. There was this large object. At the time, she barely knew what it was, but in hindsight recognized it as a flowery fabric covered couch that her grandmother used to have. The couch that had become her parents' couch for a while.

She had made it to the edge and was about to go into a forbidden zone, not that she cared, as she was an explorer off on adventure. Though when she had reached it, she had sat up for a moment to look back at her mom and dad sitting at the kitchen table, talking to her grandmother. None of them were paying attention to her as her mother held her grandmother's hand and were looking at each other. This was her chance, and she wasn't sure if she really realized it or not, but in this dream memory, she knew she had to take it. She turned back around and got in the crawl position to make her escape around the corner.

That was when a pair of large hands grabbed her from under her arms and pulled her up. She saw his smiling face, his happy eyes, and heard that deep laugh as he exclaimed, "Caught ya."

Was the memory real? Were any of them? Memories of her uncle always felt so surreal that she was never sure. So much time had passed since she had seen him.

She put the envelope on the table and stood there, looking at the rest of the garbage on it. This was her house now; it was her refuge. She was going to have to clean it, and she didn't have much else to do. There were also things she might find when she did. It didn't sound like her uncle had many of the answers she was hoping for, but maybe there had been things he had overlooked. He had all those years to research it, and he had found the talisman, so he had learned some things.

That table, that damned dining room table, so full of junk. It was as good as a place to start as any, but did she have any garbage bags? When was garbage pickup, she should call the county and find out? He had said all the utilities were paid, which surprised her. She was surprised he was even on county utility lines. With how remote the house was, she would have expected to have a generator or something, though she supposed there had to be one for the winter. She would have to check the barn for that as well.

She looked over at the kitchen; the door was closed as it always was. That swing door haunted her, and a chill filled her every time she looked at it. Just anyone could sneak into the kitchen, hide there in waiting, and she wouldn't know it until she went in. It was how Sarah had died; next it would be her turn, as she was now all alone.

She had to go in there to find garbage bags, mad at herself for not bringing any with her. That seemed like something she should have thought of at the convenience store. With how much garbage was scattered throughout the house, her uncle may not have any.

"Hey bitch!" Sarah screamed from outside. Lizzie closed her eyes, took a deep breath, and counted backwards from ten. Sarah had been quiet for the last hour or so. They all had been, but now, as Lizzie looked at the kitchen door, it was like she had been able to read her mind to know Lizzie was thinking about her.

Lizzie walked away from the yelling dead and stepped into the kitchen, taking deep breaths as she did. No one was in there. The house was still that disturbing quiet that she didn't think she would ever be able to get used to. She would have to do something about that, maybe find her uncle's laptop and stream music or something. *Wait, didn't he say he had destroyed his...she would have to order a new one?*

The kitchen was easily the cleanest room in the house. Part of that was probably from the cleaners, but the little she could remember from the last time she was there; it had been clean then, too. He had taken care of this room, no papers scattered about, but just a place that was well maintained so the food cooked there would be edible and not send anyone to the hospital for food poisoning. Though, thinking of what her uncle was going through, that may have had more to do with it than caring for the room itself. A trip to the hospital could spawn countless new dead surrounding the house.

You had gone to the hospital, and no one had died...

But there *had* been people who had died. They just hadn't died while they were there. The shadow man had waited. Had waited and, like her uncle had said in his note, had toyed with her until the right time to take their lives. How had the shadow man known when that would be? He couldn't have. He just had to be very patient.

She should lock that thought away, as she felt knowing he was extremely patient was good to remember. Though she wasn't sure she wanted to know what he was patiently waiting for. It involved her, or her bloodline. That was obvious.

She stepped all the way into the little room and noticed for the first time the little slant to the room and how much of it looked newer than the rest of the house. *This was an addition. Her uncle had mentioned something about the changes he had made to the house in his note. This room must be added on.* She thought about that as she continued to look around, letting the door go and whoosh shut behind her.

The house felt disturbing and alone again, that feeling of dread she had felt outside returning. It was deep in the pit of her stomach, and she looked back at the door to the rest of the house, wanting deeply to rush back to the other side.

This was an addition, so maybe what made her feel calm and safe there didn't apply to the kitchen. The dead man had been in the kitchen, not the rest of the house. He hadn't been able to..., but yet the dead outside couldn't get in there.

"So, whatever protected the house didn't protect the kitchen, but something else did." She said it out loud, letting her thoughts out in the quiet place. They seemed louder than they should have. She needed to start listening to music or something or else she was going to do a lot of talking to herself.

"What was it they said? It was okay to talk to yourself as long as you don't talk back?" she said as she walked to the other side of the little island counter in the center of the room. "Sure, that was it," she said in response to herself, letting out a little cackle at her own inner joke.

She looked back at the door to the house again. Her eyes kept coming back to it. With it closed, she would never know if another surprise waited for her out here. She doubted she would ever have issues in the house. The note made it sound very safe, and she believed it. The kitchen didn't feel like the rest of the house. She couldn't rely on the same protection.

What was she going to do about the door?

She walked over to it and studied its hinges. The door swung both ways, but as she studied the hinges, she wasn't sure how things worked. She understood how regular hinges did, but these were different and were alien to her. Regular hinges, she could take a butter knife to and work the pin free to remove the door. The double hinges weren't like that, and she couldn't see any access to the pin.

How could she get the door off? She would probably have to take off the whole hinge, using a screwdriver to remove the hinges from the wall. Though that seemed like it would be a project, and she wasn't ready to start modifying the house just yet. Instead, she looked around for something heavy and found a block of kitchen knives; the base being made out of wood. She grabbed it and used it to prop open the door.

"Wa-la!" she said as she stepped back to admire her handy work.

"Proud of yourself in there?" She heard the voice and turned to see who said it. She recognized it but hadn't heard it in a while. He had never been one to say much to her. She didn't see anyone standing behind her. She was still alone in the room.

Chuck had to be outside, which made sense since he couldn't come into the warded house, but still felt disconcerted that he would know she was in there. Could he somehow see inside? She was never sure what their deathly abilities were, as they always seemed to be able to do more than what they let on.

"I am, a little." She walked over to the back door and opened the interior wooden one. She forgot that the screen door was still broken from its frame. It would probably always be broken as she was afraid to go out there to fix it, and afraid to call a handyman to the house. What if the man came to the house and was killed? She couldn't call anyone to the house. Any time she did, she would be putting their lives in danger.

Chuck was standing at the door, and she looked down at him, nervous as there was no visible barrier between them. She thought he couldn't get in to attack her, but it was hard to imagine something unseen keeping him away.

"You okay?" She said to him. They hadn't really talked much since his death. He had always blamed her for it, and his anger had been obvious. Then, when Josh had come along, Chuck's role seemed to have become the protector of the other dead, as Josh had been angry with all of them. What was his role now? As he was the first to talk to her since the talisman, had he become the peacemaker?

The anger she saw that darkened all of them since their time in the other realm was present on him, too. No, he would attack her if he could, just like the rest of them. They all blamed her, as they should, but she hadn't known what the talisman would do. She was sorry, but how do you apologize for sending someone to hell for nothing they had done?

"You shouldn't have done that."

She looked back at the door she had just propped open and back to Chuck.

"Why not?"

"Not the door. You shouldn't have done that us."

"I didn't know."

"You shouldn't have done that to us," he repeated, his eyes digging into her own.

"I know. I didn't know what it would do. I just wanted peace."

"Peace! Peace! How do you get to want peace?" He screamed at her, his anger blazing as he rushed at her. She jumped, slamming her back into the refrigerator and feeling it rock.

It took a moment to calm her breathing. Any second, she expected to feel his hands on her throat, his teeth tearing into her flesh, and his...

She pushed the thoughts out of her mind as she looked back to where Chuck had been. He wasn't there, but was on the ground a few yards back. His eyes were wide as he looked around in shock.

Slowly he stood, looked back to the door, and then ran towards it, again lunging after her. This time she watched, not worried about him getting to her, and she saw him hit the threshold. With a white flash of light, he was thrown back across the yard.

This time when he got up, he kept his eyes locked on her, and she saw that fire burning hotter. He was slower to make his way to the back door, not lunging for it. He walked casually, his hands opening and closing into fists.

He reached the threshold and stopped there, studying the frame before looking back at her. Then he nodded and stepped away from where she could see him. He didn't say a word, didn't make any threats, just studied the house and the frame until he was gone.

She didn't know why, but that scared her more than if he had made the threats.

She looked at the path leading back to the barn. The letter had said she'd need to go there. She didn't feel safe doing it, not yet. Instead, she studied it from a distance. It wasn't anything special. It just looked like a barn, maybe a little smaller than some she'd seen used for farm equipment, and it needed some paint. Still, from a distance, it looked sturdy enough.

She turned away as she closed the back door and left the kitchen.

CHAPTER 27

She had made it about five steps out of the kitchen and into the mess that was the dining room before realizing she would have to go back. If she was going to have any chance at finding garbage bags, the kitchen was her best hope. With it being the cleanest room in the house, it was her best hope of finding anything.

It hadn't taken her long, and she had been quick in the room and back out. It had been a stroke of luck to find a couple boxes of garbage bags under the sink. Her uncle had plenty of them. She couldn't understand why he hadn't been using them.

He had given up. How many years had he been stuck in this cabin all alone, unable to talk to anyone but the dead? How long do you think you'll really last? He made it nearly fifteen years; you were just a little girl when he had been struck with the curse. Do you really think you'll last that long?

She had to push the thoughts from her head, as she knew the answer and already feared it. She had been in the cabin less than half a day and already it was starting to wear on her. The constant bombardment of insults coming from outside, the silence inside, and there was no one she could talk to. If only she had someone she could open up to, but the moment she did that, the moment she gave that creature another target.

Stay focused. The dining room had plenty to occupy her mind. Looking around, she could see the piles of papers and books. There were a lot of them, but there was also just a lot of garbage thrown about. She figured her best bet would be to start from the farthest corner and work her way out from there. That plan was a failure when she realized she couldn't reach the farthest corner, as there was just too much junk in the way.

"Well, crap. Fine then," she said to the empty house. She wished she had her phone. At least then she had some music she could play, and the house wouldn't feel so empty.

She went to the farthest she could go, which was near one of the chairs. The chair had scrapbooks piled on it, and well, it was as good of a place as any to start. Clear off the chair. Then she would have a place to sit and work out from there. She could work her way to the corner and then work out in all directions from there.

"So, what do we have here?" Lizzie picked up the binder and opened it. The cover was covered in dust but opened to reveal photos. It was an old photo album. The pages were yellow with age, and all the pictures were vintage. They had that look to them like old photos. It reminded her of that filter she used on Instagram a lot, though she couldn't remember what it was called. Many of the pictures were washed out, but all of them had smiling faces. Some of the photos contained people she remembered, while most were alien to her.

She came across a picture of her parents with her uncle and his wife. They were all standing there on a cliff, the beautiful skyline behind them and a lake that could be seen far below them. Underneath the photo was written on a little label, "Starved Rock Vacation, 2002."

2002. That would have been shortly before the curse passed down to him. They all looked so happy; young, and oblivious to the hell that was about to crush them and tear them apart. Lizzie ran her finger along the photo. A tear slipped from her and landed on the clear film that protected the page and soon there were more. Her parents were so happy, her uncle smiling his big tooth filled grin. Lizzie wasn't sure where she was or why she wasn't in the picture. Her mother had just begun to lose her pregnancy weight, but there were still signs of the bump that had been her.

And there was Cynthia. Lizzie had forgotten how beautiful she was and how happy they were together. They were an amazing couple that should never have been torn apart so viciously.

Lizzie turned the page to find more photos. Many of the pages were filled with ones similar to the one previous, all taken while at some national park and so long ago that she wasn't even able to walk yet. Her parents must have had her grandparents watching her, but couldn't imagine why they would have left a near newborn alone with them for what looked like a vacation.

As she progressed through the book, it showed other memories. Some of them were with her parents and some were with friends. It seemed like her uncle was so well liked as he always seemed to have large groups around him, and at the center, he was always with Cynthia, both with wide genuine smiles. Had they ever truly been as happy as their pictures made them look? She remembered him, barely, but when she did, she thought mainly of the big fight her dad had had with him.

She turned a page and saw the four of them. Her dad, mom, Cynthia, and him as they all stood. Then she saw the little girl in the background running toward them. Behind the girl was an agitated woman, and Lizzie immediately remembered Cynthia's sister, who would watch Lizzie as her parents and the two of them would go out to parties. In the background, Theresa was the sister's name, was chasing after Lizzie as she was supposed to be watching her for the day.

* * * *

"Daddy! Daddy! Save me before the monster gets me," Elizabeth yelled, though it was a struggle as she was also giggling as she ran.

"Elizabeth!" the monster, who was a young woman wearing a black formal dress, called out as she tried to chase the little girl through the crowd of people. It was hard, as she was wearing high-heeled shoes instead of her flats and trying not to bunch up her dress by running too fast. This left her moving slowly, as she was more mindful of how she would look later in the day rather than the girl she was trying to capture. "Elizabeth, get back here!"

The girl darted through the crowd of well-dressed people, while the woman chasing her had difficulty getting the other adults to move out of the way.

Because of this, the girl was able to seek out her target and rush him long before the monster had any hope of catching her.

"Woah there." The man groaned and looked down at the girl, whose age was around four years old, wrapped around his leg. The man smiled at her, bemused, and then looked over at the other man next to him. "I think I have something that belongs to you."

"Oh?" the other man said, looking down at the girl. He made a funny face at her, and she giggled as he looked back at the man. "Nah, I don't think so. I don't recognize her. She looks like a wild beast. Why don't you keep her?"

"Daddy!?" the little girl said, releasing the man she had clung to so that she could wrap herself around her dad.

"Nope. Don't know her. My daughter is a nice, good little girl who is being good for her aunt. I mean, you kinda look like her, but she would never be running through a church."

"I'm sorry Dan. She just took off."

"It's okay." Dan said as he looked down at his little girl. She could see that he was trying to give her the 'hard' look, but she also saw his hints of a smile. She didn't know it then, but later would discover that he was working hard to bite back the laugh and joy of being around his little girl, his 'Lizzie.'

"Well, we should probably make our way in to pay our respect." Tom, her uncle, said as he looked over at her dad and patted his back.

"I'll take her over to the other kids so they could play. The church opened up the youth center since there's so many here."

"Really? I mean, I don't even know half these people. I mean, who are these people? Our uncle hadn't been seen by anyone in our family for what, twenty years?" Her dad said as he lifted Lizzie into his arms.

"As far as I knew, yeah. He's been a compete recluse, hiding away in that cabin of his."

"I heard someone say that's it's all family of his wife." Theresa, otherwise known as the monster aunt, said as she reached out to take Lizzie from her father.

"I got her. I'll walk her in."

"He has a wife? Someone was actually living with him in that run-down shack?" Tom said as they walked towards the church entrance.

"I knew he had one, but she had passed away a while back. Dad never said much about it. He didn't talk about his brother much. It sounded like every time they had talked it had been a big fight."

"Da- Dang, man." Tom said, obviously catching himself from cursing in front of Lizzie. She, of course, stuck her tongue out at him and he, in return, stuck his out at her. They both giggled.

"Mr. Rogers?"

Both Tom and Dan turned around to see a short man bulging out of his suit, as it seemed like someone had forced the man to be shorter and now the fat was being forced out. Lizzie had to struggle not to giggle as the man fought to pull his pants back up and keep it from again falling too low.

"Yes?" Dan asked.

"Mr. Tom Rogers?" The man was questioning, obviously not sure which man was his intended person of interest. The brothers looked at one another and then Tom turned back, a raised eyebrow in question.

"That'd be me."

"Okay. I used to be your uncle's best friend. He asked me to draft a will and have you as beneficiary. I'll need you to swing by sometime later today to go over everything."

"Today? What kind of lawyer works on a Saturday?"

"He was a friend. He asked me to do this and said it was very important to go over what you inherited right away."

"Okay. I don't see what's so important and I'm busy today and tomorrow. Cynthia and I have plans and I'm not going to break them because I inherited some old shack in the woods. I can meet you at the office on Monday."

"Your uncle said it was important we did this right away."

"I'm sure he did. He was nuts."

"Look, I'm sure our uncle had some crazy idea that his cabin out there in la-la land was some big deal," Lizzie's father said, stepping up to the shorter man, his agitation clearly getting the better of him. "But this is his funeral. Why are you doing this now?"

Her dad looked from the lawyer to a couple that was entering the funeral home. Lizzie recognized them vaguely, but wasn't sure until they stopped to say something.

"Dan, why didn't you get a sitter? A funeral is no place for children."

"Tammy's sister is going to watch the children during the service."

"That doesn't mean they should be here."

329

"Yes, Ms. Tamarack." Her father exclaimed with a frustrated sigh that he tried to hide from the older woman. She responded by shaking her head and entering the building.

"Ms. Tamarack? What is she doing here?" Tom said, his mouth slightly agape at the shock.

"I asked her to come." The lawyer said. The brothers turned to face him again, Dan having to shift Lizzie as the four-year-old was getting heavy. "Your uncle has been away for many years, but came to me last week. He had me do his will and then asked if I'd get ahold some of his old friends. It wasn't easy, but I think most of them are here. Of course, a number of them had died over the years, but the ones I knew to still be around are here."

"Why?" Tom said, beating Dan to the question.

"He didn't want his funeral to not have anyone. He said he spent the last twenty years in isolation. He didn't want his funeral to be...empty."

"There you two are," said a very pregnant Tammy as she approached. She had a plastered-on smile that anyone close to her knew was for show. She'd been in a lot of pain with this pregnancy and was supposed to be in bed. She had ignored it, saying that if Dan was going to be there to show his respect, he was not allowed to do it without his wife.

He returned her smile as she approached. It was just as forced, neither of them wanting to be there. Lizzie hadn't realized at the time just how little anyone had wanted to be there. She clung to her father and gave that annoyed look to them all, quickly bored as there was little to do in the 'stuffy' place that was filling with people. Some weren't even dressed up but had just come in their regular casual wear. Dan noticed it now that the lawyer had said he had to talk many of the attendees into coming.

"Hey hun," he replied as he lowered just enough so she could give him a peck on the cheek.

"Want me to take a monster?" Tammy said, and she didn't wait for a reply, as Lizzie was already holding out her arms to her mom.

"You sure?" Dan looked at the protruding stomach and saw the frustrated grimace that flashed.

"Dang it," and then she looked to her belly and added, "You better be good looking like your father because your kinda a pain in the butt like him."

"Oh, really?" Dan said.

"You're lucky you're cute," she said, flashing her first genuine smile of the day.

"So, I'll see you after the ceremony?" The lawyer asked, bringing everyone's attention back to him.

"What's this?" Tammy asked.

"He needs Tom to stop by his office after the funeral."

"Fine." Tom said in resignation.

"On a Saturday?" Tammy said.

"Say's it's important." He said to her, then turned to Tom, "see you inside."

Tom nodded. "Yeah, I'll be in as soon as Cynthia's back. She had to run for smokes."

Lizzie's father nodded and headed into the funeral home, his daughter in one arm and the other one wrapped around his pregnant wife. He was going into a house of death, but right then, he felt like he had everything he could have that would make him happy in life.

* * * *

Lizzie turned the page in the scrapbook, realizing that the picture hadn't been from the funeral. She didn't know what it was about the picture that had brought back such an odd memory. Maybe it was being in the cabin and remembering her dad and uncle talking about it.

It was just another picture, one of many, just like the memories that were pulling at her. There were so many things to remember, so many things to think about. That's all she could really do now, was to remember and think. That's all that was left, being out there in the cabin, alone in the woods.

She turned the page, and then another, studying all the smiling faces looking up at her. Everyone was smiling and happy. She wondered if she would ever be able to see smiles like that again in anything other than a picture.

She already knew the answer as she closed the cover of the book and set it next to her chair. She'd keep the book, so it would be the first object to go into her 'keep' pile. As long as she didn't confuse the piles like she would sometimes do when she was organizing her apartment bedroom, she should be fine and able to look through the pictures again someday.

She reached forward and pulled the next bundle from the pile. This one was a bunch of envelopes with what looked to be unopened spam mail. She wanted to just chuck it and throw it all away, but couldn't. All it would take would be to do that once, and she might just miss that one scrap of information she would need.

With a groan, she opened the first envelope. Yep, there it was, the solution to all her problems. She had just won Publishers Clearing House. She was rich and now she could live that life of luxury.

With a chuckle, she tossed the envelope into the garbage bag and started on the next one.

CHAPTER 28

Lizzie did little jumps for joy, followed by a little happy dance when she found her uncle's laptop. It wasn't even that hard to find as it had been on the dining room table, buried under what looked like a recent stack of bills and paperwork. It wasn't intentionally hidden, just probably lost in the confusion of financial responsibility.

She was surprised too; the laptop wasn't that old. She was really going to work on her misconceptions about her uncle because when she had read in the letter that he had one; she had imagined it would be some relic that was nearly as old as Windows itself. The laptop she found wasn't even a Windows PC.

It was a Mac, something she was not familiar with, but new enough that it was so small it could easily be unnoticed under a piece of paper. She still hadn't found the charger yet, and hadn't expected to see it light up, but the moment she opened it, the screen came on. Which was a surprise, considering her uncle had said he had smashed it in the note he had left.

...And of course, it was password protected. Come on Unc, why the hell do you need to keep your

laptop password protected when you lived out in the middle of nowhere?

She looked at the screen in disbelief and wanted to hurl the slim object outside into the woods beyond. This couldn't be happening. She hadn't realized just how much she had hoped to find the little piece of technology since her uncle had informed her about it. Then finding it, all she wanted was for it to work.

Come on! I need music! It was too damn quiet out there. She wasn't creeped out anymore and being out there alone strangely didn't upset her as much as she thought it would, but it was so damn quiet. All she wanted was to open Pandora, put on a station, and have something playing in the background. Sure, she could turn on the television that was so old she wasn't even sure it was in color, but it wouldn't be the same. She had to have music to really break the void.

She needed it because if she didn't break the silence soon, then she would start to worry. She was already starting to worry, because why was there so much of it? Why were the dead out there not screaming at her anymore? What were they up to? In this growing unsettling silence, she heard the buzz of the refrigerator somehow grow louder as it was predominantly the loudest noise in the little cabin, which only added to her discomfort. What were they doing out there?

In a way, she was frustrated that all the windows were blacked out. She understood, now, the reason for it. It would be greatly unsettling if every time she looked up, she would see Sarah or Josh looking in at her, but it also made it hard for her to look out at them. What if she wanted to talk to them?

She looked down at the laptop, and pulling herself out of her funk, lifted it from the table. She wasn't sure what possessed her to do it, but she looked at the bottom. Sure enough, there was a little piece of paper taped there. On one line read a long series of numbers, which she assumed was the Wi-Fi key. Under that really caught her attention. It read Password: Cynthla.

She entered in her aunt's name and within seconds, the computer showed her an empty desktop free of too many icons. It was then that she realized that she really had very little experience with Macs. Her school mostly used Chromebooks. She had always had Windows PCs and so this Mac was completely foreign to her. Where the hell was the internet?

Oh no, if I can't figure it out, who am I going to call for tech support?

Shit.

She looked at the bar at the bottom of the screen and the row of icons there. There weren't too many, but they were kinda weird. There was what looked like a two faced multicolored blue icon, which she had no clue what that did. There was a compass. Why *the hell would I need that on a laptop*, a rocket ship, a gearbox, and what looked like a stamp with an eagle on it? Her uncle must have some weird apps on this thing, as none of those really made any sense to her.

She clicked on the icons one by one and gave out a gleeful shout of excitement when she saw the familiar plain white Google homepage.

"Yes! Jackpot!"

She quickly found her way, and within minutes, music streamed from the little speakers. It wasn't much, and she wasn't sure how to turn up the volume, but for now, it was enough. She just needed to find the cord before the battery died. She could see that it was 8% and knew that if her laptop said that, it would be dead within a heartbeat.

It will do for now, so start looking for that cord. She worked her way around the table, looking at the walls in the room to see if there was anything plugged in to any of the outlets, but there weren't any outlets. How could a room not have any power outlets? She got down on her hands and knees and looked under the dish cabinet. She wasn't going to pull it out as she was too afraid of breaking any of the dishes, but what she could see showed nothing.

"Huh," she said to herself, standing and brushing off the dust from her hands onto her jeans. "Anything in here?"

She stepped through the archway into the tv room, carefully avoiding the towers of garbage she hadn't gone through.

"So, what are you plugged into?"

The television was another cord, which led to a surge protector on the other side of the room that was plugged into another surge protector hidden under a small pile of papers. This place was a fire hazard, she realized as she followed the cord from the surge protector into her bedroom to another surge protector. This surge protector had the power cord for the laptop plugged into it, and its cord ran back from her bedroom, along the wall and through the dining room into the kitchen, where she found one of two outlets in the entire house.

She looked at all of it, the cords, and the lack of wiring in the inner rooms and just kept running the course of the cord back through her head. No outlets in the inner house. Didn't the letter say that the kitchen was an add-on that her uncle added? If he was renovating it out here, then why not add some outlets to the other rooms? They obviously had power running through them, as they had lights, light switches, and such. Yet it was only the kitchen and the bathroom that had outlets and running water.

She filed the information away, hoping that maybe she would get answers later, but answers from who? There wasn't anyone she could ask about it.

She had a nagging sense to call her brother. It was a desire to speak to him, hear that computer generated voice and just listen as he comforted her that it was all going to be okay. Of course, if she did call him, not only would she be putting his life in danger, but he would not tell her it was all okay. He would first think she was overreacting, and that it was all just coincidence that her friends were dying. He would also never believe that they were coming back, haunting and hurting her, and would be concerned that she was losing her mind. Thanks to their uncle, schizophrenia was perceived as running in their family, as everyone thought he had gone insane. What else would you think if your uncle ran around saying that his dead wife was talking to him?

She had forgotten that he had said that before he had gone off into the cabin in the woods. It had been so long ago, and her dad never talked about it.

Well, it wasn't time to think about that. She took the laptop into the bedroom and plugged it in. It was still at 8% and she had to wonder if the battery gauge even worked on the thing as no laptop had that good of battery management.

So now what should I do? She looked around the living room and the dining room. She'd barely made a dent in the mess and knew if she continued at it the way she had been going, she would get frustrated and start throwing things away en masse. She couldn't allow herself to start doing that. There might be information she would need somewhere in the thick of it, but there was just so much of it to go through.

"What are you in a hurry for, some hot date?" She said to the empty room.

"Your date is dead," yelled Sarah from outside. Lizzie hadn't realized that she had even spoken out loud, yet she must have, and loud enough that they could hear her. She bit her lip as she moved closer to the blacked-out window, the one closest to where she had heard her friend. "He's dead, and you killed him."

"I thought you didn't like him."

"You killed him, and you killed all of us. You don't even care. You killed all of us, tortured us, and now you won't even take your own life and release us. You did this to us."

Lizzie heard the tears in Sarah's voice and felt her chest clench. Even when Sarah had been attacking her the previous night, Lizzie had still seen the pain on her face, the ash on their skin, and the fresh cuts along her dead arms. Lizzie didn't know where the talisman sent her dead friends, but it had not been a vacation cruise. Not unless the cruise was through hell, and the attendants were the devil's minions.

Was Lizzie just going to ignore her now until one of them was gone? From everything they knew so far, Sarah would never fade away. She would always be there, and as it stood; she would always hate her for what Lizzie had done. Lizzie didn't think she could survive that. They had been like sisters, together forever until the end. Now Sarah was dead, but it was not the end.

"Sarah?" Lizzie's voice was soft, but she knew Sarah had heard her because the sniffling stopped.

"Fuck you, you can just go die, you fucking whore! Fucking every man around, no matter how much someone else had a crush on them."

Lizzie recoiled from the window as though she had been slapped, her hand to her mouth to cover the gasp that escaped her.

"I... no, I didn't. You know I didn't."

"I know. What the hell do I know?" The vitriol dripped from Sarah's voice as she spat out the words, yelling at Lizzie through the painted glass. "I know you don't care how long you left us there. You banished us and let us get tortured. We were in hell. I was raped regularly and when I wasn't being raped..." Sarah's voice drifted off and Lizzie could hear the fresh sobbing coming from her friend.

Lizzie wanted to go out there, reach out to her and pull her into a hug, but she knew that even if she dared to go out there, there was no way she could physically touch her. They had tried at the hospital, and it only led to both of them feeling ill. Though Sarah had been able to attack her last night, Lizzie wasn't convinced she could return the contact. She seemed to be at the disadvantage of the dead, something that didn't make her too comfortable when interacting with any of them.

"Sarah," Lizzie said when her friend had let the silence linger. "Sis, you know I would never-"

"They tore me apart. And no, I don't just mean emotionally. They would pull off a fingernail, slowly, not to hurry themselves as they had all day in whatever a day was in their existence. They would remove a fingernail, and then another. Then they would, painstakingly, with no rush and with the dullest blade, slice off my tit. Then they would do it to the other. They would chop off my toes and fingers, but not quickly. They would put the blade to the nub, and ease down on it, so it sliced through the skin and bone, not in one quick motion, but with great delight in hearing me scream, as it worked its way through the tissue.

"The only thing they didn't cut away from me was my mouth because they loved to hear me scream, and I screamed. I cursed your name in screams that were meant to awaken the devil. You did that to us. You did that to me, your 'friend', and you didn't do anything about it.

"Then, as my body lied there, they would rape me again and again. Not just in the places they should but in every hole they found and made, and when they were done, and only then, the day would reset and it would all start over again."

Lizzie stood by the window, listening, and not sure what to say or how to react. The tears kept rolling down her cheeks as she tried not to imagine her friend going through that endless torture. She wished she could block out the images, but she saw the horrors in her mind as her friend told her what she had been through. She fought against it, but it was a losing battle. She could see it so clearly and knew it would be another nightmare that would be there to keep her from sleeping at night. There was becoming a steady rotation, and this one would be added to the horrifying playlist.

"I'm sorry. I didn't know. I only wore it for one night."

"Sorry." a male voice spat from the other side. It sounded like Chuck.

"One night!" Josh yelled. All of them must have gathered by the window now. It was not just Sarah, she was talking too, and she could hear how upset they were. She had no idea what they had been through.

"One night! I was there for ten years. I know as I counted the days. Do you know how many days I watched as my son was ripped out of his mother and fed upon by demons? They forced me to watch as they ate his flesh. Each day, the same thing happened over and over. I have watched it over four thousand times. Yeah, you sent us to that hell for over ten years." His voice was gravelly, and she felt the raw emotion that emanated from him. It was harder to hear once he stopped yelling, and she knew it was because he was breaking down.

"It's okay. Your wife is still alive. None of that was real. It was all mind games." Sarah was telling Josh, working to speak through her own tears.

"I didn't know." Lizzie hadn't realized the words escaped her. "I just put on the talisman for one night. I didn't know."

343

"My wife was pregnant. My wife was pregnant, and I didn't know. How could I have known? She hadn't told me. She..." Josh had lost much of the previous anger she had heard and seemed distant, like the air had been sucked out of him.

"It was a mind game. It's all going to be okay."

"I left her alone to raise our child. The others, they're nearly grown, but I left her alone to take care of a baby. What kind of father am I?"

"I didn't know." Lizzie tripped over a pile on the floor and fell back into the Lazy Boy. It rocked back, but she never took her eyes off the window. The pain that Josh had to be feeling, going through everything he had. She didn't know how to apologize for that. It was too much. Nothing she would say would ever soothe him. He would always hate her, and all she could say and keep saying to him was that she hadn't known. What kind of answer was that?

It wasn't one...

"You didn't know." Josh said, breaking out of whatever trance he had been in. "My wife was pregnant. I didn't know, you didn't know, none of us knew," Josh said with a burst of maniacal laughter. "It seems like none of us knows anything except you're a death magnet and that seems like something you sure as hell should have known."

She heard something pound against the window, and then Josh was howling in pain.

"Holy shit," Chuck exclaimed.

"What happened?" Lizzie said, forcing herself to stand again and approach the window. She made sure not to trip over the pile she had before and noticed it was a stack of what looked like leather-

344

bound books. They looked odd, but she moved around them, focusing on the window.

"I'm sure he won't do that again." Elisabeth hadn't talked much since they had returned from wherever the talisman had sent them.

"No, he won't. Well, now we know not to even throw anything at the house." Chuck said.

"How had he even been able to pick up the rock?" Sarah said. She sounded shocked. They all did.

"What happened?" Lizzie asked again, though she was beginning to piece it together, that Josh had thrown a rock at the window. But what happened to him after that?

"Guess this means we can't torch the place," Chuck said.

"Nope." Sarah responded.

Had they been planning on burning the house down? Lizzie wasn't sure, but they sounded serious. She didn't know where they had planned to get the fire, but as the house wasn't burning, they probably hadn't figured that out yet.

"FUCK!" Josh howled. "You fucking whore of a bitch. I will get my hands on you and then I will personally feed you to them. You understand me, you slut? Fuck!"

Lizzie was backing away from the window, back to sit in the chair again. She wrapped her arms around her, shaking her head, refusing to believe the venom that was being hurled her way.

She hadn't known. How could she have known any of this was going to happen? The letter had been vague and there were barely any instructions in the initial reading of the will. She had no way of knowing. And the talisman? She wouldn't have even known about it had Josh not insisted she read the letter. It was partially his fault. He told her to do it. How was she ever supposed to know what it would have done to them?

And if he hadn't been such a jerk, then maybe she wouldn't have been so quick to put it on when she had left with Roland yesterday.

The voices outside were quieting, getting farther away. She could still hear the howls coming from Josh. Whatever happened must have really hurt him, but how do you hurt the dead? What was it about the house that did? Was it something she could use? She still wanted to check out the barn and see what was out there, but was afraid to walk the path to get there. She could wear the talisman, but had sworn to herself she would never wear that again.

She could go now, couldn't she? The voices were moving away in the other direction. She would have a clear shot to run, and the letter said she would be safe once she got in there. Now would be the time to do it.

But she wasn't moving. She wasn't getting up, and when she admitted it to herself, she was not motivated to actually get up and do it. She didn't want to do anything. She wanted to sit there and cry, but she wasn't giving into that. She was just going to sit there and not cry, to have this moment of doing nothing.

Around her there was still plenty of mess, though in the living room there was less of a paper mess and more of a *'this was where he stayed most of the time and had all the food wrapper garbage mess'* combined with the occult circle and candle mess. Strange, but she was no longer freaked out by the

346

pentagram and circle on the floor anymore. She didn't want to go near it, but as far as she knew, that was what kept the dead from getting inside, so it wasn't getting touched.

She did notice the books she had tripped over. She picked one up. It had a leather cover but didn't look like something store bought or printed. The front had a latch on it, though it was old and broken, so the strap didn't close. She opened it and saw her uncle's handwriting filling the pages.

She went back to the first page and looked at it. It was dated just over fifteen years ago and written there in a shakily written sentence was her uncle's first diary entry.

"My wife died a week ago. The night after her death, her spirit came back and has not left me."

CHAPTER 29

Since then, I've seen the shadow woman, and she has come to torment me. Cynthia tries to stop her, but the shadow woman just laughs and chants her little chant at me. She has repeated it over and over, that stupid tic-a-tac, tic-a-tor. Soon there will be many more. Tic-a-toc, tic-a-turs, I will break her from her curse.

I don't know what I'm doing, why I'm even here. I came back to this cabin because ...Cynthia... I love her so much and she has always been the everything in my day. My thoughts have always been how to take care of her and keep her safe. She has meant so much to me, but seeing her walking corpse has sent daggers into my heart and I don't know how to deal with it. Everywhere I went to grieve, she was there and there would be fresh tears as I died a little each time.

How could I return to work? I tried to go back to the foundry and just couldn't do it. Whenever I pulled back from a weld or crafting a special piece, there she would be standing next to me. She would be watching me. Those dead, sad eyes. Her mouth would be working, she would be trying to say something to me, but I could never hear her.

After a day of it, I collapsed. That second day, I looked over and saw her reaching out to me and I swore I could see a tear in her eye as her hands went right through me. I felt her touch, and it made me sick in a way I cannot describe. When she saw me gasping, she pulled back, recoiling from me, and I felt like a cold hand had just reached into my chest and ripped out my heart and soul.

I fell to the cement floor and that cold stone felt hot to my skin. I hadn't thought that stone could burn. The coworkers who gathered around me later said that I was convulsing, having some kind of attack. All I knew was that I had seen my beloved reaching out and I couldn't do anything.

It had been a strange attack, and Cynthia never tried to touch me again after it. Later that day, my boss had called me into his office and told me he was putting me on leave. He knew I was upset and that I needed time to grieve. Jim and I had gone to high school together. We had never been close but knew one another enough that he had been at my wedding. He knew I was having a hard time, he just didn't know all of it. I didn't know all of it.

But then I had gotten up to leave his office. I thought I was done. I was going to go home and that would be it. It was really, but as he came around the desk to usher me out the door, I saw his eyes. There was a red ring, not the kind of long night's drink. No, this was about his pupil.

I didn't know what to say, and I didn't have time. He walked me to his office door, and then out into the shop. Then there was a loud crash. Metal broke, and I could feel something shifting around me. The air had changed, I can't explain it, but there was some kind of electricity gathering. Then I saw one of the machines, the large ones that the finished metal went in to cool. It exploded, and I watched as a metal shard slammed into Jim's head. Other men around us were screaming as I watched death again take someone I knew.

I can't remember much else from that day. I don't know how I got home, who helped me, or if I somehow drove myself. It is all a blur and when I do try to remember; I don't trust if the memories I see are real or just things I want to imagine. As for what has happened since then, I want to say that it did happen, as it was when I lay there on the ground, alive but looking into the dead eyes of my former boss, I heard Cynthia, and heard her tell me it would be okay.

God help me, but I must be losing my mind.

They're all here. They were all with me now, outside the cabin, unable to come in. Thirteen people died that day, and I had grown up with many of them. Now they are dead, but not dead, outside this very cabin.

Oh God, I don't know what to do.

* * * *

The leather-bound book crashed to the floor and Lizzie, who had drifted off, jumped awake. She hadn't realized she had been that tired, but only a few pages into the diary, or maybe it had been just sitting down to read it that had brought the exhaustion washing over her.

She hadn't thought she could ever feel so tired. Even after studying for finals and being up for a twenty-four-hour study binge, there had been some kind of a second wind that had allowed her to go take the test. This wasn't like that, or maybe it was. Maybe she had already had the second and even third or fourth winds and it was all catching up to her.

When was the last time she ate? Any time after the diner? She remembered stopping for gas and caffeine drinks, but anything after that was a blur. Hell, she hadn't had any time to sleep. When would she have had time to eat? Scratch that and reverse it. She hadn't had any time to eat. How would she have ever had any time to sleep?

It hurt to think or even to attempt it. Lifting her head and then herself was a challenge she didn't think she could handle.

Well then, what do you think you're going to do? It's not like they have delivery out here. But didn't they? She thought her uncle's note had said something about grocery delivery. In fact, she was sure of it. Would they deliver this late, though? It was mid-afternoon already; she would probably have to call in the delivery for tomorrow and how would she pay for it? She didn't have cash with her, at least she didn't think she did. Maybe she'd gone to an ATM that morning.

She stood and felt her legs become rubber under her. She had to reach out and steady herself with the arm of the chair, and even then, swayed as she tried to think of what her food options could be. Maybe there would be something in the kitchen? Her uncle had been living out there getting deliveries. Maybe when he died, there had been a full stock. Though if he killed himself, he might have been letting it all dwindle when he went.

What was that final straw that had pushed him to do it? He had lived out there for so long, losing his wife, his brother and all those closest to him that he had to have been through it all long ago. Why now?

She couldn't imagine what it could have been and wasn't sure she wanted too. It was her fate now...

As she took each step, she kept her hands on or near something, whether it be a stack of books or the wall. Her head wasn't letting up and with each movement, a growing pounding echoed through her head like a drummer warming up for a concert. The closer she got to the kitchen, the more she was sure the drummer was preparing for a long solo as the beating grew stronger. A song, the name escaped her, but she remembered that it was Led Zeppelin, seemed to form the rhythm to the pain that danced through her head.

Damn you dad for making me 'get the lead out every damned car ride, she thought as she entered into the kitchen. In sight and sending a wave of relief through her that was short-lived, she saw the two bags she had brought from the store.

"Oh God, yes," she cried out and grabbed for the bags. The cell phone was useless for now, and she set it aside as she scoured through the rest of it. Of course, it was mainly chips, Mountain Dew, and some cans of soup that did not look all that appealing, but at the bottom of the second bag, she found what she was looking for. It wasn't a big container, just a small pouch of generic aspirin, which had cost her more at the gas station convenience store than a large bottle at any chain grocery.

She was hungry, thirsty, and needed caffeine, but right then, the headache that was screaming its presence through all her synapses took priority. She opened the pouch, grabbed the couple of pills and then hurriedly opened the Mountain Dew to wash it down. There was an instant release, and she had no way of knowing if it was any of the three or all three, but she was already feeling better.

She stood there holding the counter, occasionally taking drinks from the soda. If she moved, she was sure she would fall. Though eventually she did look at the cans of soup. They were pop tops, which was good. She wasn't sure if she had a can opener or not.

I guess now is as good as a time as any; she thought as she looked at the cabinets and the rest of the kitchen.

The Dew helped a lot. Her head cleared, though not as much as she wanted it to. She remembered that she had gotten some money out of the ATM that morning and that she would be fine in that regard. She wasn't sure if her uncle's phone worked, though she saw the old landline phone hanging on the wall like some relic from the 1980s. She worried she would actually have to look up the number for the grocery store, but now noticed the sticky note on the wall with various numbers. She was sure one of them would be the one she needed.

You can do this. You really can, she thought as she went around the counter and opened the drawer to the right of the sink. Sure enough, there was silverware, clean and ready to use. There wasn't much, a couple of spoons, a fork, and two knives, one a butter knife and the other a serrated steak knife, but it would do. She was one person, after all; it wasn't like she would need to feed an army, or the dead that clung outside her door.

Could she do it? Was she really going to live out the rest of her life in the cabin, hiding, keeping away from the world? What other choice did she have? As she looked around the tight confines of the cabin, she didn't see anything that inspired some great idea. If she went out and interacted with her friends, they would die. This was all such a nightmare.

She opened one of the cans labeled Chicken and Rice. She ate it as she opened cabinets around the room, and realized she was stocked better than she would have thought, while again surprised at how clean the room was. She also found the garbage can in a drawer and smiled as she threw away the lid she had been holding.

At least I'm not going to starve.

Not right away. She realized that she still didn't have much in the way of perishables and while she had plenty of Mountain Dew, she still needed water, as she had no way of knowing if the water there was safe to drink.

She started making a list of what she would need. Midway through, she looked up and off into the dining room.

Was it two weeks ago now that she had walked through that door to see that naked, smiling man holding her best friend and biting out chunks of her flesh? She thought that sounded right. She should be much more of an emotional wreck after everything that had happened, yet she found herself constantly adapting. Like all of this was strengthening her. She hadn't coped well, but now so much of this rolled right off of her. Was she becoming stronger emotionally, or heartless? Either that or she truly was losing her mind.

Maybe she had never cared as much about the world as she thought she had? What does that say about her? Her ex-boyfriend died last night, killed right in front of her, and here she was making shopping lists like nothing had ever happened.

Maybe that was a good thing. If all this had been too much, she would have already cracked, killed herself and now all of this would have fallen on her brother. Plus, with how this shadow thing wants to take those she cared about, it would be better if she cared less. If she didn't care for anyone, then no one else had to die.

So, yes, this cabin was her new home, and she would never be able to leave it or venture out and meet new people. Just by saying hi, it could mean that someone else would then die.

She finished the soup, tossing the can in the garbage and the spoon in the sink. It was time she lay down. Sleep was overdue, and it wasn't like the house couldn't be cleaned later. What's the rush? It wasn't like she was ever going anywhere. All she had to do was sleep and sleep and sleep. This was her new home, her new prison.

CHAPTER 30

Beep...Beep...Beep...

She heard it, a sound pulling through her consciousness when she wasn't even sure where she was or how she got there.

BEEP...BEEP...BEEP...

She smelled nothing. It was dark. There was only the sound. It continued, pulling at her.

Beep...Beep...Beep.

The sound, lulling her awake as she recognized the repeating tones, but wasn't quite sure from where. Something so familiar, but while the familiarity she knew, it wasn't something good. She could feel her heart racing. The strain of it pulled her focus as it hit her.

Hospital bed, dead friends, sheriffs, doctors, people around her, ready to die for being so close to her. She was trapped, back in a hospital room again, that had to be the beeping. That had to be where she was at. She just needed to open her eyes and she would see it. She would see them all around her.

She could hear the voice and their motions as they were frantic, quickly moving throughout the darkness. It was scattered; they were all around, and quickly running, changing directions. Chaos, pure chaos, was erupting around her.

"We're losing her. Quick, get the doctor-" came the first clear voice through the darkness.

She saw someone run past her in green hospital scrubs, and as Lizzie watched the rushing form, she saw more of them. She focused on them and watched as they moved. They came in and out of the darkness and Lizzie could see that she was not the one in a hospital bed. She was still in a hospital, but it wasn't her...

That's when she heard the scream and looked back to see the bed in the center of the room. The room was getting brighter fast, too fast, and became so bright that Lizzie couldn't focus on the people scurrying around her.

The people were all rushing to the person on the bed, and Lizzie quickly recognized her mother there, being held by multiple nurses as she screamed out in pain. Her stomach was bulging, and she was on the bed with her legs spread wide, knees high.

"Somebody get the doctor," another nurse called.

* * * *

She was in an old apartment building. It was the dream again; the same one she had been having for the last week. The apartment building was old in the way abandoned buildings were old. She was in a hallway; the floor covered in garbage. Some of it was the discards of transients and she worried that some of it was fecal waste as well as fast food wrappers. She didn't care to investigate further as she kept her attention on the light at the end of the long corridor. Though she did occasionally have to look at her feet as there was rubble from ceiling panels that had fallen and shards of plaster that had been ripped from the walls.

A breeze wafted through the plastic further down and it drifted upon waves of air. She could hear the heavy plastic as it flapped to its own course. If the fluorescent light fluttered overhead, she would not be surprised as all of it felt like a movie she had once seen. Some nights in the dream the lights did flicker, but most nights they were broken, and the glass shattered. She would cut her feet on them as she walked slowly down the hall.

It was just a dream. She shouldn't have been able to cut her foot or even feel the pain, but there she could. It was unlike any other dream she had ever experienced. This seemed so real, but unreal at the same time, and she always felt it as though she was there, smelling the puke and fecal matter under her feet.

She made it to the plastic film and abruptly the floating plastic stopped and fell limply to the floor as though pulled from whatever had fastened it above the doorway. The room was left exposed, but inside was dark. She thought she could make out a shape hiding in there, back amongst the shadows, and knew it was calling out to her, trying to pull her in its direction.

Without realizing she had done so, she had taken a step towards it. She feared taking that other step. Her foot was lifting, she felt it as she put more of her weight on the other foot. Every night she had come down this hall, she had stopped here with the wind dying away and a force inside struggling to call her into the darkened room.

So far, she had been able to resist the temptation, and just like those previous occasions, she closed her eyes and pushed the voices from her head. They screamed at her; their peaceful siren calls turning into the screech of banshees in her skull, but as she took a step back, they stopped.

When she opened her eyes, the plastic had returned, not blowing but rugged as it hung there, blocking sight of the shadows. Above the doorway, the spray-painted graffiti glowed, the green phosphorescent read, "All hope abandon, ye who enter here."

Did she still have hope? Is that what kept her moving, kept her walking past the doorway and down the hall towards the other room? As she approached it, she saw the light she was nearing cascaded from another doorway, one she approached with as much trepidation as the last, but it was different.

Where the doorway she feared, the fear had been her own, and she knew that. It was like no part of her actually wanted to go into that room, but something else inside of her had pulled her towards it. Now, as she approached this other door, she realized that the something that had pulled her to the other door was afraid of this one and it was that fear that caused her to pause before the light could touch her.

She looked around the hallway, wondering if there was somewhere else she could go. She wanted to hide, that part inside of her wanting to flee before it moved into the light. As she glanced around her, she saw the graffiti on the walls. The hallway was filled with it. Every night it was there, but every night it was different. Some of the graffiti even changed while she was there looking at it.

"We are but dust and shadows" was written there a few times. Her first night, it had read simply, "Go back, you are not welcome here." Tonight, written in the largest letters and covering most of the wall, larger than anything else she had ever seen written in this hallway was, "'Let there be light,' and there was light. God saw that the light was good, and he separated the light from the darkness."

She recognized the quote from her Sunday school classes when she was a girl, though she hadn't set foot inside of a church in over a decade. She read it a second time, and this time, as she read it, she whispered it to herself. As she did so, that dark presence inside of her that was recoiling from the lighted doorway, again faded and she found comfort flooding through her as she turned and stepped into the light flowing into the hallway.

The doorway and the room were too bright to be seen from out there. She would have to enter to know what lay beyond, but she was no longer hesitating and instead stepped into the room.

As soon as she did so, the light faded enough that she could see and was immediately taken aback at how unlike the rest of the abandoned apartment building this room was. This wasn't abandoned. Not at all. This room was fully decorated and even more, there was an old dark-skinned woman sitting in the middle of the room, looking at her.

Lizzie didn't look at her at first, and the old woman just watched as she took in the room. This wasn't old and abandoned, this was...lived in. This was a living room, though she could plainly see the little eat-in-kitchen that had a small table. That led off to the left, and she assumed that the two doors that led off to the right were for the bedroom and the bathroom.

The room they were in was modestly furnished. There was the couch that was on the left side of the room against the wall, and across from it was a television stand with a television that looked like it could have been from the black and white era of television. It was a small screen, but the back housing stuck out and the screen bowed out in the front. Lizzie didn't think she had seen one like that since she was a little girl and even then, those hadn't been as old. This one still had round knobs along the side of it.

She realized she was staring at the TV, fixated on it, and moved to take in the pictures that were hanging on the wall. There were a lot of them, but none of them had people in them. They were all pictures of places. She didn't recognize any of the places as they weren't nice places you would want to visit, but slums that looked like they were ready to fall over.

"What are these?" She blurted it out and then realized that she had forgotten to introduce herself. All the time she had her dream, she couldn't remember if she always did this or not because every time she came into this room, she never remembered what happened. For as far as she knew, this old lady murdered her in her sleep, though as she turned to take in the old woman, she highly doubted it.

Not that the old woman couldn't do it as she had no clue what she was capable of, but it was something she felt, a kindness that radiated from her. It was shocking, but just like the house, no matter how weary and emotionally obliterated she felt, this woman somehow brought a calm with her, and Lizzie felt that lift the weight from her chest.

"I'm sorry. I don't know you," Lizzie finally said.

"You do. You don't. We've met many times in here, though it's strong enough now to make you forget."

"It?" The old woman nodded at Lizzie's question as though it was an answer, leaving her to stand there confused. "Where are we?"

"The only safe place from it. Deep inside your dreams."

"How did you get here?" The old woman smiled and nodded her approval at the question.

"You're learning. That is good."

"What do you mean?"

"You no longer ask the stupid questions."

Lizzie wasn't sure what she meant by that and tried to think what the stupid questions could be. She had that sense of Déjà vu, but why could she never remember any of this when she was awake?

Curiosity tugged at her, and she felt herself wanting to ask just what the stupid questions would be, but she held her tongue. The old woman was still watching her, studying her in a way that made her feel like the woman was judging her for what she wasn't saying, just as much as what she was.

This made Lizzie study her more. She was old; her face wrinkled heavily with age, which made Lizzie want to think of her more than ancient, but refused to think of her that way, even in the privacy of her mind. Her skin was dark, her hair white, and as she sat there, she had that stoop to her where she leaned forward onto her cane as she sat there. She guessed the woman's spine had curved with age as she had seen Jessica's great aunt had done when she had aged into her nineties. This woman was older. Lizzie didn't know how she knew it, but she did.

"It will be coming soon. It will find you here and will tear us apart again."

"The shadow thing?" Lizzie asked, but again, she already knew the answer and the woman knows that she knew as she could see the frown in disapproval from the redundant question.

"Yes, it fights to keep us apart. It thrives on your ignorance and fear. It grows stronger from the souls it takes and stronger more from a change happening in this world."

"What is it?"

"Lonbraj. A darkness from before time has found its way here. One of the many darknesses that are getting a foothold on our world." The woman started and Lizzie had a sudden pain in her gut that doubled her over. Outside the apartment, there was a howling wind that slammed into the walls and the floor beneath them shook. "It has found us. We don't have long, but I will come again. Soon, you must find me out there, but for now, remember that it is a trickster. It is evil and wicked and will mess with your mind. When you think you know the rules it goes by, it will change them, for it has no rules. None that I know."

The room shook, and outside there was a hideous laugh. It was a cackle that Lizzie had become familiar with and inside her, the pain in her gut twisted into something sour. She could hear from the laughter that he was coming.

"I'm trapped. I don't know what to do." Lizzie was rasping. The pain growing and she couldn't breathe.

Each breath hurt, and each word was a struggle between pushing them from her and them being ripped out of her. "If I leave, they'll attack me."

"I know."

"The talisman-"

"The talisman is-," but the old woman was never able to say it. Lizzie fell to the ground as the other side of the apartment was ripped away, the building torn away and, with it, the old woman. Lizzie watched as she disappeared into the fog of a storm-filled night, only able to be seen from the lightning that was cascading around her.

She felt dejected. It had been so close. She finally had a chance to get some answers, but he found her. He shouldn't have. Lizzie knew she had been having this same dream for the last week, but while much of it had been different, there had been so much that was the same. Each night that she had been there, it hadn't come until much later, though it hadn't mattered because what little Lizzie was beginning to remember, the old woman said even less.

On the other nights, Lizzie hadn't been as believing and had asked stupid questions, often repeating herself. So why had he not come so soon on those other nights?

Because he was watching her. He loved to toy with her. What had the old woman said? He was a trickster. He loved to tease her. That was what all of this was about, or all that she understood. He played with her like a cat who was playing with his food, and he only clamped down once she had been close to hearing something she needed to hear.

None of that mattered now. He was there, and he was coming for her...

I'm done. I'm done just reacting to this shit. She'd had enough. Ever since that first day when her friend had been killed, everything she had done had been in reaction to something he had done. She had to take her life back. For now, that meant getting out of there and away from him. She'd done it in the hotel room. She fought him there.

"You also ran away then, too? You say you're done, but what does that really mean? You just going to keep running away." That little voice of insecurity said to her in her head.

"Fuck you." She screamed it. She screamed it at the voice in her head and to the shadow crawling closer around her. Her voice bellowed into the room and for a moment, the shadow stuttered around her, pausing at the ferocity of it. She felt her lungs exploding out in the air that formed the words and the power that came from it.

Then she turned and ran, quickly escaping through the door and running down the hall away from the two rooms she had seen so far. She hadn't seen anything past the lights before, but now she saw the end of the hall. She had to push herself if she was going to make it. Behind her, the floor was falling away. She didn't turn back, afraid of what she would see, but Lizzie could feel the floor give way every time she lifted her back foot. It was getting closer, and the end of the hall seemed so far away.

There was a roar that was building up behind her. It was in the cracking of the cement as it ripped away, the ripping of plaster as it was pulled from the walls, and in all parts of the apartment building as it was being stripped from this dream around her. That's what it was like. It was like claws were

366

reaching out and pulling what was around her away. As it did, this low rumbling growl was building, and she knew that when it climaxed, that the rest of the building would be destroyed in its fury. If she didn't get out fast enough, she would be destroyed along with it.

"You'll never escape me." She heard that rasping, deep-throated voice she knew so well in her head. No longer was there the tic-toc playful tone and she could tell that the voice, the thing behind her chasing her, was pissed.

Then the roar erupted and the walls around her and the floor beneath her fell away. She found herself falling, and she flailed in the open world. She hadn't made it to the stairwell. She had been so close that she had seen the exit sign shining over the fire escape door. She actually had the slightest bit of hope that she might have made it.

No! She wasn't giving up. S*he was close to it*. She could make it. She was falling, but she could see the remnants of the stairs and she was falling towards it. She focused her efforts, pulling in her flailing arms and legs together. It reminded her of sky divers, how they would control themselves so that they could control their free fall. She brought herself in. It was harder than she thought as there was nothing to push or pull from and she only had wind resistance to propel her. She shifted herself, and then reached out to the railing, not looking down for fear of the abyss below.

Maybe she should have looked down, as then she would have realized how pointless it was. The ground was already gone and just as her fingers would touch the metal railing; it fell away, too. The cement stairs crumbled, the stone looking like it was getting grounded into sand, then falling away, swirling into an hourglass as it filtered down into darkness below.

The railing bunched up, and then twisted until it pulled in upon itself into a ball. First, it was a rough round shape and just sat there in space, but then she watched as it rotated. First slow, but as she watched spun faster. The rough edges were pushed in and flattened out; the ball becoming smoother.

It was like clay. In high school, she had taken a few art classes and remembered that when you rolled it around in your hand, it would become a ball. The more you rolled it, the harder you pressed, the smoother the ball would become.

She was in his hands. This was his shadow place, and she was watching while he crushed the metal before tossing it away. When it was done being smoothed out, it disappeared.

Now there was nothing but black around her. It was an endless void, and she no longer knew if she was falling or floating. There were no reference points around her and no wing that blew against her. That meant she must be floating. Wind or no wind, she would feel the air assaulting her face, but what if that was wrong? She was in a place that broke all the rules, so how could she assume she would feel anything?

"Tic-a-too, tik-a-tee. What was one is now three. Oh three, yes, yes, you'll be." The voice said, returning to his annoying joyful tone. She could feel him in her mind, penetrating her, pushing to get into her deeper thoughts. She didn't know how she was keeping him away, but could feel his frustration mounting.

His frustration? What about her frustration? She had nearly gotten out of there and escaped. She had nearly learned something about what was going on. Who cared if he was frustrated as she was getting pissed?

"You!" she yelled into the nothing. She took another deep intake of air, getting ready to launch a second bellow, when a shape appeared. It was walking on nothing, but she could tell it was a man. Yet even as he neared, the details of him stayed obfuscated by shadow.

She pushed away the sense of helplessness as she dangled before him like a puppet on strings. There was no way she would ever be his marionette.

"You have no control over me." She said to him, knowing how corny it sounded. She couldn't let him see her fear or find where she hid it deep inside. She kept her eyes focused on where his should be in the shape. Orange flames appeared there, and she knew he was studying her.

This hadn't been like the other nights when she had been in this same dream. She knew she entered the room, and it would find her there to rip away the old woman, but that would be it. Then it would take her, and she would wake up screaming in the cabin.

Maybe it didn't have control over her...

She thought about standing in front of the shadow, and then she was. There was nothing below her. Her feet just felt like there was something solid there. Something she could stand on; it was something that could give her strength.

Somehow, she sensed it was smiling, but those orange eyes burned with more intensity as they bore into her.

"Tic-a-too, tic-a-tee, hehe. Soon you will see. Soon you will see, oh yessssss, soon you will see and what fun I can be."

Then the shadow was gone, and she was lying there awake in what had been her uncle's bed. Her bed now, but none the same. The room was dark and empty, the house silent except for the fan on the laptop and the distant hum of the refrigerator.

She listened to it briefly, before it was pierced by a howling scream. Before Lizzie knew what she was doing, she was up, quickly dressed in her thick robe, and running out the front door.

CHAPTER 31

Lizzie should have known better. She shouldn't have rushed outside, not even if she heard screaming. The night was cold, fall making its sharp descent into winter temperatures early this year, and she hadn't stopped to fully prepare for it. She wished being more prepared for the chill had been her only mistake.

Time would tell how costly it had been if it ever got the chance. Now she was trapped out in the dark woods, surrounded by many she had once thought of as friends. They were all dead now, and their piercing eyes were all the yelling she needed to know that the hatred hadn't subsided in the week following their abandonment to hell and subsequent release.

Though there was one set of eyes that didn't share the hate. Roland, who had joined them nearly a week ago, had not spent the time in hell, and still looked at her as though he cared. He was but one of the many that still did hate, and she knew that as much as he wanted to help her, he would be powerless. As the rest of them circled her, Josh was holding Roland back, his head locked in a massive head lock as Josh's large beefy arms held him secure. Roland struggled to break free, but he could barely match a portion of the larger man's strength.

If the others, her dead friends, could spit on her, she knew that they would. They had tricked her into coming out there. During the daytime, it probably wouldn't have worked. She was surprised it had at night. That had been some dream, and when she had woken already thrashing as the fight from the dream crossed over into her struggle with the blankets of reality, she had already been in fight mode. Her heart had already been racing, and she hadn't been thinking. She only knew that something had been wrong, and she was ready to strike back.

The scream had been a catalyst. It had also been bait. How had they known she would fall for it? Lizzie could see on Sarah's face that she was mocking her for it, the sneer showing the contempt the woman held for her. That long ago friendship they had was lost.

What were they going to do with her? Lizzie had already seen that they could hurt her. They had done that at the coffee shop, and she had been terrified of that moment happening again. Since she'd come to the cabin, she had been staying in a confined space, not even leaving to get groceries. She had yet to call in for a delivery, though if she survived this, she knew she would have to in the morning. She had eaten the last can of soup for supper and was thankful, as she didn't think she could eat another can of chicken and rice soup. There was only so much canned soup a woman could take.

This was why she was afraid of ordering. If not her, she was afraid her friends would attack the delivery driver and hurt him. She had never seen them attack anyone else and wasn't sure if they could. She wasn't about to put someone else in that danger if she didn't have to.

"Why?" Lizzie finally broke down and asked as they circled around her.

Sarah chuckled.

"Poor little rich girl," Sarah said.

"I'm not-" Lizzie started, but she was stopped by a shove from behind and grew sick with that sense of wrongness she felt whenever one of them would touch her.

"You're not? Really? I know how much he left you," Sarah spat back at her.

"You know what he really left me." Lizzie was turning with them, keeping her eyes locked on Sarah, though she knew that kept Chuck to her back. He had to have been the one to have shoved her, as Elisabeth was always just to her right.

"You killed us," Chuck said, and she barely had time to turn around before she felt the blow and saw the fist he swung. It hit her chin but didn't feel like a hand that smashed into her, but some kind of unseen force. She couldn't really explain how it was different, but it still hurt, sending her falling back on her ass.

"So, you can be hurt. I thought you-" Chuck looked behind Lizzie at Sarah. He was watching her as she walked around Lizzie to him. "Said she couldn't be touched."

I'm not going to cry. I'm not going to- fuck no, I'm not going to cry. I've been through too much shit and have put myself in harm's way, not sending them back to that hell.

Sarah glared at her as she walked around into view. She had a smirk that Lizzie didn't recognize. It was like the friend she had grown up with wasn't there. Who was this woman who strode around her, able to plan and execute a deviousness Lizzie couldn't fathom?

"It seems things have changed."

"Sarah, you all don't have to do this. I'm trying to find a solution."

"We don't need you to find a solution." Sarah said. Lizzie felt that sickening feeling and knew that one of them had grown close behind her. She guessed it was Elisabeth who was keeping very quiet.

"No, we've got that figured out," Chuck said. He nodded to Sarah. "At least your friend did."

"We don't need to figure it out because all we must do is kill you. Isn't that, right?" Sarah said and Lizzie felt a force slam into her back between the shoulder blades.

Lizzie called out in pain as she was pitched forward by the blow. She gasped and realized that she'd been hit from behind, but whoever hit her hadn't released her. They must have landed on top of her and that sickening feeling in her stomach spread through her into her chest.

"How...How... would... I know?" She panted, struggling to breathe.

"When I first came back, I couldn't even move a coffee mug. Not by myself. You remember that. We tried, just like the friends we had always been, we tried to do things together."

Lizzie didn't like the tooth-filled smile Sarah was giving her, and there was a wildness in her eyes. They were opened wide, and Lizzie was sure her friend had lost her mind. She was moving towards Lizzie, as Lizzie struggled to pull herself back. It was hard, but Lizzie could push against the force that was trying to keep her there.

"You're not getting away from me." Sarah took another step towards her.

"Lizzie. You must get inside. Trust me, get back inside." Roland was struggling to get away from Josh, but Josh was a big man, and it was like a grizzly bear taking on a wolf. Wolves can do well in a pack, but by himself, he was over matched. There was nothing he could do for her; she was on her own.

And she wasn't about to let them hurt her. She had to fight them.

Lizzie laughed. It was hard at first and initially sounded more like a wheeze that barely escaped from her lungs. The force behind her pulled back, though, and she could pull in more breath.

"What are you doing?" Sarah asked, and Lizzie laughed harder. She looked at her friend, but the question wasn't posed to her. She had asked the person behind her, and Lizzie looked back to see that Elisabeth had been the one on top of her. Elisabeth had stood up and was now looking at them both, pained.

Was she crying? Lizzie thought she could see the glisten of moisture at the corner of her eyes. Maybe there was still something of her soul left.

Thank God! Lizzie thought as she turned back to Sarah.

Why was it someone Lizzie had just met was more her ally, had more of her soul, than the person she had grown up with? Sarah had no compassion for her. That fiery intensity had only shifted to Elisabeth for a fraction of a heartbeat, and it was now reaffirmed and directed back at Lizzie. She was walking closer, faster now, only a few steps away.

Lizzie didn't have time to think, only react. Her gut told her to strike, and so she did. She leapt forward into where Sarah was, unsure if Sarah had any mass or not. She pushed forward, keeping low so that if Sarah was solid, Lizzie would tackle her out of the way. With luck, Chuck would be so caught off guard that she could get past him and run back into the house.

When she hit where Sarah had been, it wasn't that she went through Sarah, but that the shape of her disappeared from where she had been. Lizzie had felt the resistance of something there, but not the solidness of flesh. Then there was nothing, and she was fighting to keep her balance while running forward.

"No! You bitch!" Sarah was close behind her. Whatever had happened to her, it hadn't moved her far from Lizzie, and Lizzie knew that she would be running to catch up to her. Lizzie didn't have to make it far, but she was also not dressed to be out there. Each step she took was a reminder that she had left the house with no shoes on.

The cold was bad enough, not enough that she had to worry about frostbite and losing a foot, but it did make the ground hard and every bump in the dirt sharp to the bottom of her feet. Sarah didn't have such concerns, and she knew it. Dead things didn't feel pain, and she would be able to catch her.

Lizzie could feel the biting in her pants and knew that the talisman was in her pocket. She didn't know how it got there as she had put it away, storing it in the box of books she had found that her uncle had left her. She had never pulled it out, and especially didn't put it in her pocket before coming out there. Still, she felt the stabbing jabs from the teeth of the hideous thing and the desire in her chest to put it on and send them all away. All of them, get rid of all of them so she would never have to deal with them again. Then maybe she could live a life in peace out there. Even if she couldn't enjoy normalcy, she would have quiet.

She pushed herself harder to make it to the house. She was only a few feet away now. She just had to be ready to make the turn to go up the sideways stairs, and then she could fall into the living room if she had to.

Lizzie already knew what was going to happen before she felt it. She had to slow down to make that turn to go up the stairs. If she hadn't been running straight towards the house, she might have been able to get to it at an angle and she would have been okay. Unfortunately, she hadn't been thinking about that as she had just pushed to get away. Now she did have to slow, and Sarah would be there to catch her. Sarah, the cheerleader, had always been more physically fit than Lizzie, who spent much of her extra time in the library. Sarah, who liked to work out with Jessica while Lizzie would be there with them, occasionally commented while she sat off to the side reading a book. Sarah was determined to see her in pain as Lizzie tried to escape into the confines of the house.

Lizzie felt her feet go out from her first. She had been close enough that she was reaching out to shift her balance for the turn to go up the stairs. It was right when she had shifted her weight and then she was falling. She had a brief moment when she realized it was happening and knew that no matter how she turned, it was going to hurt. She had too much momentum against her; she was going to slam into the house.

The pain shot through her. First it was her shoulder as it slammed into the rough wood of the outer wall. Then her back twisted and that sent torrents of pain from all over as then her arm and legs slammed into places she wasn't even sure of. She felt like a rag doll being tossed around as she hit the wall before landing hard on the ground.

She lost consciousness, but only for a brief second or two. It was enough for them to catch her and when she came to, she was feeling the force of their blows all along her body. They were kicking her into the wall, each blow was doubled as she felt it, then the pain as it slammed her into the house. She had somehow managed to get her arms over her face, so even when she had blacked out, some part of her was thinking, but the rest of her was exposed and she felt each strike.

She fought to pull herself towards the stairs. They hadn't been far when she slowed and when she outstretched her arm; she felt the tip of them. That was when she saw the shoe come crashing down on her face and felt the smashing force. She could feel the blood spurting from her nose and swore she heard something crack. She felt lightening stabs of pain shooting through her eyes and into her skull, but couldn't stop.

It didn't stop her. She knew where the step was, and pushed through, pulling herself towards it. Each blow rocked her towards the ground and the house, but she kept going. Each lifting of her knee was met with a kick from one of them to throw off her balance, but she moved slowly, not pulling it high, so if it did fall back down, it wasn't going to cause more pain.

She made it up the first step and then the other. She only had two more steps to go and there would be the open front door. At that time and more than any other time in history, she was thankful for being out in the woods and that she had run out without closing it behind her. All she had to do was reach the platform and she could just fall into the entryway.

"Oh, no you don't bitch," Sarah snarled behind her, and Lizzie felt a force behind her head, trying to smash her face into the next step. It hadn't stopped Lizzie, and she reached out and pulled herself farther up. She was on the platform now. She had almost made it. "Shit!"

Lizzie didn't try to run into the house, or anything glorified. She was too tired and in too much pain. She saw the entryway and fell past the threshold. First, it was just her upper body, but once that had cleared, she pulled her feet and let them crash against the wall on the inside of the door frame.

Lizzie saw that Sarah had been trying to reach for her, but that was the problem in not really being able to use their hands against her. They could hit her with some kind of force, but it made it really hard for them to grab at her.

Lizzie was panting, just inside the door, not moving. Sarah stayed outside, watching her.

"Just die already."

"No..." Lizzie wheezed out and then rasped into a cough. She was thankful no blood came out. She didn't know what that would mean, but she knew it would be bad if there had been. "Not yet. Brother."

"Brother. Yeah, well, too bad. He'll be dead soon, and then what will be your excuse?"

"I'm sorry." Lizzie was catching some of her breath, now able to say short phrases, and her chest no longer felt like it was going to seize up and quit working for her. Maybe she would survive the night. Maybe. There was still a long time before morning.

"You don't get to be sorry."

"I am."

"Yeah, well, fuck you. Fuck your whole fucking family. I've never liked you. I only tolerated you because your dad. Your mom was a fucking drunken whore who slept with the whole town. Everyone knew it. I felt sorry for you."

Lizzie felt a new pain in her chest rise, and a lump formed in her throat. She was having trouble breathing again, and was not sure if it was from the beating or the words.

Her legs fell from beside the door, and she twisted her body around. It was hard. Each time she moved a muscle, they protested in agony, but she was able to turn so she could reach for the door. She grabbed the handle and pulled herself up so she could step to the threshold and look her friend in the eyes.

"Then why get an apartment with me?"

"Fuck you."

"Why still be friends with me? Why come out here with me?"

"I came out here to die. It was my fucking time. That's all I am or was, someone to die because I was close to you. Fuck You. Fuck you, fuck you, fuck you."

"I'm sorry."

"Stop saying that. I don't fucking care if you're sorry."

"Sarah-"

"You know why I got the apartment with you? Because I was fucking your boyfriend. I was the one fucking Roland, and I loved doing it when you were in class. I would fuck him on your bed, in your bathroom. I would fuck him wherever I knew you had enjoyed him, so that way I could one day tell you how much I enjoyed fucking him and taking him from you."

"But-" Lizzie looked past Sarah to where Roland was standing at the bottom of the stairs and knew right then that it was true. She had known he was sleeping with someone, but never would have- no, how could she?

Roland's eyes were staring at the ground. He refused to look at her. Had he always been screwing her? Had it all been some game to the two of them?

"Roland?" Lizzie's voice was weak, and she barely recognized it.

"I'm sorry Liz. I never meant to hurt you."

That pain in her heart twisted like someone had just grabbed it and started to squeeze the life right out of her. The tears were welling up inside her, and she knew they were getting ready to break free.

She tried to take a step back from the door, but her legs were weak. They wobbled from the strain of the abuse they had just taken, and Lizzie found herself falling hard onto her butt. She barely even registered this new pain as she was still processing what Sarah was telling her. Why had Sarah kept this from her and waited for so long to tell her? Why wait until now? There were many times that if she wanted to hurt her like this, could have said something and ended all the lies.

Lizzie forced herself back up. She was not going to lie down, not this. She was not going to let Sarah keep her down. She made it back to the threshold of the door; her face covered in tears and blood continued to flow from her nose. Still, she stood there, as close to Sarah as she could get, and stared into those eyes that radiated so much hatred and contempt for her.

"I fucked your dad once. He was a bad lay, but I didn't do it for pleasure. He had an old man's dick, and I had to do all the work. I walked into the bedroom while your mom was working the late shift and you had fallen asleep early. I walked in there, in just my bra and panties. He was asleep, and I started sucking his cock. I don't even think he was fully awake until I was on top of him, riding him until he came into my nice young pussy."

Lizzie was backing away from the door. She knew Sarah couldn't get in, but her words were still hurting her more than any knife or fist ever could. She realized she was stepping back and stopped herself, forcing herself back to the threshold. She grabbed the door as she didn't trust her legs not to give out on her again.

"Why?"

"For a long time, I did it because your mom fucked my dad. I hated you for that, but you know what? After I did it for a while, I started working on fucking up your life. I found that it was too much fun. I stopped caring about our parents and their fucked-up relationships and started to craft new ways to torture you."

This was too much. There was no way this all could be happening. She wanted to collapse again, just fall to the floor, and let the cabin rot around her. She wasn't against returning to her childish self and covering her ears while screaming, "Na Na Na Na Na."

"I even told your mom about how I fucked your dad."

Lizzie's glare shot back to Sarah, no longer avoiding her eyes. She saw the glee in how much she was enjoying this. Right then, Lizzie had never wanted to hurt Sarah or anyone else as much as she did right then, and Lizzie had a way of doing it. She still felt the bite from the talisman teeth digging into her leg. It was like it was taunting her, begging her to use it. If she did, it wouldn't just be Sarah, she would be hurting.

Roland was out there with them. He hadn't been sent *to the place* yet and was still on her side. He was trying to help her. He tried to warn her. He talked with her whenever they could and was being nice to her. She couldn't send him there or else he would come back, no better than the rest of them.

But he didn't have to come back, did he? None of them had to. She could just keep on wearing the twisted looking object and never have to worry about any of them again. Something nagged at her, though. That told her that wasn't a good idea. If her uncle hadn't told her to always wear it, but only when she had left the house for long stretches, there had to be a reason for it. There must have been some kind of cost associated with it that she didn't know about. She had already made enough mistakes by doing things without understanding what was going on.

She still hoped that there would be some answers in her uncle's diaries. She'd read through the first one, but had stopped, not wanting to read the next. So far, her uncle didn't have the talisman yet, and a lot of it talked about him taking long walks with his wife.

The other dead were upset with him, but all they could do was yell and shout at him. He was learning to accept that, though was having trouble sleeping as some would take turns screaming through the night. He was starting to experiment with watching television or keeping it on through the night as the distraction made the screams less noticeable. He wasn't rich yet, but his savings weren't hurting too much. He was learning to deal with it and talked about this man named Bobby with whom he chatted with regularly. She wondered who Bobby really was.

Lizzie looked up from Roland, who tried to hold her gaze with his eyes. Sarah was still standing just beyond the threshold. Some of the anger had edged off and that little smirk she had earlier returned. Her eyes had a joyous sparkle at the corner that Lizzie hadn't noticed before and realized that Sarah was enjoying hurting her in this new way.

"Yeah, I told her. It was right before they left for the weekend trip."

Lizzie felt her grip on the door handle tighten, and that pain in her chest twisted even harder. She felt like she had just been kicked in the stomach. She didn't want to hear this, but already knew what was going to be said. She saw it in the smile that grew wider, spreading across Sarah's lips.

"I told her just as she was getting in the car, ready to drive away. I told her just an hour before they both died."

Lizzie felt the fresh tears streak down her cheek but ignored them as she slammed the door shut. Lizzie crashed into it, her back hitting hard as she tried to use it to support her. She was falling. It was going to happen. Her legs were giving out, and she had no control. She didn't want to hear anymore, but Sarah wasn't going to stop. The dagger was firmly jammed in Lizzie's heart. This was her death blow, and Sarah knew how much this was hurting Lizzie. Not only did Sarah not seem to care, but she was also enjoying it.

"I killed your parents. Don't you see? What else would have gotten them into such a big fight and not seen the oncoming truck? I killed them." Sarah went quiet, but Lizzie knew it was only for the effect and she was right. The next bit came out in a harsh whisper. "And I'm going to kill you when the time is right."

CHAPTER 32

I wish I knew what was happening to me. Why? How come I can't even talk with someone without them turning up dead, their spirits brought back to torture me? What have I done to deserve this? Why do I even write about it?

Maybe just to preserve my sanity? Maybe these will be found one day once I've succumbed to the madness. Does me no good, so fuck these books, this writing and fuck my life.

I can't even have one friend. I truly am alone in this world.

Okay, While I don't think I'll feel any better anytime soon, I have taken a minute, made myself a shot or two of some Jack, the one friend who won't die on me, and have sat back into my chair. The bottle is next to me, ready to toast myself into oblivion.

I try not to drink obsessively, but today, I earned it. No, not earned. I didn't do anything to deserve this, but I need this. I need the stupor tonight. After all, tonight I am sure I will have a new resident to my collection of souls, as tonight is when I'm sure Bobby will be joining them.

Yep, Bobby, the one friend I foolheartedly allowed myself to have. Knew better. I know anyone who befriends me dies, but it was an accident. I'd talk to him a little on my trips into town. Everyone needs to get supplies and well, everyone needs a little interaction with other living people as well. You can't just live off of talking to the dead, even if they do talk back.

Bobby had become a friend. I hadn't realized it. Every time I went into town, he was there. Of course he was. He owned the convenience store, not that it was much of a store. It looked like it had once been an old farmhouse, and I had missed it the first time I had tried to find it. I was lost for what seemed like an hour lost before I stopped off and asked someone at the post office. Once I came back, I'd seen the little sign on the porch.

It was a place that didn't want to be found, much like the town it belonged to. A small town deep in the woods, far from any major highways and only a little road leading to and from. Had that main street that held everything, all the residents and the businesses. At the end of the street was a small school with a parking lot just large enough to turn around in. There wasn't room for anything else. Any more houses to build, the surrounding forest would have to be cut away, and no one seemed interested in doing that.

It was an interesting place. I don't know why I ramble on about it. I had grown up with my brother in a small town, but it had been nothing like this. It had been an actual town, but this store, and the houses that were around it, it felt like a community that didn't like or want outsiders. Still, they were nice. It was obvious I wasn't from there when I entered the store.

"Hey stranger. Lost or getting lost? I can tell you how to get back to the highway or farther into the woods, whichever you prefer. I prefer the woods myself. Got lost here thirty years ago, and still not sure I ever want to get found. Though I wish my wife couldn't find me."

"I heard that." Came a female voice from the other room and I couldn't help but smile as I took the whole place in. The scents, the decor, all of it overwhelming me.

"Damn, she found me again. Hey, listen fella, help me out. Run the store. I need to flee to Mexico."

"You're not going anywhere, you senile ol' coot."

It was then that I realized just how amazing these two were and knew that I had just walked into meeting some very special and dear people.

Who else would have taken an old house, knocked down most of the walls so that the first floor could be used for a general store? It had wood floors and walls. Wood was everywhere. The shelves that were lined with grocery items as well as anything else you might need in a cabin out in the middle of nowhere, were also made from wood. The cooler in the back wasn't, but next to them was a wood sculpture of an old Indian standing there looking out disapproving at the rest of the store.

The store was quaint, rustic and everything I never realized I'd wanted in a small country store. It smelled like her. There were always cookies or something sweet baking in the kitchen, and that was her smell.

I'd forgotten what I'd gone in there for, so lost in the sweet northern charm of the place. It wasn't until Bobby called out to me the third or fourth time that I pulled myself from whatever stupor I'd slipped into.

"You okay?" He said after I'd been staring lost in space for who knew how long.

"Yeah, just blanked on why I came in here."

"Couldn't tell ya. That is, unless you're planning to buy me out of house and home so we can finally get a day off from this prison."

Every time I went there, he always asked me if I was ready to buy him out. Damn fool. Damned, damned fool, should have never said a word to me. Now he wouldn't be dead. If the old man had just shut up and took my money, not been someone I could talk to over the last few months while I came to town, he would still be alive.

According to his wife, that kind, elderly woman who would call out from the kitchen while making another batch of those wonderful cookies or her special homemade bread, her husband died just this morning. The store was closed when I pulled up. She was sitting on the front porch, rocking in the bench swing that was mounted there. She had been crying most of the morning, evident by the streaks of wetness that traced down her cheek and the puffiness of her eyes.

She didn't want to talk about what had happened. She told me so, and I didn't press it. I did ask her if I could join her for a minute. It wasn't a smart idea, as I was putting her life at risk by talking to her, but I didn't trust my legs to get me back to my car. They felt like rubber, and I just needed to sit down for a few minutes.

She nodded, and I sat. Both of us rocked there for a few minutes in silence, staring off at nothing. Not a single car passed by, and I thought it was strange that no one had been here or come to visit her.

That was when she said something that had nearly dropped me, even from the bench swing.

"He always knew his life was at risk, talking to you. Everyone knows those living out where you do are on borrowed time. There's a darkness about you. Some evil that comes from that cabin. You ever notice how the birds don't fly near you, or that you never see a bear out by your place? Probably not. You don't realize how common it is to see a bear on your property, and especially not out there. Animals know to stay away. My Bobby knew to stay away, but he just couldn't help himself. He was too nice an old man. Said he'd lived a long enough life. If something happened to him for it, he was willing to take that chance."

Not once did she look at me, and I know I don't have all her words right. She said more than that, but that's how much I can remember and it's close enough. It was what she said next that killed me, and I quickly tried to escape after that.

"Do me a favor. Whatever voodoo whodoo that surrounds you and that place, make sure it takes me next, please. I want to be with my Bobby."

That was when she turned those intense blue eyes on me and I felt my chest heave a heavy breath, my insides burning. My throat went dry, but I tried to respond.

"I know. You don't have no control over it, but I know talking to me helps. Will you do that? Will you come back to me here and talk to me?"

Bobby hadn't joined the dead that followed me everywhere I went yet, and he's not with me now either. I'm sure he'll come tonight as they normally do. For now, there was only the army of regular gruesome faces I had come to know as my regulars, and then there was my own wife. I looked up at her, saw her moist eyes, and she shook her head at me. I agreed with her that there was no way I could go back there. As much as she wanted to be with her husband, I could not be the cause of this woman's death. There was enough death that followed me.

"Sure," I lied.

"Thank you." She nodded, and a small smile curved at the corner of her lips. "He wanted you to have something. You better take it now before the vultures get here later."

She stood and walked me to the front door. I tried to open it for her, but she slapped away my hand.

"No, don't be doing that. I've opened my own doors for all my life, don't need some youngin' opening them for me now. I'm not that old."

I followed her in, and at first, I was afraid she was walking me back to that old Indian statue. I really didn't want to turn down whatever she was giving me, but the last thing I needed out at the cabin was this old Indian constantly watching me. Besides, with the weird shit going on, I couldn't help it. I was afraid the damn thing might come to life. It wasn't too lifelike, but enough so that I could see it happening. My life had become too much of a horror movie for me not to expect the crazy.

Behind the statue, though, was an old clock that hung on the wall. It was beautiful and made of wood. I guessed that it was hand carved with engravings of a man and a woman. The woman stood with her hands back and her cheek turned towards the man, while the man leaned forward, giving her a kiss on the cheek. The outer corners were gold, and the large face, each hand was crafted gold arms. Hanging from below it was two rods that ended in weight balls, probably to tick away the time. The clock itself hung there, motionless.

"He called it the lovers. Someone gave it to us shortly after we got married, but don't go thinking it was a wedding present. It doesn't have any kind of emotional sentimentality to it. No, he wanted you to have it as he said the damn thing hadn't worked in nearly fifteen years. He said to give it to you and tell you that time doesn't always drag on. Sometimes it will stop so you can enjoy a little peace of happiness."

I didn't know what to say to her, and she must have seen my discomfort. I was saved though as we both heard another car pull up out front.

"Go ahead and take it. Sounds like the well wishers are starting their arrival. You'll want to be out of here before more show. Some of the more idiotic fools might try to blame you and do something stupid. People don't seem to have the sense that God gave a dog anymore, and people turn mean when they get that dumb."

392

I grabbed the clock, not yet sure why I was taking it.

"I just hope when my time comes, it comes easier than Bobby's. Maybe, if i'm lucky, I'll die in my sleep."

I wanted to ask her how he died but couldn't bring myself. I'd find out soon enough.

I left the small store as a family was walking up the front steps. The mother saw me and quickly pulled her child back, all of them giving me a wide berth as I walked to my car. I set the clock down on the back seat and left.

So, the friend I had made, the one I had let myself get to know, had died. I should have known better.

I guess I am meant to always be here, alone.

* * * *

I don't know what this existence is. Each day, I join my dead wife, and we walk among the trees, down some of the paths that are around the cabin. Each day, I have those few moments that I forget that she is dead. Then I try to hold her hand, and we never embrace. She is trapped somewhere between life and death, and I feel like I am as well. How else do you describe me hiding from life out here in the boonies with no way of surviving back in the real world?

This is no way to live. I don't know how I'm going to survive. I haven't been back in town since that day. It's been a week now, and when we return from our walks, Bobby is there. He cries so much. He knows how he died, and that his wife is hoping to join him. He wants me to return to town to talk to her, hoping that whatever curse that took him would take her as well. He doesn't understand that I just can't do that. I'm already the cause of so much death.

That is only part of it-

Bobby had died viciously, a random bear attack. His face hangs in tatters on his mutilated body. If I went back and talked to her, kept talking to her until the shadow woman takes her, she would see Bobby as he was now when she got there. And how would she look? What kind of gruesome death would the shadow woman dream up for her? He doesn't understand.

None of them do.

They all look at me with those haunted eyes. They all hate me, all except my Cyntha.

I want so badly to hold her.

How can I be surrounded by so many yet feel so alone?

I dread even going outside of this cabin. When I finish the walks, sometimes I'll venture into the barn. I've started to clean it up a little, using one corner of it to create a little work area. I haven't done too much with it, don't really know what to do. So far, I've just been tinkering with that old clock. It is such an amazing piece of old technology that it is fascinating. I think I may have even found what is wrong with it.

It is so quiet here, without any nature sounds to make the place feel natural. I think the only way to preserve my sanity is to find some kind of project to work on. Maybe the clock will be my salvation?

So alone.

Oh God, why have you so cursed me?

CHAPTER 33

The week dragged on, and already Lizzie wasn't sure what day it was anymore. She could look on the laptop, at the calendar, and see if it was a Wednesday or a Saturday. None of it mattered. Her life no longer mattered. She was trapped out there in the woods. How could anything matter? There was nothing for her there except for the undead things that kept her locked inside. They had become her guards; this cabin was her prison. What kind of life was she exiled to, and for what crime?

What time was it? She was just getting out of bed, and the light was already high, trying to pierce through the darkened windows. It was a weak attempt, only pinholes of it were able to shine through scratches that had formed over time from where pieces of paint had fallen away.

She missed the sun but knew that an open window was a harsh reminder to the dead that waited outside her door.

Her door...

At the cabin door, there was a sound. It must have been what have woken her up. Someone was pounding at it. She had thought it had just been another part of her dream, a holdover from the apartment building that she always found herself in when she closed her eyes. Each night she dreamed of the old woman, and each night the building fell away before she could get any answers. The faster she tried, the faster the building fell.

But no, this knock was real, and it was growing impatient. Whoever was out there was now slamming his or her fist down repeatedly. Any harder and Lizzie wasn't sure they were going to break through the door... Maybe that was it, maybe it was the dead. Maybe they were trying to break their way in, but had they really grown that strong?

She didn't like the thought of it, but always knew it would be a possibility. Once they had grown powerful enough to attack her when going outside, anything was possible.

Slowly, she slipped out of bed, trying to avoid the places on the hard wood cabin floor where it creaked the loudest. The dresser was next to the bed, and she eased a drawer open, pulling out an oversized flannel shirt. She slipped it on and then her jeans. The same jeans she had been in since she got there. Who cared? She was out in the middle of the woods, and she hadn't thought to bring a change of clothes when she decided to hide herself out in the middle of nowhere.

They needed to be washed. She would, some day.

The knocking continued, and she held her breath, trying to listen. Maybe it was the police. They could have found her. She didn't think it would have been too hard, after all, her friends knew she was going to a concert with him, knew they had been broken up and that she resented him, and then boom, he was left dead in a hotel room over a hundred miles away from where they lived.

Why had she run away? She should have called the cops. She hadn't killed him.

No, but was she going to explain to them that some weird shadow thing had reached into his chest and stopped his heart so that now Roland was an undead thing that existed outside of her cabin? Yeah, and how long would it be before she found herself locked up in that padded room?

The cops had probably found her lawyer, gotten the address for her cabin from him, and were now out there to take her in. She was about to be arrested. Then what would happen? She would be in a prison cell, locked away with half a dozen people who wanted to do nothing more than kill her so they could stop existing.

She couldn't open that door. She had to get out of there and make a run for it.

Yeah, like that made any sense. If she ran into the woods, her dead enemies would still be there with her. They would run her down, and it would be like that dream she had of Jessica. They'd tear her apart, ripping away pieces of her while Sarah laughed, watching them.

She was trapped.

Maybe if she stayed really quiet, they would just go away, figuring there was no way someone would be living in this decrepit old house.

She eased into the living room, now only a short distance away from the door. Whoever was on the other side of it stopped for a moment, listening just like she was.

Lizzie couldn't hold her breath any longer and she let it out as quietly as she could. She had held it too long; it was loud in the stillness of the room and now she was breathing hard to regain oxygen in her lungs. She was sure whoever was out there could hear her, and that they were listening to gasping for air.

Then the pounding continued.

"Who is it?" Lizzie didn't recognize her voice. It was tight and screeched with the words, wavering as she spoke.

The knocking stopped, and she repeated herself, sure they hadn't heard her over the pounding. This time, she had more strength in the voice.

Whatever is going to happen is going to happen. There's nothing you can do to change it now, she thought as she approached the door.

"Hello?" came the sharp, accented voice on the other side of the door. *British,* she thought, where it sounded more like he said "'Ay 'lo" more than the nasally "hello" she was used to in northern Wisconsin.

Really, she's out in the middle of nowhere, and some British chap was on the other side of her door. The only British person she'd met in real life was..., well, she'd never met anyone British. She'd only seen them on TV or in movies. There was someone British here, now? Her life was getting too damned weird.

"Who is it?" She walked slowly to the door. It had some kind of protection to keep the dead things out, but no clue if it would protect her from intruders. She was a woman, alone in the woods. Why had she never worried about men breaking in here? That should have been her first concern. Just what in the hell had she been thinking, not keeping the door locked? *Maybe he wouldn't try to get in. Yeah, and maybe he's just there to have a nice round of fish and chips*, whatever the hell that was.

The man had paused when he had heard her voice, no more knocking, but he was still there. He was listening to her approach. That was it. He had stopped to hear when she would get close.

She stopped a yard away from the door, close enough to it to talk to him, but far enough away that if he burst through, she could try to run for the kitchen or even her bedroom. Neither of them were great escape plans, but it was what she had.

"Is Mr. Hooper available?"

Who the hell was Mr. Hooper? Lizzie had no clue. The man must be lost, or just acting like he was. When had she become this distrustful?

"Sorry. No one here by that name."

"Really?"

"I think you're at the wrong house."

"Now I know that that's not true. Miss, I've been here many times before and I am inquiring about Mr. Hooper. He was working on a clock that belongs to my master and my master has grown impatient with the lack of progress."

Lizzie took a hesitant step to the door. Clocks... Something about the clocks rattled around in her head. Hadn't her uncle said something about working on old clocks? There'd been something in his letter to her about them.

"You said Mr. Hooper was working on them?"

"I don't think that was his real name. He was a weird sort. Maybe that was why he was living out here, but he had come to us as being highly recommended and thought to be one of the best in the world. He had repaired a number of other clocks for my master, and we'd become quite impressed with his efficiency and craftsmanship. He has our latest find, but he has not followed up with us in a timely manner."

Lizzie opened the door. Standing there and looking out of place with the cabin and woods around him stood the Englishman in what appeared to be a finely tailored suit. He was facing away from her, looking at the yard and woods around the cabin, and hadn't noticed she'd opened the door.

A couple of yards behind him sat Elisabeth and Chuck. Chuck was sitting on the ground and Elisabeth was lying against him. She looked like she was crying while Chuck was keeping a watchful eye on her. None of the others could be seen and Lizzie wasn't sure if that made her more or less comfortable.

Lizzie knew he couldn't see them, but it almost felt like he did and was watching them.

"I'm sorry, but Mr. Hooper has passed away."

The gentleman turned to look at her, and a shiver ran through her, chilling as deep as her soul. His gaze was intense, his eyes dark in the shadows of the overhang. His nose was small and pointed, and his mouth was tight with disapproval.

She couldn't hold that gaze for long. As he looked at her, it felt like his eyes were burrowing deep into her soul and as it did, there was a cold that tried to invade her heart. It was like a hand made of ice reached into her chest and caressed it, making it hard to breathe. Her breath came in shallow bursts as she tried to keep herself together, to tell herself she was just imagining that demonic gaze. It was hard, near impossible, as it brought back strong memories of that night, the shadow man on top of Roland as it took his life from him.

"Then I would like my master's property returned to us." The man made a move to come inside the house, but Lizzie refused to step out of his way.

"It's not in here. It might be in the barn."

"Then we shall retrieve it." The man said, taking a step back, obviously frustrated at not being allowed in. Then he looked back over his shoulder and Lizzie was again struck by the sense that he was looking at the dead couple as they were both watching them. Sarah had stepped around from the side of the house and all three of them were watching curiously as the man turned back to Lizzie.

"Okay, go back there and grab whichever one is yours."

"You won't be accompanying us?"

"You know which one is yours. I have no clue."

"I'd feel much more comfortable if you would join us. I am not in the habit of fumbling through another's domain."

Lizzie looked at her undead guards and then back at the Englishman. Would Sarah and the rest of them attack her on the way to the shed? Lizzie hadn't been there yet, but she thought she had read somewhere from her uncle that the path and barn were protected. Had she read that, or was it just wishful thinking?

She hadn't left the cabin since that night. She hadn't showered for even longer and couldn't imagine how bad she smelled. The man was being kind enough not to acknowledge it, but she had to have wreaked like the dead. Yet he wanted her to take him out to the barn and be in an enclosed area with her. He must really want that clock back.

...Or he really wanted to get you some place dark and isolated.

That didn't make any sense. She was already isolated. How much more isolated could she get?

"Su-Sure. I'll meet you out back." She didn't mean to stutter over the words, but she'd gotten trapped in the man's eyes again.

He released her by turning away. She watched him go down the stairs before she closed the door. There was no way she was walking around the house. Josh had ventured into the front yard, and they had all been watching the stranger. Curiously, as she closed the door, she again sensed that the stranger was watching *them* as well.

Now she had to meet him around the back. If she knew the man and trusted him, she'd just hurry through the kitchen. But who the hell was this guy? She wanted some kind of weapon. Even if the Englishman didn't put her nerves on end, it still wasn't smart to go out there with a stranger.

Was there a gun somewhere in the house? She'd been cleaning the house a little each day. There was still much she hadn't found, and so often she would get sidetracked by reading more of his diaries. Still, there weren't any firearms, and she hadn't seen anything large like a gun cabinet or secured like a small gun safe. So, unless her uncle practiced very poor firearm safety, she didn't think he owned one.

What kind of person lives in Wisconsin and doesn't own a firearm? Sure, maybe if you were from Madison, but everywhere else in the state had common sense. What if a wild animal came around or even a bear? That wasn't uncommon to see. They did have bears up here.

But that wasn't true either. There were bears in the woods, yes, but nearby there wouldn't be. The wildlife knew better.

So, no gun. Nothing to arm herself with.

She entered the kitchen and felt that familiar pain and a twinge of guilt knowing this had been where Sarah had died. It was brief and quickly she focused her attention on finding some kind of weapon to take with her.

"Hello? Miss? You never told me your name. Miss, are you coming?" The man was on the other side of that door. It was the door she had fallen from to get away from the smiling dead man. It was also the door that led to the barn. She knew she'd have to go through there or walk back around the house.

"Just a minute." She called back. Near the sink was the silverware drawer. Inside, she found a set of small knives. She'd debated on grabbing the butcher's knife one drawer over, but there was no way she could conceal that. A small steak knife wasn't much of a weapon, but her uncle had purchased good quality and the little blade she worked along her arm felt sturdy. She just had to find a way to secure.

"Miss, please don't keep me standing out here all day."

Lizzie opened another drawer and pulled out the plastic wrap. She hastily pulled out a stretch of it, fighting as it bunched up, but still wrapped it around her arm a few times. She hoped that would hold as she let the sleeve of the flannel shirt fall back into place.

It wasn't much of a weapon, but if this guy meant her harm, she didn't have much of a chance to begin with.

She went to the door and pulled it open. Outside was a cool October day, or was it November now? Her sense of the time had been lost being out there. The trees were nearly bare; the leaves forming a bed of dead and discarded to be walked on. The clearing around the house was covered in them, and nowhere was there a trace that animals had been through there to rustle them.

The woods were still, the air quiet, as not even a breeze dared to stir. They were in a place out of time.

"Please, I must get this piece back to my master."

"If it's so important, why didn't he come?"

"He is very busy and doesn't make public appearances, especially during daylight hours. Just know that his money is good."

Lizzie eased herself down, remembering when she had fallen out of the kitchen, when she hadn't realized that the steps were gone. The Englishman reached a hand out to help her, but she waved him off. Just being this close to him put the hairs on the back of her neck on end. The last thing she wanted to do was touch him.

As she heard the gravel crunch beneath her feet, she looked around. She saw all her dead standing in the backyard. Were they going to rush her, or rush the both of them? No, they were all just standing there, watching. They seemed to be studying the man and were as weary of him as she was.

Lizzie, you should just run right back into that house and lock the doors. Hide. Get away from him. Get away from him now!

The voice was screaming inside her head, and she had a hard time ignoring it. What was it about this man? She pushed down her fears and led them both to the barn. She had to admit to herself that she was more than a little curious as to what they were going to find in there. She'd been wanting to explore it, but feared what it might contain.

The door was unlocked, only kept closed by a large wooden board that was held in place by metal hooks. She pulled up on the board. It was heavy as she feared, but as she wiggled and worked at it, she felt it lifting from its holders. The Englishman stood behind her, and she was thankful that he didn't try to help her.

She set the bar to the side of the door with a grunt and looked back at him. He turned away from her, looking over to where Roland stood by the house. They seemed to be glaring at each other.

"You'll have to point out which one is yours." She said as she opened the door.

"He didn't leave them labeled?" The Englishman seemed to be astonished by this, which Lizzie shrugged off.

"I don't know if he did or not. I haven't been in here before."

"These pieces are worth a lot of money. Anyone could just come and claim them. You need to be much more wary, Miss."

Lizzie was beginning to get the feeling that each time he said 'miss', it was because he was trying to get her to tell him her name. She didn't know why, but she had a feeling that giving him her name was a very bad idea. It wasn't just because of her uncle having never done so. There was something else, some instinct that told her that giving this man her name meant he would have some kind of control over her.

She shook off the feeling as they both stepped into the building.

* * * *

Inside, it was a barn, not the insidious killing chamber, that had somehow filled her thoughts over the last couple of weeks. She thought her uncle couldn't be wrapped up in anything satanic or crazy garbage like that. Maybe at first, when Sarah and her had visited the place. There were crazy runes and markings throughout the house that had made them question it, but reading through more and more of his diaries, she couldn't see that man being a part of something so obviously sinister.

Her uncle seemed to be more about just surviving than getting into the dark stuff. He was like her, trying to figure out what was going on, but not having much information to work with. Many of his books in the house were dealing with Wicca and finding ways of using earth magic to push back the dark forces that followed him.

So why had she expected something truly hideous out there?

You were trying to convince yourself of something bad out here, so then you wouldn't want to see it. You didn't want to take the chance that they would attack you again.

And that was true. She didn't want another confrontation with Sarah, whom she still tried to reconcile her once friend with the monster who now led the dead outside.

"This place is a mess." The Englishman said as he turned on lights. The switch had been next to the door, but she had ignored it as she had just stepped inside, looking around, not having ever seen anything like how her uncle had designed it. She assumed it was him.

For starters, as the lights flickered to life, she was taken aback by just how much light there was. It gave the sun-filled day outside a run for its money, as there were lights everywhere. That wasn't surprising considering what she read about how he feared a shadow woman, as he called her. Lizzie still felt the shape looked more like a man, but it was hard to differentiate.

The ceiling was high, which she supposed was to be expected in barns as they were such tall buildings, and hanging from the support beams were rows of lights. There were many fluorescent lights, but there were also rows of string lights that cascaded lower. This was supplemented by more string lights that weren't hanging but were part of the actual tall ceiling, which seemed like their only purpose was to keep out shadows above the hanging lights.

All these lights shined down to a very bright area where there were no dark shapes. The wooden tables that should have had shadows beneath them were lit by under table strips of the same string lights that hung high overhead. There were absolutely no shadows to be found.

Along the walls were work benches, the area left cluttered with tools, parts, and clocks at various stages of completion. The center of the area had a table with three clocks lying on it and next to it stood two grandfather clocks that were both taller than her.

Then all of it ended. About halfway to the back of the barn was a void, an ending to everything that was light as the room just ended in darkness. It had to be a large curtain her uncle had put up, and she was curious as to what lay beyond it.

"It's a little too bright for me." The Englishman said, and Lizzie looked back to see he had retreated to the threshold of the barn. He looked ill, his face twisted in discomfort.

"You okay?"

"Yes, I'll be fine. If you would please, retrieve my master's clock. I believe it to be that one, right there." He was pointing at one that was on the table, and she was glad to see that it wasn't one of the ones that looked like it was open and ready for some major clock surgery.

"But you're sure you're going to be okay?"

He was rubbing his lips like he needed a drink. She'd seen that look, having been around one or two alcoholics in the past. It was the look of desperation that needed to have something when they knew they should try not to give in. It was usually the look one had right before they crashed and found the bottom of a bottle.

The man nodded and gave her a quick glance, but then he returned to staring at the clock.

She stepped over to the table and reached out for the one he had pointed to, but stopped as her hands neared it. There was something...off about the clock. There was some kind of energy that pulsated from it.

She could feel a rhythm coming from it, but it wasn't from the mechanical innards. The clock wasn't ticking at all. Nothing was working to tell time as far as she could see. Yet, there was something thrumming from it, like it had its own hum.

She could feel her stomach getting queasy and knew it was just being in such proximity to the item. It didn't matter if there was something wrong it with, she just needed to pick it up and hand it to the stranger. Then she would never have to see the device again and this feeling would just go away.

But there was an itch at the back of her skull, and she knew that if she gave it to the man, this feeling just wouldn't go away. It would stay with her and eat at her very soul. This clock was a part of her now, and it was evil. It wanted to devour her. It wanted to devour any live soul that ever touched the device. Any living flesh that caressed its crimson varnish would always be a part of it.

She looked over at the Englishman and saw the black gloves that he wore. He knew. He knew that if she touched it, there would be something that would happen to her. He wasn't going to touch it himself; he had worn the gloves. She hadn't thought of it before because, well, he was English. She had thought it was just something he wore and had with him, like an umbrella and wearing a top hat or whatever those hats were called they so often had on their heads.

He wore no hat, and he had no umbrella. Those gloves weren't for some formal style.

She turned back and looked at the clock. This time she studied it, but was careful not to let herself touch it, no matter how much she felt herself being pulled to pick it up.

She had been wrong before. The intense light above hadn't gotten rid of all the shadows. In fact, as she looked at the clock, it seemed like there were all kinds of them. And there were those dots on the face of it. She could almost believe that they were eyes that were looking at her, but that made no sense. Like how the arms seemed to twist up and reach out for her, stretched to become tentacles. There were all these shapes, runes on the face of the clock, tattoos of different colors, but they danced together until they too went black. That blackness joined with the hands as they elongated towards her.

She blinked and pulled herself back just as she felt it was getting near her. She had to turn herself away, and physically step back so she could breathe, the air having been sucked out of her lungs. Her head was woozy. She wasn't sure if she was going to pass out as the barn spun around her.

"Miss?"

She looked over at the man, but he wasn't a man anymore. He was a tall black shape with horns protruding from his scalp and long nails from what had been his hands. Those weren't hands anymore, as now she could see the large talons protruding.

He lifted a leg; he was going to take a step into the barn but stopped himself. It was too late. She saw now that he wasn't wearing shoes. His feet they were hooves and there was just the trace of hair coming out from under his suit leg to sprout over the hoof.

She took another step back, now close enough to one of the workbenches to reach out and grab it for support while she continued to work at pulling in large puffs of air. She continued to breathe as she closed her eyes. Mentally, she started the count. "One, there's no such thing as demons. Two, there's no way a clock was just about to invade your mind. Three, it was not about to steal your soul. Four. Five. Six, there are no such things as demons. Seven, Eight, and your dead best friend and ex-boyfriend shouldn't be outside either, but they are. Nine. Ten, there's no such thing as demons."

She opened her eyes and looked at the Englishman standing in the doorway, his demonic shape gone, leaving only those deep hollow eyes to look at her. She didn't, however, turn to look back at the clock. She didn't have to, as even before the crazy vision had started; the foulness of that design would be burned into her mind to be seen every time she closed her eyes.

The wood had been varnished in a dark crimson as though soaked in the blood of man and left to dry into it. She hadn't been able to make out many of the details, but like the runes she had seen swirling on the face, there had been similar ones burned into the wood. Each of the top corners were adorned with red carved jewels that were shaped into gargoyle like creatures whose mouths were open, long fangs extending ready to bite. Not only was the clock hungry for her, but she felt like even these depictions of creatures starved and thirsted to taste her.

Even with her back turned to the thing, she feared that it was reaching out to try for her once again. She wanted to turn around to make sure it was still sitting where she had set it down. She knew she was turning; she needed to know...

411

She had to physically reach out for the workbench to keep her from turning around. Her shoulders tensed as her body was rigid with anticipation of feeling its icy touch, but she couldn't do it. Instead, she focused on her breathing.

What the hell was that thing? Why did her uncle have it in his workplace?

"Miss, I can see you are not feeling well. If you'd just hand me the item, I will gladly be on my way."

She wanted to turn to the man and tell him to come in there and get the damned thing himself. He wanted the thing. She didn't want to go near it again and she was sure as hell not going to touch it. He must have realized what she was thinking, as he eased closer to the threshold and was looking around at the room.

"I think I see some gloves behind you. If you do not wish to touch it, you may wear those."

Lizzie turned and sure enough, there was a box of latex gloves open, one glove partially dangling out of the top. She grabbed out two and pulled them on. They felt like powder to the touch.

She didn't look directly at the clock, keeping her face turned away and only seeing it out of the corner of her eye. Even as she did so, she could see tendrils of darkness floating around it, ready to seek out a new victim to be entangled in its web.

The wood was like ice, she could feel it freezing chill even through the gloves, and she knew that even though she wasn't looking at it. Those dark tendrils were wrapping around her hands as she picked it up. Their touch could be felt on her wrists and goosebumps formed up and down her arm. The desire to turn and look at it burned in her chest. She refused to breathe, instead staying focused on shuffling her feet as she made her way to the door.

She felt the weight lift from her and nearly turned to look at the Englishman holding it. She averted her eyes but saw out of the side that he was looking directly at it. The darkness did not reach out to him but ignored his presence. They were there, but not there for him.

He produced a cloth bag from somewhere; she wasn't sure where and slipped it over the clock.

"I'm disappointed that Mr. Hooper was unable to get the clock working." He said as he continued to hold the clock. Now she could look at him and watch as he held it delicately, holding it from the bottom and keeping it close to himself.

"Yeah, well, I'm sorry his death is an inconvenience to you."

The Englishman looked at her sharply over the top of the clock.

"I could walk with you back to the house. Maybe we could have some tea?"

"I'm all out." Lizzie said, and she wasn't sure what it was, but she no longer felt safe leaving the barn while he was there. It wasn't like she felt safe in the barn, even with that clock gone. There was something about the house that when she entered it, it felt like the weight of the dead was lifted from her. That effect, she realized, didn't extend to the barn. Much of the pain she'd realized, the loss of friends, how they were killed all because of her, came crashing down on her harder than before.

"Well, I would like to sit down with you and have a chat. My employer loves to help those who are seeking to stay hidden from the world. I'm sure you have some skill that he would love to help nurture. It had been pure luck coming across Mr. Hooper, but my employer has an amazing ability for seeking out individuals. I think it would be beneficial to both of us if we could go inside."

"I'm sorry, but not today." There wasn't a chance in hell that Lizzie was going to let him in the house.

"That's too bad. May I inquire as to why?" He looked around as though checking out the additional dead who had been gathering around them while they were in the barn. Lizzie noticed that none of them ventured onto the path.

Lizzie, don't fool yourself. That's probably just a coincidence. They'll still attack you the moment they get a chance.

And she thought that was probably true. Still, she wasn't the only one watching them. He was as well, and he turned back to her, showing her the first hint of a smile she had seen on his stoic face.

"I could at least walk you to your cabin."

He held out a hand to her, now holding the clock with the other.

She didn't know why, but every sense inside her told her not to trust this man. It had nothing to do with the craziness the clock had shown her, but she couldn't shake that demonic image from her head, either.

"I'll be just fine." She said, not taking a step past the threshold.

Slowly, he closed the hand that she had left ignored. He then looked at her straight into her eyes. She could see the darkness there, lurking behind them, and then nodded to her. Then he was gone, walking quickly around the house towards the front.

She didn't leave the barn. She waited until she heard his car starting and the crunch of gravel under his tires as he drove down the long driveway. The sound never came to her.

Most of the dead had lingered near the barn, but Roland had followed the man around. After a while, he came back and rushed over to the barn.

"He's not leaving."

"What?"

"He's just sitting in his car, watching the house."

"What the hell is he waiting for?"

"I don't know."

Lizzie wasn't sure why the man was still there either, but as long as he stayed, she wasn't leaving. She was trapped there.

Trapped in the house, trapped in the barn, what difference does it make?

She pushed the thought out of her mind as she stepped away from the door. Looking around, she found nothing other than stools near work benches to sit on. She didn't feel like sitting up, so she closed the barn door and leaned back against it, sinking slowly to the floor.

"Trapped again. Trapped, trapped, trapped yet again." She chanted as she closed her eyes and rested her head against the hard wood.

CHAPTER 34

She was back in the apartment building; the walls were covered in the graffiti that changed every time she was there. It was *the* dream again. The nightmare that always tried to explain something to her that she never quite understood.

Again, there was the rustling of the plastic, carried on wind she didn't feel. It was all the same. She didn't even bother looking into the plastic room to see the darkness hiding there. It was where the shadow man stayed when he was not tearing apart her life.

She walked right past it and straight to the apartment door. It was numbered 23. Strangely, she didn't remember the number before. What had been on the door before? She felt like she had looked at it, but thinking about past trips down this hall were blurred into obscurity. She wasn't sure if she had ever looked at the dark red door or not.

It opened for her when she turned the knob, and she walked effortlessly into the room. Inside, the old woman was sitting there in her chair, drinking something that looked like tea. It was steaming, hot and fresh, and the old woman was blowing on it before each sip. In the kitchen, Lizzie could hear someone moving around and the clang as though they were putting away pots and pans. Maybe the granddaughter was back there after having just served her grandmother.

The old woman looked up at Lizzie as she entered, a look of shock on her face, but she didn't spill her tea. No matter how much the old woman's hands shook, either from some illness or the effort of being there, the tea never spilled. Lizzie had a quick thought, wondering if that was the case in the real world, and wasn't sure if she would ever find out.

"You are here?" She asked and Lizzie didn't know why she did it, but as she entered the room, she turned and closed the door behind her.

"I guess so." She said as she turned back to face the woman. There was something different this time, and she could feel it. She didn't have that tension she normally felt when she was there. Sure, it was a dream, but even in a dream, your heart can race, and you can feel fear. This was calmer, more relaxed. She didn't feel like she was rushing, and when she closed the door, it wasn't to keep something from getting to them. It was simply, she realized, out of courtesy.

"You are here, while I believe it is at its weakest. Smart. Maybe now you will come to me..." the woman said, but as she spoke, her voice trailed off. Lizzie realized that the woman didn't mean to say what she had just said. Lizzie didn't know why, but she suddenly didn't trust the old woman as much as she had on previous visits. Without all the tension, she could focus on thinking, not being rushed. The woman no longer felt like her savior before being eaten alive. No, now Lizzie felt like she had been running from a bear just to run into a wolf's den and was standing before the open mouth of the Alpha, staring down its long row of teeth.

Before, she had longed and looked to the old woman as being a way to save her, but why did this old woman care about her? What was she getting out of helping Lizzie?

"You are here, but something is different. You aren't where you normally are. There is something near you, something just as dark, as dangerous as it is." The old woman said, squinting as she was studying Lizzie. Lizzie thought about turning around and running back out of the door. Where would she run? To the darkness down the hall? Where else did she have to go?

"What do you mean?" Lizzie approached the old woman cautiously. The woman in the kitchen was stirring something in a pot. Lizzie didn't know how she knew it was a woman but realized that she did and knew who it was. It was the woman she had seen on the street when she had been with Jessica. It had been the one they tried to save. The one who had screamed at her and run away in terror, but what was she doing there?

That was when Lizzie realized she could smell something, too. It was lingering in the room, like that of burnt meat. It didn't smell right; the meat smelled sour, like it had rotted. It mixed with the fragrance of piss wafting in from the hallway and Lizzie was sure that had this not been a dream, she would be gagging.

The old woman seemed to notice Lizzie's discomfort, and then somehow all the offending smells were gone.

"Sorry about that. Normally, I am prepared for you. I have to be, to fight it as long as I do. You caught me off guard. Wasn't ready."

"I've taken naps during the day before. Why had you not come then?"

"I don't know. Something is different this time. This time, you found me."

"Why? How?"

"Maybe your mind is getting used to the connection. Maybe you are starting to seek me out when you sleep. Could be many things. Some things we may never know." The old woman said as she took a long drink of her cooling tea. It stained her lips when she drank, as when she pulled the cup away. They were red from the thick liquid.

"So why am I here? I remember you. I remember dreaming of you, but why?"

"You are cursed. Your family is cursed. I cannot say much more. It is weakened during the day as it is a creature of the dark, but it is not sleeping and is not powerless. I still cannot say too much. You must come find me."

"How? Where? I don't know who you are." Lizzie couldn't help but keep glancing at the cup. She assumed it was tea, maybe coffee, but neither stained your lips red. What was in that cup?

"I cannot tell you that. He is waiting for me too. He will strike then as he had done before."

"He?"

"He, It. It is whatever it chooses. For your uncle, it often took the shape of a woman to torture him. For you, it molests you as a he."

"Why?"

420

"He is a trickster. I tell you this every time and you must remember it. He plays only by rules he designs. You cannot trust what you know of him. He plays with your mind not because he needs to, but because he enjoys it. He feeds off the dead. He does not need you to fear him. That he does for his own pleasure. He is old like me. He gets bored. He entertains himself with your suffering, I think."

"Okay, so how do I stop this? How do I get my life back?" Lizzie said and took a step forward towards the old woman. She dropped to one knee and was about to reach out and grasp the woman's hands in desperation with her plea, but stopped herself as the smell of copper caught her attention. She again looked at the half-empty cup. There were red stains on the rim of the glass. Dark red. It looked like blood.

The old woman smiled as she took another long sip.

The sounds coming from the other room stopped and Lizzie suddenly had the sense that someone was listening to them. Someone or something. Before she had known that the person in the kitchen was that girl Lizzie had seen, the one she knew of as this woman's granddaughter, though she couldn't remember how she knew that. Now she wasn't so sure as she saw the old woman tense at the silence in the room.

"I cannot tell you. Not here. You must seek me out, but for now, you must go."

"But how do I find you?"

"Silly girl, look around you. I'm not hard to find." The woman was laughing, and the red liquid dripped down from the side of her lips. Maybe Lizzie was wrong, and this wasn't a dream, as it sure felt like it was quickly becoming a nightmare. At any time, she felt like the old woman would stand up and start chasing after her.

Was everyone in her life evil? How had she fallen into such a world of darkness? She didn't know who to trust. She thought this woman would help her.

Lizzie hurried out into the hall, escaping the sudden chill she had felt in the room. The goosebumps from her arm had spread throughout her body and she had to control herself from shivering.

Back in the hallway, she had the déjà vu sensation. It wasn't the same as when she had gone in. She felt like something should be there, something she was afraid of, something that always chased her down the hall. This was when the darkness would be after her, and she thought she could feel a taint of its presence.

No, it wasn't there. She felt the pull again to the plastic covered room, but she ignored it. She just stood there, looking around. She wasn't sure where to go. This is where the dream would usually end. She would leave the apartment and get chased. Without the chaser, she wasn't sure what to do.

On the wall across from the apartment was a myriad of graffiti. Whenever she went there, she would read what was scrawled there, usually something dark written in large letters covering much of the wall. It was hard not to notice it, but as she looked closer at it, there was more to the graffiti than she had noticed before. There were other sayings that were smaller, some written under the larger dark sayings, and some integrated into it.

As she looked, she saw that much of it was written in beautiful letters, painted in a bright blue. There were poems of the light and of peaceful dreams. Poems about flowers, green grass fields, and a calm river during the morning dawn. Then she noticed it. Hidden small amongst the lovely writings was an address.

The old woman's words came back to her, "Silly girl, look around you."

Lizzie started to chant the address to herself, afraid she would forget it as the world around her slipped away.

* * * *

Lizzie woke up on the floor of the barn and shivered from the chill. She saw her breath as it left her mouth; the mist swirling around her face. She hadn't remembered it being this cold before, and now it seeped into her. Her jeans felt wet beneath her, and she wasn't sure of them really being moist or if it was due to the cold floor beneath her.

Slowly she stood, using the door behind her to guide her up while she wrapped her arms around her. Her head felt heavy, her thinking slow as the realm of dreams struggled to keep hold.

She was still chanting the address. She realized it, and moved faster, looking around her franticly until she came across the pad of paper on a side workbench. She hurried and wrote down the address.

"Wha la!" she exclaimed, happy with herself that she had finally pulled that scrap of information from the dream. Then her happiness evaporated as she remembered the woman laughing at her, blood covering her teeth and lips as Lizzie had rushed to flee the apartment. Was this really the woman she would hope to have some answers for her? She was relying on her to be her salvation.

What was the woman's motivation for helping her? Why was she so willing to get involved with the darkness? She had to have a reason. Everyone had an angle. She wasn't going to just lift this curse from her out of the goodness of her heart.

Could she trust this woman? Lizzie wasn't sure of the answer.

She looked up from the pad of paper and at the curtain she was now much closer to, having rushed over to the paper.

It wasn't a curtain. It wasn't anything. It was pure darkness. No matter how many lights were in the barn, the back half was lost to it.

She was much closer to it than she now felt comfortable. It was... unsettling. How had she not noticed before that there was nothing? Not nothing in the way that the room was empty, but the room was completely gone. This wasn't right, and she suddenly worried that she was going to get pulled into it.

It was drawing her closer to it. It wanted her to be a part of it. It was why the paper had been so close to it. The darkness had moved it. She sensed that her uncle would never have been so close to it. All the workbenches were empty this close to it. It had been the one to move to the pad of paper.

Lizzie, that's insane. You're losing it again. Take a deep breath. It's just a curtain. You'll see... But it might not be a bad idea to go back into the cabin.

Lizzie stepped away from it and back to the door. Her feet felt heavy, her body slow to leave the darkness behind.

"It's where the shadow man is from," said another voice inside her head. This one was different, a stronger voice that felt like it was more than her own thoughts. She didn't know why, but she trusted it and believed it. This is the darkness she had felt when she had tried to stop it. Somehow, this was the darkness from the time before light had come into this world.

She opened the door to the barn, wanting to hurry back to the cabin, when she stopped. It was snowing outside. It was the first fall snow, but there was already enough of it to coat the ground in a layer of white.

It seemed too early for the white powder now covering the ground as it hadn't been that cold before today. Now the temperature had significantly dropped and there it was.

She looked at the couple of dead people walking around the house. They grew bored, she could tell, and while they hated her for what she had done, they also tried to keep themselves busy. Elisabeth and Josh were walking hand in hand. She noticed that her dead friends didn't leave footprints in the snow. That was interesting, as the undead things had felt real enough to kick her ass.

So, the dead didn't leave footprints... Well, if they didn't, then whose footprints did she see walking around her house, up to the back door and then continuing?

Someone else was there...

CHAPTER 35

"Hey, so what you up to?" Sarah asked. She was smiling that broad smile she often wore, especially when they were out of school. Lizzie looked over to her, as she had just finished hefting the last of the suitcases into her parents' car. Her parents were going on a weekend getaway, which was frustrating as Lizzie had just turned eighteen last week and wanted to go somewhere herself. Now she was going to be stuck staying home and watching her brother.

"Nothing. I'm stuck on nurse duty."

"Eww, that sucks. Just for the night?"

Lizzie pointed to the suitcases. She never knew why her parents had to pack so much shit when they were only going away for a couple of days. It was like they were running off somewhere and would never return. She swore her mother had most of her clothes spread out into two bags.

"For the weekend."

"And they packed that much?"

"I know, right? I swear they're running off and leaving us here."

"Maybe. You can be a handful." Lizzie looked at her friend and gave her a playful shove.

"And you're not? They're running to get away from you, most likely."

Sarah started looking more closely at how many bags were in the car and what kind of stuff they were taking with them.

"You know, your mom packs almost as much stuff as you do for a one-night stay over at your aunts."

Lizzie glared back at Sarah but couldn't hold the expression as she broke out laughing.

"Hey, you try going to her house and not packing everything. She has no internet. Really? Who today lives with no internet. It's like going to visit the stone ages. I have to bring some kind of entertainment, and I pack extra in case she decided she also didn't need electricity."

"Who are you girls talking about?" Lizzie's dad came out of the house, and he smiled at them. Did the look linger on Sarah just a little bit longer than when he smiled at his own daughter? Lizzie couldn't tell, and why did that matter? Lizzie smiled back, looking at his pale face. She knew he had been upset lately. Something was going on and as much as both her parents tried to hide it, she could tell. They hadn't been fighting in front of her, but there had been a lot of hushed words and then silence when she entered a room.

"Aunt Theresa," Lizzie said as she reached up to close the back of the SUV.

"Hold up, let me put these in there," her dad said. She stopped, and he tossed in his laptop bag as well as her mom's iPad case. "There's nothing wrong with your mom's sister. She just has her own...quirks and doesn't trust the outside world."

"Much like Uncle Tom." Lizzie added as she closed the door.

"I hope not. He's got his own problems."

"Oh, really?" Sarah asked. "You know, I think you're the only family on the planet that can claim not only one hermit relative, but two. It's like you two were made for each other."

Was that a dig? Lizzie looked at Sarah, who was studying her father. Lizzie didn't know why, but she had a thought trying to break free from the back of her mind. A little voice was trying to speak up and tell her that something was off between these two.

But that was crazy, and Sarah was right. It was like her only two extended family were both trying to hide themselves from the rest of the world. It really was strange. She barely thought of her aunt as she hadn't visited her in over a year and was often only sent there while her parents went on long trips.

"Yeah, well, we can't pick our family," Lizzie's dad said as he was double checking his pockets. Lizzie knew the ritual as he was checking to see what he might be forgetting. He was still talking to them, but mentally he was checking off a list in his head, going over everything he thought they might need. Sometimes he would mumble it aloud, and other times he would even say it aloud mid conversation.

This time was different though, as she watched him from having that unfocused look to completely dazing out. He drifted away from them, his words growing vacant as he looked off into the distance. Then he snapped back and looked at them as though he was surprised they were still there.

"Maybe you should go to your aunts this weekend. The both of you, take your brother with."

Lizzie had looked at him, her mouth dropping open.

"No way, you know I got that thing tomorrow and Sarah and I plan on going to the movies later." Lizzie didn't want to mention that she had planned on going to a book reading on Saturday as her thing. Sarah was her best friend, but she still would tease her about going to see her favorite author read a chapter from his latest book. Books weren't Sarah's thing, as she was more about clothes and make-up.

"I'm just thinking it might be better…"

"Dad, I'm eighteen now. I'm a big girl."

"What's going on?" Liz's mother asked as she came out. She handed her husband his cell phone, and he smiled. The mental light coming on that the object he had been trying to find had been realized and found.

"Dad thinks I should go to Aunt Theresa's when I have stuff planned this weekend." Lizzie said, her lower lip already extending into a pout. She knew it was childish, but also that her mom would often cave to it. That pout was the reason why she had not just her favorite book series in not only hardcover but also the collector's edition signed by the author. She knew how to get her way.

"Don't worry hun. I'm sure he's just kidding."

"I don't know. It wouldn't be a bad idea, and it'd make sure someone was watching out for Brian."

"They'll be fine."

"Besides, Lizzie's got me to take care of her." Sarah said, nearly bouncing with the giddiness of a teenage girl trying to emulate a toddler in a candy store.

"I guess," her father said, exasperated, as he walked around to the driver's side of the car. Lizzie's mother usually drove when they were going on trips, but Lizzie had overheard her complaining of a headache earlier. She'd asked her dad to drive, and grumbling, he'd said okay.

Now he was looking like he'd eaten something that hadn't agreed with him, his face pale and grave. He let out a burp that looked painful and after opening the car door; he paused to place his hand gently over his stomach.

"Dad, you okay?"

"You okay to drive, hun?"

"Mr. Rogers, you're not looking too good."

"I'm fine," he said, forcing a smile as he looked at each of them to reassure them.

Lizzie gave her mom a hug but kept looking at her dad. He seemed to be holding the car door for support with his one hand and had pulled his other away from his stomach to play with the car keys.

"Have a good weekend." Her mother said, her smile tight as she kept following her daughters' glances with a concerned look of her own.

"You too. I love you and I'll keep a good eye on B."

"Promise? You're not just going to leave him with the nurses all weekend, you'll actually hang out."

"Sure."

Lizzie hurried around the car and gave her dad a big hug. He smiled down at her and that was when she saw the red rim around the center of his eye. She knew what it meant. They were going to die. She knew it and she tried desperately to grab her father, to stop him from going. She tried to turn to her mom and tell her not to get into the car. She wanted to steal the keys and throw them into the bushes in the neighbor's yard.

She didn't do any of it, and it was then that she realized she'd become a passenger in her own body. The events progressed without her being able to change any of it. She was screaming, but her mouth never moved. Her father gave her that little peck on her cheek as he often did, and then he looked over to Sarah, jokingly telling her to keep an eye on his little girl.

"Sure thing," she'd said, while flashing that half smile, she'd use whenever she was playing at being mischievous.

Then he got in the car, her mom already in the passenger seat and fighting with the seat belt lock as it refused to fasten.

Lizzie could see that same woman, the incredible person who gave birth to her, hanging impaled on a tree, the seat belt having not held her when the semi slammed into the driver's side of the car. The force of the sudden collision had thrown her, and she had gone high into the nearby woods, a limb spearing her. She didn't die immediately, but suffered in agony, calling out for Lizzie as she struggled to pull herself free.

Lizzie smiled and waved, "You guys have a good trip," her mouth said while she tried to plead with her parents, her mind begging them not to go.

Her dad climbed into the driver's seat, and she saw with complete clarity, his legs trapped under the steering wheel while his torso, severed by force alone as he had forgotten to wear his seatbelt, was through the windshield and in the front grill of the semi. His head was crushed into metal, eyes liquified by force and drizzled down his face like white cream and mingled with red blood and green antifreeze.

Lizzie was gagging in her mind, watching helplessly as the car backed down the driveway. Sarah, at some point, had come up behind her and wrapped her arm over Lizzie's shoulders.

"Don't ya worry. I'll take good care of you." Sarah had accentuated the word 'good', and Lizzie looked over her shoulder to see that grin growing as she looked at Lizzie. No longer was it the Sarah of her childhood standing there. This was the new one, the one Lizzie had only recently come to know, and Lizzie no longer trusted that smile as Sarah's smile grew, revealing sharpened teeth. The mouth opened wider and wider until all that remained was darkness and Lizzie was falling into it.

"We'll have all kinds of fun..."

* * * *

That smug smile. It had always been Sarah's thing to flash that smile that always said she was a little smarter than everyone else in the room. She would just walk into some place and cock her hip to the side, smile, and Lizzie had felt the air as everyone waited for her next move. Sarah, who she had always thought was her...

She'd been putting off dealing with the revelation that Sarah had something to do with her parents' death. Even as she remembered it, she still could only partially believe it. It seemed so impossible. How could someone who had been so close to her have kept something, her true nature, so well hidden?

That was over. As Sarah walked around from the side of the house, she was flashing that same annoying smile. Lizzie was done not dealing with it. It didn't matter if the Englishman was out there walking around the house. Let him have her. Let him have the clock, the house, every damned thing he wanted. Right now, she only wanted one thing, and that was to put that bitch in her place.

Where had this anger come from? A tiny voice in the back of her head tried to challenge her, but she pushed it away as she stepped out of the barn, her eyes locked on Sarah. For a moment, when their eyes met, she saw the fear come into Sarah's eyes, and then it was gone, as well as the smile.

"So, you killed my parents?" Lizzie growled as she rushed across the snow-covered grass. Sarah was already backpedaling. Lizzie sped up as she saw the other girl getting nervous. "You killed them? You!?"

It was as much of an accusation as it was a question. She reached where her friend was and went to slap her. Sarah was quick, and she ducked the blow, spinning around out of reach of Lizzie. Lizzie had overextended putting her weight into it and stumbled into the side of the house, which she hit with a solid thump.

"Look who finally grew herself some balls." Sarah said, regaining some of her composure. "Time to chop them off."

Lizzie didn't get to turn around. She was still trying to get her balance, using the house to guide her, when she felt a force from behind her slam her into the wall. Then her hair was pulled back. She couldn't see what had her, but she heard Sarah laughing as she was tugged forward, her face pressing against the siding.

"Yeah, you still harping on it. Yes. I killed them. I'll kill you too."

Lizzie felt her scalp light on fire as her hair was pulled back and then she was falling. Nothing held her up and her ass landed on the ground, hard, a few feet back from where she had been being grounded into the house.

Sarah was standing over her, smiling as she looked down at her.

When Sarah touched her or grabbed her, Lizzie wasn't sure how to describe it. It wasn't like a hand had grabbed her, where she could feel the texture and solidness of it. If someone off the street came up to her and slammed her or choked her with their hands, she would feel the warmth, the hardness of their touch, the roughness of the callouses on their skin. It would be something tangible and, if someone did that to her, she could fight back, bite the hand, and dig her nails into it.

When Sarah attacked her, it never felt that way. It had to be because Sarah and the rest of them were dead because when they attacked, all she felt was force and pull. She saw, when she was facing them, the hands they used, but she never physically felt them. She didn't know how else to describe it. It was like some invisible force was being used, but it wasn't them directly.

Lizzie wasn't sure what she had been thinking when she had run out there to attack Sarah.

Because you hadn't been thinking. That's what you get when you let your rage do that for you. You end up on snow-covered ground, cold and wet and getting your ass kicked.

The voice was right, and Lizzie realized she should be scared. Sarah had her trapped. She was on the side of the house now. The front and back door were both out of view. She had nowhere to go, and Sarah must have known, as she was lauding it over Lizzie with that pretentious smile.

"Now, what are you going to do?"

Lizzie wasn't sure what she could do, but she twisted herself in a roll so she could quickly get her knee under her. This got her standing in a run, and she was going to run away. Then there was a tug around her midsection, and she could feel herself turning, being redirected toward the wall again. She kept running, an immeasurable weight wrapped around her, but she continued to fight. Each step was a tremendous amount of effort. *I bet you miss those work out sessions Jessica always tried to get you too.* Her teeth were clenched, and she felt the sweat beading on her forehead.

"Where do you think you're going?" Sarah grunted from behind her. Somehow, Sarah was managing to hold her. With how small Sarah's frame was, there had to be more to it to slow Lizzie down. It felt like she was tied to an anvil as the harder she tried, her breath now coming in short gasps, the little ground she gained.

So Lizzie did the opposite. She switched momentum, pushing herself back and pitching her elbow high. It was something she'd seen Jessica do on the few occasions she'd seen her friend train and knew that it was what self-defense coaches would teach in this situation.

436

The blow never connected to anything solid, but she did feel the grip on her let loose. This resulted in her again being off balance and losing her footing. She fell only inches from the siding, *but hey, at least you didn't hit the wall this time.* She barely had time to process the thought as she was already moving, crawling towards the front of the house, working to get on her feet.

"You fucking bitch." Sarah said behind her, and Lizzie knew she was close. Before she was all the way up, she twisted and lunged at where she'd heard her voice. Sarah was right where she thought she'd be, but she was quick, sure-footed, and had the agility of someone who had danced nearly all her life. She was out of Lizzie's way, and once again Lizzie fell to the ground.

Lizzie was beginning to feel like a bull. She was being toyed with. She could tell that Sarah was just having fun playing with her while she waited to take her kill shot.

...Or was she waiting for something else?

The snow continued to fall around her, and she felt the chill as the little flakes melted on her arm. Was it just her imagination or was it getting darker around her? The tree's shadows grew longer, stretching forwards her.

Why would the trees have shadows? It's snowing. The day was overcast. Where was there light to form shadows? There wasn't anything she could see, unless-

He was coming...

She felt it in her stomach, a growing anticipation expecting him to appear at any time.

She had to get back into the house. It would be safe there. She'd be warm, and it would all just go away.

Lizzie turned to see that Sarah was watching her, her hip cocked to the side and her hand resting on her side.

"What? Finally figured it out?"

Lizzie didn't know what Sarah was talking about, but didn't care. Lizzie had to go through her to get to the house.

Lizzie dashed for her. This time she went in like a linebacker going for the tackle. She kept her body low, her arms wide, and moved quickly to go in for the hit. She had fire that burned in her eyes, and she kept sight of Sarah as she moved. So, when Sarah didn't move but was somehow gone, when Lizzie ran through where she should have been, she knew this was a fight she could not win.

Lizzie kept running. She hadn't overextended this time or stopped when Sarah had disappeared. She kept her footing and put on the speed. She was aiming towards the back of the house, having started in that direction, and refusing to take the time to turn around.

"Get back here, you bitch!" Sarah called after her.

"...Not ...on... your... life..." Lizzie panted from exertion; the fight having worn her out more than she'd realized.

"I'm going to get you!" Sarah yelled.

Lizzie didn't turn around, though she could feel that Sarah was catching up to her. She couldn't stop. She made it to the corner and then neared the back door of the house. She knew she hadn't locked it.

The closer she got, she put on another burst of speed to reach it. She could feel something brushing against her shoulder, like someone reaching out to pull her back, but wasn't quite able to reach her. She might have been imagining it, but she wasn't going to take that chance. Once she reached the door, she would lose all speed as she had to stop to open it. She would fight the bitch then.

So, when the door opened in front of her, a dark shape she couldn't make out standing just inside the threshold, Lizzie didn't take the time to worry about it. She just felt a strong tug against her shoulder when she launched herself in the open doorway and quickly scrambled to get her feet past the unseen barrier.

"Close it. Close the door, close it!" She screamed.

The door slammed shut behind her, and Lizzie turned to glare at the intruder in her house.

CHAPTER 36

"What was that all about?" The voice was familiar, and Lizzie didn't have to wait for her eyes to adjust to the dark to know who her savior had been.

"Jess...? What are you doing here?" Lizzie said as she reached to the counter to pull herself up. As the adrenaline was wearing off, the pain in her knees throbbed and she could feel slivers of cuts burning along her arms and in her palms.

"Really?" Jessica said and there was a bite to her question. Lizzie ignored it as she rushed forward, attacking her in what was the fiercest hug she could manage.

"I thought you were dead." Lizzie felt the wetness on her cheeks as it soaked into the sweater her friend was wearing.

"What the hell? You have some serious explaining to do." Her friend was barely returning the hug, her hands just barely resting on Lizzie's back as Lizzie remained buried in her friend's chest.

"You're not dead. Oh, thank God you're not dead. I was so worried about you. Is Dennis okay?"

"What? Of course, Dennis is okay. Why wouldn't he be?"

That's when Lizzie felt herself being pushed away, and she allowed it, standing up and taking a step back to lean against the counter. She wiped away the tears from her cheeks and looked at her friend. She couldn't stop smiling. Jessica was there. She was standing in Lizzie's kitchen, and she was alive.

That dream Lizzie had had been so real. She had been in Jessica's head and been a part of her while her friend had tried to kick ass. She sure as shit had done better than what Lizzie had just done. How had Jessica ever survived that?

Because it hadn't happened. It had just been a dream. Her whole life had drifted away to feel like one long nightmare. Just what was real anymore?

"He controls the dark spaces and dreams lie in those places to live. Beware your dreams." Lizzie heard the old woman's voice in her head, reminding her of something Lizzie had forgotten.

"Are you okay?" Jessica said, but she didn't reach forward, and she hadn't really returned Liz's hug.

"Yeah, I'm fine."

"Really? Because I just heard you yelling at someone and then I saw you jumping in the back door as though you were being chased."

"Thank you for that." Lizzie couldn't take the way they were both awkwardly standing there and so she stepped around the island and grabbed a glass by the sink. She filled it with water, already dreading the foul taste of the tap water... but she was doing something and hiding her face so that Jessica couldn't look at her.

"For what? I didn't see anyone. No one was out there."

"Hey, did you see a large, dark-colored car when you pulled in?"

"What? No. The driveway was empty other than Roland's car. OMG, why did you take his car!?"

Lizzie finished filling the glass and took a drink, keeping herself turned away from Jessica. She wasn't ready to turn around. Inside her was a war of emotions, with no clear winner as to how she felt. She wasn't sure how much of that was visible, so instead she was feeling them all, at once and in turns. She wanted to throw the glass against the wall, while crying a river of blood drenched tears and hugging her friend. She wanted to fall to the floor and ball herself into a corner, and she wanted to stand there hiding her face in her hands, hidden from everyone and everything that wanted a piece of her.

She wanted to do so much, so instead she did nothing. She stood there and looked at the water as little air bubbles floated in her glass. The water was sour, tasting of both rotten eggs and lead. The pipes were bad, and she'd run out of bottled water.

"Liz?"

Lizzie looked over her shoulder to see that she wasn't the only one who was having a hard time talking. Jessica stood there, her mouth opening and closing like a fish out of water, but no sound escaped them. Her eyes were pleading like she wanted an answer, but wasn't even sure what question she should ask first.

"I'm okay. Really." Lizzie said.

"No, you're not."

"I am," but even as she said it, she knew her friend was right. She wasn't alright and hadn't been since the first time she'd entered this house.

"You look like shit."

"Thank you."

"No, really. You smell like you haven't showered in weeks. You're still wearing the pants and jeans you wore when I last saw you, and your skin is baggy and pale. Have you left this house since Roland died?"

"I told you, I'm fine."

"Liz, stop it!" The volume and command in Jessica's voice brought Lizzie up short. "You're not fine. Don't lie to me."

Lizzie tried to answer. She did. Her mouth opened. She closed it when nothing came out, then she opened it again as she wanted nothing more than to say once again, "I'm alright," but this time mean it as she said it.

But when nothing came out, she lowered her eyes and rushed past her friend to leave the room, no longer able to stay in the kitchen. The house itself felt small and stuffy, and even as she stepped into the dining room, it felt like there wasn't enough room for them. It was making it hard for her to breathe.

"Liz, don't just walk into the other room. Talk to me." Jessica followed her into the dining room but wasn't quick to go any further into the room. Lizzie had been trying to clean up the mess she had found in there when she had inherited it, but it was still a mess. There was just so much to go through. She'd read a few of her uncle's journals and had read a few of his books on witchcraft.

There were still piles and piles of books and clutter that made walking through the small room difficult. Lizzie had gotten used to making it through the mess, but Jessica had to work her way through to where she'd gone. It wasn't far, and with Jessica's

444

grace, she was standing next to Lizzie as she was looking down at one of the journals. It was bookmarked with a picture of Lizzie's parents.

"Liz, I know you've been through a lot, but you need to talk to someone."

"Last person I talked to died. Everyone's dead. Everyone but you."

"Liz, you can't blame yourself."

Liz refused to look at her friend, but kept her eyes locked on her parents' picture. How old were they? It looked like the picture had to have been from before her brother was born, as none of the grey had started in her father's goatee. She'd never seen this picture before, and everyone looked so happy. She hadn't read this journal yet and opened it to the page it marked.

"Can't I?"

"No, you can't." Jessica tried to twist Lizzie around to face her, but Lizzie pulled herself free from Jessica's grasp.

"You should go."

"No."

"I said, you should go. Go, or you'll be like the rest of them." Lizzie nodded as she looked over her shoulder towards the window.

"And I said no." Jessica watched where she was stepping and moved to stand in front of the window Lizzie had turned to. Briefly, their eyes met, and Lizzie quickly turned away, fighting to hold back more tears. She cried a lot, and she felt like she needed to stop doing it so much.

"You'll die. They all do."

"Liz, come on. Everyone dies. Just because someone dies, it doesn't make it your fault, no matter how close or how much you cared for them."

Liz just laughed. If only her friend knew the realms of crazy Lizzie had started to call home. Her life had become a resident in the insane.

She looked around her, knowing that what she was looking for would be nearby. Jessica watched her, though Liz knew she was growing impatient. Why wouldn't she just leave? Liz had told her to go, and it would be for her own safety. She needed to get Jessica out of there, but maybe she could explain some of it to her. Maybe her friend would even understand.

Lizzie remembered why she hadn't told Jessica everything the last time they had seen each other. Lizzie had still thought she could live a normal life then. Well, normal as she could with dead people constantly with her, yelling in her ear when she tried to have conversations with people.

Lizzie found the diary she was looking for. It was the first one, the oldest of them all. She briefly turned the pages until she found where her uncle was talking about losing his wife and her coming back to him. She quickly skimmed through the pages, running her fingers across the tear-stained paper before she handed it over to Jessica.

"Here."

"What's this?" Jessica took the book and just briefly looked at it before looking back at Liz.

"It's my uncle's diary. It talks about his introduction to all this craziness."

"What does your uncle have to do with anything? You just inherited his house and money, not his insanity."

"Sometimes crazy isn't so crazy when you're on the inside."

"What? Is that like, if you're crazy, you don't know you're crazy?"

"Something like that. Just read it."

Lizzie left her friend there and went back into the kitchen. She felt like she should eat something, but wasn't sure she could. Her stomach hurt, and she wasn't sure when was the last time she had forced herself to eat.

Jessica followed her, the book unread in her hands.

"Liz, I don't care what happened to your uncle. I'm worried about you. You can't stay out here. It's not healthy, I mean just look at you." Jessica held up her free hand as if indicating that Lizzie's appearance was proof of some point, and maybe it was. When was the last time she'd showered?

She opened the cabinets and found the two remaining cans of food that she had thought had been finished off. One was for Spaghetti O's and the other was canned soup. She ignored the soup and grabbed the fake pasta.

"Ew, really?"

Lizzie popped the top and tossed it into the sink while grabbing a spoon off the counter. *It looked clean. Well, clean enough...*

She forced a bite, still not enjoying the rolling around in her stomach, and looked up at her friend.

"What? I'm hungry. Read the damn passage."

"At least wipe your mouth."

Lizzie had felt the dribble on the corner of her mouth but had been talking. What would it take to get Jessica to read it? Lizzie didn't care if a little sauce had settled on her cheek. She wanted Jessica to read the damned thing, and motioned so using the spoon.

"What's so damned important in this?" Jessica held up the book, her finger marking the page Lizzie had opened it to, so at least she was curious.

"It's about Sarah."

"Really?" Jessica looked at the pages. "This book must be over five years old. How is this about Sarah?"

"It's about what happened to his wife. It happened to Sarah."

"So what? You have to let it go. There was nothing you could have done. My God Liz, do you really think you're responsible for what that bastard did? Is that why you're hiding out here?" Jessica put down the book and stepped over to Liz, her arms wide for a hug. "You didn't do anything. You're not the reason Sarah or Roland died."

"You're wrong." Lizzie said, fighting to hold back the tears. It was getting easier, as only a few tears threatened. Maybe she didn't care anymore, or maybe she was just past the point where tears came every time she thought about their deaths. Maybe she could even tell Jessie what's been going on without becoming a complete wreck.

Lizzie knew she was being silly about it. As soon as she opened her mouth, she knew it would be a mistake. Jessica would never believe her, and she would either think she was nuts or... No, there wasn't anything else she would think, but maybe then she would leave and be safe. That's what Jessica needed to do. She needed to get out of there before the shadow man did his voodoo, heebie jeebie, killing thing.

"Jess, you're in danger and the longer you're here, something could happen. Please, just go."

Jessica dropped her arms, giving up on the hug that Lizzie never stepped into, and they both stood there studying one another.

"No." Jessica said. Lizzie was taken aback by Jessica's stern look.

"Yes, please."

"No. I'm not going. You need me. I brought my bag with me. I'm not leaving you out here all alone."

"Jess, you can't do this."

"Yes, I can. I'm taking a break from school, and I'd already quit my job, so yeah, I'm staying."

Lizzie looked at Jessica and noticed that Jessica was wearing more make-up than usual. It seemed especially heavy under her eyes, like where a woman would cake it on if she was hiding a black eye, or something else. Had Dennis been beating on her? Did she need a place to hide out?

Oh my God, if he has been hitting her, I'm going to kill him. It flashed through her mind so quickly she wasn't even sure the thought was hers. Even as she thought it, though, she couldn't believe it and had that feeling that something else was going on.

"Jess, is everything alright?" Lizzie set down the can of Spaghetti O's, untouched since that first spoonful, and stepped forward, taking Jessica into a hug.

"I'm fine. I'm just worried about you."

"Dennis hasn't hit you, has he?" The hug was gone, and Jessica nearly jumped back out of Lizzie's arms, her eyes wide.

"What? Where did you get that idea?"

"Well, Your, Um? Why would you quit your job?"

"I quit because that asshole Kevin tried to feel me up."

"Did he hit you?"

"No, but I nearly dropped his ass there in the center of the store. No, no, where in the hell did you get the idea that someone hit me?"

"Your eyes."

"What about my eyes?"

"Um, I don't know. It's ...just..."

"I've been having trouble sleeping. That okay with you?"

"You sure?"

"Yeah, I think I'd notice if someone had hit me. I don't regularly go out looking for fights and I don't let people hit me."

"Okay. You'd tell me if someone had, right?"

"Liz, this isn't about me. I'm here because you just disappeared. How could you just run off like that?"

Lizzie let Jessica go and step back to collapse onto the counter, her legs weak and her chin dropping to her chest.

"I watched Roland die."

"What, did he have a seizure or something? Did you call the paramedics? Wait, why were you in the same room with him? Did you ...guys...?"

"I watched it kill him. Most the others he didn't do it directly, but he seemed to be telling me something

450

when he killed him. It smiled at me. I could feel it. It wanted me to see it."

"Liz, what are you talking about?"

"The shadow man, or sometimes I think of it as the Tic-Toc man. He's not a man, though. It is death, and it surrounds me."

"When did you get so poetic?"

Lizzie looked at Jessica, their eyes locking on one another. Lizzie felt her own intensity burning off of her. It reminded her of how she would be on a project, and how annoyed she would be when someone tried to get her focus away from her work.

"Poetry is as dead as life is around me. The shadow man is real. It is a monster hell bent on spreading darkness, and it is using me to do it."

"Maybe I should leave. I think I need to get you some help. You know the police are looking for you. Your brother too. Maybe they can get you what you need."

"I'm not crazy. I thought that at first. I thought I was losing my mind. I'm not though. There's this thing, and no one seems to know how to stop it. I don't, but I need to find out. It wants us all. Just somehow, it is trapped here, and I seem to be its anchor and food source. It started long before Sarah and even my uncle."

Lizzie nodded towards the book. She hadn't noticed when Jessica had set it down on the counter.

"Liz..."

"It started for me the day Sarah and I came here. Sarah was killed by a dead man who had dug himself out of his own grave. I thought that would be the last time I would see her. Later that night, she came back to me, and has been here ever since."

"Wait, you're saying you've been seeing her ghost?"

Lizzie shook her head and then went on to tell her friend everything. It would be the second time she'd told anyone. Maybe this time Jessica would live long enough to help her.

CHAPTER 37

How do you convince your best friend that everyone close to you has been killed because they were *close* to you? Okay, so maybe it sounded crazy, but it was true. They were dead, and now they were undead, and it was all because of interacting with her.

Lizzie wanted to scream, as the frustration was growing, and it felt like the breath of each word was producing this pressure inside her chest. It was building, and each time that Jessica interrupted her, it wanted to escape in a fierce blast of anger.

Jessica had fought Lizzie through the whole retelling of what had been happening the last few weeks. Lizzie wasn't sure if it was because she couldn't believe it or because she refused to believe it. Lizzie would tell her about Sarah's death, which Jessica understood Lizzie's hard time to talk about it, but when Lizzie told her about Sarah's reappearance she had baulked.

"So, you really think Sarah's still alive?"

No, she wasn't alive. If Jessica would just listen to her. Lizzie had told her she was undead, still appearing to her and talking to her. Though, telling Jess about her had created a pause in the story. A pause that had Lizzie stop and look at the person with whom she thought of as one of her best friends. She couldn't stop herself. She had to know if any of it was true, if their friendship was true and if Jessica had known anything about 'it'.

Lizzie had always felt like it had been weird that these two amazing and beautiful people would be friends with someone so shy like herself. Why had Jessica been her friend? She had always thought it was because Sarah was her friend. So, if Sarah had been playing her this whole time, had Jessica been in on it?

"Did Sarah ever talk about my parents? Or say anything about my dad?"

Jessica had been surprised at the sudden turn in conversation, but had rebounded quickly enough to not sound like she was making something up.

"Not really?" It was a question. Lizzie could tell by how she said it. She stretched out the *really* and made a face as if to ask why Lizzie was bringing it up. "I mean, I know she was devastated when they passed away. We both loved your parents. Sarah always thought of your mom as her second mom, though I think she'd of rather had your mom over hers. You know, there were always rough times for her at home. Well, you know, you were always with her."

And Lizzie had always been with her. It was why she couldn't believe the things Sarah had been saying lately. It didn't make sense. How did it even work, for Sarah to have done what she said?

Lizzie shook it off, telling Jessica to never mind as she continued then with trying to tell her about Elisabeth and Chuck.

In total, it took her nearly forty minutes to get through the story. She hadn't mentioned anything about the strange Englishman or the clock. She still wasn't sure what to make of it, or of the barn with the black wall. She had felt different there. It was like the house felt safe, magically safe even if she had to put it into words, but outside felt like 'his' playground and he was waiting out there to play with her. Then there was the barn, and it was cold, dark, and there was something else in there entirely. Whatever was in there was waiting for something. It wanted something to happen and when it did, it was ready to emerge. When that happened, she wasn't sure when that would be, but she knew it was bad.

Whatever he was, and no matter how bad the shadow man was, whatever was in that barn was much worse.

It sounded crazy. So much so that she didn't tell Jessica for sure that it would be the final straw for her friend to be shipping her off to the looney bin with the padded white walls and floors.

"You're crazy, Liz. I love you, but you're crazy and I think you need help." Jessica had said. Lizzie had just finished eating the last of her can of fake spaghetti sauce and had tossed it in a garbage bin. Next to it was a garbage bag that was filled with similar cans and other refuse. She hadn't been sure what to do with the garbage out there, so for now she left it inside.

Lizzie stared down into the darkness at the bottom of the garbage bin. It was a fresh bag, so the can had gone to the bottom and was almost completely lost to the dark plastic.

She felt like she could relate. Her life was beginning to feel like it was lost to the dark plastic. Why had she come all the way out there to the cabin? Was she going to hide out here for the rest of her life like her uncle had? It seemed like a good idea at the time, and she'd hoped that when she got back there that she'd have found some kind of answer. She would walk right into the cabin, open one of his books and *"voila!"*. There it was, the answer to what was going on.

She had found an answer, at least. The answer was that he had never really known what was going on either, neither had his uncle who passed it down to him.

Though someone must have, as she had the voodoo necklace. Well, she assumed it was voodoo. She kept having dreams of the voodoo woman and she assumed the woman made the necklace.

Why do I think she made it? She hadn't thought about it before, but as she was reviewing all the crazy around her, she realized that she did believe the woman had made it. She had been involved in this long before Lizzie had run into her granddaughter, and that necklace felt like it belonged to the old woman. Like it was calling out to be back with her.

"I'm not crazy." Lizzie answered, realizing Jessica was still in the room and watching her.

"I didn't say you were. I said it sounded crazy. I just think you need to talk to someone and get some help. There has been a lot going on and it would be a lot for anyone to handle alone."

"But I'm not alone. I haven't been alone since they died. They're always out there."

"They're outside right now? Why don't they come in? You said at the apartment they were there with you."

"I don't know. There's something about this cabin. Maybe it's why my uncle has weird symbols carved into the wood throughout the house. Who knows? I do know that they can't come into the house and kitchen, and that dead things can only make it into the kitchen, but not the rest of the house. I think the kitchen was some kind of add-on or something and the magic works differently out here."

"Either that or it has something to do with the plumbing. If there was some kind of protection spell, then it wouldn't be effective in a room that has pipes of running water running in and out of it."

Lizzie looked at her friend, her mouth dropping open.

"I'm not saying that I don't fully believe you. I don't know what I believe. I'm just saying that if there is some kind of protection on the house, it may not be as effective in rooms with a lot of pipes running in and out of it."

"And how would you know that?"

"I don't. Duh. But come on. You've seen just as many dumb horror films as I have. There's like, rules to witchcraft mumbo jumbo. If you have a circle, you can't have things breaking it or the magic won't work. Well, it wouldn't be an actual circle, but if there's magic and protection, then this room has a lot of pipes, I would guess, running in and out of it. I'm guessing the bathroom would be the same way."

Lizzie looked at the door that led into the bathroom. The color drained from her face and the vision she had wasn't comforting. She could see herself in there, doing her business, when the undead man, a huge smile spread across his bloodstained teeth, came crashing into the room and grabbing her.

Then there was the shower, and suddenly theme music played in her head. "Eh, eh, eh, eh" and a knife coming swooping down like out of that Hitchcock movie.

Maybe she wouldn't be taking a shower anytime soon. She hadn't felt comfortable enough in the cabin to take one yet, and another few *years* wouldn't hurt anything. Well, maybe it would affect her sense of smell, but that'd be worth it.

"I guess that makes sense."

"You know it does. Come on." Jessica led her out of the kitchen, and exhaustion must have been kicking in as Lizzie let her.

"Where are we going?"

"You're taking a shower."

"No, I'm not."

Lizzie stopped moving, and they both looked at each other. It was obvious that Jess was concerned about her, but Lizzie wasn't about to go into that room and get naked. There was just no way.

"Liz, I don't know what you've been through, but I know it's a lot. I understand what you think you've been through, and we'll talk about it more when you get out- but right now, you stink. You stink more than this house does, and as long as you have warm, running water, then the shower will do you some good. I'll stay with you. Nothing is going to happen, to me, or to you. No one is going to attack you."

Lizzie didn't believe her, but somehow found the small woman was surprisingly strong as she pushed her through the house to the small room just off the living room.

"I don't think we have hot water." Liz said as they neared the door.

"Really? None?"

"I don't know. Haven't tried, but there's no basement and I've never seen a hot water heater. I'm not sure."

"Well, guess what? There's only one way to find out."

Lizzie tried to think of another way to stall, but it was too late. They were at the door. Jessica stepped in front of her and pushed it open, and then beckoned Lizzie to enter. She did and Jessica followed, the room suddenly cramped as if it was never meant for two people cohabitation.

"I knew it'd be small, but this is like both of us trying to fit into a port-a-potty." Jessica wasn't wrong as she was forced to nearly sit over the small, dirty and rust stained toilet that Lizzie had slowly come to trust. Her first couple of days in the cabin she had just hovered over to use, but after Sarah and the rest of them had beat her, she hadn't had the energy to keep it up and now was used to sitting on it.

Then there was a little sink, and above it there had once been a mirror that in the past had been removed and now was open to the contents. All of it was her uncles. She had no toothbrush and hadn't done anything about her teeth since she'd gotten there. It was probably a good thing there wasn't a mirror. The more she was beginning to realize it, the more she felt like she could imagine what Jessica was seeing. She really must have looked like one hell of a mess.

The sink wasn't what she was in there for, and she turned to study the tub. The room had obviously not been designed for the thing when it had been built and once it had been installed; it allowed just enough room for her to sit on the toilet and her knees just touch the cold porcelain. The curtain was hung on a makeshift steel rod that was fastened to the wall, and the shower head hung from a wire dangling from the ceiling. It was one of those loose kinds that you could hold while using it, and the head was discolored from years of inactivity and age. Just like a ring of orange around the tub, the head of the shower was covered in rust. None of it looked appealing to use.

"Maybe we should just go to a motel? There's one around here, right? Get a room, you can take a shower, maybe even get some sleep in the bed?"

Liz shot Jessica a look.

"You know I can't-"

"Oh yeah, I know. Sorry. Just look at this. It looks like it hasn't been used in years and is from a lifetime ago. Shit, I bet this tub is from before you were born."

"Yeah, it is probably older than that." Lizzie said as she bent over and started studying the contraption at the back of the room. It was hooked to the shower, and she had no idea what it was there for. It looked like some kind of pump. She clicked the little switch on the top and it whirred to life.

"What's that?"

"No clue."

"Water pump maybe? I know my great aunt has a cabin and they have one of those hooked up to it. Maybe you do have hot water, I think it's supposed to work with some kind of specialized hot water heater."

"I have no idea."

"Well, you turned it on. Try it."

Lizzie looked around as the pump continued to run. Eventually, she found a bar of soap and a bottle of shampoo that was crusted at the top. She grabbed for it, and Jessica shook her head.

"Give me a second. I brought my own."

Jessica left the room, and a second later, Lizzie heard the front door slam. Her heart quickened as she realized that Jessica had gone outside. *What the hell was she thinking? Hadn't she just been told about what was out there?*

Lizzie rushed from the room, nearly knocking over one of the piles by the easy chair. There were more books on witchcraft as well as a diary on top. Lizzie barely noticed it as she made her way to the front door and nearly crossed the threshold.

She stopped herself and cursed at the front awning. It was great to keep people from seeing into the house when they were in the front yard, but made it impossible for her to see where Jessica had gone.

All she could do was stand there and listen as she heard what sounded like a beep and then car doors being unlocked. There was a scraping, and then a kathunk kathunk as something heavy fell to the gravel.

Lizzie cringed as she could imagine Sarah or Josh, even Chuck, if he got back to that rage induced person she had seen when he had first died, attacking her and that was her falling to the ground. They could be swarming over her, tearing her apart. Even the shadow man could be out there or one of his dead lackies like what had killed Sarah. Anything could be happening, and Lizzie was trapped in there, powerless to stop it.

Why had she gone out there?

Did Jessica have the red rings around her eyes? Lizzie hadn't noticed, but she couldn't help but think about when they had been in the parking garage. Jessica hadn't been acting herself. It was almost like something was influencing her to put herself into a dangerous situation. No, not just any something- the shadow man, he was doing it. He had controlled her then, and now her friend was in danger again.

Lizzie inched closer to the door, wanting desperately to poke her head out and peek around. Her pulse was pounding, and she felt her heart trying to pump its way out of her chest. She tried to listen, but it was hard over the loudness of her own breath and the silence of the woods.

Then she heard it. Something was being dragged across the gravel.

Lizzie grabbed both sides of the door as though she was getting ready to launch herself out there. She was pacing back and forth, her movements growing more frantic as she wanted to propel herself past the threshold.

She knew Jessica was in trouble. What was it going to take for her to run out there and save her? Was she really going to stand by while another of her friends was killed, this time while there might be something she could do?

She gripped the threshold tighter, preparing herself. Her jaw was clenched, her teeth threatening to grind down to nothing as she tried to will herself to just do it.

The dragging sound was getting closer. What were they going to do, drag Jessica over to her and kill her so she could watch?

Come to think of it, most of the deaths had happened with her watching. Maybe that was one of Shadow man's turn-ons, to have her watch. He did love to torture her. It was like he fed off her pain, enjoying her suffering at watching those around her die.

I can't take this anymore. I have to do something.

Her foot crossed the threshold, and she felt that foreboding fear slam into her. It didn't matter what was out there; she had to hurry. Her friend's life was in danger.

She was in the entryway created by the little yawning and turned to rush down when a shadow appeared at the bottom. Her momentum paused as her heart leapt into her throat.

Then the shadow became a person, and Jessica stood at the bottom of the stairs. She was dragging her rolling suitcase, the wheels barely any help in the rough gravel. She stopped short when she saw Lizzie at the top of the stairs.

"Woah. You okay?"

Lizzie didn't wait. She dashed down the stairs, grabbed Jessica's free hand and pulled her so they were both rushing to get back inside.

Once they made it past the threshold, Lizzie nearly collapsed on the floor. Instead, she made it into the chair and finally allowed herself to burst into tears.

"Liz, what the hell? I just went out to get my suitcase."

"You could have died."

"I just went out to my car."

"Elisabeth and Chuck, they died just at the end of the driveway. Sarah died in that kitchen. Being around me, there isn't any, 'just went out to my car' moments anymore. They're always out there, and the shadow man, he's everywhere."

Jessica let go of the suitcase and lowered herself to look into Liz's eyes. She grabbed her hands and waited until Liz looked up and their eyes met.

"Liz, I'm not going anywhere. You need to calm down. You're not the cause of these freak accidents. Okay?"

"You still don't believe me."

"I believe you need to stop blaming yourself."

"You still don't believe me."

"Not really, but I'm here for you and I'm going to help you."

"You need to believe me."

"Okay, fine. Then I believe you."

"No, you don't, but you will."

Lizzie stood quickly, nearly knocking Jessica out of the way. Before Jessica could say or do anything, Lizzie was at the front door. She rushed outside and was gone, down the stairs and past what was visible with the awning.

"Come on out, you bitch!" Jessica heard Lizzie yell. "Sarah, come and get it!"

Jessica's mouth dropped as she hurried to catch up to her friend.

CHAPTER 38

Does anyone remember the summers when you were a child? As an adult, they are always distant memories when time seemed endless. The summer was filled with years of fun and school was just days between each warm vacation. The pool was a place to ride bikes too, and home was where you had tea parties with other girls from the neighborhood who would come to your backyard.

When looking back, do you ever remember the bad times? Sometimes you'll vaguely remember a squabble you had with your bestie if it was really bad and cause you to go home in a huff, but there were too many good times to think about. Why waste time of thinking about when Sarah had called you a poopy head and stormed off? Why, when you could think about the time you were both at the pool, splashing back and forth, giggling as she had just threatened to tell Tommy Walker that you had a thing for him and thought he was cute?

Lizzie had grown up in Steven's Point for nearly all her life, though they didn't live too close to the downtown area, but on the north side near Atwell Park. Their house was on Jordon Lane, not too far from the university, so her dad didn't have too far to go to work. He liked being close enough that he didn't have a long drive, but far enough away that students wouldn't be pranking their house. Which, they didn't except for Halloween, and even then, who could know for sure if it was students or just random mischief.

Lizzie's brother hadn't been sick yet, but they still had never been close. He was younger than her, but still he was the bully of the house. He had learned to pick on her from the moment he had been able to talk, and their mom always took them to play dates where it seemed like she was maybe one of two girls. All the other kids had been boys and Brian had fit right in. It never took him long to make friends, and before she would know what was happening, she would be getting rammed by three to four toy tractors.

And what was the worst part of it? Her mom would just laugh and find it funny. Could she not see how much Lizzie's brother was a little demon trapped in that body? He was a holy terror and was torturing her and their mom just thought they were playing.

Then there were the times that Lizzie fought back. She would get hit by some Sesame Street doll that had been flung across the room and she would throw it back. Yeah, she would whip it back at him, get him good with it. He would take the hit, and then would wail like a banshee. You would think he was mortally wounded and never going to recover, as her brother had a set of lungs on him that would make Renee Fleming proud. This would then follow, with Lizzie being whisked away into the corner chair where she would face the wall for another time out. The longer she cried, shouting how it just wasn't fair, the longer

466

she sat there thinking of all the different ways she was going to get her revenge.

She never did. She never got the chance. Anything she ever tried was always met with failure, her plans always thwarted by those wailing lungs and never being left alone with him.

It got to become so frustrating how her parents never saw her side of it, that when Lizzie had turned seven, she had started to explore the neighborhood on her own. She would do whatever it would take to get away from the little beast. Her parents never seemed to care. She was free to roam on her own, just as long as she didn't get into any trouble. That was kind of an unsaid deal. She didn't get into any trouble and that she was home before dark. She could work with that.

Well, she also couldn't ride her bike further than the end of the street. That was a given as she wasn't allowed to cross Stanley Street or Prais Street, so she really only had a couple of blocks to get away, and there were no girls living in any of the houses there. She could ride up and down the street all day and all there were was boys that ran and played. Sure, they were okay, better than her brother, but who's saying that they wouldn't become just as vicious if she started playing with them?

It was unending, each day the same thing. She would ride her bike, and she would see the same group of boys, some of whom would meet up at the park and throw around some balls or play on the playground. She would also be at the park, but she didn't say much to most of them. Some tried to talk to her, but she would shy away whenever any of them would try to throw around a ball to her or try to chase her.

Some of the older kids teased her and it was unwarranted when they started to call her 'freak girl.' She wasn't a freak. They were just all scary boys, and boys liked to hit and fight. She watched how they played with each other. They were always wrestling around and throwing each other to the ground. How could she trust them not to do that to her?

Then Sarah came to her street. It had been a bad day at the park, and it was really hot outside to make everything worse. At the park, Billy, one of the boys who regularly tried to get her to play with him, hadn't accepted it when she had told him 'No.' He wanted her to join their game of tag, and no, was not an acceptable answer.

When she had said it to him again, this time louder and stronger, he had pushed her down, then lowered himself to yell in her face, "Tag, you're it!" Then he ran off and all his friends ran away from her.

She hadn't chased them but stood back up and started to cry. Her butt hurt. She hadn't known he was going to do that and falling had stung. So, she stood there, watching them all run, expecting her to follow, and she didn't.

That was when it got bad, because all the boys gathered when they realized she wasn't chasing them. They started pointing at her, laughing, and calling her names. Jeremy, another one of the boys, left the group to walk over to her. He was the shorter of the group and had sometimes even been nice to her, so she didn't run from him as he approached.

She had a moment to think that maybe, just maybe, this boy was going to be nice to her. He was even holding his hand out to her, so he was going to help her up, and he did right before he pushed her down again.

"Tag, you're it!" He laughed and then ran away, the rest of them, some having moved closer to see what Jeremy was going to do, laughed with Jeremy.

"I was already it." Lizzie cried. She sat there, not even trying to get up. What was the point? They were all mean and just going to make fun of her. Eventually, she heard them moving farther away. A new 'it' was running around, one boy chasing another, until they caught them and pushed them down.

She watched it off and on for a minute or two as her tears dwindled. Finally, they stopped when she realized no one was coming to save her, and that she no longer needed saving. Maybe she should just go home and see if Brian was playing on his Nintendo. Her parents would never buy her one as she wasn't a boy, but when no one was home, she would sneak in there.

It was on her ride home from the park that she stopped and saw one of the coolest things she had ever seen. It was a large pink castle, easily as tall as she was. There was no way a boy played with that, and it was being carried out of a large truck around to the back of a house she had never paid any attention to before. She didn't think anyone had lived there, but now there was a girl there!

Lizzie stopped her bike and watched as more things came off the truck. She could feel the air in her mouth as it was going dry. It was open and she couldn't help it as she watched the large girl dining set that was being carried out next by the large men who just kept coming and going out of the backyard.

"Mom, where are they taking them?" yelled a girl's voice from behind her.

"Sarah, don't you dare get out of this car until we have completely stopped. Close that door right now!"

Lizzie turned and saw a large SUV pulling up to the curb. The back door was already partially open and the moment the vehicle came to a complete stop, a little girl roughly the same age as herself came sprinting out. She didn't even notice Lizzie at first as the girl was in a full sprint towards the backyard, where the two men had disappeared with the large castle.

"She's going to be a handful today." Lizzie heard the girl's mother saying.

"Are you up to this? I can watch her and take care of the movers. You can lie in the back, get some rest."

"I'll be fine. I'm feeling okay today, and then tomorrow, we'll go see that specialist and I'll be all better."

"I'm not Sarah. You don't have to talk down to me."

"I'm going to be fine. It's all going to be okay."

Lizzie looked at the girl's parents, who were so lost in looking at each other that they never noticed she was there. That's okay, she figured if they didn't notice her, then they wouldn't mind if she followed to where the girl went to.

Lizzie rested her bike on the grass and walked to the backyard. It was larger than hers and fenced in, so she had to go through an old wooden gate that needed to be repainted. The paint was brown and peeling, but as Lizzie walked through it, what was there and what she imagined was there became very different things.

As soon as she saw the castle in the middle of the yard, the two workmen disappeared to her eyes, and she saw a lush landscape around her with a meadow of beautiful green grass. Unicorns were grazing in the distance, and they nodded to her as she approached the kingdom. The other girl was standing there by the large castle, smiling, and twirling around as she sang to the music of Cinderella.

"Hi, I'm Lizzie." She blurted out, and the girl stopped dancing and looked at her like she had suddenly been caught doing something embarrassing. Her cheeks went red, and her mouth hung open.

Oh no, Lizzie thought, *I just barged in there and now this girl, the only other girl in the area my age, is going to hate me for the rest of my life. This was it; I'd ruined it.*

"Hello?" the other girl said nervously. She quickly recovered, and a smile stretched wide as she started hopping up and down. "Do you want to be a princess?"

"I don't know... does the castle's library have any good books?" Lizzie hadn't really learned to read that well, but she loved stories. If she was a princess, they would need to read stories to her day and night.

"Books? Why would you want books?" The girl scoffed, but then looked like she was considering what Lizzie had asked. "But it's a large castle, I don't see why it couldn't have a library... and unicorns, and cotton candy and ... and... and..." Sarah started to name off all the wonderful things it could have and as she did, Lizzie looked around seeing them floating in the air.

It wasn't long before they were both running around the yard, and when the movers had brought the tea table with the box labeled "teatime (back yard)" on it, that they were preparing for their own tea party.

"Yes Princess Elizabeth, this is a very fine brisket and glass of tea," Sarah said. Lizzie giggled as Sarah took a bite from her pretend cookie in one hand while holding her teacup in the other. Her pinky was raised, and she was pouting her lips in what Lizzie guessed was her snooty queen face.

"It is Princess Humperdink," Lizzie replied, making her own queen face, "but I do believe they are called biscuits, not briskets."

Sarah looked at the invisible cookie held between her fingers and then back at Lizzie.

"I thought they're called briskets. Biscuits are large and fluffy. I want an English cookie," then dropping back into her faux English accent, she continued, "Only the best briskets can be found acceptable for the queen."

"Yes, my queen." Lizzie said, but then dropped her own faux accent to continue, "My dad's a professor at the college. He meets all kinds of cool people and another professor there. She comes over and brings these really cool cookies, but... she calls them biscuits because that's what they're called where she's from. She's from London I think."

"Really!" Sarah says, losing her character momentarily.

"Yeah, she's really cool. She always talks British, and she calls things really weird. Like she calls our TV a telly."

"Oh, wow."

"Yeah."

"Well, should we go inside and watch cartoons on the telly?" Sarah asks, slipping back into using her faux accent.

"Sure."

They both stood from the short table and started running towards the house. They made it halfway when they could hear the yelling from inside.

"Really? We're not living here for twenty minutes and you're already flirting with the neighbors."

"Flirting! I was just being nice to our neighbors. She was asking if her daughter was here playing. She'd seen her going into our backyard. I'm not the one running around with my damn tits nearly hanging out. You had one of the movers walking around with an erection."

"Fuck You!"

The girls had both stopped when they heard something made of glass fall and break inside the house. Lizzie didn't know why, but she felt tears forming in the corners of her eyes and she backed away from the open door. Sarah looked at her. Her eyes were also wet. Neither of them wanted to go inside.

"Maybe we should go to your house and play," Sarah said. Lizzie nodded her agreement and Sarah rushed to where one of the movers had set her bike. Lizzie's bike was still out front, and she had a momentary worry that one of the neighborhood boys had hidden it on her when she didn't see it. They'd done it before, and she turned around frantically, looking for it.

"Looking for this?" Sarah asked her, and Lizzie stopped to see that her bike was near the front porch. Someone must have moved it, maybe one of the movers. Didn't matter as she was just happy to see it.

"Aren't you going to tell your parents where we're going?"

Sarah looked over her shoulder at the large house. They could still hear her parents, but now the voices were muffled and the words indistinguishable.

"They'll figure it out. We won't be far."

"I guess that's true." Lizzie said.

They were part way to Lizzie's house, and Sarah hadn't said anything since they had left. Every time Lizzie looked at her, she found her new best friend looking back at her parents' house, or looking off into space and wiping away tears Lizzie could tell she wasn't supposed to see. When Sarah would notice her looking, she would flash a smile and act like nothing was wrong.

Lizzie didn't know what she should do. She didn't say anything about it, and after a while, the smile Sarah gave her lingered on her face.

"Hey, do you think your parents would mind if I stayed the night?" Sarah asked as they were setting their bikes down near the garage.

"I don't think so. We can always ask," Lizzie said.

"I hope so. I think I'd really like to stay the night."

"Then let's do it."

Sarah surprised Lizzie as she quickly ran over to her and gave her a huge hug. Lizzie wasn't sure how she was supposed to react, so she went with it, and returned it. When Sarah pulled away, there were more tears and Lizzie barely heard her whisper, "Thank you."

"Hey, let me show you my room. My uncle got me this amazing Princess Sofia, and I can show you some of my favorite books."

"Books?"

"Okay, well, just wait. I'm sure you'll love it."

"Sure, let's go."

They both rushed off, the sound of giggling laughter echoing through the house as they ran up the stairs to Lizzie's room.

CHAPTER 39

"Sarah!" Lizzie yelled as she felt the sudden rush of air around her, the wind howling through the trees surrounding the clearing. She was pissed, as the emotions raged through her, a torrent that combined her pain and frustration that had been building over the last few weeks. Many of her friends were dead, and she was hiding because even in death, they weren't gone, but physically trying to hurt her. Everything that she loved and cared for was being torn away. She was being stripped of what she had always taken for granted as being there for her, and it was turning her into this mouse who hid, and she no longer recognized.

But the mouse was always her. You just never allowed yourself to see your true nature. The voice of her insecurity said, again trying to beat her down and pushing her to go back inside. Well, for the second time that day, she was done hiding inside.

"Get your boney ass out here! Sarah!"

"She's dead." Jessica said. She stood at the bottom of the stairs to the cabin, looking at Lizzie. She looked troubled as she watched her friend twisting around, calling out for their dead friend. She would take a step towards Lizzie, but then stop and pause. It was obvious she was unsure of herself and whether or not she should rush over and comfort her friend.

Lizzie would look at her. She could tell what Jess wanted to do and damned her for it. She would never be able to get her to see what it was she was going through unless she was given the chance. If Jessica came to her now, it would... It would... Lizzie wasn't sure what it would do.

Lately, every time she went outside, she had been attacked. Could the dead also attack Jessica? If she was near Lizzie, would they go after her as well?

"Stay there!" Lizzie said, as she watched her friend come to a decision and had taken a step towards her. "Just give me time."

"Time for what?"

"To show you."

"Oh? What are you going to show her?" Sarah said as she walked around from the side of the house.

Lizzie looked at what had once been her best friend as she strutted in her direction. It was the walk of a panther as it approached her prey, knowing it was trapped and had nowhere left to run. Lizzie locked eyes with her, and never looked away, Sarah's death scars still hideous to look at. They no longer fazed Lizzie as she grew more hardened, her emotions no longer getting the best of her.

If it doesn't kill me, it only makes me stronger, she chanted in her mind, telling all her other insecurities they needed to back off.

"This isn't you."

"Oh, you still think we're friends? We were never friends, but if we had been, you really think a friend would have put up with all this and still be your bestie? You sent us to HELL Liz. *HELL!*"

"I said I'm sorry. Josh even asked for it. You all thought the talisman would somehow cure what was going on. You wanted it as much as I did."

"I didn't want that! I'm sure none of us did."

Lizzie noticed that none of the others were coming around with Sarah. It was just her and what had been her best friend. That seemed odd, and she didn't know quite what to make of it.

"But it was what you asked for. You were hoping for peace, and I needed some quiet for my own sanity. I thought it would be like when we traveled. That you would just be gone. That you'd be somewhere else and then just bounce back in. How could I know it would have done that?" Lizzie noticed that the desperation and pleading were gone. She was no longer begging for her friend's forgiveness. It was simple, this is what happened. She was going to tell her friend the truth and was at the point that it no longer mattered if Sarah believed her or not.

The Sarah she knew would believe her.

Goose flesh prickled along her arm, and she had a feeling that something was wrong as Sarah approached her and got right up into Lizzie's face. Lizzie could see the flaps of skin vibrate as Sarah spoke, and it looked like there was something there underneath Sarah's skin.

"Hell, Liz. You sent us to hell." Lizzie looked at Sarah, keeping her eyes locked onto the dead woman's. "Now it's time for me to send you there."

Lizzie felt the blow as it slammed into her stomach. It knocked her off the ground, rising into the air before she fell back onto the hard earth. The blow had hurt, but the landing felt much worse. She had a moment to think she had just broken her tail bone when she felt that feeling of being grabbed by unseen force and dragged.

"Lizzie! Lizzie, what's going on!" Jessica called.

Lizzie opened her eyes, not realizing she had closed them when she landed and looked. Jessica was hurrying towards her. Lizzie held up her arms and shook her head 'no' the best she could. Jessica stopped, but she looked pained to do so.

"Oh look, she has finally caught on. So nice for you to try to protect her."

The force let her go roughly and Lizzie had no way of stopping herself from having her head slam against the ground. Stars briefly flashed in her vision and lines of color swirled around her as she tried to ignore the pain now spiking through the back of her skull.

"Why-" Lizzie gasped, struggling to form words, "Why are you doing this?"

"You know why," Sarah said, as Lizzie felt her head slam down again. This time her vision briefly went black, and she swore she heard something snap.

"But...you're lying." Lizzie said, and with as much effort as she could from being at such an odd angle, she pushed against the force as it rushed her head hard to the ground. It did little to slow the oncoming pain as again her head cracked against the earth.

She didn't lift her head this time, as it hurt too much. Instead, it was pulled up by her hair. Sarah was saying something about Jessica not being safe there, that it could still get her in that house, but Lizzie could barely comprehend the words. Her struggle was more with consciousness than with what was being said.

How often had Sarah ever lied to her?

It was a brief thought that the pain was quick to push away as her mouth filled with a coppery taste.

Some semblances of survival made her move. She could barely feel her body as her mind was numb and felt loose inside her skull. Still, she moved. It was slow, her whole body was racked with pain, but she continued to grab handfuls of dirt, pulling herself away from Sarah.

Her vision was blurry, but she saw the shape of a car and continued towards it. She had to reach it. It wasn't far. If she could get to it, she could escape. It was only ten feet away. She grabbed another handful and then another, willing herself to keep moving forward.

"Maybe I should go over there and play with blondie." Sarah said. It was a hovering voice somewhere above her. Lizzie couldn't tell where it was, but felt that it was close.

"Where...are...the others?" Lizzie said, as red spit darkened the dirt.

"Lizzie, stop this! I believe you. Now get inside."

"I think blondie would like to have fun under the sun. What do you think? Tic-toc, time is running out on the clock." Lizzie heard Sarah's voice, but felt the chill. Something that had been nagging at Lizzie clicked into place, a thought from the back of her mind realizing itself about how Sarah had been acting.

"You're not Sarah." Lizzie gasped, her breath pushing up a cloud of dust below her. She stopped reaching for more handfuls and turned herself around so she could look up at the dead person standing above her. The sun beat down, so all Lizzie could see was the outline of a person. "You're not Sarah."

"Tikkity toc, tickity tit. Better just get over it." The thing above her said. It still sounded like Sarah, but now it echoed with that same voice she'd heard coming from the shadows. It was him. He was inside her.

A chill ran down Lizzie's back, but she clamped down on the fear that tried to push her. Instead, her mouth tightened, and she ground her teeth to where she heard them straining, threatening to shatter under the force. As she did, she twisted the rest of her, so she was on her back, keeping her glare on it.

"Tic-toc, tic-ted. How about your friend?"

The woods erupted around them. Birds that had been quiet in the trees took to the air, their cries shrieking through the darkening sky. There were so many of them. They created their own breeze, and it blasted the trees, shaking the branches as they circled above them. It was like a tornado rising higher until it peaked, closing off the clearing and taking away the light from the sun. It was a swirling cloud of crows that surrounded them.

"Lizzie!" Jessica screamed from where she was by the house.

Lizzie looked at her and the thing above her stepped away from her and was quickly moving in Jessica's direction. Lizzie knew it wanted her, and now she had just set her friend up.

"Run! Get inside." Lizzie yelled, quickly getting to her feet. She was running, though her head still felt full of cobwebs. She ran as best she could. Every other step she would stagger one way or another, but she fought to chase after what looked like her friend Sarah as she ran towards where Jessica stood.

Jessica had never been a person of inaction, and Lizzie was glad to see that none of this took that away. She had been watching the birds for as they had risen, but she hadn't stood still, waiting to see what they would do. She had already been backing towards the door. As soon as she had heard Lizzie, she had turned and run.

Sarah moved fast, but Jessica was already on the stairs as Lizzie followed her.

Then Jessica stopped and looked back at Lizzie. What the hell is she doing?

"Get inside!" Lizzie yelled again, but Jessica stood there, looking at Lizzie and then at the birds in the sky. Then it dawned on Lizzie why Jessica wasn't rushing to get back into the house. She didn't see Sarah. She looked back to Lizzie and held out her hand to Lizzie.

"Hurry up!"

"She's coming for you! Get inside!"

"Lizzie, hurry!"

"Watch out!"

Lizzie stopped running. Sarah would get to Jessica first. Lizzie was all over the place, her staggering getting worse as she tried to run, the world threatening to spin like a top as it trembled beneath her. Her head felt like an anchor on her neck, and the more she ran, the more her body called for her to just lie down out there on the ground and pass out.

She couldn't, though. She had to stop it from getting Jessica. Jessica needed to get inside. *Damn*! But maybe, if Lizzie stopped, Jessica wouldn't stay outside waiting for her. Maybe she'd realize that she needed to get in where it was safe.

"Lizzie!"

Lizzie looked up. She had been easing herself down, her body deciding on its own that it needed to sleep. Hearing Jessica call out to her shocked her awake enough to upright herself and look in the direction of her friend, who was rushing towards her, afraid to see Shadow Sarah preparing to attack her.

Sarah was gone, making Lizzie even more confused. She knew she'd been there. *Where has she gone?*

Jessica reached her and brought her arm around her in a sideways hug that held her up. Quickly, with Jessica's support, they were taking steps towards the house when the first bird struck. It came in hard and fast and hit Lizzie's arm before falling to the ground, dead. Lizzie barely had a chance to look at it when she heard Jessica cry out and the arm around her briefly grew slack to realize she'd been hit.

"It hit me." She said in disbelief and Lizzie looked at her friend's arm to see the red streaming down it. Then she heard a thump ahead of them and saw where one of the birds missed them and hit the ground directly in their path.

Lizzie struggled to push more of the confusion out of her head. She needed to focus and think, and they needed to get inside.

"Hurry!" she said, relying less on her friend and trying to walk faster. They weren't far from the house, only a couple yards, but as more birds fell into their path, she knew it was not going to be easy. Another bird struck her in the middle of her back and had hit with enough force that her legs momentarily buckled beneath her. She was going down.

Jessica pulled her back up and took two steps of her own, keeping Lizzie tight against her. Then Jessica was hit by another bird, and she was launched forward. She hit the wall of the cabin, and Lizzie rushed to catch up. When she was pulled back, the strength of the grip pulling her hair caused sensations of pain along her scalp, setting it ablaze. She fell hard, landing on her butt nearly two yards from where Jessica had fallen to the ground.

That's when Lizzie realized her friend wasn't moving. She had hit her head when she had crashed against the house and crumpled to the ground.

Lizzie struggled to pull herself forward towards Jessica when two birds crashed down. One hit a foot in front of her, the other smashed into her hand. She howled in pain and pulled her hand back to her chest. She was sure it was broken. It hurt like nothing she ever felt and had gone numb.

A shadow washed over her, and she felt herself forced to the side, falling flat to the ground. She looked up, and there was Sarah again, standing over her, a dark sneer barely able to be seen with how she was now surrounded in the darkness.

"Time to watch your friend die. Tic-a-too, tick a tee. Oh, what will it be? Tic-a-too, tic-a-tat, curiosity killed the cat."

Sarah turned from Lizzie and looked up at the sky. Light started to burst through the darkness above and, for a moment, Lizzie thought maybe they would be saved. Then she saw why the darkness was leaving. The birds were rising higher into the air, breaking their dome overhead as they rose out of sight.

Lizzie knew they were not leaving. Even though they were flying away, it was only to get higher. They were preparing, and soon they were going to crash down. They were all coming for them, no longer in ones and twos, but now they were coming in mass. It would literally be a murder of crows as they came down to kill.

Jessica was about to die, and there was nothing Lizzie could do.

CHAPTER 40

"Jessica! Jessica wake-up!" Lizzie yelled and her voice burned in her own throat as she tried to scream harder than she had ever screamed before. She was not about to watch another one of her friends die, no matter what she had to do.

She tried to reach out again to pull herself along the ground, but her injured hand refused to work. She was forced to bring it back to herself, tears falling as she worked to ignore the pain. Each time anything shifted around her hand, new sensations stabbed into her, making it hard to ignore, but she bit down on it, biting into her own lip until she tasted copper.

"Jessica, please. God wake her up. Please God!" Lizzie called. She was not a religious person. Jessica was the one who never missed a week of church. Lizzie hoped that maybe that loyalty would reward her. At least Lizzie prayed for Jessica's sake. "Please!"

Lizzie heard laughter behind her and knew that it was mocking her. Overhead, the large black birds were crying out, squawking as they reached the apex of their flight. Lizzie didn't have to look up to see that they were coming back now, formed in their final formation.

"Please Lord, help us." Lizzie muttered under her breath as she shifted in her place on the ground. She didn't try to pull herself along the ground anymore. The cobwebs had cleared, and she was able to think so maybe she could run. She had to try.

She rocked back and forth once, shifting her weight, giving herself momentum as she propelled herself forward. She caught herself by putting one leg quickly forward and then she did it! She was on her feet, nearly straight into a run.

Her legs were still unsteady, but she was nowhere near the mess she'd been minutes ago. In fact, she wasn't even sure how she was standing as she could feel her knees buckle, yet she never fell. It was almost like there was a hand holding her, keeping her up.

It had to be her imagination, and she didn't have time to dwell on it as she rushed as fast as she could to Jessica. The birds shrieking above grew louder as they neared.

She heard a moan as she neared Jessica, then saw her leg move. Maybe she would make it in time, she thought and pushed herself even harder. Then she saw Jessica shakily look up at her.

Lizzie paused when she saw the dullness in the eyes as they looked back at her. Her stomach tightened. She knew that look. It was the look of the dead, of being controlled by the shadow man.

"Something dark is coming, and your shadow man wants to control it." A voice spoke inside her head. She didn't recognize it, but somehow, she trusted it. She felt a warmth wash over her and much of the pain she had felt lifted. Her hand was no longer numb, and her feet somehow felt light as she could feel herself running faster. "Trust."

"Tic-a-too, tic-a-tee. What was one will be three." The shadow voice screamed from behind her. Lizzie ignored it as she reached Jessica, and Jessica came to life the moment Lizzie touched her. It was like an electric shock went through them both. Jessica shook her head and then looked at her. That look was gone, and her determined friend looked at Lizzie with that raw hunger of needing to survive.

"We have to run now!" Lizzie said as she pulled on Jessica to stand. Jessica was already working to her feet, so she worked into Lizzie's grip just as the first wave of birds hit the ground around them.

The shadow thing growled in frustration as none of the birds came close to touching them. Each bird crashed into the ground, their bodies breaking on impact, leaving the corpses to surround them as they ran the few yards to the door.

"Come on!" Lizzie screamed. She was dragging Jessica, or Jessica was dragging her. It was hard to tell as they clutched one another, pulling each other forward. Lizzie wasn't sure how they weren't tripping over one another. Jessica's skin felt warm to the touch, and it felt like they both had begun to glow, the light tossing off the shadows that formed around them.

"We can make it!" Jessica screamed! "Help us Lord, we can make it!"

"No!" They heard a mangled cry behind them. It was a voice like they had never heard before. Part of it was Sarah's voice, but it was mangled with other voices, all of them coalescing into this one sound that reverberated, shaking the ground around them.

They were so close to the door. They just needed to push themselves to cross that last gap so that they were inside.

"Up the stairs!" Lizzie yelled at her friend and hoped she had enough strength to climb them. If not, she would have to shove her friend and hope she fell forward enough that Lizzie could drag her through the open door. Oh God, she hoped the door was still open.

A sinking feeling flooded her stomach. She couldn't tell if the door was open or not. What if Jessica had closed it? What if the wind had blown it closed? A thousand more what ifs tried to rush at her like the birds crashing around them, and she had to push them away. She could see them getting up the stairs just to have the door closed in front of them. It wouldn't open no matter how hard she tried, and as she fought with the door. They would be stranded out there, and there would be no stopping the murder of crows as they flew down.

"Trust." She heard that voice again, and it was like a whisper in her ear opposite to the side of Jessica. She thought she could now recognize the voice. She just couldn't place it. It was right there at the tip of some knowledge, like a word stuck just out of reach. It was on the tip of her tongue. She knew it, but also knew that right then she didn't have the time to focus on who that voice belonged. She had to get into the house and get to where it was safe.

They came to the first step, and to Lizzie's surprise, it was Jessica who was pulling her up the rickety wooden stairs.

"Come on, we're almost there." Jessica yelled down to her as she was pulling Lizzie up them. Lizzie wanted to yell at her, telling her she could get up them herself. She thought she could at least, but Jessica tugging at her was pulling her off balance and she wasn't sure she could make it. She made it up the first step, but then tripped over the second that had her leaning heavily into Jessica for the third.

Inside the front shelter around the stairs, there was a thunderous explosion of sound, followed by three more in rapid succession. It echoed throughout the enclosure and pushed painfully in their ears. They could feel the noise as it shook everything, rocketing through themselves as they had been rushing up the stairs.

Both stopped, and it only took them a second to identify the large dents in the roof of the shelter and realize that the birds were now aimed at the surrounding metal. First the four birds, then more started striking down into the metal. After six more hits, a little hole appeared where one of the bird's beaks must have hit hard enough and in a weak enough spot that it broke through.

It felt like they had shotguns going off all around them, as they could feel the shock waves. Lizzie thought her eardrums were going to burst, and both of them stopped on the platform before the front door covering their ears as they began to bleed. More holes appeared. Dents were forming all around them. Lizzie had no clue how much longer the structure would hold, but the pain that was drumming through her head made it impossible to concentrate. They were so close. Her eyes were closed, as it was hard to focus on anything other than the sounds and the pain they caused.

"It's open. You can do it. Trust. Go through the door. Trust. You can do this. Just step through the door, and the pain will go away."

Lizzie wasn't sure how she could hear the voice over the noise. It still felt like a whisper in her ear, but hearing it relaxed her. She could feel the tension ease, and the surrounding cacophony dulled to the point that she could see that the door was open. They were right there. All they had to do was take the step, and both would be inside. Jessica had her hands away from her ears and was looking at it too before looking back at Lizzie, a relieved smile breaking through the fear.

Jessica stepped across the threshold first, quickly followed by Lizzie. As soon as they were in, the noise outside faded. The drumming of the birds on the metal stopped en mass, and they heard thumps of what Lizzie guessed was the rest of the birds dropping to the ground. There was no reason for it, but she knew that the rest of the birds would be dead. She would..., no, it would have killed them and let them drop as he no longer needed them. He would kill just because he could, and because the two of them had just pissed him off.

* * * *

They both stood just inside the doorway to the house, gasping for air. Time passed, but seemed to move around them as neither of them paid it any attention. Lizzie thought they were both afraid, too. After the birds had died, there was an eerie quiet that had descended, only interrupted by the sound of the refrigerator in the other room clicking on and off. It was unsettling how the world had gone from an earth-shattering, ear-splitting cacophony of madness to nothing.

Lizzie never took her eyes off the open door. She was sure that once she did, something, maybe even more birds that had somehow survived, would rush at them. At one point, Lizzie thought she had seen a wave of small spiders rushing in across the floor. She had been too tired to panic, and somehow, it hadn't scared her to see them. She blinked her eyes, and they were gone. No, not gone, just not there in her cabin. The spiders were loose elsewhere in the world, yet somehow, she was close to the darkness that was a part of them.

She shook her head. Way too many cobwebs were spreading through her mind, and too many weird thoughts.

"You okay? How's your hand?"

Lizzie looked over and saw that Jessica was trying to look at her hand. Lizzie remembered how much pain had been going through her when they had been trying to escape the outside, remembered that she thought it had been crushed when the bird had slammed down on it. Yet, since she had started hearing that voice, the pain had faded.

She looked at it now and didn't see anything wrong. There were scratches on the back of it, obvious that the bird had crashed into it, but it didn't look broken. She remembered the pain, remembered looking at it before. It had been a wreck. Some of her fingers had been at the wrong angles and she had been sure she would never be able to use her hand again.

She flexed it slowly. Everything worked. All her fingers closed to form a fist. It was sore, but the hand worked.

She formed a fist and lifted it to show Jess, but Jessica wasn't watching her. Jessica was watching the door, and Lizzie turned to see why.

It was there. It still held the shape of Sarah, but there was darkness around it now. Somehow, Lizzie knew that even if this thing stood in the direct sunlight, those shadows would still cross its face. That darkness was something the sun could never push away. It was older than the sun. Lizzie knew that, and it made her stomach clench as she stared it down. Her knees were weak, but she was not about to give in to the fear.

The thing was furious with them as it took turns glaring at them. It stood just on the platform outside, not daring to attempt to cross into the house. Whatever protected them remained strong, but that didn't stop it from standing there seething.

Finally, it spoke, and Lizzie wished it would remain silent as that voice drilled into her skull, the painful agony like a nail being hammered through her temple. It screeched with the voice of a thousand voices, all screaming in chorus. Were they all the voices of the dead? Who knew how long the thing had been killing, how many generations had fallen victim to the curse, but now they all spoke.

"Tic-a-too, tic-a-tee, you are now trapped with thee," it said. It was staring straight at Jessica, and Lizzie felt her heart sink. Lizzie hoped she was wrong about what that would mean, but knew she was right. Jessica would never be able to leave now. She was cursed, just as Lizzie was.

It smiled at her, those orange eyes of fire burning suddenly through Sarah's own as its glare drilled into her. Then it was gone, but the afterimage of those eyes burned like sunlight into her vision even after she tried to blink them away.

They both stood there in silence as they continued to watch the empty doorframe. Finally, Jessica did move. She walked across the room and slammed the door shut.

"We are going to kill that damned thing." Jessica said as she went into the dining room and grabbed one of the journals Lizzie had piled in there.

CHAPTER 41

I am so damned tired of this curse. So God Damned, mother fucking tired of it. It is unrelenting and I ~~know~~ no longer know where reality ends and my life begins because I no longer feel like I'm a part of what is real. Everything is lost to me. The dead are all around me, but even my wife has lost her patience in continuing on this way.

I struggle to find reasons of some way to ~~stopp~~ this madness. I had cable installed and now the cable man is dead and joined the masses outside. He was a husband and a father of two kids whom he'll never see again. Then there is the one who installed the internet. Things that I wanted to try to keep me from slipping further into the depths of despair and guess what... now he's dead, too. He was a kid, working at the cable company during the summer. His boss was his father who now mourns a son. Ben is his name, or was, and is, who the hell knows, but now his life is over. He wanted to go into business. He will never get that chance. It was all taken away from him because he got too close to me.

And what defines closeness? Sometimes it feels like the shadow woman will take anyone who is just close to me, other times they are at a distance, but yet I knew them and had spoken to them recently. The rules of this crazy game are always changing and I was never told how to play.

It's trying just to make me crazy. I swear it feeds off my misery just as much as the dead around me. It wants me insane. Sometimes I think I already am. What sane man would live alone out in the woods talking to the dead?

And now I've had these strange dreams. A woman, I keep showing up in her apartment. I tell her to get away from me; she isn't safe, but she knows the shadow thing. She says she has something for me and that it'll help me.

Nothing is going to help me.

If it wasn't for this curse, I'd kill myself, but it is because of the curse that I want to die. If I die, who'll inherit it then? Danny? One of his kids? How do I do that to them?

* * * *

Jessica put down the journal. Tears were streaming down her cheek, and she tried to wipe them away, but there were too many. She gave up and reached for the tissues nearby. The page already had crinkled spots where her tears had fallen.

She sniffed, then blew her nose.

"How many years did your uncle live like this?"

"I don't know. Fifteen years or so," Lizzie didn't look up right away, but when she did Jessica could see in the fading light, beads of moisture streaking the dirt on her face.

Behind Lizzie, Jess could see the orange glow from the kitchen as the sun made its lumbering journey below the trees. The light in the dining room was on. Lizzie must have flipped the switch while Jessica's nose had been in the handwritten pages, and the interior light gave the appearance of growing stronger as the radiance outside drifted away.

Night was coming, and Jessica feared what that might bring. This thing was stronger in the darkness, and it nearly killed them earlier.

"Have the lights ever gone out in here?" Jessica said. She couldn't help but look between the different light bulbs that were already casting their illumination throughout the room.

"Not that I've seen. I don't know."

"You got spares, right?" Was that one in the living flickering? She couldn't tell. It could just be her imagination, but she swore it was dimmer than a few seconds ago.

"I don't know. Maybe."

"Well, what if the lights went out? Then couldn't it get in?"

"I don't think it works that way."

"But how do you know for sure?"

"Well, for starters, I don't make a habit of sleeping with the lights on."

"You don't?"

"No. I hadn't really thought about it, but I've never gotten the sense that it was light keeping it out. There's something else about this cabin."

"Has he mentioned it in any of these?" Jessica asked as she held up one of the new journals. Her uncle had upgraded his writing books to the newer ones, and this one looked like was made from faux leather.

"Maybe. There are so many of them and much of it is just him talking about long trips in the woods, talking to his wife, who had been the first one killed by the curse."

"I wonder what happened to his dead. You would think that they would still be here torturing you. I mean-" Jessica stopped talking and Lizzie looked over at her friend. It was almost like she could see the wheels turning as Jessica looked at the table and then around the rest of the room as though she were scanning for something. Lizzie didn't think she was, though. Her eyes were moving quickly as she was running through whatever had occurred to her. It was like Jessica wasn't looking at the table, but through it as she was lost in her own thoughts.

Lizzie had known Jessica a long time and while some would assume that with her bubbly nature that there wasn't much going on upstairs. The more you knew her, you'd learn that she was a very aggressive person who was one hell of a fighter. If you knew her long enough, you'd learn the airhead was mostly an act, and that she was smart. It wasn't book-smart. Jessica was not one who enjoyed sitting down for long periods of time, but she could figure her way out of things pretty well.

"How could your uncle walk through the woods?"

"What do you mean?"

"You just said he was always taking long walks with his wife. How? You walk outside and you're getting attacked. First by Sarah, who I couldn't see, and then by possessed birds killing themselves to kill us. Why was none of this happening to your uncle?"

Lizzie wasn't sure. She looked at the books around her and then back towards the door, which they had slammed shut after being chased inside. There was a chair leaning against it now and a pile of books in front of them. On a conscious level, Lizzie knew no one was getting in that door, but that didn't stop her from letting her friend block them in. It made her feel safer too, but as she looked at it, she realized her friend was right. Why was it being more aggressive for her?

"I don't know."

"Something's changed, but what?"

"Maybe because I'm a woman?"

"You really think the things gone all crazy because you're a woman?"

"No, but it's the only thing I can think of."

"There's got to be something else."

"Why? I mean, it doesn't play by any rules I can follow. The voodoo woman told me it was a trickster, playing by one set of rules only to change them on you later. I don't know, maybe it's jealousy. It went after you-know-who with a vengeance."

"No, I can't believe it. This is the 21st century."

"And we're dealing with an ancient being. Maybe some kind of sexism worked its way in through the years."

"Well, that's bullshit."

"Yeah."

"That's bullshit!" Jessica yelled again, this time projecting her voice loudly towards the ceiling. Lizzie thought she could be imagining it, but she swore she heard laughter from outside.

"It was my uncle before me and his uncle before him. My uncle always referred to it as a shadow woman, but I always see a shadow man. There's definitely some kind of... kind of game going on with the gender, but I don't believe that alone is why it is being more aggressive with me."

Jessica looked at Lizzie for a minute, then the door and now back to Lizzie. It was like she was studying her, having some kind of internal debate in her head. Lizzie was getting frustrated as the music had paused, the quiet was growing loud around them, and that gaze was unsettling her. She was just about to scream at her friend to interrupt the stillness when Jessica took in a large breath.

"Sarah."

"O-kay." Lizzie said, stretching out the word with the confusion apparent on her face with a cocked eyebrow.

"It played the male for you, but now you said it yourself, that it's using Sarah to get to you. You said there was no way that was Sarah, right? That Sarah must not be out there like the others. It is using her to try to get to you because you showed no interest in the guy version."

"I still don't think it's about gender."

"Liz, I don't care how old this thing is, but everything is about sex."

"I doubt an evil curse, or thing, or darkness from beyond time is after me because it wants sex."

"I don't know. If I've been around for a few centuries, I'd be horny."

Lizzie rolled her eyes and tossed one of the diaries at Jessica. It felt good to giggle at her best friend. It was almost like a weight had lifted slightly from her chest and she was able to breathe a little easier. Some of the weariness she hadn't realized had been bogging her down slipped away. She actually laughed as Jess swatted the book away.

It fell to the floor. It was one of the older ones and the binding had already been loose. The pages ripped from the glue and spilled out across the room. One of them floated to the center of the threshold between the living room and dining room and rested there.

Lizzie looked at the page, and her laughter stopped.

Part 3

CHAPTER 42

Brian sat at the window, watching the birds. He was always there, in his room, watching birds. It was his life. What else did he have to do? He was trapped and alone, not just in this place, but in his own mind. He was a prisoner of his own body, constantly screaming to be free.

"Scream as I scream, but no one listens to me." He would have said to the empty room, but to talk would have meant he would have typed it out using the one fingertip that he did have enough control over to use. It would have been typed, not spoken, and then the room would have heard the computer-generated voice that was now what he thought of as his own.

How much of him was even presented to the world? How did the world see him, just the crippled in the chair, or did any of them ever see what he was inside?

What did they matter? He was an outcast inside and out...

A new bird chirped as it landed close to each other and the two fought over some unseen worm. The fight drew him out of his reverie, though he knew it would only be temporary. He had woken up again in a foul mood. He couldn't explain why he had been waking up in such temperaments, but felt the blame had something to do with his dreams lately. He couldn't remember them, but would wake up shivering and sweating.

"And how is my young athlete doing this morning?" A booming, chipper voice called out behind him. Brian didn't turn around to look. He couldn't, not without moving his whole chair, but he also didn't have to, to know that the voice belonged to Jerome. "We ready to get up and take on the day."

Jerome wasn't this insensitive to all the patients he cared for. He was a good guy, and his jokes were often tailored to his audience. Brian could take the joke and most days the barbs would be returned in a jousting match of insults and sarcasm, all good natured. However, today wasn't a good day. Instead, there was an anger that was building, that dark feeling that was following him out of his dreams. It made him want to snarl and lash out at the world, and for right now, the world was Jerome.

"You shouldn't say that," came the computer-generated voice from the speaker attached to his chair. It was followed by a single tear that ran down his cheek.

Jerome had continued into the room as he had talked and had gone to the clipboard next to the bed, writing some information into the log sheet there. At the sound of the voice box, Brian watched through the reflected glass as the man looked up in surprise at the boy sitting in the wheelchair. Jerome's mouth had opened in shock, and Brian could see how much pain spread across his face.

"Bro, I'm sorry. You know I was just kidding." Jerome set down the clipboard and walked over to Brian, coming around and lowering himself so he could look into the boy's eyes. "You know I don't mean stuff like that, right? We just always kid. Something getting you this morning."

Brian could feel like more tears threatening to stream out of him in a flood of emotions he himself didn't even understand. He could feel them right below the surface, but not the cause of why they were there. They were bottling up, just like the anger he was feeling. All of it, fighting as to which emotion was going to break free, and at the same time he didn't want to release any of it. Not now, not in front of Jerome when it had been Jerome's own words that had brought all of this to the surface.

"What is wrong with you lately" the little voice inside him asked as he looked back at Jerome. No, he glared at him, the anger taking the forefront of the storm. He refused to even reply as he just stared into those dark ember eyes that looked at him with compassion.

The moment lingered and doubt creased along Jerome's face until he stood and backed away. Brian could tell the big guy was thinking, which wouldn't surprise Brian, as Jerome was a pretty smart guy. He was normally fun and geeky, full of comic book knowledge, and always up on the latest movies coming out. Not only that, but he knew about stuff and was a deep thinker. Jerome had once told him that he was minoring in philosophy in college before he decided to dedicate himself full time to helping people, and sure, while much of that could have been bullshit, Brian didn't think so. He believed him because Jerome was also very earnest.

So as Jerome stood up and looked outside at the grass that was covered in fall-colored leaves, Brian knew he was deep into his thoughts about something.

"When was the last time your sister came by to see you?" Jerome asked, looking back at Brian. Brian wanted to scoff. He tried too, and he even typed in "ha, ha" into his little keyboard, but all that came out was the digital laugh that sounded eerily creepy.

"That's what I thought. Don't seem right. I mean, don't get me wrong, I don't know her, she's not my sister, but sure seems selfish how she stays away. Just doesn't seem right." Jerome was again looking out the window and his voice had grown distant as he kept his gaze locked on the trees.

Brian looked in that direction and was struck by the shadows. They were dancing. He could first see how the ones that stretched out from the woods into the grass swayed back and forth and gyrated like people in a seductive rhythm. Bodies of darkness were intertwined, wrapping around one another as though moving to their own song. They were beckoning, reaching out to him. He could see it. He could even feel it inside his chest, burning inside his soul. He felt something inside him shift, and though, while knowing it was impossible, he could feel his penis growing stiff.

The shadows pulled him in, and he found himself looking at the trees. Was that a man he saw there? It was far enough away; he couldn't be sure. The man was hidden, but somehow Brian knew that if he did see him, he would still not be able to make out any details.

There were other patients, members of the long-term care society, just like himself. Many of them would be walking along the paths, escorted by one of the many orderlies. They were out there, mulling around like cows out to pasture. Though as they all walked, everyone avoided the shadows. He even watched as Nelson, a zombie of a person so out of touch on meds that he never responded to anyone, shocked the orderly he suddenly sidestepped out of the path of a dancing shadow that had stretched towards him.

They all were avoiding them and avoiding the woods. What was out there?

Brian adjusted his wheelchair so he could see Jerome, who was still looking off to the woods.

"Jay." The digital voice called out for Brian. "J-man, come on."

Jerome looked at him, the jolly smile Jerome normally had was spread wider into an unnatural tooth filled grin, and there were so many teeth. Brian was sure there were more teeth than what was right and that there might have been another set of teeth buried deeper within. Jerome's kind eyes were gone, burned away by a purple flame that burned in his eyes.

Brian's friend was disappearing before him and something else was replacing him. It wasn't the thing in the woods, but did this belong it him?

Why are you so sure of that? He didn't know, he just was. This was something else, and it was wrong for this world.

"Hey B-dawg, what's wrong?" The thing said, its voice stretched and broken, somehow rattling as it spoke. It was like the voice was formed as wind blowing through broken glass, shaking then shards as sound stretched into words.

It sent a shiver through Brian. He knew he should run, and he did want to get away, but he also knew how pointless that would be. Even now, as terrified as he was and shook in terror, none of it was visible as his body trapped him. He had nowhere to go. He was more a prisoner in his own body than he was in the room around him. He had been trapped long before this creature appeared.

"You see me..." the thing said, but Brian noted the surprise when it struggled with the words. Each syllable was slow and paused. It reminded Brian of how his older speaker system had been, when the system spoke each word as he typed rather than waiting for him to finish what he had typed. It had made for long stretched out sentences all because the machine kept saying a word, pause, then say another word.

"You see him too." The creature who had once been Jerome looked towards the trees. "It thinks it is master just because it found it first and has been here longer."

The creature looked back at Brian and Brian knew Jerome was lost. The burning eyes were melting away the skin around the sockets and the mouth that had torn wide to accommodate the new set of growing, sharpening teeth was continuing to bleed. Blood was dripping from its gums and the lower jaw was red as it spat out when the thing spoke. There was no return from this transformation.

Brian knew he should be scared, and for the skip of a heartbeat, he had been. Then he hadn't died. The thing was there, and it wasn't attacking him. So, the fear slipped to the back of his mind, still there, but lulled as he watched the thing talking to him. Maybe it was part of his condition, or it was because he was used to being trapped within himself and that was worse than whatever this thing could do. It could just be that logic had won out, and he realized that if he was alive and this thing was still talking to him, then it needed him. Whatever was the case, he found himself not the terrified mouse looking back at the predator, but as the grizzled vet, staring at the end of his life.

It knelt close, and Brian could smell the blood on its breath as it spoke.

"It does not control me. It wants you." Blood spattering Brian's face as it spoke. "It wants you to its collection. Some think it is a trickster, but I've known it too long. It is a collector. It wants you for its collection." Brian felt the chill from the thing's eyes and wished he could turn his face away. He couldn't. He was locked in, and his eyes were fixed on staring into the cold flames.

How could cold burn into him? He wasn't sure, but he felt it. There was no getting away from what he felt. As much as he wanted to, there was no escape.

"I'm not going to kill you. If I kill you, then you become a part of it." It said as it backed away from Brian. Brian tried to take in a quick gasp of air in relief, but found that his body was fighting him. Instead, his breathing was still quick, struggling to keep up with his racing heart. He was more terrified than he realized, but it was all alien to him. His body reacted, but his mind felt detached. Like it could watch this thing as it moved and transformed, while still being able to study it and think rationally. The thing had just told him it was not there to kill him. Then why was it there?

"What then? If you are not going to kill me?" Brian asked. He did. It took him a couple seconds to comprehend it, but he had spoken the words, and that they were not projected from the speaker. He had not taken the time to type the message out, but instead had just blurted it out. Something he hadn't been able to do for over three years, but the words had come to him, and they had left his own lips.

He felt the tear as it stung his cheek and knew there would be a tidal wave behind it. He had spoken. That was a miracle, and one he had given up on long ago. He had moved more than just a few muscles. If he could do that, then what else could he do?

The thing was looking back at him, and that wide, tooth filled smile stretched wider, tearing more skin.

"I want you to get something for me."

"I can't."

"You can. What would you do to get your body back? Would you kill?"

Brian shook his head 'no,' before he realized he was doing it. Then his eyes opened wide in disbelief and suddenly he wasn't so sure he wouldn't kill to have his body back.

"You would. I can see the doubt. You think you wouldn't, but you would."

"No." Something about hearing his own thoughts come from the thing's mouth gave Brian a newfound resolve. Having his body back would be great, but he realized he would never be able to live with himself if it meant taking another's life.

The thing just nodded and went back to walking around the room. Brian hadn't noticed before, but even when it had been close to the window, it still moved to stay away from any direct source of light. It always moved around them, working to stay in the shadows, even if the shadows were faint in the well-lit room.

It went to the door and closed it.

"No? Well, we'll see, but I don't need you to kill. I just need you to get some things. Things that *it* can't get. Things that we want. Things that we need. Things that a few people have...including your sister."

CHAPTER 43

I have always been a tinkerer. If I had parts to something, I always tried to put them together. Unlike my brother, I always found it better to put things together than to take them a part. When we were kids, I would build up these towers just so that he could come along and smash them, tumbling to the ground. It was just childish games, but I think it always said a lot about me that I liked to create rather than tear things down.

I was always so proud that Danny went into teaching rather than embracing his destructive routes.

When I first started fixing clocks and stuff, it hadn't been something planned. I had not expected to find this way of making money that would make living out here in this cabin to be so easy. When I first came here, I had a little bit of money and nothing else. I don't know what I would have done in that first year had the clock thing not happened.

Maybe it's just that I have been here too long, but I am starting to think that the clock restoration thing may not have been such a coincidence. A lot of it had started with when that Englishman started bringing me clocks to fix. I hadn't thought much of it then, and the money he paid, while I thought was crazy, I had later learned was on par with what people made in the business.

I guess it never occurred to me before that I had no idea what I was doing. I had not done anything like that before, and here I was doing it professionally. Why was I good at doing this? Sure, I was a tinkerer, but I shouldn't be able to do these things, or know how to fix them. I can look at a clock and just know what is wrong with it. Well, not all clocks, just these old coo-coo ones that people keep bringing me.

But when I started, I had started in this barn. Why had I not paid the darkness any attention then? I never noticed so many things until I found that note. It was like everything around me was hidden by some dark veil that I was not accustomed to seeing. Now that I know what I should have been looking for, everything seems so obvious.

I was a fool, blinded by my ignorance. For that, my soul will eternally be damned.

I have been here too long, yet I still find new things to occupy my mind and new things to make me think differently about what is happening here. I was a fool and will always be.

I have even found something in the wall. Something I think I should have seen earlier. Who knows how long it has been there? The pages in the journal were yellow and nearly fell apart when I pulled it free. What would have happened had I not lost my temper? I never would have known it was there.

But now I know- I know my uncle wasn't the first. I doubt he even knew much of what had been going on. I vaguely remember the note he left me when I got here. I'd lost it long ago. How many years have I been here? God has abandoned me, as have my memories. Each day is the same as the last, and I don't know if it is morning or night. I've died here long ago. My body has yet to catch on.

But I digress. It is easy to do as I write in these damned things, filling these pages, only to clear my mind of thoughts. No one will ever read this shit. Yet, here I am, babbling on again and again.

"When masturbation has lost its fun, you're fucking lonely." Isn't that how the song goes? I don't even listen to the radio anymore as it is all garbage today. The same old shit sang five ways that all sound the same. Who the fuck is the president anymore? Does it even matter?

See how easy it is to lose your mind?

So, I found this journal in the wall. I think it must have been my great grandfather's or something like that. No, it must have been his brother. Maybe it was my great grandfather. Seems like this curse always moves uncle to nephew. I don't know if there is a reason for that or just a coincidence.

The clocks. The well. The darkness in the barn. I never thought of how the clocks worked into everything. I don't know if I ever really know how they do. I can't give the Englishman his clock back. I do know that much. Not all of it. And that crazy old woman, I need to keep her away from it as well.

Was I wrong about the shadow woman...

I'm not making any sense. Maybe I should get some sleep and start all this again.

* * * *

Let's start this again, from the beginning. I found something yesterday. I found a journal. It was buried in the wall. I would never have found it had I not, in a fit of rage, thrown a chair across the room. I'd stubbed my toe on the damn thing and had been furious enough to pick up the chair and throw it. Having not seriously exercised in over ten years, I was surprised when the chair landed on the other side of the room, its leg smashing into the wall. I was even more surprised when I pulled it away to see a book nearly falling out behind it.

I've been suffering from a lot of depression lately, getting quick to anger. I should never have thrown the chair, but I did. I guess it was a good thing as I read the journal. I'm not sure if I'm happier knowing the history now, or if ignorance had been bliss.

The book is old. There are holes in some of the pages. I am ripping out the pages that tell the story of how things first came to be here and put it in my own journal. I doubt anyone will ever find this, but then, I don't know if the author of the original journal ever thought that way as well.

"Give me what I want, and I'll go away." I can't remember what movie that line is from. I don't know why that even popped into my head just now. I don't know why I wrote that down.

Dawn is coming. Maybe I should get some sleep.

****

Jessica looked up from the page she was reading to Lizzie, who was holding the brittle, yellow pages that looked like they were ripped from another notebook. The paper had grown so thin over the years that Jessica could see that there was writing on both sides; the ink having stained through.

"Can you read it?" She asked. Lizzie had been staring at it, and after attempting it a couple of times, she nodded back to Jessica.

"So, what is it?"

"I don't know. Do you think-" Lizzie started to ask, but she wasn't even sure what she was asking. When the book had fallen, they both thought it was odd that it had loose pages stuffed into it. Now they were staring at it in awe.

They were both thinking it. Could these pages really hold some kind of answers to what was going on? From the journal it fell out of, it looked like one of the new ones. It may even be the final one.

Did he write that shortly before he killed himself?

"Well, what does it say?" Jessica asked.

Lizzie read it, her mouth going dry as she did, then she handed it over to Jessica. Once they were both finished, they both looked at each other, their jaws dropped, the color having drained from their faces.

"Holy shit." Jessica finally said. Lizzie just nodded her head, took the pages back from Jessica, and read them again.

CHAPTER 44

My wife was killed by darkness today. It had been this thing. It wasn't a man that killed her, and as I'm sure others will suspect me of her disappearance, it wasn't me either. I had seen it, though, and if I tell them to look at the bottom of the well, I don't think they will find her body there either.

My wife is gone. No, I'm not sorry the old witch is dead. Hell, if I wasn't a God-fearing Christian, then I might have done it years ago. Damn, that woman could yell, and she was never happy when I moved us out here into the woods. She never understood, and now she never will.

* * * *

I wrote those words years ago in another journal. It had been lost recently. I had burned it, as well as the lies they contained.

I did kill my wife. I couldn't take her anymore, so when she fought with me while pulling water from the well, I pushed her, and she fell over the cement blocks. I could hear her screams as she fell into that darkness.

It was after she had fallen that I had seen the evil that lie in wait. When she fell, it must have woken as dark appendages emerged and chased after me. It was only when I was out of the shadows of the trees that they stopped and I was able to stand there, out of breath, watching as they struggled to get me.

These cursed things are of the dark place, and as such, these things of evil cannot enter the light.

I had stayed there much of that day, watching the well, studying it, seeing what it would do next. As the day wore on, and the shadows stretched, those tentacles reached farther. I feared that eventually, once night came, they could reach the house, and then I too would succumb to the darkness.

I did not sleep in the cabin that night. Instead, I went to the closest town with an inn. I stayed there, telling anyone who asked that Margaret and I were quarreling and that I needed a break. Word got back to Kathryn, her sister, and she found me to ask if she needed to go out there and console her sister.

I hadn't thought yet what story I would tell about Margaret and had floundered at first when asked. I was never good at lying or thinking quickly when it came to this. How could I be? Kathryn must have seen my distress, as she took pity on me. She, in turn, asked if I was the one who needed consoling.

I consider myself to be a man. My father never raised me to cry on some woman's shoulder, even if she was kin. Men buried their tears as well as their pain. Showing anything else, then you were being less than a man. That's how it was, and while I still had no child of my own, that was how it would continue to be.

So, I am ashamed to admit that when her hand touched my shoulder, and I looked into her eyes, something broke inside of me and I could not stop myself. The tears came, and I found myself burying my face in her large bosom.

I did not take comfort in her bed that night, though I could feel we both wanted it. I have never cheated on my wedding vows, and even in Margaret's death, I was not going to put my soul in that immortal damnation. Especially not when I knew that evil truly did exist.

She left me there, and I was thankful, but filled with longing as I watched her go. I thought she would have been going home. She lived nearby, with all her animals. She was often taking in strays, and had I gone with her, I would have been just another lost soul living there.

That night, though, as I tried to sleep on that uncomfortable plywood board they called a bed, my wife appeared to me. She wasn't alone. Her sister was with her, and after the initial shock that they found themselves together in my room, they were both curious. It didn't take me long to realize that they were apparitions and that my soul was already damned. It also meant that Kathryn had traveled out to the cabin to check on her sister after she'd left me there, and she too was no longer with the living.

As the two of them squabbled, I knew sleep was ever going to be a phantom, for if I was to be haunted, these two were going to be a pair to drive me quickly into insanity.

I did fear, however, that if they had both been killed by the well, the evil trapped there may not be content with just these two. I might be next. Once I was taken, who then? I have a large family, eventually someone would come visit. My brother would make the trip next year as we celebrated the New Year. What would stop him from falling victim?

As I lay there awake, I thought of a plan. I did not know if it would work, but by the holy ghost, I prayed that it would.

After hours of drifting in and out of consciousness, I finally rose and dressed. Since I hadn't planned on the day trip to the inn, I was forced to wear yesterday's clothes. They were wrinkled and smelled of dirt and fear. I could smell her still on them, but I refused to say as much as she stood there, staring at me from across the room.

It was one thing that I killed her, but to have her now haunt me with those accusing eyes made each breath a tearful, painful one. Somehow, though, I was able to steel myself and do what needed to be done.

My first stop was to the parish. Father Thomas was an early riser, and I knew him to often take a stroll around town, stopping only when he was back at the church. There he kept a table and chairs out front of the building where he would sip his coffee and watch the early morning rise to wake. When he finished his walk, I was waiting, already seated at his table. I stood and greeted him, realizing by his stern look upon seeing me that it had been very rude of me to just be sitting there.

I didn't tell him everything, but I told him that I felt there was an evil spirit that had come to reside in my home. To my surprise, he was aware of the darkness that lurked in the well. I had not been the first to approach him. It was a blight on the township and the area in general, and everyone knew what was there without saying what was there.

How did they let me buy the place? How did they let me take my young bride there? The answer was simple, though the priest did show some remorse as he said simply that someone had to. Someone had to live there, or the evil would spread.

He then explained to me that I was the gatekeeper. I live in this house, and that the house is protected from such evil. It has long ago been blessed by his predecessor, and he has also said his vows there and will do so again if it would make me feel better. I told him it would.

Feeling encouraged, or it might just be because of knowing that I am not alone, I bought an axe and returned to my cursed home.

See, having my house blessed protected me, but that wasn't my whole issue. I still had a place of evil in the clearing near the trees. I had fallen victim to it, and I now knew I wasn't the first. The priest said that there were a number of disappearances in these woods and we both knew where those bodies could be found. The well was a source, and it would continue to feed.

I do not know why other options hadn't occurred to me. I only thought of one solution. It involved an axe, my sweat, and doing something I had not done before and was unsure how to do. Yet I was somehow able to and know what piece I would need to craft when I needed to craft it.

It felt like my hands were being guided. I liked to think it was the lord guiding them, though the sickness in my gut told me there was darkness at its root. One way or another, by the time it grew cold for winter, I had completed the barn, trapping the cursed well deep within.

By the time it was done, the priest and two-thirds of his congregation were with me, as well as the local constable. A few others as well, including a few traveling salesmen. All of them had died while I worked, none of natural means. The constable had been investigating the deaths and questioned me. Next day he had been trampled on by horses to join the legion of the dead that night.

Only a few held ill will against me at first, though it didn't take Margaret long before she had all of them looking at me with venom. Her vileness blamed me, that it was my evil act of pushing her into the well that started this.

My memory grows hazy of this to know for sure if I pushed her into the well, or if the tentacles reached out and took her. The priest has tried to come to my defense, but I can see the doubt on what is left of his face. He had died while visiting my home, blessing it. A tree I

527

had been cutting down had fallen awkwardly and still much of the trunk still needed to be chopped.

The new priest in town refuses to make the trip out to see me, though much of his congregation had come. Many of them are now permanent residents. I don't know what started when Margaret fell into the well, but it has been spreading and getting more aggressive.

The barn is finished. I hope that it will help protect against the evil getting worse. I was such a fool. What evil have I unleashed upon this world? Oh God, forgive me for what I have done.

CHAPTER 45

"Is there more?" Lizzie asked. She'd been watching Jessica as she read the pages of journal entry they had found, while making glances towards the kitchen in the direction of the barn. She wasn't sure how, but she was sure she felt the darkness throbbing out there, aching to get to them.

"Yeah, I just need to get a drink. Reading this. It's disturbing and really worries me. What is out there? Have you been in the barn?" Jessica said, setting down the pages and moving into the kitchen. Lizzie followed her and got herself a glass of tap water.

"Well, yeah, it was where the clock had been. Didn't I tell you about the creepy guy who came out here? The old Englishman-" Lizzie shuddered at the memory of him. "He just gave off this really uncomfortable vibe. I can't even say why, but he also wanted inside the barn, but I think feared it as well. He wouldn't come in there, not once the lights were turned on, and he wouldn't step foot inside the house."

"Things of evil can't enter here." Jessica said, taking a sip of her water while looking out the kitchen window towards the old barn. "I wonder why he couldn't enter the barn, though. It sounds like that's where the evil is contained."

"It doesn't really feel contained."

Jessica nodded her head in agreement.

"Jes, what am I going to do?"

Jessica turned to look at her. Lizzie could see that Jessica wanted to say something. She struggled for words until finally they came out in a frenzy.

"We need to get a priest involved."

"Really? God is the answer. When has he ever done anything for me?" Lizzie scoffed as she reached to pull down her own glass and ran the water.

"You just heard what he's done for you. This house was blessed by a priest. God is what keeps you safe."

"Yeah, just as safe as the voodoo woman's charm. I'm still trapped in here with those things outside wanting to kill me, and some kind of shadow thing who wants to do only God knows what."

"But he is here. His presence is in this house." Jessica waved at the room around them.

"So, God is holding me prisoner here?"

"That's not what I said."

"Yes, it is. You're telling me that there is some great almighty and that because of him, there is this evil thing out there. Why because of him? Because the big man upstairs won't smite it down, or cast it away, whatever he does with this stuff, I have to hide here in some remote cabin, stuck in such a way that I can't leave because if I do, people will either die or I will be attacked. Oh, and guess what? You're trapped here too, because in case you haven't noticed, you're the only friend of mine that hasn't died, and the only reason why I can think that is, is because you are trapped in here with me. So, there you go. There's your God, and you know what? Fuck him."

Jessica looked stricken. Lizzie could see the color rising and knew that she was angry. Surprisingly enough and to Lizzie's amazement, she was mad enough to not immediately yell back at Lizzie. Which, in a way, was worse, because she calmly sat down her glass of water and walked out of the room not looking in her direction.

Lizzie stood there for a minute, looking at the door her friend had just walked through. She could hear Jessica moving around in the other room, but expected her to come back. After she didn't, Lizzie grew nervous.

"Jess?"

"Yeah?" Something was wrong. Lizzie could hear it in her tone.

"Hey." Lizzie followed Jessica into the other room, getting ready to apologize to Jessica, not really sure what she had said to upset her, but obviously something was going on. Lizzie stopped when she saw that Lizzie was going through the diaries, looking at a few pages in each one, then moving on to the next.

"I'm going to find that crazy voodoo woman and show you that she is not the answer."

"What do you mean?"

Jessica stood glaring at Lizzie.

"You have this in your head that nothing can help you- that God can't help you. You have all this evil around you, and your only thought is this voodoo woman has some kind of answer for you. She doesn't. The sooner you accept that, the sooner you will be able to pull yourself out of this mess."

"Jess, I'm cursed. My family is cursed. You read the pages. That guy, some distant relative, who the hell knows, he had a priest out there and guess what, the priest was also killed. Everyone who tries to help is killed."

"There is a way out, and God will be the answer."

"You can't honestly believe that."

"I do."

"Then you're an idiot. When did you get all Jesus freak on me?"

"What did you just say?"

"I said, when did you go all religious? Is this Denny? Did he get you into all this?"

"I met him through my church, which I've gone to since I was a little girl. You would have known that, but you and Sarah were always so involved in yourselves that you really never got to know me, did you? Don't get me wrong, you've always been good friends, but you never asked what I was doing Sunday mornings, or why I would never meet up with you guys on Wednesday nights."

"Well, no, you said you were busy. It was your thang."

"Yeah, well, God is more than just a 'thang'."

"I get it. You're ultra-religious. I'm not. Jesus isn't just going to come swooping in here to save me."

"No, but he might help you save yourself."

"It's not going to work that way. God doesn't work here."

"Then why can't they get in this house?"

"One of them did, and Sarah is dead because of it."

"What do you mean?"

"This all started here when Sarah and I came here. Remember? That guy attacked her. He killed her. He was naked when he did so, which is something I will never get out of my head, that penis over me, the maggot swiveling out of its head. God, I don't think I'll ever be able to have sex again. But that happened there, in that kitchen, and you know what, God didn't come save me, and that thing was able to get in despite your 'God's protection.'" Lizzie said as she air-quoted.

"Yeah, but he was just a man. Men can be corrupted. That won't stop them from coming onto blessed earth."

"No Jessica, he was dead. That's what the sheriff said. He had been a freshly buried corpse and had somehow dug himself out of his grave to be in here when we got here, and he killed her."

Lizzie was trying to hold it together, but the tears were streaming down her cheek as much as she tried to fight it. The more she did, the stronger the sobs became, the memories coming back to her as she had watched life fade out of Sarah's eyes. She had watched her friend take her last breath just yards away from where she was standing now. Whatever mental barrier she had put up to protect her from those memories withered away, and now all those emotions she had bottled up were rushing at her.

She couldn't handle them. She collapsed into the closest chair, letting the wave of emotion slam into her.

Before Lizzie could see through the tears, she could feel Jessica's arms wrapped around her, but they weren't just enveloping her. Jessica pulled Lizzie up into a hug and she didn't let go. It was long and soothing, and Lizzie could feel some of the tension trapped in her shoulders release, but with it, a new torrent of tears.

"Come here." Jessica stepped away but had slipped her hand into Lizzie's so she could pull her. Jessica was leading her into the other room, but Lizzie couldn't stop herself from asking.

"Where?"

She saw where. Jessica was taking her into the bedroom.

"Come on. You need to lie down."

Lizzie followed her, and once in what was now 'her' bedroom, she rested on the mattress. She hadn't noticed how it had smelled before, but she thought she could almost taste the generations that had slept there, all tortured by this affliction. It was trapping her, and she felt herself balling up, pulling herself inwards. She was never going to be able to leave this place ever again. This was her prison, but her only crime was one someone in her bloodline had committed a long time ago.

New tears fell onto the brown stained pillow, she could feel them streaming down her cheeks. Behind her she felt the bed shift and then warmth. Jessica was behind her and wrapped her arms around her.

"You're not going to try to make out with me, are you?" Lizzie said. She knew she was trying to be funny but could hear how badly the off-the-cuff joke came out even to herself. "Because I never took you as swinging both ways."

"Shh. Just relax. We'll figure this out, okay?"

"How can you say that?"

"Because I have faith, and for the record, I've always thought of you and Sarah as my sisters, and sisters can lie with one another when one needs it. There is nothing sexual about this."

"If you say so, and thanks." Lizzie said. She could feel that fear and worry that plagued her fade. She also felt herself slipping off to sleep and hadn't realized how tired she'd been. "I'm going to die here."

"Liz- do you know where this voodoo woman even lives?"

"Wha-?"

"Where does she live?"

"How do you know about her?" Lizzie asked. Her voice was just above the whisper, and she knew she was saying the words but wasn't connected to them. Part of her had already slipped away, losing herself to sleep, and what was still awake seemed like it was talking from a dream.

"You told me about her. Remember the talisman. I'm going to go see her. You think she has some kind of answer for you? I'm going to go see her."

"Please don't. I can't lose you too."

"You are not going to lose me. You're not going to lose anyone else. We're going to stop this."

"She's at-" And that was the last Lizzie could remember as she drifted off into sleep. She thought she could hear the old voodoo woman laughing at her, but then the sound faded, and the darkness enveloped her into unconsciousness.

* * * *

Lizzie wasn't sure, but didn't think she had slept too long. It was still light outside, though the clouds made it hard to know for sure where the sun was. It didn't matter, the little bit of sleep that she did get reset her. It helped to calm her nerves. After all, maybe Jessica was right. Maybe they could find a way out of this.

Lizzie eased the blind back one of the few windows not blacked out and let it slip back into place. She did it slowly, trying not to make too much noise. Jessica must have fallen asleep behind her, as she could feel the warmth still pressed against her back. It was more comforting than she'd like to admit having her there. Lizzie wasn't sure if she could handle being alone anymore. She needed someone to help her through this. She didn't know what she had done to deserve a friend as good as her.

Lizzie worked on, continuing to move silently as she slid from the bed and out of the small bedroom. The house seemed so quiet, quieter than it had been since she first arrived at the house.

It made sense. Since she'd been there, whenever it had been silent like this, she had found it oppressive and creepy. The stillness drove her to the point that she thought her own mind was buzzing inside her head. So, since she'd lived there, her laptop had been playing some form of music, always playing quietly in the background.

The music had stopped at some point during her nap, and for the first time, Lizzie found the lack of noise comforting. She quickly made her way through the room to the kitchen. Her mind kept wandering as she walked.

How were they going to break the curse? Jessica was so confident that they would, but how? She believed her god would. Did Lizzie?

There was something that happened with the birds. She couldn't quite remember what, but there had been something out there. There was just no way Lizzie was ready to call it Divine Intervention. If it was, God had waited his sweet time before he had stepped in. There were quite a few very good people whose essence was outside that could still be alive if God was going to step into things. They could all still be alive.

Lizzie wasn't sure she could put her faith in a god who let that happen.

She stepped into the small room, listening as the squeal from the door hinges broke through the silence. It was much like the first time she had entered this room, and for a heartbeat of a second, Lizzie saw the naked man standing there. He was again standing over her friend, Sarah, on the ground with her eyes bulging, nearly exploding from their sockets.

Lizzie closed her eyes and counted back from five. He wasn't there. There was no way he could be. He was dead.

He'd been dead the first time. That hadn't stopped him then and it might not have stopped him now. Though I can't smell him...

Before he had that terrible odor to him. She remembered it as that sweat and rotting meat. It would have been gut wrenching had he not already disgusted her with his naked appearance.

She opened her eyes, and he was gone, not that he had ever really been there.

Well, you had a few moments of peace, she thought. The tension was already returning, tightening her back and burning through her chest. Her eyes were already dampening from more impending tears.

Her water was near the sink, and she was thankful that it was still mostly full. It was even slightly chilled, which she enjoyed as the clear fluid rushed down her throat and into her empty stomach.

"That's the stuff." She said to the empty kitchen and was already starting to look around for something to eat. She still needed to call in a food delivery, something that she had continued to put off, afraid of what would happen if she did.

Lizzie continued to think through, taking a virtual inventory of her food situation, but there was movement outside. There was someone arguing. She turned and she could see two men out there fighting. They were in the shadow of the barn, so she couldn't really see them and just barely hear their voices. They weren't yelling at one another, but Lizzie felt it was only a matter of time. First the shouting would come, and then the hitting. Wasn't that how men always chose to solve things? A bunch of men, always trying to fix problems with their fists and not their head.

She moved to the door, getting ready to go outside when she remembered earlier. This... this was all probably just another trap, trying to lure her out there. She still hurt from the last time they did that, and the time before that. She kept falling for it. When was she ever going to learn not to rush out there?

It was in her nature. If she heard someone in trouble, she... no, that wasn't right. Jessica was the one who would run out there and fight. What is wrong with her? Lizzie was the mouse. She always hung back. Why did she keep running out in the middle of these things?

Could it be because it was your friends out there, and you don't want to see them hurt? She supposed that could be a part of it. That didn't stop it from being stupid.

She let her hand fall away from the back doorknob and retreated to the kitchen sink. Just because she wasn't rushing out there, it didn't mean she still wasn't concerned for her friends. Most of them were her friends. They were dead, but that didn't mean she didn't worry about them.

Lizzie wanted to see what was happening out there, she wanted to know who it was that was fighting... but instead, even going against how much it nagged at her to know, she focused purely on getting herself another glass of water. Maybe the cool water would wash away from that pulling sensation that was trying to force her to look outside. If it felt just as refreshing as before, maybe then she wouldn't look out the window, or worse, go back to opening the door and taking that step outside.

The water was bitter, almost sour in her mouth and she set it aside, frowning at it for disappointing her. She couldn't ignore it anymore. There was more noise out there, now voices were shouting louder. She could hear someone yelling her name. Then, to her surprise, someone was yelling Jessica's name, and it was a voice she recognized but knew it shouldn't be here.

"Dennis?" Lizzie said to herself quietly as she rushed to the back door, this time pulling hard on it, flinging it open so that it slammed against the counter and shaking the glass above. She moved to the threshold of the frame, keeping a careful eye as she reached it, making sure not to cross.

She didn't have to go any further to see him. He was right there. He had been near the barn and was rushing away from it, hurrying to get to the cabin. Roland and Josh were close behind. They all stopped when they saw her at the door. Roland, those sad eyes of his, looked at her. He already knew the truth of how Dennis was here, but Dennis was oblivious and obviously confused as his wide eyes tried to look at her and everything around him at the same time. They were always moving, looking all over, trying to take everything in at once without missing anything.

"Lizzie, I'm not sure how I got here, but I need to see Jess. She said she was coming to check on you, but then I never heard anything, and- is she here? I need to see her."

Lizzie opened her mouth to say something, but just closed it right away, not able to form the words. She was trying forcefully not to let the emotions get the better of her. Why should she? Wasn't this becoming an everyday thing? Of course, another one of her best friends was dead. Of course, they were there to be with her.

She looked at the large wound on his neck. As he had been speaking, the words had whistled out of him, some of the air escaping from where someone had cut his throat. It was just another one of the many ways that her friends were dying.

Nope. She couldn't deal with it. She shook her head and closed the door.

"Lizzie!" Dennis yelled; the anger was obvious as his voice grew harsh. Well, he can be mad at her. He was going to be out there for a while, he would eventually get over it. She just wasn't ready to deal with him yet, and he would have to wait until she was.

For now, she had another issue. Jessica. Lizzie had to tell her, but how? This was going to shatter so many of her beliefs. Lizzie knew that her friend felt safe by all of this just due to her own reliance on her god, but Dennis shared those beliefs. His loyalty hadn't done anything to protect him.

It was going to ruin Jessica.

You could always not tell her?

That was true, but how long would that last? Eventually it would slip out and then what, tell her he had just gotten there? That might work, but Lizzie didn't trust herself to lie that well. Not only that, but Jessica was risking a lot to be there with her. Jessica deserved to know.

Lizzie just wasn't sure how she was going to tell her.

She's going to blame you; you know that right?

"Yeah, well, she should. It is my fault. None of them should have died. None of them should have. They should all be alive. I should have just killed myself when this whole thing started."

She thought about that for a moment as she entered the living room. She wasn't really looking for anything as she looked around the quiet house. If anything, she was looking but not seeing. She didn't pay attention to any of the mess that was cluttered around her. She had cleaned up much of it, but there was still so much stuff. Now they took their time as

541

they cleaned, hoping that her uncle had found some other clues as to this existence.

I should have killed my brother and then myself. Then this damn curse would have just ended.

Lizzie shuddered at the thought but couldn't stop herself. What would have happened if the curse didn't have anyone in the bloodline to continue? What happened then? Was that the solution? For all this to end, she had to become a murderer like the first cursed. What if she was wrong? Look at where his murder got him? Look at what it has done to the rest of his descendants. Killing her brother was not any kind of a solution.

How could you even think that was the solution?

She needed to tell Jessica. The longer she put it off, the more she would think about it. In truth, Lizzie was starting to feel like she had had enough of thinking. Her thoughts were starting to have their own thoughts. She wanted to be done with it.

Jessica still hadn't left the bedroom, and Lizzie went to wake her.

"Jess-" Lizzie started as she stepped into the small, dark room. She stopped, not able to finish as she stood there. Then something must have snapped, and Lizzie found herself on the floor. The tears were already flooding from her, and she shook her head, not accepting the truth.

"Jessica. How could you?" Lizzie said to herself as she pulled her knees to her chest and crept into the corner. For now, she wasn't ready to accept anymore. First Dennis was dead and now... now Jessica...

CHAPTER 46

Lizzie wasn't sure how long she had been sitting there in the corner before she finally stood. She knew it had been a while as her butt was sore, with pins and needles running up her foot and thighs. None of her pain, or the time she had been sitting there, changed the fact that the bed was empty. Jessica was gone, leaving Lizzie alone in her house of death.

She had to have been there. Lizzie had felt her, felt the warmth of her when she had gotten up. How was she gone?

Lizzie didn't know how she had felt her then, but she was gone now. It couldn't have been phantom warmth. That wasn't even a thing, was it? Maybe Jess was just in the bathroom. Maybe she had gotten up while Lizzie was in the kitchen. She should check the bathroom. Yes, she should check there...

But she knew it would do no good. She wasn't in there. She could feel it, and as the light outside was fading, so was her life. The room was growing dark in the waning afternoon light. It would be full dark soon. There was a part of her that welcomed it. It was becoming too hard to keep fighting. Not when everyone close to her or helped her would just keep dying.

Lizzie had no doubt that she would see Jessica soon, and that she would have joined the dead outside. Now it was only a matter of time. Then, with Jessica gone, who would she have left? All her closest friends were dead. Who would it take next?

Lizzie turned on the light and stared back at the bed. Just how long had Lizzie slept? How long had she been out before her friend decided to leave? Had that been her plan before, trying to get Lizzie to lie down? Jessica had been adamant about going to see the old woman. Had she gone to see her?

Lizzie tried to think back. Had Jessica still been adamant about going to see her? Even after they had read the note, had the desire still been there? She thought Jessica had chilled, but Lizzie could have been wrong. When had they fought? Was it before or after?

The last few hours were fuzzy in her mind, details just out of her grasp as she tried to force herself to remember them. With the midday nap, it made everything feel like a new day, that all that stuff happened yesterday or something. The timeline was not clear in her head.

What did it matter, anyway? Jessica was gone. Soon, another one of her friends would be dead.

All she would have left would be the dead ones outside. She could hear them bickering out there. Most times, she always had music or some show playing just to cut down on the stillness of the cabin and the noise outside. With Jessica there, she had turned it off.

Now that silence was growing heavy, and she could feel the pressure of the walls closing in. The space of the cabin felt smaller, the rooms tighter, with not enough space for her to move through.

She had to get out of the bedroom. The dark interior felt like it was reaching out to her, that the light hid shadows that were coming alive. The room itself was getting stuffy. She was sweating, yet she was fighting a chill in the air. Her heart was thumping in her chest and the walls trembled around her. She couldn't tell if it was the cabin or her own eyes playing tricks. It was impossible to tell, as her own body felt like it was betraying her. What was happening to her?

She rushed out of the room, coughing, unable to breathe. She took only a few more steps; the world spinning around her before she passed out, crashing to the floor.

* * * *

Lizzie tried to move, but everything was stiff. Her body was sore, the hard ground below her unforgiving. Where was she? Her mind was not processing, not allowing her to think of who she was or where. The fog that clouded her thoughts did not want to dissipate. *Am I waking up? Where am I?*

Her eyes wouldn't open. They felt glued shut, and there was this pounding that was pulsating through her. At first, she thought it was her headache, throbbing enough she could not only feel it in her teeth, but all the way down to her toes.

At least I still have toes. At least I'm still alive. But really, did she still want to be alive? Life just meant that she was still alone.

Jessica! Jessica had left her there to be alone.

Some of the thickness in her head pulled back, and she started to remember the panic attack she had had. That had been, by far, one of the worst she had ever experienced. *God, I hope that never happens again.* Though she knew she couldn't even make that promise. After all, what was going to happen when she did see Jessica again, as one of the dead?

Dead inside, dead inside, what you gonna do with the dead inside... A song floated through her head, the track suddenly on repeat. Even worse was she couldn't place the song, and she was sure those weren't the correct lyrics.

And please make that damn pounding go away! She wanted to scream at it, to just stop shaking her. Her body hurt enough.

She finally opened her eyes. She had been right. She was lying on the hardwood floor. Not comfortably either. All of her was sprawled out like she hadn't caught herself when lying down there, her face flat to the floor, her back twisted as though she had been in mid turn when she crashed.

All of her hurt... but the pounding. Now that was strangely alien. It took her a few more moments to process that it was the floor shaking with the pounding; the vibration shaking through her.

Someone was pounding from outside.

"Hello!" she heard a gruff male voice barking from outside. The voice sounded angry. Who would be so angry?

Oh God, it had to be someone who knew about the dead. Oh no, maybe one of the loved ones found out somehow and were now out there to get their revenge. They were going to kill me. I'm about to die.

Lizzie suddenly found herself fully awake as she pushed herself up from the floor, a slight trail of drool the only remnant to show where her face had been.

"I see the car out here. Now open this door. I know you're here." The gruff voice growled from beyond the door as it assaulted it with a fresh barrage. "This is Sheriff Lowe. We spoke at the hospital. Now open this door."

Lizzie knew she was fully awake, but she still felt like the fog was swirling its way around her head again and her chest was tight. It was like she couldn't breathe all over again, and she saw the darkness in the corner of her vision. She was on the verge of passing out again. Maybe SHE needed to go to the hospital again. It wasn't right for her to keep passing out, or nearly passing out.

She worked to force herself through it, standing up, but she had done it too fast. The world spun around her and before she realized what she was doing; she had reached out to the wall and caught herself.

"I can hear you in there."

"Just-" she tried to call out, struggling to form the sentence, "Just a second" in the hopes of getting herself a reprieve from the fists slamming on the door. Each pounding beat was like a fresh wave of drum lines that struck through her head, working to rebound off her aching skull.

She couldn't get it all out though, and was left moving closer to the wall, leaning on it for support. She rested her head on it, enjoying the sensation of the cool wood. That was until the fresh round of pounding caused the cabin to shake again and vibrated the wall.

"Open up. This is the sheriff, and I want some damn answers. Open this damn door." She clearly heard him say, though afterwards, she swore she could hear a muffled, "Damn kids today have no respect for the law." It was as though he said this to himself, and even through the pain, she formed a slight smile.

Come on, Lizzie, get your shit together. All you have to do is open your door and let him in. She knew that wasn't true, though. She had to let him in, but then she had to talk to him, and what did he want to talk about? How much did he know? Well, he was there, so he had to have an idea of what was going on. He had grown up around here, hadn't he? She had no clue, but even if he hadn't, if there were as many rumors as the journal made out, then he had to have heard things.

She would never know until she opened the door.

Her head wouldn't stop spinning, and she wondered when was the last time she ate? How long had she been on the floor? Could she be so off because of food?

FOCUS!

The voice screamed at her, and it pulled her out of the fog she knew she had been slipping back into. Enough, at least, so she could push herself from the wall and start stumbling towards the door.

* * * *

"Hello," she said, her voice sounding weak to her own ears as she stared up at the tall, uniformed man standing outside. She barely remembered him from the hospital, but recalled how she hadn't liked him then. Elisabeth had to save her from him then, pulling him out of the room, telling him that Lizzie still needed time to recover. Lizzie didn't recall him ever coming back, though, to ask more of his questions. Maybe he had, and she had just been out of it. That time in the hospital felt so long ago, and everything after was just lost, captured in this haze of confusion she couldn't seem to escape from.

What did she remember?

She hadn't remembered him being so tall. She knew that much. Her memory was fuzzy, but she recalled him towering over her, his presence filling the hospital room as Sarah was trying to calm her down.

Lizzie had hidden in the bathroom. She had been terrified, but it hadn't been the sheriff that had scared her. There had been something else there, some other creature, and it had been after her.

All those memories were a blurry mess, and she wasn't sure how many of them were reliable. She had no clue what drugs that had been pumping into her. There was something about snakes. She had thought they had been around her, trying to attack her, but she had been in a hospital.

The sheriff watched her, not saying anything, and she realized that she had just stood there with the door open, allowing her thoughts to wander after saying hello. He was studying her, that much was obvious, but why, she wasn't sure.

You do realize that Roland's car is still parked out there. That you had driven it here after leaving him dead in his hotel room. He must have run the plates by now. He knows that you stole it. What else does he know? He's here to take you to jail.

How long would she even stay in jail before a padded room would be needed?

"Can... Can I help you?" She asked. She had started shifting back and forth, uncomfortable as the man was staring at her, not saying a thing.

At least he's alive, not like all the dead who were standing out in the yard watching the exchange.

"Arrest her!" Josh was yelling. He was obviously afraid to get too close to the house, as he kept his distance when he yelled. He was doing his best, though, to get the sheriff's attention, trying to pick up rocks and toss them at the house. The best he could do was shuffle them around, which only Lizzie noticed.

The rest were quiet, watching with interest.

"We've met before." He finally said. Lizzie didn't think it was a question, but she answered it anyway, unsure of what really to say to the man.

"I think so. I think you came to ask me about my attack."

"And about your friend dying?"

"Yes, Sarah."

"She was killed here, in the kitchen." Lizzie winced as the sheriff said, kitchen. He nodded towards the room behind her. At first Lizzie didn't feel comfortable that the man knew the layout of her house. It made sense, though. He would have been in there when they were investigating the m-... death. She struggled not to think of her friend as being killed that way.

"I've been looking into your friend's death. We don't get many murders around here, so when one happens, I like to be thorough."

Lizzie doesn't know what to say. She nodded, as though she's understanding, but didn't move, still standing there at the threshold. It took all her concentration to listen to him, as her mind wanted to travel back in time to when Sarah was still alive. Her friend, going with her to movies, or just shopping as they would talk about what new infatuation either of them had.

"I think I told you about your killer. He had been dead for less than a week, but somehow his corpse came here...and killed your friend. How does that happen?"

Lizzie felt herself wanting to scream at the sheriff and at everything around her. She wanted to run up to him and yell into his face, "Because I'm cursed asshole, and all kinds of weird shit happens around me with the dead. I have a backyard full of them. Do you want to come and see? I'm sure if you stay here long enough, you'll join them. I bet you would like that, wouldn't you, motherfucker?"

The rage, as sudden as it was, was invigorating. The fog that had kept pushing in on her thoughts was suddenly forced away and she was suddenly looking at the man standing in the threshold with a sudden clarity. Why was he here? What did he know? Why wasn't he asking her to come in?

Suddenly, all the warning bells were flashing through her skull as something was off about this man. He must have seen it too, seen the shift in her eyes, as he changed his stance and his hand dropped to rest on the revolver holstered on his belt.

"What...What are you trying to say?"

"I'm not sure yet. That was odd. First, I thought that you and your friend had dug him up as some kind of kinky sex thing. Sick, but who knows what you city types do to get your kicks? Tim Hicks, the medical examiner, did say, however, that it did look like the ol' coot did climb himself out of his own grave. All the physical evidence supports it. So... Why did he come here? What brought him here?"

"Don't know, deputy. Any other recently dead bodies start waking up? If any of them stop by, I will make sure to let you know."

"Sheriff. Sheriff Lowe. I apologize for not introducing myself. You are Elizabeth Rogers, friends, those still alive at least, call you Lizzie. You inherited this house and now live here, I gather, as no one has seen you around your apartment in over a week. You used to date a..." The sheriff pulled out a small notebook from his chest pocket. She already knows what he is going to say. It was obvious as he had been looking into her. Why her? He already said he'd figured out about the old man, so there was nothing more for him to investigate.

He also didn't answer your question when you asked him if there had been any more dead bodies to get up and leave the cemetery.

"Roland, who died one week ago from what looks to be a heart attack in a hotel room. That's his car-" the sheriff said, nodding over his should to the car parked out from. "Parked right over there. You were with him when he died."

"I was."

"Then you stole his car."

"I was freaked out. I needed to get out of there."

The sheriff stood there for a while, looking at her. That stern look never changed. The man could be carved out of marble. He definitely looked like he had been around for a while, his weathered face, the wrinkles that show age with his pale skin.

"Taking the car was illegal, but his parents said they wouldn't file charges if it turned out you had taken it. They say hello, by the way, and are worried about how you are doing."

"I'm doing okay."

"Hiding out here in the woods."

"I said, I'm doing okay."

"Yeah, well, they said if I found it with you, you can keep it."

"How would any of that be in your jurisdiction? That was down in Milwaukee, not way the hell up here."

"You're right. I was looking into you and came across the case. I let the Milwaukee PD know that I would try to help them out. That case is going to be closed, just like all the cases that surround you."

"Okay. Then why are you here? You obviously know I haven't done anything."

"Other than stealing the car."

"Which you just said was okay. What are you doing here, sheriff?"

Who is this woman and where had she been in the last two weeks? Lizzie was proud of herself. Maybe it was just easier to stand up to the law when you've been dealing with the dead and creepy other things from beyond this world. After that, the sheriff seemed not as imposing.

"The cases were closed, and I'll admit, I'm not from this area. I moved here just a few years ago, caught up in an opening for the sheriff's department for the county. Seems that it was hard to find a local willing to patrol this area and no one could tell me why."

"Okay. Why are you telling me this?"

"I didn't ask any questions then. You see, I needed a job, and most places asked too many questions about one's past. Up here, though, they didn't care about my past. They saw my experience, and that I was willing to patrol the area without question. I was hired within days.

"It's a quiet area. Nothing really happens. There are no major highways in my zone, so I never have to worry about speeders. Bothered me at first, as I wasn't sure if this district enforced any kind of quota, but the people who hired me had no issues. I felt like I wasn't doing my duty, but I quickly learned I could just sleep away my shifts and no one would care. I was in the dark zone, and as long as someone was here, they didn't care what I did."

Lizzie was suddenly not feeling so well. Her stomach rolled, and she felt like she was closer to his man than she wanted to be. Her face was flushed.

She swore that look had changed. He was looking at her with hunger. She could see it in his eyes. That they had shifted. The brown had changed as the black of his irises expanded. His voice was growing more gravely, and she watched as he swayed forward and back.

He reached out and put a hand on the door frame to steady himself.

As soon as his hand touched the wood, he brought it back, clutching it to himself. Lizzie saw smoke from between the fingers of his other hand. Was it just a trick of the light? She didn't think so as his pupils shrunk, returning the brown to his eyes, and he was now clearly snarling. The look was feral as he licked his lips.

"Then your friend died." He growled. "It seems like there are a lot of people who die around you. Have you noticed that? The nurse and her boyfriend, they brought you home and then were killed in a bad accident. Do you know how long it has been since the last accident in this area? It was over ten years ago, and do you want to guess where it occurred? I'm sure you already know. I'm sure you know a lot of things.

"Not a lot of people die around here. Statistically, it's one of the safest and healthiest counties in the U.S. Though it is a small county, there are not a lot of people left. Those that are, they don't like to come out here. Do you want to know why?"

Lizzie was pretty sure she knew why. She wanted to step back from the sheriff. She was no longer convinced he was a man. She wasn't sure what he was, but he wasn't human. If she turned her back on him now, she felt, no, she knew that he would be on her, attacking her, ripping her to shreds. It didn't matter what protection the house had. It looked like it only hurt him, and she didn't think that would stop him. Not if she allowed him to give in to his nature. He was a predator, and you never turn your back on a predator.

"Why?"

"Because people die when they come out here. Just like little Tommy Wallace. Do you know who that is?"

Lizzie shook her head.

"He delivered your groceries last week. He died this morning. Another car accident. He was run over by a semi-truck. Not much of the body was left. He only had one arm attached, both of his legs had been ripped off. It was like when he got caught up in the truck's large tires, it ground him up. He had been riding his bicycle, so that was with him. His face had spokes from the tires sticking out of him, one of his eyeballs had been affixed to the end of one like a shish kabob.

"I had to scrape that poor kid up off the gravel this morning, and you know what I realized? That all this death, it all comes back to this place. That it all comes back to you."

"People died before me, sheriff." Lizzie could barely find her voice. She didn't remember getting the groceries, but so much seemed like a dream anymore, she wasn't sure what was real. Had she ordered groceries? Last she remembered, she had been digging through the kitchen because she had been out of food.

"That's what I'm told. Doesn't matter. It all comes back to you now. To this place-"

Lizzie blinked away her thoughts to look at the cop who was standing at the door. She noticed his hand was still resting on his revolver. He hadn't flicked off the strap, but she could see his finger hovering.

"Does it?"

She saw his tension, and it was like watching the wheels turn. She realized that his predator self didn't need to come into the house. A bullet from that gun would have nothing to stop it. He could end this all now, and it would be over with for her. She might be able to find peace, but then it would be her brother's turn. How would he ever be able to protect himself? She saw as the sheriff must have come to a conclusion. His shoulders relaxed as he started to study the house around her.

"It might not. I know about your brother, too. I know about your whole family. So here is what we're going to do." He said as his hand fell away from his revolver.

"Whenever you need groceries or something brought to the house, you call me at the sheriff's department. I'll bring it out. You don't call the grocery store, you call me. You do not leave this house for any reason. You don't go anywhere; you don't do anything. If you feel like you need to get out, too bad. Think of this as your jail cell, because you are now under house arrest. You got that?"

Lizzie wanted to argue with the man, but she kept thinking of that little boy. She knew she would be seeing him again soon. Jessica and now he. Two more to join her legion of horrors outside.

"What if I say no?"

"Is that what you want?" the sheriff said, bringing his hand back to his revolver. Lizzie understood the threat, though in truth, it wasn't needed. She agreed with the sheriff. For whatever he was, this might be the best solution.

She shook her head no in response to his threat.

"Good."

"What do you know about all this? What do you know that you're not telling me?"

"That's none of your concern," the sheriff said. Then he went down the stairs, keeping his back away from her. She watched him until he was out of sight, blocked from view by the metal slab.

With him gone, she closed the door. She thought she would collapse like she had done before. Instead, she looked across the room at the pages scattered on the table.

What is it about this place? The answer seemed simple, but was it? This house was death, and those resided in it were its plague that it spread across the land. This house was death, and she was the disease.

CHAPTER 47

The new priest in town refuses to make the trip out to see me, though much of his congregation had come. Many of them are now permanent residents. I don't know what started when Margaret fell into the well, but it has been spreading and getting more aggressive.

The barn was finished. I hoped that it would help protect against the evil getting worse. I was such a fool. What evil have I unleashed upon this world? Oh God, forgive me for what I have done.

* * * *

Lizzie read those words again, looking at the wrinkles at the edge of the page. The man had obviously been crying when he wrote them, and the last word had a long stroke from the 'e' like he had dragged the pen on the page. He had obviously been upset, and how could he not have been? He had been the first. Yet, he knew so much more about this than anyone else.

His entry had seemed so final, like that had been the end of it, but Lizzie was surprised as she turned the page over, that there were quite a few more pages. These were not as nicely written, the ink splotchy in many places and the handwriting barely recognizable as it was written in a rushed scrawl.

She was finally able to work out the first sentence, and gasped, nearly dropping the page in her hand.

* * * *

Today, I fucked a shadow woman, and my soul will now no longer be my own. My family is now and forever cursed. Hell is all we have to look forward to, and it was all because of me and what I have done. My soul be damned.

I hate such foul language, but it seems apt for the world I am now cursed too.

When I finished the barn, I thought that by locking away the darkness of the well, that I would find peace. Instead, I have created a place for the darkness to rise. Within days of the completion of the barn, the darkness was no longer deep in the depths of the accursed object. It was now brimming to the top.

The moment I entered the barn, the last board having been hammered home not five minutes, I saw the well. It looked like water had risen, but I knew better than to get near it. That well was older than this house, and not once had it ever held water.

Even still, I could see that the dark liquid moved. From the door to the barn, I could see the pitch black of night on that surface. There was no light there. There was very little light in the barn itself, but nothing penetrated that surface. It didn't even reflect the little bit of light that was present. It was like a black nothing, and I could feel the cold presence that emanated from it.

I didn't know what else to do. I don't know how long I stood there, just watching the gentle lapping of the water. It could have been hours or days lost in just what was a few seconds of me standing there. Time was gone, and I could feel the distance receding between me and it.

I might have been lost then had what sounded like a large bear come crashing through the woods nearby. I never found out what made the sound, but it had pulled me back, and I was able to blink myself out of whatever trance I had been in.

I wasn't any closer to the well, but it had changed. I saw them now. There were little strands of black that had emerged. They were moving through the air like strands of web from a spider. They seemed like they were floating on the breeze, but that couldn't be right. The little bit of wind was flowing into the barn, and these strands were flowing away from the well. They were moving throughout the barn, and towards me. The closest one was only a foot away.

It was like a web, strands forming throughout the darkness, and I was the fly it was trying to lure. Where was the spider? That I could not see.

I was getting pulled into another trance. I realized the moment that the closest strand nearly touched my cheek, and I still hadn't moved back. Just feeling it get near me, I could feel how cold it was. It was like ice had just touched me, and the strand was still inches away.

I stepped away from the barn, afraid of it and what I might have just done. The evil was spreading. Had I just given it a home to grow? Was I fostering it like a weed? I have never been much of a gardener, but was I nurturing this thing like you would a tomato? Tomatoes need sunlight, so you plant them where they will get it. Whatever this is, it needs darkness. Did I just build a place where it could grow and become whatever it was to become?

I needed help. Those who were dead around me they were all telling me I was going to hell. Once a new

561

person arrived, Margaret was quick to tell them about how the evil had been awakened. It didn't take long for an army to hate me, spouting vile and obscene threats.

Much of that changed when I backed away from the entrance to the barn and the first strand tried to leave. It burst into smoke when it touched the sun's light and around me, the God-fearing residents of the town watched in horror as it recoiled back into the confines of the barn.

"You need Patrick." A quiet voice said near me. I turned and saw that it was Margaret herself, her crushed face looking in horror as the darkness writhed. "You need him here now before it gets dark."

She was right, and the moment she said it, I knew what she meant. The sun would only be overhead for so long, then that creature would be free, and I slept only yards away. Who knew what it would do to me once I found myself wrapped in that cold darkness.

I knew I had to go into town and find Father Patrick.

* * * *

I did go into town, and I had found the priest. I'd already spoken to him before. He knew my situation. I pleaded with him, telling him there was no other way. He was bringing forth the end of the world if he didn't come back with me. I told him everything, confessing everything to God and the priest. I did all of that, and it was for nothing. He would not come back with me to this cursed place. I can't even say I really blame him. I wouldn't have come here if I didn't have nowhere else to go.

I must admit, if I'm being truly honest with myself, that I'm surprised he didn't throw me out of the church. He told me that just that morning, Miss Maisel had passed away in the night. He had now lost nearly half of his congregation, and he himself was not sure what must be done. More and more of them are dying from some disease that has been sweeping through the perish. Some in town have started calling it the sleeping sickness. Others have called it the Roger's curse. I don't know which is true. Is it my curse? Have I started this? What was there that I could do about it? It was obvious by the fear I saw in that young priest's face that he would not be of any help.

I had thanked him, and prepared to leave, when he did offer me one thing, and at this point, as useless as I felt it was, he offered to pray with me.

I don't remember much of the prayer. I think I've already established that while I go to church occasionally; I am not much of a praying man. Something about that prayer did strike me, though. I don't remember the exact words, but the priest had said something. It was a passage I could tell that he was reading from the Bible. Something about bringing light to the darkness or casting out the darkness with light. I don't know why, but something about him saying that, as I kneeled there with him, well it got me to thinking about ways of possibly doing just that.

How do you get rid of darkness? You bring light to it. The barn didn't have electricity, not yet at least, but that didn't mean I couldn't set fire to it. Fire. Set the whole thing on fire, burn it all down...

Or that was my first thought.

As I made my way home, I thought about why I had built the barn. Or tried to. It was hard, as I couldn't recall too much of what had possessed me to do such a terrible idea. There were safety concerns, worried that others might fall into the well, but seriously, how often did that happen? There had to be other reasons, and I didn't think it was all wrong. It does trap the evil during the day. I just needed to find a way to make whatever barrier was in place stronger.

I was stuck on the idea of fire. I couldn't get the picture out of my head, this huge blaze burning away, burning it all away. In my head, starting the fire, turned into this monstrous beacon of light that lit the whole area and rose high into the sky. It was glorious, this halo that would surround the world and push away the darkness.

It was foolhardy, of course, and I knew I would never do it. That didn't mean there wasn't some merit to the idea. I didn't have much time left before dusk would turn into night, and while I had an idea of what to do, I wasn't sure of how I was going to do it.

I don't remember doing it. I don't remember going to the store or purchasing any of the supplies, but as I neared the house, I smelled kerosene. On the floorboard was a jug of the stuff. In the back seat, I saw long sticks and a pile of rags. I don't know where it came from. Even if I had gone to the general store in town, I doubted they would have had the cloth, not in the dirty, disheveled state of what was in my back seat. The poles were also dirty. So, none of it was new.

Where had I gone after I left the church? As much as I tried to remember, it was like there was a dark patch in my memory. It wasn't even that something had guided me. This was flat out, I had no clue where I was or had been.

Something was wrong, and it would have troubled me more had I not just put the car in the park and was looking at the haggard cabin.

I could burn it all down...

I knew as much as I wanted to as I got out of that car and walked my way around back, listening to the angry screams from the dead as I did so. Burning the barn would be a mistake. If I did, what was in there would be free. Whatever had kept it trapped before was withered away now since Margaret's murder. My only chance was the barn. It was the only way I could contain it.

I stopped when I reached the back corner of the cabin to look at the barn. The shadows had grown long, and I had forgotten to bring the torch making supplies with me. They stretched out from the front of the barn, filled with the dark flailing tendrils of evil... There was not a chance in hell I was taking another step towards any of that without fire leading the way.

Maybe it was a good thing I hadn't brought the supplies the first time. Before, I hadn't had a plan, but as I watched the things shifting through that darkness, I got an idea. I would need my hammer, and it was only going to be a temporary solution. Probably would work only for tonight. I couldn't know for sure. It might not work at all.

I grabbed the supplies and brought them to the back and then went to grab my hammer. I thought it would be in my toolbox, and when I went into the cabin for it, thought it would be on the kitchen counter where my box sat open.

It wasn't there...

Hadn't I only finished the barn this afternoon?

I had, and all of this had started when I had gone into the barn, my hammer still in hand. What had I done with the hammer, then? I knew the answer, but didn't want to acknowledge the truth.

Of course, when I stepped outside and looked at the barn, I could see my hammer. Not at first, but as the dark tendrils flicked back and forth, I could see it there at the threshold of the barn. I had dropped it...

There was already not enough time to get this done. How could I ever do this... And now I had no hammer? I needed it if my plan was to work.

The thought of going back into town for a new hammer was appealing, but I knew there was less time for that, and I would never be able to contain this thing if I did that. I had to get my hammer back.

"And hey, look on the bright side. At least I'll be able to see if this whole torch idea was even going to work." I had said it out loud but had meant it as a thought to myself. Kathryn and Margaret were both near me when I said and they both snickered.

"Serves you right. You're going to die," Margaret said.

"You need to do this. If you don't, everyone else will die." Kathryn said. I could see the pain in her eyes, and knew she was worried. Both of them were, which surprised me with how much Margaret would love to see me die horribly.

I didn't have much time. I quickly went to work on making my first torch.

CHAPTER 48

I have never made a torch before, but the mechanics were simple enough. I wrapped a few strands of the cloth around the long wooden pole and then tucked in the lengths to the top. It was crude, and I figured I would hammer nails in once I had recovered the hammer. I just needed to get my hammer back first. The crude torch should work until then.

I went back inside and grabbed matches from the kitchen drawer. This was still my first year at the cabin, and winter hadn't fully hit yet, but figured whoever had been here last must have had a long winter with a lot of power outages. I had found matches spread throughout the house and various kerosene lamps when I had moved in. As I ran back outside, box of matches in hand, I looked at the torch I had just made lying on the ground and stopped.

I had kerosene lamps in the house...

My plan had been to light the torch, work my way to the door of the barn, and recover the hammer. It was not a great idea, and I'd been concerned about setting down the torch at some point once I had recovered the hammer and needed to use it.

Yeah, not the brightest idea when I realized I had lamps in the house and I could use the lamps just in the way I had planned to use the torch. Though, unlike the torches, I could set the lamps on the ground when I was done with them.

I rushed back into the house and quickly found two of them. I lit them both when I was back outside and looked back at the barn. The shadows had stretched another foot since I had returned and were now reaching close to where I had set down the supplies for what would be the torch barrier I had planned to build. With the shadows, I could already see those long strands of darkness inching towards them.

"Shit." I muttered under my breath and rushed over to where they lay, setting down one of the lanterns. I was already losing faith in my plan, as the lantern was not giving off a lot of light in the daylight around it.

My stomach twisted into knots, and I could already feel the chill coming from all those strands of darkness that were lurking in the shadows. There was going to be no way I was ever going to reach the hammer.

I had to. There weren't any other options.

I lit another match and fired up the two lanterns. They ignited quickly, and I heard the hiss as the lamps started to burn away the kerosene from the interior wick. It was like the fire was sucking away my breath, as I could feel my heart quicken.

The day was getting cold, and I knew why. I refused to look up as I left the one lantern lit by my supplies and stood with the other two in my hand. I kept my gaze focused on that fire as I moved towards the door for the barn.

It didn't take long for me to be surrounded by the darkness. When everything was gone around me and I could see my breath in a mist in front of my face, I looked up to see that the strands had grown so thick in the shadows that the entrance to the barn wasn't visible. I separated the two lanterns as I walked, and their light was now bright in the dark, so maybe my plan wasn't as harebrained as I had originally thought.

I had only taken a few steps, but it felt like I had entered somewhere else. The light was gone; the temperature had dropped and the world I had known felt like it had slipped away, replaced by this evil place where color was lost to a void. What little shapes I could see were only shown to me in gray, seen through a thick shade of darkness. I knew where the barn was, but that it wouldn't take much for me to be lost in this shadow world.

I felt the ice-cold touch as one of the tendrils slithered past my leg. I looked down, momentarily taking my gaze away from the direction I needed to go, and saw nothing. That is to say, I saw nothing below my knees. The darkness was encircling my ankles and rising.

I lowered one of the lanterns and felt resistance as I brought the light down. These strands of darkness weren't just pieces of air where there was an absence of light. This darkness was alive, and the bottom of the lantern touched it as I tried to see my own shoes. I could feel the friction as whatever these tendrils were slithered out from beneath the bottom.

There was a growing odor around me. As I had entered the darkness, it had smelled like a stronger sense of the forest during the fall, the growing lingering smell of leaves decomposing. I can't think of a better way to describe it. However, as the darkness moved around me, and I lowered the lantern to free my own legs, I could smell something burning. It was a mixture of horrific odors that swirled together to attack my senses, and I had to work not to vomit. I smelled rotten meat, the burning of leaves and cinnamon as they all came together from where I could see the light striking the dark strands.

I knew the light was hurting this thing, but it kept around me. I could lower the one lantern as far as my ankles, but to keep the other one raised so my body did not fall in shadow, I couldn't get any lower.

I was losing sensation in my toes. The cold was getting unbearable, and even though it was only my shoes covered in darkness, the chill was running down my spine.

I had to rethink this, and was trying to lower myself by bending down. Maybe I could duck walk my way to the entryway. Or so that was what I had been thinking. It was funny, thinking of something so ludicrous as the days of when I was a kid, and would play games with my brother where we would run around cackling like geese. Right then, something so childish could actually save my life. Of course, I wasn't thinking about that at the time, I was only thinking how I could do what needed to get done...

I never had the chance to find out. I bent my knees and tried to lower myself. I was trying to get myself lowered to do the duck walk, but I couldn't bring the lamp lower. No matter how hard I pushed, the darkness would not let go. The smoke rose from the tendril wrapped around my ankles, and the smell of burning, rotten meat got stronger, but I could not lower the lantern. I tried raising it and lowering it down in a slam to reach the ground, but it hit the same spot and would not go any lower.

I raised the lantern to try again, and that was when my world was turned upside down.

The tendril yanked hard, throwing me off my balance, and I lost both of my lanterns. The one that had been lowered just fell to unseen ground as the darkness had absorbed it out of my sight. The other lantern had flown away, quickly lost in another direction. I had no idea what came of either one of them and I didn't have time to care. The darkness had me.

I had fallen quickly, but never saw the ground. I don't think I had ever reached it. No, I know I hadn't, but I could feel the movement of the dark strands beneath me as the thing wrapped around my ankles pulled me along.

I could feel that I was moving, but had no sense as to how or where. You never realize how much you rely on your eyes for the world around you. I have learned a new respect for the blind as, without being able to see; I was in a disconnect with most of my senses. I only had the feeling that I was moving, but nothing to allow me to confirm it.

It felt like I had snakes slithering all over my skin, that the darkness was full of them, and they were wrapping themselves around me. I could feel that the air was growing thick, but I continued to struggle to breathe through my nose in the fear that if I opened my mouth, one of these dark things would slither inside. It was hard, though, as all I wanted to do was scream.

I thought I was going to freeze to death. The cold only grew colder. I thought I could feel parts of my skin freezing and breaking off, but was too numb to know for sure. My mind was telling me that all of this was too much to take, so it had stopped trying. Part of me was just wanting to give up, but I was too stubborn. I couldn't move. I was helpless and trapped, and afraid that if I did move that the cold tendrils would do more to me. To say I was afraid that they would sodomize me sounds ridiculous, but I feared anything and anywhere these things would go.

My heart was beating so fast, I thought it would burst free from my chest. The wetness of tears trying to form frozen at the corner of my eye. There was nothing I could do, and it was only getting worse.

I had to do something, though. I knew I had to.

571

I could say that I did try to struggle, at least I tried a little. The moment I did, I realized that the tendrils were not as close to me as I feared. There were the ones under me, those I could feel, as they slithered and there was the one around my ankles, but above and around me there were none. I could flail back and forth, and there was nothing to keep me from moving.

I wish I could say that I remained calm, and that a lesser man would have been flailing around in fear. Well, I was the lesser man. Finding that I could move, I thrashed back and forth, and hit with fists as I spun around. I couldn't see anything or feel anything. I swung, trying to get in a good blow. It was pure desperation and fear. I tried to kick, but the cold iron grip was like a steel trap. I tried to claw at what was under me, grunting through bared teeth, but could not dig into anything. Though as I did, I felt the tendrils move over my hand and in between my fingers. I pulled my hand back and fell back to lie in the darkness.

I began to wonder briefly if I really was moving. The shifting of the creatures under me may just be making me feel like I was in motion, but how could I be sure?

What did it matter? I was still in the dark. Still held by them, and I could feel my head starting to spin. Trying my desperate escape had only thinned the air more. I was going to suffocate in there.

I had to do something. I had to think.

Or do something without thinking. Which is more so what I did. I tried to be quick, hoping I would have the element of surprise. I tried to pull myself up, reaching for the tendrils wrapped around my ankle. My fingers were bent like talons, and I aimed to use the little fingernails I had like claws. I aimed for where my ankles would be, ready to dig into flesh or pound away at what was there.

I never got the chance to find out. I could feel my ankles release, dropping to whatever constitutes as ground. Was it on a bed of darkness or something else? I still couldn't see anything but black, and the numbing cold on my back. Whatever had been moving beneath me was still. All I had was the stench and darkness. I hadn't even realized that before there had been this white noise and even now that was gone. I was left in perfect isolation to everything. I could move but feel nothing, see and hear nothing. I was in the perfect void and wondered how long until I would drown in it.

Then a whoosh of stale air hit me, and I could breathe. The air was dry, and I had no idea where it came from. Not until the thousands of strands pulled away from around me and I found myself in a dark world different from my own. I knew this, because I could see the well, see where I had started the barn, but the back half of the barn was blown away, like something had exploded out of it.

I... I don't know how to fully describe what I saw. It was too much for me to comprehend. There was no light, yet I could see. The world was dark, but somehow my mind could make it out. There was no color, there was no brightness, there was only existence. It was like I was somehow seeing without my eyes, but with my mind... and it hurt. It hurt like hell.

The brighter something should have been, the more it hurt to look at it. I avoided looking up, for fear that where the sun would be. I was sure it would throw me into painful insanity that I would never recover from. Instead, I looked around, trying to squint my eyes so that the brightness wasn't too much. I couldn't grasp that I wasn't seeing with my eyes, as it was no good. As I looked around, tiny blades of pain seared their way into my temples.

What I saw around me was the dead. I saw all of them, and they were all staring at me, that look of hate

573

for what I had done to them...I tried to close my eyes to avoid it, but again I was not seeing with those useless organs.

"Tik a tat, tik a tee, I wouldn't if I was me," said a raspy voice around me. I quickly turned back, but didn't see anything. There was only the well and the front of the barn. Between the two, I noticed for the first time a wall of darkness that stood as the barrier just a little way past the well.

Before I could obsess over the barrier, a hand emerged from the well. At least, I thought it was a hand. It wasn't of flesh, but of darkness, like a shadow of a hand. It was there for a second and then the hand was gone.

"Tik a tit, tik a tat," said the voice, and this time I heard it behind me. I felt its touch. It was cold, but not as cold as the tendrils had been. I felt it as it ran along my shoulders. I looked over one, and then the other.

That was when...that was when I saw her. The shadow woman that stood behind me, and while all of her was dark, her features unable to be seen even with my mind vision, I could still make out the razor-sharp teeth as they bared into a smile.

"How about that..." it said, finishing whatever unGodly nursery rhyme. I-

* * * *

Lizzie looked at the page in her hand and turned it over and then back again. She started searching through the other pages on the table and then picked back up the journal where they had fallen from. She did this a couple more times before putting it all back on the desk.

That was it. That was all that her uncle had left in the journal. What happened? Who had been the previous owner of the curse and how had he survived it? Had he survived it? Obviously, he must have rebuilt the barn if whatever darkness had been coming out of the well was now contained there. The barn must have been rebuilt and some kind of barrier spell had been put in place to keep it from getting out. Right?

Are you really believing in magic and spells now? What's next? Are you going to believe in the boogeyman? It was logical. Lizzie heard her rational voice in her head, trying to point out how silly she was getting with her thoughts, but what has really been rational lately. Her life was nothing but a series of crazy, mixed with evil spirits, rising dead, dead friends who don't stay dead and so many other things, when all kinds of insanity surround you, how do you continue to believe that life is rational.

Maybe I should just commit myself to a psych ward.

It hadn't been the first time she had thought about it. Maybe there was even some logic to it. If she committed herself, she would be locked away. Then no one else could get hurt...except the nurses, guards, doctors, and anyone else who came to visit her. What if her brother visited her? Then he would be on the things' radar.

There had to be more. She couldn't lock herself away, it would only bring bad things to the one person she still cared about. The only one left alive, that is.

Jessica. She's not dead yet. Maybe she wouldn't be, and maybe her faith would protect her.

Lizzie tried not to scoff at the idea, her ancient cynicism working to get the better of her. She had to keep positive that Jessica would be okay.

Just don't think about it then...

Lizzie reached forward to grab the journal the pages had fallen from. Maybe there would be some context... something had to have more information for her, and it had to be in there.

She was about to give up when she came across the page that must have contained the loose ones. It referred to finding them in the wall and how her uncle had dug looking for more, but there was nothing. He doesn't say too much about the pages themselves until she turned to the next journal entry.

* * * *

When I read the journal, I thought I might have finally found some answer for this curse. Instead, I am left with more questions. The police have started to visit me; I keep having these terrible dreams, and this Englishman keeps wanting me to fix these old clocks. There's something wrong with the clocks, I can feel it. There's something wrong with all of them, but it's like they are drawn here. I thought for sure there would be some answer, but there was nothing? Why hide the pages if you are not going to finish it?

I've asked a few of the dead, some knew the area. They recall my uncle, told me about how he was some creepy old writer who killed his wife and lived out here as a hermit. Now I know there's more to the story, but there are holes.

Dan told me that my uncle wrote under a pen name, and it was really creepy stuff. It scared people. They said it got into their heads. That when they read it, people felt like they could see, even dream about, the monsters. Drove some insane. It was very Lovecraftian, referring to old demons and creatures so large they filled the skies.

He also wrote about darkness and a well...

I began to wonder how much of his stories was written in his books.

Dan couldn't remember his pen name. He thought it was Michael or Mike. Something like that. Really weird last name, though. Ennencock or something.

I'm thinking about going to the library tomorrow. Maybe I can find one of his books. If I'm lucky, maybe he'll have written the rest of it down. Maybe someone has it published?

I don't have much hope. Hope is for the ones who are not cursed, and I've been cursed since the moment I entered this cabin.

CHAPTER 49

Lizzie knew it was a bad idea, but when she woke up the next day, she felt like she had to go outside. She figured Jessica would be out there by now and they needed to talk. There were some things she needed to get off her chest... After all, how could she? How could Jessica just abandon her like that? How could she sneak out when Lizzie was at her weakest? How could she run off when she knew she would die? How could she be so selfish?

Lizzie lay there in bed, not wanting to get up, as she couldn't stop thinking about Jessica and all her questions. It just kept running repeatedly, over and over. She envisioned her confrontation with her, and—she had no idea how it would end. Jessica couldn't give her a hug.

However, Lizzie was stopped from making her way to the door as Sarah stood in the doorway.

Sarah looked just like she had the day she died, if not a little worse. Unlike what Lizzie was used to seeing, Sarah looked like her eye was still hanging from its socket, the orb now gray and withered. She was withered, life having been sucked out of her. Her lips were dry and split open. Her skin was ash, and her one remaining eye was sunken and dull.

"How are you in here?" Lizzie asked, pushing past her initial shock, and standing tall to stare down at this thing that wore her friend's face. It was still hard to believe that the shadow thing was doing something, trying to trick her with Sarah. Who knew how long it had been doing it?

"Liz" It tried to say, but the jaw was dislocated, and Lizzie could hear the grinding of bone as it forced out her name. It was trying to say more, but seemed frustrated with how hard it was to form the words.

"I said, how the hell are you in here?" Lizzie shouted and rushed across the room. She reached the thing that looked like her friend and didn't stop to think about what she was doing. She got there, and pushed, only as she was too late into the motion that she realized she was going to push at nothing and that she would be sprawling forward. She was already bracing for impact with the ground when she reached her friend.

To her surprise, she didn't go through Sarah, but it was Sarah who was forced backward to land roughly to the ground. The dangling eye snapped off the decaying strand and rolled away on the floor. Lizzie watched it for a second and then turned back to Sarah, who wasn't getting up. She had turned on the floor and was leaning on her side, her hair covering her face.

After a moment of Lizzie standing over her, her fists clenched, ready to start swinging, Lizzie realized that Sarah's back was heaving up and down and she sounded like... Was she crying? Yes, Lizzie could hear her. Sarah was sobbing, not trying to get up and fight back.

"How are you in here?" Lizzie demanded through gritted teeth. She felt her own chest. The more she wanted to cry watching what looked like her friend on the ground, the more the anger was internally seething, preparing to blow up inside her.

It was a conflict of emotions inside her, and it was clear who the winner would be. The pain of her grinding her teeth, wanting to smash things out of her frustration, was such a rampaging desire that it was hard for her not to just walk over, grab a chair, and slam it on the back of the imposter.

"Lizzie, stop, please." Sarah said. The words sounded coarse, grating through what was left of her throat.

"Why, so you can try to kill me in here too?" Lizzie yelled. "You never stopped when you were about to kill me and Jessica."

Lizzie kicked her foot out and pushed Sarah so that she lost her balance and landed on her back.

"You haven't stopped killing my friends, or anyone else," Lizzie growled as she stepped over Sarah. She was looking around, trying to find something to smash down onto this thing on the floor. At first, she wasn't going to get violent, it wasn't in her nature... But this thing was in here, in her safe place. Not only that, but it was also weakened, probably by breaking through the protections. This was her chance. This was finally going to be her way of ending it.

When her fist slammed down into the chest of the thing below her, it felt like she was hitting brittle candy. Dust erupted from where she hit, and she heard the popping sound as bones shattered under the impact. Sarah's rotting shirt caved into the dents she created, and yet she brought her fists down in another strike. The room was filling with the sounds of children's cereal, the snap, crackle, and pop of bones breaking.

"Please-" it gasped as though it struggled for breath. Lizzie had to fight back a giggle, seeing it try to plead with her. "Liz- Liz stop. Tinker b- bell."

Lizzie pulled her hand away, revealing the carnage of the chest beneath her. There wasn't much left of the shirt, and the bones were mostly dust, allowing Lizzie to stare into the beating heart and lungs of what had once been her friend. It was her friend. -or maybe it wasn't. The shadow man had done an excellent job of fooling her in the past.

"Tinker- bell." It hissed as it quit struggling beneath her, not that it ever really put up much of a fight.

Tinkerbell...

Sarah only called her that when she was really trying to get under her skin. It had started as a childhood name, one that Lizzie hated when her parents would call her it, yet they still would. When Sarah heard it, she had done so too for a brief time, until Lizzie had once gotten so angry that she pushed her down. It had been the one time that Lizzie had really done something so out of character as to push Sarah. It had shocked them both, and Sarah had laughed it off, saying, "All right, I'll never call you Tinkerbell."

And Sarah hadn't... mostly

But was she now calling her that, or was the shadow thing getting into her head again? It had been years since the incident, but this was eerily similar. Lizzie hadn't consciously been thinking about it, but she didn't know how the shadow man did its thing.

She would never know, as the voodoo lady was right, and it always changed things up. You never knew what its limitations were.

...Was...It...Getting...In...Her...Head...Right...Now? How would she know?

"Liz, please...it's...me." Sarah rasped below her, fighting through struggling breaths.

Lizzie looked down and saw the pain twisted onto what was left of her friend's face. This Sarah did look different from what she was used to seeing outside. The dead outside had all been healing since their deaths. It was weird to see that each day they looked better, but the Sarah beneath her looked worse. Kinda of like a zombie that had been left out to rot, how it decayed as it walked around. Sarah was not looking any better. Hell, her eye popped off. Who knows where it had gone to?

Oh God, I'm going to have to try to find that later before it starts stinking up the house...

Lizzie stood and backed away from Sarah, taking a quick glance around the room, trying to see where it might have rolled. It wasn't directly visible. It must have rolled under something.

"A... little...help," her dead friend rasped, and Lizzie looked down to see that Sarah was trying to get up, but was having a hard time moving with her chest caved in.

Lizzie reached down and started to lift her, pulling her towards the recliner. As soon as she put the slightest pressure on Sarah's shoulder blades, she heard the popping sound and knew that more bones were breaking.

"I can't lift you."

"...Get...Chair."

Lizzie wasn't sure if she meant to get Sarah over to the chair or to bring the chair to her. She decided the latter would probably be easier and lowered Sarah back to the floor.

The chair was a large recliner and would probably slide no problem on the hardwood floor, had there not been piles of books still spread throughout the room? Lizzie had been doing as much as she could in the weeks that she had been in the cabin, but there were just so many books and she was always afraid that the one book she threw out would be the one that she needed.

Of course, now there were so many of them in the way that she had to push piles into other piles and listen as they all toppled over. They fell like dominoes, so as soon as one pile went, more followed as they went into each other. Two of the piles fell into the path she was trying to clear, and she cursed as she reached forward, trying to brush those books off to the side. It was nearly impossible. There was just no place to push them all.

"Come on!" Lizzie grunted, trying to force her way through the unmovable piles of books. She still had Sarah working to drag her, but Lizzie could hear more popping sounds and could hear the wheezing from behind her.

"Liz- stop... tinker."

Lizzie stopped, feeling the wetness she had denied herself earlier start to form and the first tear streaking to its downfall.

Lizzie sat there for a moment, sitting back on her knees, before turning herself around to face Sarah. Both shoulders were now crushed. The arm Lizzie had wrapped around her when she tried to drag her to the chair was more cloth than anything else, the rest having disappeared. The corpse looked so small now, her width almost no wider than her head, as there were no longer any upper torso bones to widen her out.

"Tinker... ease me down." Sarah said, and Lizzie let out a sudden, tear-filled giggle as she did.

"I told you not to call me that."

"...Then... listen... next time."

Lizzie had a hard time looking at her friend. It was too much like watching an old corpse that was still breathing. There was almost nothing of her friend that was recognizable, and it was hard to believe considering her friend had only been dead a few weeks. Surely corpses didn't rot this quickly...

"...I... I'm ...not...here." Sarah said.

"What do you mean, you're not here? I don't know how, but you are in the cabin. You know, where the dead things can't get inside. Or is it just evil..." Lizzie said, taking glances at her friend, but each time, she would quickly look back at the living room window. The curtain was drawn, but she could tell through the lack of light that it must still be night outside.

"...You're... not... here..." Sarah rasped. Lizzie was about to respond, but the words were trapped in her throat and before she could say anything, Sarah was able to get another breath and finish. "I.. don't.. know.."

Lizzie looked at Sarah and then around at the house around her. She started to notice that things weren't right. When she looked at the books around her, they were all generalized. There were no titles on any of them and they could have been the same old couple of books taken out of some ancient archive somewhere. Which wasn't right. She hadn't had time to look through all the piles in her uncle's house...her house, but she had been around them enough to know they all didn't look like that. As much as her uncle loved to steal old library books about demons and witchcraft, there were also plenty of other trade paperbacks, but Lizzie didn't see any of those.

They weren't in her uncle's house...

Then where?

"Sarah. You're ... are you real?" Lizzie looked back at the faded, lifeless eye of her friend and the empty socket. She tried, and it was hard, to focus on the one good eye. Sarah, the eye of her friend, did seem to be looking at her. Her friend, not the creature that used her shape as it tormented her outside, but her friend, the one she saw die, was staring up at her. This was her. It had to be her.

Sarah didn't speak, and Lizzie could see why. Her breathing was getting weaker. Could the dead die? Was that what was happening? Lizzie didn't think she could handle losing her friend again.

"Are you dying? What is happening?"

Sarah shook her head.

"Al- dead..."

"You know what I mean. What is this? Where have you been? You can't leave me all over again. I don't know what's happened to you. You were here and then you were gone. All those other dead bastards came back. Why can't you?"

"......ot... back. Trapped." Sarah wheezes.

"Where? How are you trapped? You're right here? You can't be trapped."

Sarah shook her head and looked up. Lizzie followed her gaze and saw that now they're not in the cabin, but Lizzie quickly recognized it. It was hard not to. They were in the back half of the barn. She could see the well, the darkness floating at the top like vapor being released over boiling water. Small tendril shapes occasionally rose up but fell back into the mist.

Lizzie didn't have to look, as she knew she would see the busted out back half of the barn. Just like she knew if she looked at the sky, there would be no light. It was all darkness around them, but she could still see. This was the dark place. The one where the original cursed had been taken. This was a very bad place.

"Are we really here?" Lizzie yelled as she looked back at Sarah.

"I... am." She said.

"How did we get here? I need to get us out of here. We can't stay."

Lizzie was near shouting. She had only read about it, but that wasn't what terrified her. There was a sense of wrongness to the place. A feeling that she needed to get out of there before she was noticed. If it found her there, then it would have her, and she could feel its hunger.

What was it? What do you feel?

She felt the foulness of it. She could smell it in the air. It was how there was no wind, there was no smell. There was a complete blandness to everything around her and it felt like a vast nothingness that had her and was pulling her deeper in. It was a void...No; it was *the* void...

What had it been like when she saw inside the shadow man? She had seen... she tried to forget about that moment, but it had burned into her soul.

She had seen the darkness before and what would be again...the time before. This wasn't the same, but familiar to it. There was a similar wrongness to this other world that reminded her of that place. She couldn't place what it was.

"You...need to go..." Sarah warped a wheezing breath. Lizzie feared it was her last, as she wasn't making any more sound. She wished she could see her faux sister with her eyes instead of whatever this mind vision was. Even in her decaying state, Lizzie wanted that one last chance.

Instead, Lizzie bent over and gently kissed the forehead. The brittle bones cracked with just the slightest of touch, and Sarah's eye shot open. She let out a blood-curdling scream and Lizzie couldn't help but drop her and back away. More bones shattered as what was left of Sarah's body landed in a whimpering corpse, her sobs of pain suffocating Lizzie as she watched.

"I thought you were dead."

"Am-" Sarah wheezes.

"But, really gone."

"Ca-t" Sarah said, barely able to form the words as her face contorted in pain.

Lizzie felt her skin crawl with a tingle. It wasn't that there was a breeze, but a change in the presence around them. Lizzie could feel something getting closer, and she struggled to keep her focus on her friend.

"Can't? What do you mean you can't? You can't die yourself out of existence? I don't understand."

Sarah couldn't move. She was immobilized by pain and each breath showed that it was another lesson in agonizing torture.

What could she do? She wasn't a doctor. She wasn't even a good friend. She could have been better, done more for her. Now she couldn't even touch her without shattering another bone.

Sarah was looking at her in terror. Her lips were moving, but no sound escaped them.

It took Lizzie a moment to realize that Sarah wasn't looking at her... She was looking past her. Something was behind Lizzie; she could feel it. That electricity that was building up was now a fire upon her skin. Her hair was alive, and she felt that voice inside her screaming at her to get out of there.

But this was a dream. It had to be a dream. That was the only thing that made sense. The realities shifting around her; her lost friend coming back to replace the thing outside. All of this wasn't real. She was just dreaming it.

No... The fear was real. That pain she felt in her chest as her heart beat so passionately that it wanted to leap up out of her throat was real. Her inability to breathe because of the terror she felt forming from whatever was behind her, all of that was real.

"...........arah... what have you done? Where are we? Where have you pulled me into?" Lizzie asked.

Sarah didn't answer. Her eyes never pulled away from whatever was behind Lizzie. Lizzie wasn't sure Sarah could answer, but knew that her inability wasn't what kept her quiet. Lizzie could feel the sensation of immobilizing fear as the waves of it washed over it.

"Elizabeth..." The voice wasn't around her, but inside her head. The sheer massiveness of it shook the very foundations of her skull and she thought her

589

head was going to explode with the volume it smashed through her thoughts. It shook the reality around her, and blurred even the darkness to the point that even it could not be seen.

Lizzie feared what came with that voice. She knew it was behind her, and that it had set its sights on her. It was coming, and it was coming for her.
She didn't want to turn to look. Her sanity would be gone the moment her eyes fell upon it, snapping like a twig under foot of a giant. She was but an ant to whatever it was, and soon she would know just how it felt to be at the insect end of the magnifying glass. It was coming...

She didn't want to turn and look, but she was in the other place. She wasn't seeing things with her eyes. Her mind controlled what she was seeing. She didn't have to turn her head or gaze upon it with her physical body. Her mind could do it all without so much as a twitch. It was already starting to do that, turning, seeing the woods and clearing around her as her mind gaze slowly shifted.

She knew she would see it soon, and then all sanity would be lost. She saw the shadow man hovering near the woods, but this other thing, it wasn't him. This was something more, something larger, and it was about to force loose her grip on her reality. Just a little more and she would see it...

"LIZZIE!" screamed another voice inside her mind. This one she clearly recognized. This one was Jessica, and with it, Lizzie felt herself ripped out of where she was, losing her grip on the other world...

CHAPTER 50

Lizzie was... She wasn't sure where she was. The world around her hadn't settled yet. The images were distorted in a haze that she couldn't quite make out anything more than shapes, but she heard voices around her. They were shouting at her.

It was hard to focus. Her head was screaming at her in pain. Nothing was coming together. Dream and reality were swirled together in a confusing mess, and she couldn't tell which direction she was in. She could be hanging upside down as far as she could tell.

Was she awake? Was this another dream? The pain that was stabbing through her temples reminded her of that agonized sensation of being pulled out of a dream too soon. So, she was awake, right?

There was so much screaming, both in her head and around her. She heard her name. It was a familiar voice, but she couldn't place it. She knew she should know that voice. Why couldn't she put a name to it? What was wrong with her?

The fog felt like it was getting worse, not better. The gray haze around her thickened. It felt like she was being pulled somewhere.

"Elizabeth," the old voice said. This one wasn't around her, but in her mind again. She recognized that voice as well, and a sudden chill went through her. She knew she didn't want to go back to that voice and was relieved that it no longer boomed inside of her. It was distant, but the pull she felt... That was it. It was trying to pull her back to that other place. It wanted her back. She had to desperately focus on not getting sucked back there.

But where was she now?

"Lizzie!" She heard the familiar voice, the one that was there with her now. It screamed out to her again. It was calling for her, but who was it?

Jessica

The recognition was like a knife that stabbed through much of the confusion in her head, and with it, she started to remember. She still couldn't see where she was, but knew there was much going on due to the shapes around her. There was so much movement. The room was alive around her. Everything seemed to be moving.

Focus! Jessica is calling for you!

She needed to get herself together. She must have been pulled out of a dream, so she had to be back in her cabin. Was that smoke that was around her? Was that why she couldn't see?

She felt something. It was on top of her... No, something surrounded her. When she tried to move, it held her in place. She couldn't move her arms. Whatever it was, it kept her from seeing more than shapes.

Lizzie started fighting against it. She pulled, trying to break her arms free, but it was strong and fought against her. She tried kicking out her legs and even just being able to pull them apart, but they barely moved. Whatever surrounded her stretched as she tried, but it was like a rubber band and immediately snapped back.

"Lizzie!" Jessica called out.

From the shapes she could see, it looked like she was one of the larger shapes on the other side of a room. Lizzie guessed it was a room. Some of the shapes were moving up and down objects, and there were light sources in rectangular shapes that made her think of doorways. Lizzie could start to put some of the pieces together as she continued to wiggle free of her confines.

"Jessica! Help me!" Lizzie screamed. As she did, she felt a part of her hand break free and Lizzie's whole body suddenly shifted. She came crashing down, not realizing that she had been sitting up in her restraints and had not fallen over. She gave out a slight puff from landing roughly on the ground but didn't let it stop her as she used the few fingers that were freed to start working at the fabric.

That's what it felt like. As she pulled at it, it felt like strands of fabric that were stuck together. It truly was like some gooey string because, as she pulled at the strings, they stuck to her fingers, and she kept having to pull them apart to keep it from resealing itself.

"Lizzie, watch out!" Lizzie barely had time to process that her friend was warning her before she felt the needle pricks and the weight of something moving swiftly up the side of her legs to her torso where her hand was quickly plucking away at the strands. She almost had her whole hand free by now and was starting to pull at the strings that were constraining her wrist and waist when she felt this warm flow of something wet and sticky hit her hand. It washed over it and quickly stuck between her fingers, drying in seconds for her to realize that the wet goo had been the same as the strands she had been fighting against.

"No!" Lizzie called out and twisted violently. She felt the needle pricks tighten as she moved, which made her shake harder until she felt the weight lose its grip. She could barely make out the shape as it rolled across the floor away from her and she didn't watch it as it stopped. If she had, she would have seen the eight legs lift it up and the shape moving back towards her.

She didn't need to see it to know what it was. The knowledge was working its way into her thoughts as she was putting it together, and the realization hit. She was struggling frantically to get herself free of the web that was cocooned around her.

"Stop struggling, my dear. It wants you back, and I don't want you here. Not until you bring me back what I lent to you." The voice was from the other side of the room as well. Lizzie couldn't tell where it was in one of the shadows she couldn't see through the webbing. She recognized the voice. She knew she had heard it before, but where? She needed to see her. Who was that? Where was she?

She didn't have time to get caught up in questions. She needed to get out of the web. She needed to help Jessica. To save her before the shadow man got to her.

"What 'it'? What do you mean?" Jessica yelled at the other voice. "Liz, you need to wake up! Get out of here. You are safe in the house, but not in your dreams. You need to wake up!"

"Oh, hush now." The older voice. Who was she? She was definitely an old woman. Lizzie could place that much, but how did she know that voice? Where had she heard it before... "Lizzie and I know each other well, don't we? You've been coming here since your first cursed night. You just don't remember most of your visits now, do you?"

The voice. It had an accent before, but the accent was gone now. Lizzie was sure of it.

Lizzie realized where she was and knew who she was talking to. She couldn't remember if the old voodoo lady had ever given her a name, but she remembered her and the old apartment. The layout made sense as she could see the light from the doorway leading into the kitchen and the other light rectangle going to a back hallway. The old woman must be sitting where she always sat, over in her chair, out of the light and always a part of the darkness, but not completely one with it.

"Wake up!"

"Jessica!" Lizzie tried to yell back at her, but the web she was caught in was making it hard to breathe. If she was dreaming, how could she have trouble breathing? But her lungs were growing tight with the lack of air.

The spider climbed back on top of her, and she felt the warm goo again as it splashed onto her. The spiders were hers? What was the old woman talking about? What was it?

Lizzie desperately kept twisting and turning, her movements becoming more vicious as she struggled against it. The spider was on top of her, and she felt its pincher like legs digging in as she thrashed. It was struggling to stay on her, but she was committed to getting rid of the damned thing. She had to find a way.

She pushed herself to sit part way up; it was the most she could lean forward and took much of her will to do it. She did it for as much as she could, and then threw herself back at an angle so that she slammed back to the floor. She couldn't see what had been behind her but felt it, as there must have been more of the large creatures there. She felt them as they crushed beneath her.

More crunched as she rolled back and forth on the ground, and she felt the one on top dig in harder. She feared it drew blood as the needle-like legs had to have broken her skin. She pushed through the pricks of pain and continued to shake and roll. She was doing everything she could to twist her way free, fighting with all she could to escape.

"Lizzie, wake up! Just wake up and you'll be okay. You'll be back in the cabin. You can't be here right now. You can't do anything for me." Jessica yelled. Why wasn't she helping Lizzie? Was she cocooned as well? She was still on the other side of the room.

"That's enough out of you. Daughter, shut her up." The old woman yelled. Lizzie couldn't see or hear what they were doing to her friend as she viciously fought against her constraints. No matter how hard she shook, she couldn't find any give. She kept twisting, pushing and pulling against anywhere she felt even the slightest wiggle, but it was no use. They were layered so thick that there was no way she was now going to break through.

"Now, little one. We have talked many times before." The old woman said, and Lizzie knew she was talking back to her now. "We have talked, and I have tried to play nice. I've tried to make you think I served your best interest. I don't, really. I just want what is mine returned to me. I lent it to your uncle, and now I want it back. You bring me the talisman...maybe I will let you free of this web. It's that simple girl. Bring me what I want, and you can all go away. I won't need you anymore."

Lizzie finally twisted just right and felt herself spin so that she landed opposite of how she had been. The spider had stayed with her for the ride, and she felt that satisfying crunch of it as she landed on top of it.

She barely had time to savor her victory. As it had crunched beneath her, two more spiders landed on top of her. To make it worse, she was now on her stomach with less leverage to twist around. Now, with the two heavy creatures on her back, it made it near impossible to move even back and forth. She tried, but it was so hard to breathe. She was finding that it was getting harder to move, and she wanted to drift away into a stupor. She could feel the new fog of exhaustion trying to take root and she had to rest to keep away from drifting into its deluge.

"It wants you. It's trying to pull you back to the other side. It thinks it already owns you and has made a claim. My claim predates it, no matter what side it is on. I claim you, and I claim my talisman."

"Why?" Lizzie gasped and let her head fall forward, resting it on the carpeted floor.

"Why do you care? You don't believe in any of this. This is just a dream to you. A nightmare ruining your life. Give me the talisman and I can make it all go away. I can give you back your life. You'd like that, wouldn't you?"

Lizzie felt herself losing the fight. Fatigue burned through her muscles and confusion was getting into her thoughts. It had to be because she found herself contemplating what the old woman said. She sounded right. Lizzie never asked for any of this, and she wished nothing more than to return to her life. She wasn't even completely surprised when she heard herself ask a question.

"Would my friends be back? Would they be okay?"

"Tsk, tsk. No, my dear. What is done is done. Dead is dead. There is nothing I can do about that. I can free you from this curse, but nothing more."

"What about Jessica?"

Lizzie heard a movement, and then there was a thump. She never saw what was happening, but felt it as another spider jumped on her back.

"You don't have long to choose. It is pulling you back. You can feel it, can't you? It wants it too. It knows it is the key."

"What key? What about Jessica?"

"What do keys do, dear? They unlock doors."

"What door, what's the key?" Lizzie was feeling the lack of air getting to her and was taking frantic short breaths. The air tasted funny to her, but of course it would. It's her breath. Her own bad breath and it was killing her. She didn't remember much about biology and physics, but she did remember that much.

"As to your friend? She's lost now. She thought her religion would save her, but there is more to this world than crosses and even the persecuted must face hard times. God won't protect anyone here. Not your God."

"What have you done to her?" Lizzie gasped. Her lungs were burning. If this was a dream, how could she be suffocating herself?

"Would you like to see? Daughter, help her see. It would be worse for you if you allow it to take you."

Lizzie saw a shape moving towards her and felt as the needle pricks on her back deepened as it did. The shape paused, looking at them, but then continued. Lizzie could tell that the daughter was nervous, and she kept her distance from the things on Lizzie's back.

Lizzie briefly wondered about the rest of the spiders in the room. When she had first woken up there, she had seen shapes all around her. Now much of the room was still floating between intense darkness and intense light.

The daughter reached her and bent down. Lizzie could feel her tugging at the web around her face, though Lizzie was starting to forget why. She had stopped breathing; her head was spinning. She felt the darkness taking her, and she was fighting herself as she slipped into it.

The first rush of breathable air struck her face like a slap back to reality; her face was on fire. That brain crushing headache returned as she opened her eyes with a snap. The air awakened her senses and everything in her body was alert with waves of pain. Combined with the countless pins and needles that stabbed at her through every nerve ending, the spider's legs were excruciating. Because her body had oxygen again, all her senses were alive.

She had to close her eyes. The pain that stormed through her was too much. She screamed, calling out to God, and all that was around, "Ahh! Holy shit, that hurts, GOD!"

And from across the room, she could hear the laughter from the old woman as she cackled in delight.

"Whose god?" The woman teased. "Her God is not here. Not in this place?"

"God... is... everywhere."

Hearing Jessica's voice, as weak as it sounded, brought Lizzie through the pain that was already starting to subside. Her body was coming alive, and with it, the sensations of more than just her waking muscles. Lizzie was able to open her eyes and see what they had done to her.

She wished she hadn't, and quickly closed them again knowing that she would never get that out of her mind. That image, that brief second that she saw, would be with her until the day all this was over, and she found herself a part of that other place. It would haunt her seconds, traveling with her as the obscene horror, the macabre Christmas would never go away.

After all, wasn't that what it had looked like? In that brief glance she had seen. The dangling red of Christmas decorations hanging around the room, twinkling of lights as they danced throughout and the green plants of holly hanging from the doorway.

But decorations were never wet... No, they were never wet...

And that was what she couldn't reconcile. Why would the decorations be dripping? Well, it wasn't water. Water wasn't... No, no, ...no... she couldn't finish that though. Finishing that thought, thinking about the red liquid that dropped from around the room. If she thought about it, she would know what it was...

But you already know. It's why you shut your eyes. It's why you're hiding from the image burned into your thoughts.

She didn't want to acknowledge it, but she knew the voice was true.

The dripping red streamers were Jessica, her intestines stung around the room, dripping... The twinkling lights were all the sets of spider eyes as they moved all around them. Just knowing what they were, all the different sizes and how many of them there were made her skin crawl. They were all around her. Even on the web, she could feel tiny spiders moving along her skin...

Then there was the green thing. She had filed it away as holly, but there were no words for what it was. She tried to file it away as something natural, a vine that was hanging down over her friend and not covering her face. That it wasn't pulsating with a dark glow that flowed in and out as Jessica still breathed. It wasn't something that had teeth that jutted out from it, and there weren't mouths with fangs embedded at various points in Jessica's body. That it didn't reach up into the ceiling with part of it snaking away in a branch that ran to the old woman who sat in the corner, cocooned in roots that invaded her body.

No. None of that could be possible, as the perversion of it was too much. None of it could be real. None of this was real. It couldn't be...

The old woman was right. There was no way God could ever be there. No God could ever allow for the unreality that Lizzie had seen.

She found herself counting down from ten, and when she had reached one, starting over and counting down again. Maybe if she just kept counting, it would all go away, that the nightmare would end, and she would be back in her bed.

She would be in a different nightmare, but at least then, it would be one she had grown accustomed to. How long had her uncle lasted? He'd lasted decades, right? She just had to keep surviving.

"...3...2...1..."

"Open your eyes." The old woman said. Lizzie listened as the spiders around her were beginning to frenzy. The ones that were on her were climbing back to her face, probably to cover it again. Lizzie felt it as well as heard the crunch as the closest spider flew off her. Then the next and finally the third one.

"Tsk, tsk, daughter. They are here for her. They can have her. She's seen that there is no God. Her friend's God has died long ago. He will not do anything here."

"God ... is ... Everywhere." Jessica said, though how she was even alive, Lizzie wasn't sure. Not with what she saw. It must be keeping her alive somehow.

"Tik-a-tat Tik-a-tee. Where must you be..." The voice slithered into the room, and Lizzie didn't turn to look at the open door. She could feel the cold even through the web and knew it was standing there. The shadow man had found them.

Instead, Lizzie watched the old woman and saw how she tensed up the moment it appeared in her doorway. The daughter never saw it. She was still fighting with the spiders, as they had turned their attention to her. Out of the corner of Lizzie's vision, she watched as the daughter swung wildly at any of them as they drew close to her.

"What reason you be here, trickster?" The old woman spat.

"Tik-a-tee, Tik-a-tu, I am here for you. You took what you shouldn't and now it's due."

The old woman turned to look back to Lizzie and Lizzie felt her heart tightening in her chest.

"Mother!" the daughter cried out, and Lizzie heard as the woman near her dropped, the spiders now leaping on her.

"Daughter! You let her go trickster!"

The shadow man laughed, the bone grinding laugh causing a wave of nausea in Lizzie and had her gagging a hearing the unnatural sound.

"Tik-a-tu, tik-a-tee, you have never understood who I be. I have no control over these." It said, and Lizzie didn't have to see it, to know that the wicked smile, the white teeth that could somehow be seen on the face that could not, would be smiling at the old woman. It was taking glee in this.

"Estufa!" the old woman yelled. Seconds later, Lizzie felt the heat and watched as the room around her was ablaze. Fire had erupted. Each of the hundreds of spiders were lit up as the flames burst from their bodies. The daughter let out a horrendous scream as she was covered in the spiders, and in the flame bursting from them spread.

The old woman looked from the shadow man to her daughter, her face twisted in pain. The shadow man's laugh grew louder, and it was painful for Lizzie to hear it. She imagined she could see the room shaking but wasn't sure if that was her own skull vibrating, threatening to rupture from that terrible sound.

"Get out of here! Go, you terrible thing, and take her with you." The old woman yelled as she pointed to Lizzie. Lizzie barely knew what was happening, barely saw how the flames had reached the dangling organs of Jessica and quickly spread along the grotesque vines. She didn't have a chance to see much of it, as she felt herself being ripped away. As she left, she heard the old woman call out to her.

"You made a mistake, you. You're about to see, as they are all coming for you now. You thought you have seen evil. You haven't seen anything, and they all know you now. They know what you have, and they will all be coming to claim the prize."

The last thing Lizzie heard as the old woman's laugh faded away was her friend's faint voice, a whisper, but somehow still reached Lizzie's ear amongst all the chaos...

"Thank you, God." Her friend had said. Then Lizzie found herself again in the darkness.

CHAPTER 51

"You cannot be serious." Sarah said, letting out an exasperated sigh.

"Yep." Lizzie said, looking at the steering wheel clutched in her hand. Her knuckles were white, and she was doing everything in her power to bite back tears. This was all her fault. They all knew it.

"No, you can't be. There's no way this could be happening." Sarah said, still obviously shocked in disbelief.

"I don't think she's kidding." Jessica said from the back seat.

"I'm not. Hey, do you have any cell reception?" Lizzie said, having finally pulled out her phone to look at the display.

"Nothing. No bars." Sarah said, holding out her phone for both to see. Jessica looked at it and then looked at her own phone that she was pulling out of her clutch.

"Crap." Jessica said before putting the useless device back into her bag.

"So, what are we going to do?" Lizzie said, looking back at the dashboard and at the flashing display. It was flashing, because the car had been trying to warn them it was getting low on fuel, but Lizzie hadn't paid any attention to it. Now they were stranded out in the middle of nowhere after having decided to take a back road home rather than staying on the interstate.

"I told you we should have used a GPS." Sarah said, looking at the woods.

"I thought I knew the way. It just, it all looks so different at night."

"Lizzie!" Sarah exclaimed, crossing her arms in a huff.

"It'll be okay. Someone is going to come along." Jessica said. She sat back in the seat, a shiver running through her. The chill was already seeping its way into the car now that the constant blast of heat had been cut out with the death of the engine.

"I'm sorry, okay? I thought I knew the way." Lizzie said. She was on the brink of tears. She could feel them building up inside of her, welling up, getting ready to burst free.

"It's okay Lizzie." Jessica said.

Sarah looked frustrated, but after a long second, her shoulders slumped and she looked over at her friend, forcing a smile.

"Yeah, it's okay." Sarah said reluctantly. "Besides, I got to see my boyfriend tonight. This is worth it."

The smile became real as well as the hand that emerged from the back seat and smacked Sarah on the shoulder.

"Your boyfriend? Oh no, Shawny baby is all mine."

"Yours huh." Lizzie said, trying to laugh though she was still pushing down the frustration and tears. It was obvious to anyone that knew her that she was about to lose it but was trying to keep enough of it together. Her friends were trying to cheer her up. She needed to let them. "Well, he can be your boyfriend, but Shawn will be my husband."

"Whatever." Jessica said, laughing.

"Yeah, whatever." Sarah agreed. "Yeah, maybe tonight was worth it. Do you think we should have gotten a hotel room?"

"We said we wouldn't. It was all about the road trip." Jessica said, but she gave quick glances to Lizzie as she was saying it, trying to give Sarah an obvious hint, one that Sarah didn't notice, but Lizzie did.

"You know I couldn't have afforded that." Lizzie said. She heard the defeat in her own voice for as much as she had been trying to hide it.

"That wasn't why we didn't get a hotel." Jessica said a little too quickly and Lizzie caught the barely perceptible glance she gave Sarah that told her it was one hundred percent the reason why they hadn't gotten one.

Lizzie had only been a part of the discussion once and at that time Sarah had repeatedly told Lizzie that she would pay for her share of the room. Lizzie had told her no, even going so far as to second question her even going. There would be other concerts. She didn't need to go with them all the way to Chicago just to see some hot guy who could sing like an angel. She could live without it.

Lizzie had left the conversation feeling sad, but had put it behind her, only to have Jessica show up two days later with the tickets, quickly putting off the discussion of the hotel by saying they'd just drive back that night. It was only a five-hour drive, they could handle it.

Why had they gotten off the damn interstate? Damn construction backing up traffic for hours. They were close enough to home; they had all thought they knew the back roads well enough. GPS on their phones hadn't been any help, it had just wanted to route them back to the interstate they were trying to get around.

"A hotel would have been nice, but we didn't. What we need is gas." Sarah said. She was tapping at her phone again, the frustration heard throughout the car with the increasing volume, the taps of her long nails on the small screen.

"What highway are we on?"

"I think highway N," Jessica said from the back seat. She had pulled back her own phone and was scrolling through it. She let out a sigh and let the screen go dark. "Useless, I can't even pull up Maps."

"Duh, no data." Sarah said, still tapping at her own screen.

"Yeah, but I thought it still might show me the area. Nothing. Just blank screen."

Lizzie looked again at the surrounding woods. There was just so much of it. What direction should she go in? She didn't remember seeing a gas station by the interstate, but she also hadn't been looking. If there weren't so many trees around, maybe they could find a town. They could be right next to one, and all these trees would block any trace of it.

And what was she going to do? She had to do something. She did this to her friends, stranding them out there. There had to be something. She just needed to think.

"Maybe." Sarah said, pulling Lizzie out of her thoughts.

"What?"

"Jessie, here, thinks that tomorrow, we'll all be laughing about this."

"Maybe even today, once we get home."

"We are in the middle of the woods with no gas and no idea where to go. What makes you think we'll be home today?" Sarah turned to look at Jessica, her focused eyes locking Jessica's own.

"We will."

"How."

Jessica looked uncomfortable, and Lizzie knew why. Jessica was always sure when it came to her faith. She would talk about it with anyone and everyone, but when it came to pushing it on someone, she often fell silent. Sarah was the opposite. She was quick to mention her spirituality and how, through it, would never find her stepping foot inside a church.

So, whenever Jessica was going off faith in a conversation with Sarah, she tended to bite her tongue. Lizzie could see her doing it now.

"We just will." Lizzie said. Jessica shot her a grateful glance before pulling out her phone again and tried to tap it into some sort of submission.

"Glad you two are so confident." Sarah put her phone back into her clutch before lying her head back on the seat.

"What are you doing?" Jessica asked.

"I am taking a nap until someone comes to save us or rape us. Either way, I'm getting some sleep."

"Sarah" Jessica exclaimed with a teasing slap on her shoulder. Lizzie chuckled at the exchange, but she couldn't help that nagging feeling in the pit of her stomach, the butterflies that were buzzing. She had already started thinking the same thing, but unlike Sarah, she couldn't make light of it. What if someone did come along? What if a group of someone's?

They had left on Friday. It was in the middle of the night, Saturday morning. It wasn't too farfetched that there were a group of drunk guys out there just looking for some kind of 'fun." What if that was who found them? They could be... No, she didn't want to finish that thought of what could happen to them. The end result of what happened would still be the same, the three of them left out in the woods, shallow graves that would be found only if their car was. If not then, then maybe if they were lucky, their bodies would be discovered in another month when hunting season began. Even then, what were the chances...

Not good.

She needed to do something.

"I'm going to get gas," Lizzie said, barely having time to realize that she had said anything. Her friends both looked at her, their eyes going wide.

"No, you're not." Sarah said.

"Lizzie, you can't go alone."

"Do you even have a gas can?"

"No, we need to just wait here. Someone will come along."

"Jess, that isn't a plan either as who knows who will come along, but Liz, you can't go alone. Do you even have a gas can? No, I know the answer. You don't. So, what are you going to do, have them pump it into your hands?"

"We just need to wait here."

"I'm going." Lizzie said and turned from looking at the road ahead to look each of them in the eye in turn. Both of them looked away, not able to meet the challenge they heard in her voice.

"This isn't a good idea." Sarah said.

"Yeah, I know," Lizzie said and could feel the conviction she had in her voice already starting to waver.

"Liz-" Jessica said, unable to finish the sentence.

"You know that you can't go alone. You know that."

Lizzie did know that. It was the same reason she could never go alone from classes at night. Young woman who walked alone at night were never heard from again. It was a sad truth. She knew it just as well as the rest of them in the car. It was the same reason she always had pepper spray in her purse... and why it was so frustrating that all she had with her was her clutch while her purse sat in their apartment who knew how many miles away.

But something had to be done. She got her friends into this; she had to get them out of it. This was all her fault. This would always be her fault. She always brought them down, didn't she...

Where were those thoughts coming from?

No, she needed to focus on the road ahead. It wouldn't be that far of a walk. She was sure there was somewhere up there, someone she could find to help her.

There wouldn't be, though... She would have to help herself. She would have to be the one to help them. She would have to be the one to save all of them. It would always be the burden she would have to bear. Even after all their deaths, it would always be on her shoulders.

She reached for the door handle, but before she could pull it, she heard two other doors open. She turned and saw that both her friends were exiting the car from the other side.

"What are you doing?"

"You're not going alone." Sarah said.

"Were coming with you." Jessica said.

"I need to do this. I got us into this. I need to get us out. You guys stay here."

"Nope. Doesn't work that way. We're in this together. What happens to one, happens to all." Jessica said.

"What, now we're the three musketeers?" Sarah said.

"Hell no. What are we, men? Na, we're better than that. We're women, and we kick ass," Jessica said.

Lizzie got out of the car, and they all looked at each other over the roof. It was dark. They could all barely see each other, but she knew they all shared the same worried smiles.

Lizzie also noticed that the butterflies were going away. That whatever was going to happen, maybe they would be okay. After all, they would be there together.

"You don't have to do this," Lizzie said again.

"Yes. We do. Where you go, we go. You're my sister. For now, and forever, we will be here for you." Sarah said.

"Ditto." Jessica said as she hurried around the back of the car. The next thing Lizzie knew was she was getting pulled into a huge hug. It didn't take long before she felt another set of arms around her as Sarah joined in.

"We'll get through this," Jessica said.

"We always do." Sarah said.

"Then let's do this," Lizzie said as she pushed them away, looking at them and their resolve. Though as the world faded into darkness around her, she saw Sarah, the corpse and Jessica, the dying deserted body, both staring back at her. Her heart quickly sank as she realized they were both gone.

"We'll get through this..."

"For now, and forever..."

Part 4

CHAPTER 52

Lizzie woke up feeling exhausted and sore. Part of her was still swimming in dreams, and part of her knew she was back in reality. She was in a cabin; she thought it was the bedroom she had thought of as her own since her time there. The room was dark. She could just as easily be in that other place. Was this the other cabin?

Though, as she thought about her time in the other place, she didn't recall seeing the cabin. There was the back half of the barn, Sarah, her rotting dead friend, others farther away who she couldn't tell who they were, and...

DON'T THINK ABOUT IT. Thinking about it is one step closer to bringing it into this world.

But what was it? What was beyond the doorway?

Lizzie slowly sat up as she studied the room. It seemed like the regular world. Had she really been through all of that, and it was still night out? She could only vaguely remember going to bed the night before. No, she couldn't remember going to bed. Last she remembered, it had been morning and Jessica had gone. There had been that creepy cop and then... what?

She kicked off the blanket so that it fell to the floor and saw she was still wearing her clothes from yesterday. She reached to turn on the light, pushing back the shadows of the room. So, at some point, she had been awake enough to get to bed. She even believed it.

Yet something still felt off. There was something wrong. She could sense that there was still something she was missing.

She stood and moved cautiously into the living room. The house was still as it should have been with only her there. Normally she had music playing or would leave the television on, just to keep the silence at bay, but tonight there was nothing. Even the dead outside were being uncharacteristically quiet.

All she heard was a scraping sound. Soft, but unsettling, coming from the kitchen.

She wondered how normal it was. Could that sound have always been there? Had to be, right? Since what would be able to get into the cabin? It was protected. She was safe there. The cabin had been safe for generations, the cabin and the barn. Nothing could get in.

Unless she was still dreaming, though, she was pretty sure she wasn't.

This was why she always had music playing. At least that way the noise would be just lost in the background of the house, where it probably belonged.

Lizzie turned on her laptop and within clicks, the soft sounds of Shawn Mendes drifted throughout the room.

She never took her eyes off the door to the other room. Slowly, she took a step towards it, reaching out cautiously to push it open.

The scream was held in her throat, fighting for its release, and her first thought was that this had to still be the nightmare. There was no way this could be happening again.

The naked man... The dead man who had killed Sarah, was on the kitchen floor. His skin was gray and sagging, as the weeks of being dead had bloated and was separated from the muscle underneath. It had been over a month since the last night she had seen the walking corpse, but it had only grown more disgusting, twisting her stomach just to look at this thing.

How? How was he there? Nothing else could break the barrier. She hadn't thought about it too much, though if he had been dead that first time, she should have... None of the other dead could get inside. None of the other evil could break across that threshold, but this corpse had done it not once but twice... How?

Did it really matter?

It did, but it wasn't something she could afford to think about right then. She couldn't get hung up on the questions. This naked man was pulling itself towards her. The time in the ground had not done it any favor. It was moving slowly towards her, but not at its leisure. As soon as it saw her, the smile had widened, and it clawed frantically at the floor, trying to pull itself faster towards her.

"Fuck you," she said. Quiet at first, almost speaking to herself, but the anger was boiling up

619

inside her. It erupted, and she screamed, howling in frustration and fury, "FUCK YOU!"

She ran forward, not caring that she wore no shoes, and slammed her bare foot into the smiling man's mouth. She could feel the pain as the top of her foot smashed into the sharp teeth, then as they gave way, caving inward from the force of her kick. His head rocked back, and she had to lean forward, grabbing the kitchen island to keep herself from losing her balance.

Her foot ached as it touched the floor, blood streaming to the floor. She looked at the damage and saw that there were chunks of his teeth imbedded in the top of her foot, gashes and chunks of flesh missing. With the blood continuing to gush from the wounds, it felt like her foot was more mangled than she could really see in the darkness of the kitchen.

She looked back at the man. He had stopped frantically coming for her, and looked up at her, his smile still there, his mouth glistening with blood. Her blood. There were teeth missing. Much of the top row was gone, but he still smiled. Then he came for her again, this time lurching the short distance to where she was.

He caught her off guard. That kick...it should have stopped him, kicked him backer farther, something. She wasn't ready for him to keep coming, and as she tried to step back, she used the wrong foot. The pain shot up, and she felt her knees give as she cried out.

Lizzie landed hard but didn't stop pushing herself back. It didn't matter; the thing had been close and was already reaching out for her feet. She was flailing them, trying to use them to keep propelling herself back, as they never seemed to be able to get any traction on the smooth floor.

The naked man grabbed her ankle, and she felt its cold, grimy grip. His hand held her like a shackle, strong and firm, but she could feel the sliminess of his dead hand, and thought she felt something else moving below it, under the skin.

Her stomach shifted in disgust, and she met its dark eyes. It was reaching for her other foot, trying to hold on to the one it already had. It was not letting go, and it continued to pull itself closer until it was nearly on top of her.

"Fuck YOU!" she yelled at it again, and aimed her free foot into its face, bringing the heel of her foot down hard on what was left of its nose. Then she reeled her foot back and did it again, and again. Four strikes, and the thing was still trying to pull itself towards her.

Her other leg wasn't kicking as hard to free itself as she kept it as leverage, and each time she prepared to kick, it used it to pull itself closer. Each time, it pulled itself into her foot that was aimed straight for it.

"Just die! Die like the rest of them." She screamed, placing one final kick before turning and scrambling to pull herself away. She broke free from its grip, its hand unable to contain her when she turned, and she used that to pull herself further away.

Now she just needed something to fight with-

There wasn't any way she could get around the kitchen to where the knives were in the corner. She didn't have anything. Shit!

She needed to get out of there and away from it.

-No, she needed to fight the damn thing. She could already feel its fingers trying to grab her, the tips just grazing the bottom of her feet as she fought to keep them away.

She pulled her knees up, lifting her legs out of its immediate grasp and used that momentum, shifting herself to sit up. It wouldn't be long before that thing was on top of her again. It was always so quick, faster than she thought the dead should be able to move. Definitely faster than those old crappy movies made out that zombies could move.

This wasn't a zombie, that was for sure. She had no idea what it was.

Its face was crushed, the front part of the skull having collapsed from her repeated kicks, and its eyes had fallen back into the cavernous depths of where its brain matter must have once been. She would have expected to see something there, inside the large hole that had been made, but instead there was nothing but darkness. Then there was what was left of its mouth. Many of its teeth were missing. Yet, it kept opening and closing, trying to bite down on whatever flesh it could find.

She had watched it for so long, caught up numbly in the obscene sight in front of her, that she didn't watch what it was doing. What it had been doing since she had discovered it. It has still been working its way towards her. Even without seeing her, it still was coming, its hands searching.

Both of its hands grabbed her legs, breaking her out of the trance. It was nearly on top of her. Its bloated skin dangled from its bones, and she felt its coolness as it touched her. Its chest rested on her bare feet. It reached out again, grabbing her shirt and pulling her to stare into the darkness of what was left.

She heard screaming and was shocked to realize it was her own. That darkness that stared back at her from inside the skull was maddening, and every time she looked at it, she felt herself slipping again, losing herself to its pull, her mind drifting from herself.

The naked man reached up with its arm, reaching higher onto her shirt, trying to pull her closer to it. It was working hard to pull itself further on top of her. It reached out again, pulling itself higher up...

That was, until she slugged it. The blow had been wide but had to be. Both its arms were inside, close to her body. All she could do was a swinging hit, her fist clenched tightly until it came into contact with what was left of the skull.

She heard the satisfying crunch of her fist slamming against what was left of its skull moments before the lightning bolt of pain shot up her arm. Her fist was on fire, and she barely had time to see her thumb at an odd angle as she opened her fingers, before it disappeared with the rest of her hand into the darkness that leaked from its skull.

CHAPTER 53

Something was pounding. At first, she thought it was a pounding inside her skull, warning bells ringing, telling her to get away, to run and get as far as she could. But the pounding wasn't coming from her skull. It was from fists as they pounded at the front door, slamming so hard against the wood that the door shook in its frame.

Lizzie couldn't turn away. She barely noticed the noise that vibrated throughout the whole house. Instead, her eyes were fixed on where the darkness stretched to her elbow, the tendrils of it reaching farther up her arm as it slowly climbed. She could feel where the darkness engulfed her. It was cold enough that it burned like fire up her arm. She could feel the slippery slime inside the darkness, but when she tried to pull her arm free, it was like a vice grip held her in place.

The knocking stopped just long enough for a rough voice to growl loud enough that it reverberated through the house, "Miss Rogers." Then the pounding resumed.

"Stop!" Another voice yelled, this one she recognized, though she knew it to be fake. Fake Sarah was standing in the doorway, though with how her fists rested on her hips, it did look like her best friend.

"Sarah?" Lizzie said, the confusion evident in the soft voice that could barely escape her lips. Why was she suddenly so tired? It was like her thoughts were trying to fade away from her and her eyes growing very heavy. She was fighting off sleep when she heard Sarah's voice again.

"Stop! Release her!"

Lizzie's eyes shot open. She hadn't realized that she had closed them, but the pain shooting up her arm, engulfing everything below the elbow, caused her to scream out.

Fire! Her arm was on fire!

The flames shot up from where the darkness had slithered from the naked man in, and even though the flames weren't touching her skin, the heat from it came through the darkness. It was an icy hot sensation that made her feel like her skin was melting away. As she saw the darkness drop from her in little flames dripping to the floor, she could smell her own flesh burning.

"Get away from it," yelled the fake Sarah, and even as Sarah said the words, another voice spoke through the same mouth, this one she recognized and made her skin crawl.

"Tic-a-tat, Tic-a-tee, you better flee."

Lizzie didn't look at her friend. The vice like hold on her arm slipped, and she pulled free. The flames were engulfing the dark shape she had seen escaping the naked man's skull, and it had let her go.

She didn't stay to watch it burn. She quickly rushed back from the thing, not stopping at the door, but continuing to push herself back until she was in the safety of the living room.

Something about being out of that kitchen relaxed her and a warmth washed over her, allowing her to take a deep calming breath. She heard sizzle and pops like a deep fryer coming from what was melting on the other side of that door... but it wasn't coming after her. She didn't think it could get farther than the kitchen. Whatever magic that worked to keep the house safe always felt stronger in the core rooms. It wouldn't cross that barrier.

She took another long calming breath, but it was interrupted by what sounded like a large, heavy object slamming into the front door. She turned and could see the tips of claws poking through freshly made cracks in the wood. They were smoking, and she could hear whatever was on the other side of the door, howl in pain. The door shook as it wrestled to pull free, which it did, leaving small slits in the door through which she could see the darkness of night outside.

Her breath caught as she looked at that darkness, knowing that any second now, it too would seep into the room, quickly surrounding her, taking her in upon itself. It was coming for her, desiring to consume her and there was no place left to run, nowhere that she would ever be safe.

But the darkness never came, and her insides burned. She let out the breath she'd been holding, and out came the tears she had been holding back. She bent over, nearly on the verge of vomiting on the floor.

"Elizabeth..." a deep voice, gravely, as though they came from a mouth that was not used to forming words and struggled with her name as it spoke from outside the other side of the door. "I... Can... Hear... You... Not... Safe... You-"

The words were cut off as another howl shook the front door.

Lizzie took one last deep breath while bent over, then stood, wiping away the tears.

There was more pounding on the front door, and then a brief pause before the claws pierced through the wood again, this time not getting stuck, but quickly pulling back, taking large chunks of the door with them.

Now she could see that there was something large out there, its features were lost in the dim light, but she thought she could see as it moved. It didn't matter if she saw it or not. She could see the damage it had done to the door and could hear its heavy breathing. There was a burliness as it snarled, and she could feel its growing frustration emanating to where she stood.

"What are you?" She called out. She was answered with a snort, following by a sky shattering howl that pierced through her.

"Not... Safe..." She heard it growl again, forming the words with effort.

She didn't feel safe. Even the comfort the house afforded her was wearing off, and she had nowhere to run. The thing out front was warning her, but she didn't think it was to be trusted, either. The holes in her front door assured her of that. It was pounding to get in. It was after her, there was no denying that, but she also couldn't go out the back door. The thing in the kitchen was making sure that wasn't going to happen. She had nowhere to go...

She had to wait until dawn.

The darkness was never going to let her do that. The twisting in the pit of her stomach told her of that. Something happened. There had been a shift, and something had changed. She didn't know what, but she could feel things pulling themselves there. It was like the air was growing thick, every breath a struggle as the tinge of evil tainted so much of it.

"Good lord, step away from there, vile beast."

She heard the voice outside, instantly recognizing the crisp British accent from the man who had been there days before. She couldn't remember his name, but that he had been there to get a clock...

She had been terrified of him, but her thoughts fogged over as she tried to remember what it was about him that had made her so uncomfortable. He had wanted something, something she thought was odd. He'd said it was part of the clock, or maybe she had dreamed that he said it was a part of the clock...

He had wanted the talisman... It had been obvious the moment he had seen it in the barn.

Was he back now, this late at night, for it?

Outside, the growl that came from near her front door was loud enough to rattle the windows in their frames.

She saw a face in her thoughts. It was hard to explain, but it was there, suddenly, a shapeless face, one she had never seen before. It burst in, and she could see it there, but knew it wasn't there with her eyes. It was like it was suddenly burned in as an image into the wood of the door, and it was looking right at her.

Outside, the beast howled, but it was cut short as shots rang out. The explosion from the gun as it fired each bullet disrupted the quiet of the woods in a cacophony that was even more unnatural than all the strangeness that had come before it.

"GO!" screamed the head from the door. As it opened its mouth, she couldn't help but see the elongated fangs.

What was happening? None of this could be real. These things, the creatures she was seeing, didn't exist. In no reality were any of them real...

I must be dreaming. This must be another dream.

The heavy shape of the beast slamming into the door did not let her question what was real or not. The door shattered inward with the shape falling into the cabin, and as it did, the human shaped wolf burst into flames. The fire quickly spread to the floor where it fell. The journals around it were quickly engulfed, the fire spreading fast, leaping towards her as though it was directed to pull her into it.

She had no choice and stopped hesitating. As the flames leapt closer to her, she was already moving to the kitchen door, her feet quickly carrying her without conscious thought of where she was going. She paused only briefly after flinging open the door to again face the naked corpse. She avoided looking at it as she rushed through, running for the back door. Fake Sarah was still near the threshold of the open door and laughed as Lizzie ran towards her. Sarah wasn't saying anything, but the other voice couldn't help but cackle at her, "Tic-a-too, tic-a-tee, looks like you finally listen to me."

Lizzie didn't stop. She escaped into the backyard, adrenaline pushing her until she took that first step down. Then the pain she had forgotten, the hurt foot drenched in blood from where it was cut open, shot through her like lightning through the night sky. Lizzie cried out, her knees buckling out from under her, sending her tumbling off the side of the unstable stairs.

The world continued to spin long after she finished falling, and she felt her neck and back locked in uncomfortable pain. Her arms were somehow under her, and they refused to obey her as she tried to move them. Her legs were above her and the pain from her foot somehow went distant as everything else in her body was screaming at her.

Something crashed inside the house. She could hear the fire as it was rapidly spreading. So much history, her uncle's journals all rapidly burning away. Secrets she hadn't read were being savagely burned away from her. Maybe there was more to be uncovered. There was so much that had happened in that house, things she had yet to find...

And she was trapped out there unable to save any of them as she fought with her body.

She wiggled, trying to shift her weight. Her back felt like it was folded into itself. Was she paralyzed? Was she going to be like her brother, needing someone to always take care of her?

Her hand came free from beneath her twisted form, and she was able to shift the other way to pull the other one. She still was unable to move her legs, though she felt them pressed against her. At least her upper torso still registered the pain. That was a mixed relief as she struggled to pull herself away from how she was pinned in the metal staircase. She could feel something sharp pushing against the lower part of her back, and as she tried to pull herself free, realized it must have been the corner of one of the steps.

"Tic-a-too, tic-a-tee, what a mess you be..." That voice that grated into her nerves echoed from above. She didn't have to look up to know that Fake Sarah was standing over her, probably perched on the stairwell.

There was another crash from inside the house, something large falling, she imagined. She thought of the large bureau that held all of her uncle's glass wares. Not her uncle's, but his long-dead wife. He had kept those for how many years, something he used to remember her the way she used to be. From the sound of it, that would all be lost now.

She struggled to turn herself again, only to be rewarded with the stabbing pain in her back to scrape across. She felt the heat as it did so and could sense the blood that was dripping down.

"Here, let me help." The accent was English, and she knew the man she'd heard out front was next to her. She felt his cold hands as they touched her, and in her current state, could not suppress the shiver that ran through her. The hands were strong and pulled her away from the stabbing step with ease. She found herself being lifted, and her legs stretching out beneath her as they should have been. She was relieved by the sudden pins and needles that stung through her as the sleeping appendages awakened, the blood flow moving as it should.

The relief was short-lived as he stood her upright. She was close to him, closer than she had allowed herself to get before, and she could smell him and feel the wrongness that surrounded him.

He smelled like sulfur and moldy earth that entwined itself in a flesh shell. His arm around her was suffocating as she could taste vomit as it rose in her throat. It was like he pulled away all the breathable air around her, and she had to close her eyes to keep from turning and vomiting directly into the man's tailored suit.

You need to get away from him-

She knew she needed to... His icy skin, and if the smell didn't make her sick, just his presence would. He was death incarnate. Having him touch her nearly put her into a frenzy, as she feared she could not get away.

"Excuse me, Miss. Rogers, but if I may have a word," he spoke softly, dropping his head so that he spoke directly into her ear. She couldn't hold back anymore, and this time the contents of her stomach did erupt from her, spilling out onto the grass, her bloody bare feet, and his expensive designer loafers. Her body shook, and she was on the verge of convulsions, taking hold over her body. She couldn't control herself, her muscles shaking, nerves pummeling through her. Was all of this because she was this close to him...

"Calm down. We must talk. I need that piece." He said, his tone direct and forceful. The arms around her strengthened as they started to squeeze the breath out of her. They were inescapable, but they eased her shaking on the outside. On the inside, her body was tearing itself apart. Everything was on fire just from his touch.

"Renfield, let her go." Boomed a commanding voice. She forced herself to look up, and through her vibrating eyes, she saw a dark shape emerge from around the corner. He looked familiar as well, but she couldn't place it.

"Of course, master." The man holding her said, and she felt herself being lowered to the ground. As his arms withdrew from her, she could feel him take a step back, and the world stopped quivering. Or she did-

She looked at the man, and she recognized him. The sickness in her stomach took another turn, and what was left threatened more vomiting. It was the man's face she'd seen in the door. She couldn't see his fangs, but she knew it was him.

She must have hit her head, or she had to be dreaming. Vampires? There was no such thing, and nothing as cliche'd as a vampire with a Mr. Renfield to do his bidding. That was straight out of Dracula.

She never had the chance to think more about it as a fiery shape leapt from the back door and slammed into the vampire. She didn't watch what happened, as she used the distraction to quickly rise and run away. Renfield was a few feet off, and he looked unsure if he should grab her or help his master, who was now fighting with the flamed beast. She wasn't concerned about either of them, but she didn't chance running past him either.

Instead, she turned and ran towards the woods. It would only be a few hundred feet. Then she could lose herself in the darkness of the trees.

"Tic-a-tee, but one makes three. Tic-a-too, tic-a-tee, don't think you can flee..." chanted behind her. She didn't need to turn and look to know who was cackling with laughter.

It wasn't easy to run. Her feet were bare, torn open, and hurt like hell.

"Lizzie! Lizzie! What's going on?" Roland called out to her, and she saw him out of the corner of her eye, running to catch up.

"It's time to go."

"Go where? How?" He caught up to her, and she refused to look at him. Unlike the others, he died without being mutilated, his deadness still looking like the guy she had the hots for. It was easy to forget that he was dead.

"I can't deal with this. I'm losing my mind. I'm hallucinating Roland. I'm fucking hallucinating."

"Liz, I'm not sure what's going on, but I don't think you want to get any closer to those woods. Liz, stop." Roland was behind her, and she turned back to see the horror etched on his face. Behind him was the house. She could see the fire raging inside, though the creatures she thought she'd seen were gone.

There you go- just figments of your imagination. Your world is now Willy Wonka, pure imagination...

The thought was not a comfort.

Roland wasn't even looking at her. She turned to look behind her.

At first, she didn't see it. There was darkness and trees, the trees only visible from the little light of the flickering flames that reached that far.

No... there were two glowing red orbs, just a few feet into the line of trees. They hung there, and she didn't need to see the rest of what they belonged to know what it was. After all, wolves always traveled in packs. Of course, werewolves would as well. The one who'd busted down her door was no exception.

She took an unconscious step back from the woods as she noticed more sets of eyes appearing.

They were moving closer and within seconds, emerged from the darkness of the forest.

"I don't think you should go this way." Roland said.

"Lizzie!" Elisabeth yelled. Lizzie turned and saw, with the help of the fire from inside the house, the burning werewolf that was on the ground and the tall Englishman standing over it, its gun drawn and aimed at the beast.

That was when Lizzie felt the cool rush of air around her, and the beasts that had emerged from the woods were moving at an unearthly quick pace. They were rushing towards the man with the gun, and he turned in time to see them coming for them. He barely had time to react before they were on him.

Lizzie heard him scream, calling out for his master, whom she didn't see. *Where had he disappeared too...?* She had a feeling in the pit of her stomach that said she would find out soon enough, and that she wouldn't like it.

Elisabeth was by the barn, and she was motioning for Lizzie.

The barn... The barn had been protected like the house was. These things couldn't get in there. She'd be trapped, but she only had to survive until dawn. Then she'd be safe. The sunlight would keep the darkness at bay. These were all creatures of the night, weren't they?

"She's right. You have to get to the barn," Roland said, but she was already moving. Keeping her focus on the pack of wolves as they tore at the man. She could hear his flesh being ripped apart, their hungry growls turning into frustrated whines as she saw pieces were thrown away.

The frustration was growing. Their whines turning back into howls of anger. Their hunger was strong, and not satisfied, and Lizzie knew she had to make it to that door, or she would be their next snack. She only had a little farther to go. The pain in her feet lost to the adrenaline, as she could see what her fate would be if she didn't make it.

"Only a little farther. Don't look at them, watch the door. I'll keep an eye on them." Roland yelled. He was calling behind her, keeping his attention on the beasts.

She tried to keep her gaze on the door, struggling against the urge to look their way. The sounds of ripping flesh were slowing, and she could hear the heavy breathing of the creatures. She could almost feel their eyes on her.

"Miss. I must implore you to hand over that talisman." The vampire said. He had emerged from the darkness in front of the door, just suddenly stepping out of the shadows, and Lizzie found herself struggling to stop herself. Her feet threatened to slip out from under her on the slippery ground, yet somehow, she stayed standing. She stopped and watched him as he stood in front of her.

"Hand over it now. You will die, your brother will die. Every member of your family will die. Though your death will be the most monstrous and agonizing, as I will keep you on the painful edge of death until I've brought every one of your family members to die at your feet." The vampire said. His eyes burned into her, and she could feel something more as he spoke; he was pushing, fighting to enter her thoughts...

It wasn't working. Why?

She felt something sharp jab into the palm of her hand. She looked down and saw the necklace in her hand. The sharp, dead legs of the scorpion were twitching and pressing themselves out as she held it tightly. She didn't remember grabbing it at any point when leaving the cabin, but here it was. She saw how the vampire was looking at it, like he yearned for it as strongly as he yearned for the blood in her veins, but he wasn't attacking her for it.

It was protecting her...

Behind her, a long howl broke through the tension, and she couldn't stop herself from turning. The wolves were done feeding, and were forming a half circle around her, their red eyes focused on the vampire.

She turned back to the vampire, thinking he would be concerned with how the wolves were looking at him. He never took his eyes off her, so he didn't see the blackened wolf emerge from the darkness behind him. Smoke emanated from where the fire had burned bright just minutes ago as the creature crouched down, preparing itself. The vampire never saw it as it leapt.

CHAPTER 54

"Lizzie! This is your chance," Elisabeth yelled, breaking her out of the trance she was in watching the horror movie that had emerged in front of her. The one werewolf had leapt onto the vampire with the rest of the pack quickly swarming, joining into the fight. Though as she had watched, and as quickly as one werewolf would tear into the thing's flesh, it healed beneath it and the werewolf would quickly be thrown off. The vampire would toss them like rag dolls halfway across the clearing to where they landed. Lizzie could hear their whimpering howls as they landed, some not getting back up.

There was nearly a constant sound of bones shattering and being reformed, whines and howls, and a continuing growling that she couldn't tell if it came from the vampire, the wolves or both.

Blood was splattered throughout, the rancid smell so strong even to her human senses, and each footstep closer toward the barn was another step into the river of red that ran away from the fight.

A crash came from behind her, and at this point, Lizzie didn't even turn to look. She just kept walking.

"You've got to be kidding me." Roland said in disbelief, making it again to her side.

"What is it?"

"That thing from your kitchen. It's pulled itself down the stairs."

"It won't get to me in time." Lizzie said, surprised to see that she was already at the threshold.

"Stop!" She heard the vampire yell, but his calling out to her was cut off by a viscous growl. This time she did hear the other creature exasperate in what she assumed was shock.

She crossed into the barn with a satisfying smile, feeling the sudden chill in the air. It was that soothing sensation, not unlike what she felt in the house. It allowed her to take a deep breath as she lingered there, enjoying the sudden triumph in knowing she was once again somewhere where she could feel just a hint of safety.

She was there for less than a second when she felt hands like iron wrap around her waist. The hands instantly burst into flame, but that didn't stop them from lifting her, dragging her out of the barn and tossing her yards away from the entrance.

She had barely landed before she felt rough, cold hands on her. They were tearing at her, pulled at her as they grabbed. The smell of rotting flesh surrounded her, and she struggled to twist herself free, any second expecting the darkness she had seen inside the cabin ooze around her. She didn't have to see it to know the naked man had her.

"Get away from her! She's mine." The vampire hissed, appearing over her. His arms were still burning, but he was unfazed. His black soulless eyes fixated on her as it ripped the other creature from her and threw it aside.

The vampire was a mess. Most of his clothes were now in tatters, torn away by the wolves. Most of the scratches had healed, but there must have been limits to his healing as there were cuts that were still not closed and dark blood dripped from them.

"Tic-a tee, Tic-a-toe, I don't think so..." a familiar voice cackled. Lizzie turned, expecting to see fake Sarah hovering nearby, but she was nowhere to be seen. None of her dead friends were around. There was nothing around her... The house, the woods, it was all gone. They were all surrounded by darkness.

Lizzie first looked at the naked man, expecting to see that all of this was erupting from him. She was surprised to see that he looked like he should have, a lifeless corpse that was no longer moving.

"No, this isn't how it's supposed to be." The vampire said as he pulled away from her. "I was supposed to get the key. I was to unlock the door. It was supposed to be me. I've spent decades tracking the key and the door!" It yelled into the nothingness that surrounded them.

"Tic a too, Tic-a-tee, what is time to me-" The voice cackled.

Lizzie slowly stood. She could still see the entrance to the barn. Everything else was gone. She thought about making a run for it, taking her chance.

The vampire turned back to her; its lips curled up in a smile.

"I knew it was time. That talisman is mine. Give it to me."

Lizzie looked at the object still in her hand, surprised she even had it, but at the back of her mind, knew she would always have it. Like the house, the curse, and everything else that had been happening to her. Once this thing had found it, it was a part of her.

Was it, though? This seemed like one part of her she could give up, and why was she fighting to keep the damned thing? She didn't even know what it was. What was the point?

"Here, take the damn thing." Lizzie said, holding it out to it.

It looked suspicious and moved slowly to take it from her hand.

"Do you know what this is?"

"Not a fucking clue, and at this point, I don't really care. I've never cared. I've never wanted any of this. Just take the fucking thing and let me have a life. Even if everyone dies when I talk to them, at least this fucking thing will be gone."

The vampire smiled at her, drawing attention to the two long fangs that stretched over the center of its lower lip.

"You're not going to let me live..." Lizzie said, barely a whisper as she felt herself growing faint.

The vampire shook its head as its hand covered hers and pulled her into its cold embrace. She felt him as he lowered his head to meet her neck. He was going to bite her. She had a second to wonder if it would be like in the movies, because she realized that it was such a crazy thought. There were many movies, and not all of them romanticized the creatures. The closest she had ever seen to the monster who now stood over her was the original silent film, and that she'd only seen because Roland used it for one of his own short films.

Somehow, she didn't think this thing would only leave her with two small holes. Those teeth were large and looked like they were used to tear into someone's flesh, ripping away to get to the free-flowing life from within her veins. These were the teeth of a vicious animal that didn't care to leave its victims alive. Death followed this bite, and she already sensed that hers was coming in the next few seconds of its touch. It's icy cold grasp as two hands reached out and grabbed her upper arms made her gasp in the suddenness of the movement.

"Brian..." she whispered as she closed her eyes. It would be his turn now. This curse would be his. How would he ever survive it? He would never be able to pull himself out of society, as he would always need someone there to care for him. How would they be able to live...? Anyone that helped him, got close to him would die.

She felt the tip of the teeth on her throat, hovering, waiting to bite down. *Damn this thing for taking its sweat ass time with all this.* Damn it all to hell, as she knew it was playing with her. Messing with her mind, playing with its food.

She felt one of the cold claws ease its grip and slowly move its way down her arm. The motion sent a tingle down her limb, the chill of it threatening shivers throughout her body. The claw like hand was rough, its skin like sandpaper, yet as it moved down her arm, she could only feel numbness from where it touched her.

It was going for the talisman. She could already feel it nearing the hand that held it, and the talisman itself was twitching in response. The closer the thing got to it, the more it twitched, almost moving like it was excited or afraid of the creature that was about to take ownership.

What did she care? She could already feel the tensions drifting away from her. None of this would be her problem anymore. Soon, she would feel those teeth, and it would be over. She was starting to look forward to it. She didn't need any of this. She could be lost in nothingness, and it would all just go away. She was beginning to like that idea. Maybe then her friends would find peace.

"Tic-a-too, tic-a-tee, what was one is now three..." A familiar scratchy voice cackled, and she could feel it pull painfully at her consciousness, dragging her unwillingly away from whatever fog she was drifting into.

No, she didn't want this. *Let it all just end. Let me be.*

She felt the cold grip of the claws loosen, then let her go so that she was falling. Her eyes fluttered open, and as she fell, she watched as the vampire looked at her, its black eyes caught in a face gripped in fear. Then she saw the naked man behind it, and the darkness that was pouring out of it oozing its way over the vampire.

"And what was three will never be...."

Lizzie looked to where she heard the voice and there, she saw the shadow man, no longer wearing the skin of fake Sarah. He stood near the corner of the house, watching them. Even close, she knew she would never see details from his shadow form, but somehow, she could sense his smile and glee at watching these things near her consume one another.

Her stomach rolled. She thought she might just be sick. Then she felt the cold and looked back at the naked man and the vampire. The vampire was nearly gone to the darkness, but it wasn't stopping. She could see that it was already moving across the ground towards her.

She quickly pulled back her foot from where it was close to touching and didn't waste any time getting to her feet.

Lizzie ran. She wasn't far from the barn, but she had to run away from it to get around the merging creatures. As she did, she found herself getting closer to the shadow man, who was also moving. He was, wait, was he running towards her? She had never seen him move like that, but he was moving to catch her.

"Come on Liz, run! You have to make it to the barn!" Roland yelled from somewhere distant.

Lizzie pushed herself, her feet burning, each step starting to feel like she was stepping on knife blades as the grass was sharp on her open wounds.

She had worried for a brief moment, thinking she wasn't going to make it, that something new, some other unforeseen evil, would appear to keep her from safety as she neared the door. She didn't look back at the shadow man to know just how close he was; she just kept running. Her lungs were on fire, threatening to burst, as she waited for whatever was going to keep her from the threshold this time...

And then she made it. She burst through the doorway and landed hard on the ground, tripping over her own feet as she fell into the barn. She crashed hard, and it hurt, but none of that mattered because she made it... She was safe.

CHAPTER 55

Her breath was ragged. Something was wrong, and she didn't feel right. It had nothing to do with the pains she felt throughout her body. Those were all external wounds and aches, but this was inside her. Something was burning. A pain was flaring up in her chest and she could feel it heating up from within her.

She looked at her hand and saw she was still holding the talisman. Part of her wished she had left it behind out there. Somehow, no matter what, it stayed with her. It was like it was becoming a part of her, joined to her with this curse.

As she looked at her hand, she could see why. Part of the talisman had pierced her skin while the legs of what had looked like the once dead creature were wrapped around her hand. When she opened her hand, as she did experimentally, the small object didn't fall to the ground. It was clinging to her.

It *was* alive. She saw it twitch as she watched it, then witnessed as the veins in her arm darkened, the surrounding skin turning purple as it moved up from her hand.

"Help! Roland!" She yelled, not sure what he could do. What any of them could do? It didn't really matter anymore, but at least they were out there. She wouldn't be alone, no matter what was coming or happening to her. "Roland please!"

"Tic-a-too, tic-a-...tee... No one here but little ol' me." Came that familiar cackle, but she refused to look up at it.

"Roland! Elisabeth! Josh!" she cried out, as she finally did look up, not at the shadow man who stood in the doorway but past him, trying to see any of her friends still out there. There was no one. She was all alone. Now, when she needed them the most, they were gone. Hell, she didn't even like half of them, but they had been there. Now, where were they?

She felt a pinch in her hand, and she realized she already knew the answer. The thing, it had them again. Even though she wasn't wearing it as a necklace, it was around her flesh. When she refused to wear it, it found a way to wear her.

The shadow man continued to stand there, laughing at her, its burning eyes burrowing into her.

She was too close to it. She had to take a step back from the creature. She knew it wanted it. It wanted her, though, not to kill her. She had long figured out that it took pleasure in tormenting her. She was the cursed one, and its existence seemed to take great joy in tormenting her in all the various ways it could. It was like she was some plaything for it, a cosmic toy that he mused over.

That's right... It was a cat, and she was the mouse caught in its claws. Occasionally it would give her just enough room to escape and every time she did, it would pounce again and bring her close to those waiting teeth.

Its large smile was wide as it watched her. It didn't seem to be too upset that she was just out of reach. She could see how it relished her anguish. It was enjoying this... Dammit! It was enjoying her pain.

"No!" she said sternly and felt her stomach twist deeper into knots while she stiffened her spin. She was standing straighter, now looking down a fraction at those burning eyes. "You are done feeding off me."

The talisman twitched again in her bad hand, and she could feel the pinchers burrowing deeper into her skin. It felt like they were growing inside her, spreading into her veins like roots taking hold. She clamped her teeth, trying to ignore the pain as she reached out with her good hand to a nearby table.

To her surprise, the shadow man didn't react to her. He just stood there, that wide smile getting wider with more teeth.

Of course he is. I could yell at it all day, telling it that I was done feeding it pain. That didn't stop this damn thing in my hand...

She had to get rid of it.

It twitched as though it sensed her thoughts, and she looked down to see that her hand was turning black, and the same darkness was spreading up her veins. It was burrowing inside of her. She turned over her hand and could see how it was almost completely under her skin, burrowing like a tick and working its way to be a part of her.

Oh my God, what am I going to do then?

She stumbled back. The world was spinning around her, and she started to feel as though she couldn't breathe.

"Tic-a-too, Tic-a-tee, not much time left for thee." The shadow voice said, but then from those same lips, a different voice spoke. She recognized it but was hard to place. There was no way the voice could be there. There was just no way.

Then the shadow man stepped forward, crossing the threshold into the barn. As it did, the shadow burst away, the darkness disappearing into the air around him to reveal her brother.

Lizzie took a step back, her stomach in knots as bile tried to rise in her throat. She recognized her brother, but saw how he was twisted. This wasn't the same boy she would go to the care facility to see. It was more than just him walking, which he was doing steadily towards her in a slow fashion that reminded her of an old horror movie serial killer. No, everything was wrong.

He's not talking. Yes, that was part of it, but he also had a tooth filled smile that didn't touch his black eyes. Those eyes remained focused intently on her, and that smile, she knew that many teeth were not natural. He'd never been one for smiling before, but that many teeth, she wasn't sure he could even close his mouth.

"Brian?" she asked as she took another tentative step away from him.

He didn't pause as he took another step towards her. She was amazed he was even walking, though as he did, she could see how unnatural it was for his frail body. Each step reminded her more of Frankenstein's monster than that of a normal person. He didn't bend his knees and with how his eyes never strayed from her; she felt like he wasn't the one in control.

Was Brian even in there?

"Brian?" she pleaded. She took another step back and had reached the end of the table. She only had two options now. She could go around the table, forcing him to chase her or continue back. She didn't have much room there either, as the wall of darkness was only a few feet away.

She chanced a brief look over her shoulder and could have sworn that the darkness was rippling. That the black was pulsating, waiting for her to cross its threshold. Her or Brian, it wanted one of them.

"Tic-Toc, Tic Toc." The shadow man said. Lizzie looked back at her brother and his smile. She could see blood on his gums and lips from where the extra teeth were forcing their way into his large grin. He wasn't the one who spoke though and over her brother's shoulder she could see that the shadow man had reformed at the threshold, watching them with that mirrored smile that her brother had.

She took a step to move around the table, but her brother in a quick movement pushed one of the half-completed clocks so that it flew off the table and crashed to the floor. The sudden motion and the clock crashing near her foot caused her to jump and take a step back, leaving the safety of the table.

"Brian! Why are you doing this? Brian!" She yelled at him, trying to pull some sense that there was any part of her brother in there. "Please!"

He was getting closer. Sure, his body was tiny and fragile. He had been trapped in that wheelchair long enough that she was surprised he had the muscle strength to walk this far and to keep going. Still, he was, and it didn't look like he was struggling.

651

Without realizing she was doing it; she took another step back and could feel the cold emanating from the darkness behind her.

The talisman dug deeper into her arm, and she couldn't feel her hand anymore. She had to glance down quickly to convince herself it was still there. It was purple and she could see that darkness was coursing through her arm and cutting off everything to her hand. She was going to lose it. Her hand would be dead to her after this.

This was just too much; everything was suffocating her as the world was closing in. This all had to be a bad dream, but the pain in her feet and arm were reminders of what was reality. It was near impossible to think through the pain coursing up her arm.

"Brian," she whimpered as he reached out to her and grabbed her. His hands were strong, and he was able to pull her the little distance towards him. It made her unsteady on her feet and she found herself held up by his grip. Those hands wrapped like steel around her biceps, trapping her arms. That grip, it felt like the naked man had her. Those fingers felt like large cables meant to restrain her.

"Tic-a-Too, Tic-a-Tee. It's time to set the old ones free." The shadow man cackled in a way she had never heard before. It seemed ecstatic with glee to where she could hear the anticipation in its raspy voice.

Brian's smile widened. She watched as the skin broke, splitting as more pointed teeth filled his mouth. Blood dripped from the corners of his mouth where the skin ripped, expanding the ever-growing smile. There had already been so many extra teeth, and his mouth had been disjointed, but now it was trapped in that hideous grin.

"Brian. Don't do this."

"Liz-e" her brother said, though it was hard to understand as his voice was thick and his lips didn't move as he spoke. His face didn't register that he was speaking. It was like he was wearing a mask of himself as her name spilled out. "You- Do this to me."

Lizzie shook her head, and she could feel the tears that had already started to run down her cheeks.

"No-" she started to say, but the grip on her arms tightened. The talisman twitched, sending even more pain through her, and she thought she was going to bite through her tongue.

Her knees grew weak. She could feel them trembling and didn't trust herself to stand there much longer. She wasn't sure if she stood there in front of her brother or if he was holding her up.

He took a step forward, and her legs dragged under her. They were closer to the darkness. She could almost feel the intensity like electricity, and it registered what he was going to do. She shook her head in protest and struggled against his grip.

"Brian, don't do this. Please! Let me go." She struggled to pull her right arm free. Her left was dead to her. She tried to use it, but it was like nothing was there but the pain that fought to cloud her thoughts. She had to keep pushing that down so she could stay focused on Brian.

"Tic-a-too, Tic-a-tee. He only listens to me." said the shadow man from the threshold, but it was chorused through the strained mouth of her brother, the enlarged mouth moving to the words. Spittle and blood spat out as it said them, more teeth growing, widening the sickening smile even more.

Brian started to take another step, and that was when she brought her knee up and made solid contact with his testicles.

There was a moment when her brother broke through the darkness. As the thing that looked like Brian bent over in pain, she could see the black pupils disappear and his bright blue eyes shine through. She thought she could even see a few of the teeth withdraw back into the gums, shrinking the enlarged mouth.

But the grip on her arms never slackened. As she watched him bend over in obvious pain, she immediately twisted first left, then right, pushing herself to break free. She kicked out her feet, working to get them down so she could leverage herself against his slender frame. With how fragile his body appeared, she should be able to just knock him down, push him out of the way.

He was like a stone; she pushed using every ounce of strength she had left in her, and somehow, he didn't budge. He never even lifted and there had been on more than one occasion back at the long-term care facility that had helped him from his chair to his bed. She should be able to at least break free.

Her strength faded. Her shoulders sagged and her knees failed her, giving out so that he now fully supported her. She knew she had had her chance; she had seen her brother return and now she watched as the eyes filled back with the darkness and he was gone.

A new wave of tears washed over her, and her head fell. She couldn't look at him anymore.

"Lizzie! Lizzie!" A familiar voice called to her, and Lizzie's heart fluttered at hearing it.

"Jess!" Lizzie mumbled, afraid to look up for fear of seeing anything that would give her hope of somehow surviving this.

When did you give up?

She heard that familiar nagging voice, the overly optimistic one that made her sick.

"Lizzie! You need to get away from him! Come on, Liz!" Jess yelled.

"You can do this!" Roland cheered.

She heard more of them. Her dead friends that had been with her since the beginning. They were all there. She could even hear Josh as he was yelling to kick her brother in the nuts. If he only knew she'd already done that, he would not be so adamant that she should do it again. How were they joining her again? Where were they?

And how could she disappoint them? Because there was no escape. That's how.

"I can't." Lizzie said, feeling as her toes dragged across the rough floor.

"You can! Just pray!" Jessica yelled. To Lizzie's surprise, it wasn't Josh to be the first one to rebuke her for it.

"What's praying going to do? She needs to just lift him up and body slam the son of a bitch." Chuck yelled. Lizzie could see over Brian's shoulder as Roland was towards the back of the group, but it wasn't because he was trying to stay away. He was preparing, and as she watched, he started running towards the threshold.

She wanted to call out to him, stop him from doing something stupid, as she had no idea what it would do to him. Brian must have sensed it, as his hands left her arms to quickly grab her by the neck. They collapsed around her windpipe, and she instantly felt dazed as her oxygen was cut off.

"And now I lay me down to sleep." Lizzie vaguely thought, though she didn't know the rest of it. Lord's Prayer... that was never going to help her. She realized it was true as his hands grew tighter and she was gagging, trying to pull in at least one mouthful of air.

Roland slammed into the threshold, and it sounded like a fly hitting a bug zapper. The barn shook, and she watched as the lights flickered. She heard laughing as they did, but she stayed focused on struggling to pull away the hands from around her neck.

Her world grew blurry. It felt like a dream as she watched Roland back away from the door. Was he smoking? He was never a smoker... No, his body was smoking, which was not surprising, as she could see bone and muscle as flesh was melting away. She could see his eye sockets, now bulging as the meat sizzles away around them. His eyes looked huge as they looked at her in fear.

How could they even be there? They were trapped in the talisman. She must be imagining him. How much of all of this was she dreaming?

The room was getting darker. Maybe he had knocked out the lights... No, they were on; she realized as she looked up at them, the fluorescents still booming with lights.

Her fists were hitting Brian's arms, and he didn't even flinch. He continued to hold her, squeezing the life out of her.

She had to have a way... She couldn't die like this, and why now? Did the shadow man do this to Brian just to have him be the cursed one? That didn't seem right. Not with how the shadow man acted. Not with what she read in the journal.

"Life came into being because of him, for his life is light for all humanity. And this Living Expression is the Light that bursts through gloom— the Light that darkness could not diminish!"

Lizzie heard the words ringing in her ears. She wasn't sure where they came from. She thought Jessica, but it didn't sound like her, and Lizzie questioned if she even heard them at all. They drifted there somewhere between her wakefulness and her slipping unconsciousness.

Did she imagine his hands slipping, loosening on her throat? Could he be letting her go?

She struggled to whisper his name, but still couldn't gasp it from her lips. She tried in a desperate hope to push with her mind, screaming "Brian" with as much mental energy as she had.

It was the last thing she did. She caught the look in his eyes, the anger and hate that filled those black pupils. Then somehow that large, smiling mouth twisted into a snarl. She felt herself move backwards, and the world went dark...

CHAPTER 56

At first, Lizzie thought she was dead, though the pain in her feet kept her from giving into that belief. She wished she could say she was asleep. At least then, she could believe that all of this had been a nightmare. If it was, it was one hell of a bad trip, and she sure as hell hoped she didn't remember any of this when she woke up.

It was the arms that were wrapped around her that told her she was not dead or asleep. First, a pair grabbed her under her arms, then another lifted her off her feet. She had felt herself starting to lift but stopped when more arms wrapped around her, this time in hugs.

"Later," she heard Roland say. We need to get her away from that thing.

"Ouch!" Chuck said.

"What happened?" Josh said. He was the one at her feet. She had her eyes open, but the surrounding darkness made it so that she could only make out their shapes.

"I touched it and it burned."

"Well, leave it there. It's probably a good thing it fell off her."

"Oh, Lizzie!" Sarah was saying. She was one of the groups of arms that had wrapped around her, fiercely hugging her.

"Later. We need to get her away." Roland hissed. Roland. She could feel his arms holding her up. How could she ever have broken up with him? There was nothing more she wanted to do than to nuzzle up to him and purr in his ear, meow like a cat as they lay naked together in a bed.

"Um, guys!" Dennis called out.

"Yeah, I see it. Now, will everyone help me get her away? I think there are some trees over here."

"How the hell do you know that? I can't see a damn thing." Josh said. She realized that she was beginning to see him more clearly. Her eyes must have been adjusting, as she could see more of him now. All of them as they hustled around her. They were moving her, though struggling to carry her as they made their way away from...

Holy shit, what the fuck is that?

The thought screamed through her as she saw the swirling vortex of darkness deeper than the black that surrounded them. It was obviously what she had just come through, but on her side, it hadn't been swirling like it was, and it looked like it was growing.

They emerged from the back half of the barn, and there she could see things more clearly. There was still darkness, but it was more like a world of dark grey. Color was gone, to be replaced with shades of forever night on a full moon.

Lizzie noticed as they were pulling her away that the back half of the barn looked ancient, the wood rotted where there was still wood. Most of the barn looked like it was blown away. Like something had

660

exploded out years ago, and now the skeleton remains stood there, waiting to collapse.

"Ah!" someone screamed around her. She thought it was Elisabeth but wasn't sure as she turned her head to look.

"What the hell is it?" Josh said in disgust, and she could feel the hands holding her jostle her as they started to move faster.

"Come on, we need to get her to one of the trees before they get too close." Roland said.

"You know she's not as light as she looks." Dennis grunted, and she knew he was close to letting her go.

"Roland." She purred. So much was going on around her, and she tried to focus. As she tried to bring herself to sharpen her thoughts, a tranquility kept invading her. It made her want to do stupid things... like purring at her ex-boyfriend, with whom right then all she wanted to do was tackle him and fuck his brains out. Damn, her libido was on fire, and she squirmed as she could feel the desires growing stronger.

"Lizzie, what the hell are you doing?" He said. She could hear the struggle in his voice as he fought with her. She was trying to reach for him while he wrestled to keep hold of her and continue to carry her.

"We should just put her down." Dennis said.

"Lizzie, you need to focus." Jessica said, and Lizzie turned to her, but it was a struggle to see. She was different than the others. Her form was darker. She was almost transparent, though that wasn't right. Lizzie couldn't see through her; she just had a hard time seeing her. It hurt her eyes, pulsating a pain deep into her temples.

"What's going on?" Lizzie said, feeling her first sense of clarity since being wherever they were. She wasn't sure where they were, but the growing dread that filled her stomach told her she wasn't in Kansas anymore.

Wisconsin, she lived in Wisconsin. Why would she think she lived in Kansas?

Damn, it's just an expression. Her inner voice seemed to argue too much as she pushed to clear her thoughts.

"Fucking end of the world shit is going on," Chuck yelled, but Roland was already talking over him, hushed tones into her ear.

"I don't know. Everything just changed, and this doesn't look good. That thing back there. There's no way that was your brother, but whatever it was, it pushed you through that doorway, and then there was this explosion of darkness that erupted. It was, like, it just sucked the light out of the room. We were outside, then we were in and then we were on the other side, and you were there on the ground, that damn scorpion thing lying on the ground next to you. I mean, I don't know what the hell is going on, but this is some fucked up shit."

They had reached the end of the clearing and Roland was easing her up against a tree, lowering her so she could sit on the ground. She didn't feel like sitting, though; she wanted to know what the hell was going on. She needed to see it for herself...

"There's something wrong here." Jessica said.

"Oh yeah? What was your first clue?" Josh was looking around, bouncing from foot to foot as he nervously scanned the woods.

"Well, I think the fact that we're dead, she's alive, but we're all hugging each other like nothing's happened gave us the first clue." Sarah said as she lowered herself and started checking Lizzie out, touching her like she couldn't believe that she could.

"Wait-" Lizzie started to say but stopped herself when she saw her group of friends standing over her. Pieces were coming together as she looked at them. They looked and felt as solid as she was, and it wasn't like on the other side when they touched it. Here it felt like flesh on flesh, rather than a feeling of pressure against her. "You're alive."

"Or you're dead." Elisabeth said as she leaned down next to Sarah. Unlike Sarah, who just poked at Lizzie, Elisabeth reached for Lizzie's wrist and checked for a pulse. She looked surprised, then reached for Sarah's wrist, then her own.

"What?" Chuck asked from behind her. Elisabeth reached for his wrist next. Then she looked at all of them, her mouth opening and closing as she struggled for words.

"I don't know." She finally said. "It doesn't make any sense."

"See, we're all dead." Josh said.

"Stop!" Lizzie turned to Roland, but he was looking away from them, watching something she couldn't see in the woods behind her. "I hear something."

"What is it?" Elisabeth asked, holding herself, shivering as she looked around them.

"I hear something moving. Now be quiet."

The rest of them were watching him, but as the silence descended upon them, they found themselves turning to look deeper into the woods.

Lizzie tried to move, shift herself so she could turn to look around the tree, but the slightest shift sounded like a firecracker exploding from the dead leaves beneath her. It would often garner herself a quick dirty side eye glance from Roland who kept watch.

She could hear it, too. It had been quiet at first, but as the silence grew, she could hear it. It wasn't distant either. There was a shuffling sound, something moving through the grass. Then, as she listened, she swore she could hear more of it. They were moving, something behind them moving in their direction.

"I think I see it," Roland said.

"What?" Josh said as he stepped closer to Roland. Roland looked at him briefly and then back at the trees.

Lizzie thought she could see it too, but she couldn't make it out. It didn't move right, it wasn't walking, but glided through the brush as it approached. It wasn't like one shape but many of them, as she could see how it moved across the grass.

But living things didn't glide. Not like this. Birds swooped through the air, but this was more like something sliding, slithering through the tall grass, rustling... like it was on its belly... like a large snake.

No, not one large snake. This sounded like hundreds of them, and they were all moving through the woods, coming towards them.

Lizzie felt her body tense as they neared. She kept trying to look around the tree to the dark woods behind her, but each time, giving up and looking at the people around her. Some of them had been strangers once, but over time, they had all become first her friends and now her family. She almost felt like their protector, now that she heard something that approached.

She used the tree, pushing with her legs as she worked her way, wriggling back and forth to move her way up so that she could stand. It was difficult. The bark on the tree was dry and dug into her shirt, pulling on it, the fabric catching on various pieces. She grunted with effort, and Roland noticed.

"What do you think you're doing?" he asked, reaching an arm out to ease her back down. She waved it off and glared at him.

"If you're going to do anything, help me up." His scowl deepened, but he reached under her arms to pull her up so she could stand and lean against the tree.

"Thanks." she said as she worked out of his grip. Her balance wobbled, her knees shook with weakness, any second threatening to collapse from under her. She knew it, but she still pushed through, using the tree to steady her as she limped around the side of it.

"Liz?" Sarah said behind her.

"What do you think you're doing?" Roland asked.

She ignored them both as she stood there looking into the darkness in front of her. It was so strange to her but looked like her woods around the cabin. She should know this place, yet it was so alien. Maybe it had to do with the darkness itself. Like the clearing, it was dark, no signs of light anywhere, but she could still see.

She watched as the tall grass was moving, shifting, coming towards her. That was it. It wasn't something moving through the grass towards them;

it was the tall grass itself moving. It was racing around the trees, shuffling as it made its way closer.

Her breath caught in her chest.

"What do you think it is?" Josh asked. He had moved towards the back of the group. *Of course he was. The loud mouths who talked like big men were always the ones to stand behind when shit got real. It's why they always survived. Cockroaches were always the hardest to kill.*

She had nothing to base this thought on, and tried to push it from her mind, to focus on what was moving towards them. Like before though, whenever she tried to focus on anything in this world, her thoughts fought against her, like some kind of barrier kept her from taking everything in. She shook herself, even pushing away from Roland, who reached to keep her in his arms.

"I think..." Lizzie started to say, but again, that annoying fog crushed down on her thoughts, pushing like a knife, now painfully forcing its way into her temples. The pain was sharp behind her eyes, and she had to close them to finish what she was saying. "How are you here? How are you so... alive? Where are we? How can any of this be? We don't have time to be worrying about any of that now, but holy shit, what the fucking fuck, fuck, fuck is going on!"

Lizzie hadn't realized she had bent over during her outburst, but as she opened her eyes, she stood and turned sharply, already mid-step back towards the barn.

"Liz-" Roland started to ask.

"I'm heading back to the barn," she said. She could feel the moisture on her cheeks from fresh tears. She quickly wiped it away, but paused as her hand came away dark with blood.

"Honey, you okay?" Rolan asked. She pushed him away and continued into the clearing. Her feet stung from every blade of grass that felt like fresh slices into her open wounds. The pain was intoxicating as it helped distract her from the annoying presence that kept pushing in on her thoughts.

"I'm going home," she said.

"What are those things?" Elisabeth shrieked. "Chuck! Get away, they're here!"

Lizzie turned around just in time to see it, and the pain behind her eyes screamed at her as she watched it attack Chuck.

CHAPTER 57

Lizzie couldn't make sense of what it was she was seeing. It defied everything she knew about reality. At least, what reality was in relation to living things and biology.

She couldn't so much see what was attacking Chuck, as it looked like soil with long gray grass about a foot high rising out of it. That was until Elisabeth reached out and tried to pull the thing from Chuck's cheek. That was when those long blades of green grass writhed and wrapped themselves around her arms.

Elisabeth screamed, and it was clear why as the green tentacles started to turn red with her blood. What Lizzie could see of Elisabeth's arm through flashes of the quick moving, writhing limbs was of her pale flesh getting ripped away as it thrashed at her.

That was all happening as Chuck himself was being eaten by the actual creature. As Lizzie took a step closer, she could see the small pincher-like appendages that extended from the other side of the dark creature that immediately made her think of crabs. They were snapping at Chuck's face while pointed legs burrowed beneath his skin to fasten the creature from coming loose.

Chuck and Elisabeth were both screaming. Elisabeth was briefly able to pull the thing away from Chuck's face, though Lizzie wasn't sure if it was because she was still trying to pull it off him, or because she was trying to get her own arms free. Either way, in that brief instant, Lizzie saw the underside of the thing, and her stomach twisted in revulsion. It was like every part of the monster's underside that she could see was moving, grinding teeth. They were sharp, inch long razors that all chewed into Chuck, first around his ankle, but as he fell to the ground, it had worked its way up.

This was one patch of tall grass had two of her friends in its grip. Lizzie looked up from her fallen friends, unable to move as she was locked in horror at the grisly scene in front of her. However, Lizzie couldn't help but notice the movement along the ground beyond Chuck. She started to shake in fear. From what Lizzie could see, there were hundreds more of the things, all of them moving quickly, getting closer to them.

"Roland!" Lizzie called. He had still been by the tree and had stood there mesmerized by the attacking creature. It was probably a good thing, as Lizzie feared that had he tried to help either one of them, he would have been pulled into the death trap as well.

It might have already been too late. She watched as one was nearing his feet. She could already see as the swaying grass turned into those strong tentacles, reaching for his bare ankles.

Roland must have sensed it being near as he jumped back at the sound of Lizzie's voice, just in time to keep the monster grasping air where Roland's ankle had been.

It wasn't the only one though, as two more were already trying to reach past the first monster. One of them kept coming towards them, but the other, its grass tentacles wrapped around the distracted creature. Within seconds, its teeth were buried in the backside, and the two monstrosities were entangled, tearing into one another.

"What the hell is this shit?" Josh cried out, quickly scrambling to get away from the two lovers being devoured.

"Doesn't matter." Sarah said.

"Bullshit it don't."

"They're creatures of the dark. You don't need to know anything more than that." Jessica yelled. Around them, the chittering noise of the approaching creatures grew to be deafening. It was becoming painful with the sound mingled with something else. There was some other thrum in the air. It was a noise, but it felt like much more. It was so much clatter that as the monstrosities neared, the sounds became a chaotic symphony of nosebleed levels that pulsated through their thoughts.

It was hard to concentrate on the scene before them, let alone think of what to do. It was hard to more than to just observe as some of the creatures veered off from coming straight towards them, to feed off the two now fresh corpses. As the new ones approached, they attacked the one lone creature. Then Lizzie noticed that the first one, while it had been eating off the corpses, had also been changing.

As one neared, the first monster reached out a clawed arm from a shoulder that suddenly appeared. The held one shrieked as it was pulled closer, its tentacles slashing and gouging this new appendage until it was pulled in. By then, the teeth that had once been attached to no discernable mouth now were reformed, filling a wide, gaping mouth inside what looked like a deformed human skull.

Lizzie might have stayed being distracted watching the creatures until she was wrapped up by one, but Sarah grabbed her as Jessica pulled at Roland. Josh was the only one who was lost in watching, and he was too far out of reach for them to grab him. He'd been stepping back, moving away from the devouring, but it wasn't fast enough. Maybe it was too fast. Maybe he should have been watching the ground around him as much as he was watching the grass in front of him. Either way, he was swallowed.

He had taken one step back, but his foot never touched solid grown. He let out a quiet hiss as he lost his balance and continued falling back. Then he was screaming.

The ground wasn't just dirt and short grass. Lizzie watched as teeth had formed a circle around where Josh had been stepping and the moment his foot had come down, it had disappeared into the throat of the ground itself. The teeth rising and clamping down on Josh's thigh, the long needle like jaws tearing through the flesh and bone until the leg was severed from his body.

Then there were more of them. Jaws along the dirt opening and closing, shifting towards him so they could devour him. Every bite of skin torn away; another mound appeared.

"Oh my God!" Lizzie exclaimed. Roland looked at her and caught what she was looking at.

"What is it?"

"The ground. Everything! It's all alive. I don't know, it's like the more we bleed, the more blood falls. Holy shit, it's all coming after us." She said.

"We need to get out of here." Sarah said.

"But where?" Roland said.

"Back through the barn." Jessica said.

"My brother's back there, and you are all dead."

"We have to go back."

Lizzie followed her gaze to the barn. Anything to get away from watching Josh get torn apart. They were already moving in that direction. The living grass, the shifting ground, they all moved towards them. The barn seemed like the only place to go. Unless they could go to the house. On the other side, it was a haven, maybe-

But where was it? Lizzie looked past the barn to where the house should have been, but it wasn't there. It was dead grass in the frame of the house, but there wasn't anything standing, no walls to keep anything out.

"Lizzie, keep up!"

She felt hands pulling at her, but didn't know who they belonged to. She halfheartedly took a step in that direction, and then another. Then she looked to see the barn they were all making their way toward. Light was flickering from it. Was that the light from the other side? She couldn't tell.

She was moving in that direction. They were pulling her, but that wasn't the only force pulling her.

It felt like there was a wind behind her as well. She had noticed it before, but now it was getting stronger. Forces were gathering, everything shifting, like the darkness she couldn't see around her was moving in upon itself towards the barn, towards the doorway. She was getting caught up in and, like a leaf on the wind, it was pushing her.

Then she felt the rhythm. The air flowed strangely, circling around them. The dirt that was not growing teeth and trying to devour her and her friends was rising in dust, making the air hard to breathe.

Lizzie couldn't see it, but she knew something was above them. It was there, and she knew not to look up. Something told her that the little voice inside her that struggled to keep her sane was screaming that whatever was up there would stretch the fabric of her reality to a point she might not accept.

How everything else was in this place, she imagined that whatever was up there was nothing but teeth, and if she looked, she would see them about to reach down and chop all of them in half. She imagined that..., but knew that whatever it was, it was something much worse. The size of it alone would rival the realm of reality.

Whales were thought of as being massive creatures that dominated the ocean, but what was above them, what neared them, would make those enormous creatures pale in size. As it moved closer, she sensed they wouldn't be able to move from the shear velocity of its flight would squash them like bugs to the bottom of a foot. What came for them, it would make those large whales seem like a minnow in a pond.

They were getting so close to the barn, they just needed to keep running.

"Jessica, what is it?" Sarah cried out as they all ran.

"Whatever it is, don't look up," Lizzie yelled.

"I'll look." Roland said, but Lizzie grabbed him and pulled his head around so that he was looking at her. Her lungs burned as so much dirt littered the air.

"Keep running."

"What about those other things?" Jessica yelled. "They're getting closer."

"Get back to the other side."

"You just need to get back. We came over with you." Sarah yelled.

"Let's all get back," Lizzie said as they reached the edge of the back half of the barn. Lizzie didn't stop at all to inspect what looked like the edge of some explosion that had ripped open the back half. She rushed in, hurtling herself into the absolute darkness of the building.

"Okay, there's the doorway." Roland yelled. The sound of the whooshing air was growing so that it was hard to hear anything over it. "You just need to go through it."

Lizzie could see where the light doorway was, and she watched as darkness was pouring through it, breaking through the barrier to the other side.

"STOP!"

It wasn't so much a voice they heard, but the word echoed around them, rumbling with the shaking earth and sky. Every part of her felt it and knew there was more than just them there.

"What was that?" Sarah asked.

"It doesn't matter! Just go!" Roland yelled. It was getting hard to hear them over the gushing wind. Breathing was hard, as the air felt like it was getting pulled from Lizzie's lungs. She couldn't talk.

"Stop."

This time, the barn shook. Dust fell from the rafters above her to immediately be sucked into the light vortex in front of them, and she could hear the creaking of the support beams as cracks formed in the wood.

"Whatever you do, don't look at it," Lizzie yelled at them, refusing to turn around. Her head was screaming in pain, and she didn't have to rub at her face to know that she was bleeding. She could feel the wetness around her eyes and dripping from her nose. She could see it in her friends as well. Each of them, blood flowing from their ears, eyes and nose, even dripping down from their hair. Just hearing the thing speak to them was causing them to bleed from their hair. What would happen if they saw it? She didn't think their sanity would survive.

Jessica was the first one to reach the barrier, and she rushed into it...only to be thrown back against the wall.

"Jess, you all right?" Sarah called out. Boards rattled around them, the wind getting stronger, pulled at the old wood. "Jess?"

Jessica wasn't moving. Lizzie turned to go to her, but Roland grabbed her and pulled her back to the barrier.

"We don't have time. You have to get through."

Lizzie looked up at him, her heart twisting, and she wanted to kick him for touching her, keeping her from her friend.

"Get your hands off me." She tried to scream at him, but it was lost to the wind as several boards from the roof were suddenly pulled free off, exposing them to the night sky.

"Lizzie, you have to go through."

She ignored him and tried to step towards Jessica, but he grabbed her again and wouldn't let go. She fought to get out of his grip, struggling to break free from him, but his hands were strong and firm.

Sarah was the first to reach Jessica, and she knelt beside her, pulling her into her bosom. Blood was flowing from the back of Jessica's head, but as Sarah held her, Jessica opened her eyes and looked up at her, a small smile creasing her lips. She spoke softly, and only Sarah could hear her, but instantly she looked up and over at Liz.

"Go!" Sarah yelled. "She says you need to go. It'll be fine, but you need to cross over."

Lizzie looked from her to Roland, then to the barrier that stood in front of them. She didn't want to leave her friends behind, but it seemed obvious that they were not meant to come with her, to join her on the other side. Wasn't that what she had learned from her uncle's journals? The dead belonged over there... that was why her uncles came there, to see their long dead in a place where they were real.

Though it seemed different for her... Why? Why was this place so dangerous to her?

She pushed down the thoughts. It was easy. The pain, the needles that were shooting through her head, made thinking hard to begin with. Just being over there was an exercise in mental anguish.

Just one step. One foot in front of the other. That was all it was going to take. She just needed to move forward and then she would be on the other side. She would be home.

She reached out her hand as she stepped forward, moving to step into the light.

CHAPTER 58

She reached forward, expecting her hand to pass through the barrier and that she would be pulled to the other side just like before. Instead, her hand struck something cold, hard and smooth, like a barrier of glass that kept her from crossing over. She didn't get thrown back like Jessica, but there was something there, something solid that kept her from going back.

She noticed that it wasn't the same for the darkness around them. The edges of the barrier were a blur of constant motion, as she could see it getting sucked through, being pulled through.

"Lizzie... What are you looking at?" Sarah asked.

"It won't let me through."

"It has to." Sarah yelled back.

The surrounding sound, that rushing of the darkness being pulled to the other side, intensified. She thought it would feel like wind funneling past them. It sounded like it should, but she couldn't feel it. She could feel something, a change to the air, but no, it definitely wasn't wind...

Lizzie wanted to reach out to the end of the gateway, but pulled her hand back as she felt the eternal cold emanating from it. Just getting closer to it made it unbearable to touch. Touching it, all it would take was one little touch and she could imagine her fingers breaking off from being instantly frozen. They would fall to the dirt floor, shatter into even more pieces, and then...

"GO!" Sarah yelled, and Lizzie felt her friend's hands pushing at her from behind her. They were rough with her, and Lizzie could hear the desperation in her voice. Lizzie nearly did fall forward with the first push, but the second one she had braced herself for, struggling to keep from getting pushed into the barrier.

"Stop it!" Lizzie looked at Roland, pleading with him for help. He looked confused at the scene, not sure who he should help.

"STOP!" the voice boomed from above. "YOU CAN NOT LEAVE!"

"Just what is that?" Jessica said as she cried out again, this time grasping at her ears. Through her fingers, Lizzie could see blood spurting out as she shrank to the ground.

"Be careful!" Lizzie called out, dodging out of the way from another one of Sarah's push attempts. Lizzie didn't see any of the things that had eaten Josh, but that didn't mean they weren't there. They hadn't seen them there out there either until they had already taken a large chunk from Josh's face. Jessica was squirming on the floor, swaying back and forth. Lizzie lowered herself, reaching out to her friend.

"It's going to be okay."

"Liz, we don't have time for this. You need to get through that thing. We need to get you safe. Get you safe, then we'll be safe. That seems to be how it works."

"Is it? So that was you that was attacking me over there? Was it?" Liz yelled back at Sarah while she gently put her hand on Jessica's shoulder. Sarah shied away from returning her glare. "I didn't think so. Now shut up."

"Roland, help me. We need to get her through the thing."

Liz ignored them both, staying focused on Jessica. She stopped her crying, but still wasn't looking up to meet Lizzie's eye.

"It's going to be okay." Jessica allowed herself to be pulled into Lizzie's arms. Lizzie whispered it again into her friend's ear, "It's going to be okay," as she could feel its effects. Her friend's shoulders relaxed, and before Lizzie realized it, Jessica had turned, pulling her into a tight hug.

It took Lizzie a few moments of holding her friend to realize that Jessica was mouthing something. She could feel Jess' mouth moving as Lizzie held her to her chest, and she pushed her back to look at her blood-soaked face. Her eyes were covered in red, crusted over by the drying ooze of concealing blood.

"What?" Lizzie yelled, trying to force her words over the increasing volume of the vortex of darkness.

Lizzie tried to make out what her friend was saying. In her mind, she heard things like, 'That's what I've always told you,' and, 'of course, it's going to be okay.' Lizzie could even picture her friend screaming, 'Please God, save us!' Jess was always trying to push Lizzie into religion. Though as she watched her, she realized that Jessica wasn't screaming or saying anything to her. Jess had her eyes closed and was whispering something only to herself. She was praying and Lizzie thought she knew what prayer. She could hear Jessica in her mind as she chanted it over and over.

"And though I walk through the valley of the shadow of death, I shall fear no evil." The words just kept repeating like a scratched CD, looping a track over and over. Lizzie could hear them, even though the non-wind screeched around them. It was like the voice was in her head and she found herself repeating them, chanting them with her.

If there was ever a time for God to step in and help the little people down here, she thought as she joined in saying the words again, saying them with hope that with each repeat of the phrase, she would feel things calm down around her.

Instead, the wind of darkness intensified. She could see the edges of the portal were getting darker. More of the surrounding darkness was soaking through to the other side. There was still a lot of darkness around them, but she had to wonder just how much would go through before the world would be washed away by it, cleansed into a world of eternal darkness like the one she was in. Was that the goal? Was that what it wanted? To take over the world of light?

She could hear loud moans erupting from outside the back side of the barn and thought back to the grass with teeth they had just escaped from. Were there more of them? Were they still coming for them? Of course they were. Why would they have ever stopped?

"What are we going to do?" Roland yelled. She looked at him and saw that Sarah was clinging to him. Lizzie had Jessica and Roland had her best friend. Maybe they had been sleeping together. Lizzie didn't know anymore, and she didn't know what to trust. Did it even matter in the grand scheme as the world was fading around them?

"How should I know?" She yelled back at him.

"This is all because of you?" Sarah yelled at her. It didn't have the bite to it that fake Sarah had when she had taken her friend's place. Still, the words hurt. They were true. All of this was because of her and her family.

"I know."

"We need to do something." Roland said. He was looking at the portal, studying it. He must have been seeing what she had about the darkness going through. "I don't think we have much time."

"And through I walk..." Jessica continued. This time Lizzie could hear with her own ears as Jessica was getting louder with her chants, and now that Lizzie could hear it, she felt a burning inside her. A rage welling up. She had tried chanting it. She had turned the phrase, and what had happened. Not a God Damn thing! How was it going to help Jessica? She was dead. They were all dead but her. None of that mattered.

"Jessica. We need your help! Come on. We need ideas. We can't just pray our way out of this. It doesn't work that way," Lizzie said, shaking her friend so that she would look at her. "I need you here. We need you here."

"Fear no evil..."

They were surrounded by evil. How did you not fear evil? Lizzie shook her friend, trying to get Jessica to look her in the eyes, but she wouldn't focus. Her gaze was downward, and Lizzie pushed her back in disgust. As soon as she pushed her away, Lizzie could make out the shape of her mistake just before seeing its large mouth open to reveal the rows of large, glistening teeth.

"Jess-!" Barely escaped Lizzie's lips when she saw the grotesquely large, misshaped head move towards her friend. It had snuck in and moved into the darkness of the barn.

Jessica was oblivious to the teeth that were about to rip into her. Lizzie struggled to shift back her balance so that she could grab her friend, but that was when she saw more of them outside. She could have sworn they all had just been teeth in the grass before, but now they were something else. Like zombies, these figures moving towards them all appeared to be dead and stumbling as their lifeless forms learned to walk again. She would have written them off as just monstrous forms, but there was something she recognized about them. She vaguely knew the shape of the monster that moved behind the one that was about to devour her friend.

Then claws shot out from behind, reaching through both wood and air to surround the large mouth that was about to make a chew toy out of her friend, and within a heartbeat, it was gone. A large hole in the surrounding wall was the only evidence that there had been something monstrous there before.

Outside, they could all hear the sounds of gnawing, growling, and ripping as the two creatures were tearing at one another.

Roland was the first to recover, the shock holding the rest of them in place as he slowly sighed. "What the fuck?"

Jessica was still writhing on the ground, her face contorted with pain. Sarah went to her, and Lizzie broke out of the trance of what she had seen. She moved to the hole and could barely make out the motion of the two creatures. They were still growing. What had once been just teeth in the woods were now gangly creatures that had grass dripping from their corpses that stood over nine feet tall. They had large mouths and wherever she could see through the grass, teeth jutted out from bone and skin. They were formed in human shape, two arms, two legs, but large claws that were each a foot in length. They were devourers, and it was clear they were only there to eat what they found...

But there was something else, something she saw, but refused to see. She couldn't focus on it. Her mind couldn't grasp it. Just looking at their faces caused her brain to hurt like a knife was stabbing into her eyes, and she had to turn away to keep from going mad.

She had to be wrong...

It wasn't possible...

"Lizzie!"

Roland came over to her, but he wasn't the one that was yelling. He wrapped his arms around her and pulled her away.

"Roland! Lizzie! Help me get this thing off her." Sarah yelled.

Lizzie looked down and saw the scorpion shaped talisman that she had been wearing when they came through. It was alive, and it was on top of Jessica, its pinchers snapping at her face. It was half a foot in length, and would tear off much of her face, if not for Jessica struggling to keep it away. Sarah was trying to get to her to help, but another devourer, one much smaller than the ones outside, was on the ground, fighting to get the talisman as well. Sarah fought to keep it at bay. There was something odd about this one, and Lizzie noticed why it was on the ground, pulling itself towards them.

Its legs were gone, only the upper torso remained, and it had pulled itself all the way towards them. It had the face of Josh, and she had to shake away the distorted proportions as it fought. The face was long and distorted, teeth jutting through the skin and where his face had been eaten away before, a new mouth had formed with rows of teeth.

The eyes were still there. Josh had always hated her, and that hate burned with red, the eyes near glowing, and as he saw her attention on him, he changed his focus from grabbing at the talisman to lunging for her.

His grip was like iron, reminding her of the old man in the house... the naked man... the one who started all of this, and just like that, Josh was pulling himself onto her. All the teeth were grinding together, but the mouths were open, getting ready to grind into her. They were like saw blades gearing up to tear her apart.

Roland had reached around Josh, pulling it from behind, but he quickly pulled his hands away. They were covered in a dark liquid that she could smell was his blood. Lizzie looked and could see smaller mouths along Josh's body. Nearly every place she would want to grab and push him away was another mouth. He was covered in hungry, chomping teeth, ready to devour her.

She had to push at his shoulders, which was one of the few places she couldn't see any teeth. Roland was trying to do the same, but his hands were covered in small wounds, and he winced as he tried to grab. They weren't making any progress in getting him away, but they were keeping him from getting her.

She tried to kick out at him, but missed as she had aimed for where his legs would have been. She was glad she did. As she got her balance back, her leg back to pushing her back, she saw the large tendril like thing that came out from his torso. It grabbed at her leg, trying to pull her.

"What the hell!" She barely exclaimed and twisted her body away. She shifted her weight again, and the thing that had been Josh lost its leverage. Roland gave a hard pull, and the thing rolled to the floor. It didn't take long to recover and was quickly turned back to them. In that brief second, they saw his lower torso, and the large mouth that it had become, the tendril being like some kind of massive tongue it used to help push it along the floor. It was helping to push it to turn towards them, and Josh was back to glaring at her.

"Fuck this!" Roland said.

They tried to get ready for its attack.

"I really need some help over here!" Sarah yelled.

Something slammed into the far wall, and they all heard the sound of splintering wood.

"Fuck! What now!" Lizzie yelled.

"Lizzie!" Sarah yelled again.

Lizzie turned and saw the talisman had shifted and was snapping at Sarah, which was good, as it was not on top of Jessica, so it was easier to hold it back. What was bad was the tail had wrapped itself around Jessica's throat and the tip was poised above her face, inches from striking. Lizzie didn't think it was poisonous, not after that tail had embedded itself in her arm for so long, but with how large it had grown, a stab to the eye could rip it out.

Jessica's face was turning blue. The tail was choking her. Jessica was struggling to pull herself free with one hand while keeping the deadly tip from striking with her other.

Lizzie reached forward to the talisman, but before she could reach it, the barn shook as more of the far wall exploded inward, covering them all in shards of wood.

Lizzie had covered her eyes, and when she looked up, she saw that Roland had done the same. Sarah hadn't been so lucky, and wood covered her face with specks of blood already dripping from fresh wounds.

There was growling from what had ripped open the wall, and Lizzie tried to look, but a cloud of dust had stirred. She couldn't see much; however, Roland must have been able to see what was out there. He quickly called out to Lizzie, "Don't look!"

That only made her want to look more, but she did what he said and looked away, back to the talisman, trying to rip Jessica's face off. Out of the corner of her eye, she saw some kind of movement, the Josh thing moving towards them, and then it was just gone. Lizzie started to look up, unable to stop herself, but

Roland's hands were there, gripping her face and forcing her to look at him.

"Just focus on me." He yelled. "Focus on me."

She nodded. She wanted to hug him, but the sounds of Sarah whimpering and Jessica gasping for her kept her thoughts from giving into her own comfort. She turned and pulled at the tail. It was rough, the dry shell of the thing was sharp. Pulling on it fell like pulling on broken glass edge. She had to grip it though, and she did, struggling to pull it away. Roland's hands joined hers, and she could suddenly feel it loosen its grip. Sarah joined them. All three of them pulled at it, and it might have been Lizzie's imagination, but she swore she could hear the thing shriek as though it was in pain, and slowly as it tried to move. It appeared like the thing was shrinking in their collective ...hands...

"...1............3- pull" Lizzie called, and they gave a unified pull. There was no denying it this time, Lizzie thought, as she could feel it now. The tail started to give. It was slowly uncurling itself.

She heard Roland give a sigh of relief as it took a step back on Jessica's chest and shook itself, like it was a dog shaking off the rain. There was a rattling sound, a creaking of the ceiling boards above them. Then the scorpion thing started to tick, like an old clock. The tick-toc sound like time was winding down. The steady click, click, but growing slower as it pounded out the final hours...

The wind around them quieted. The darkness didn't feel like it was rushing around them anymore. There was a stillness growing that for a moment, Lizzie thought maybe even the things outside had stopped trying to kill them, or one another.

No, they were still out there. She could sense it, just like she felt the hairs on the back of her head raise and knew something had just shifted. The large force outside was getting closer, but it wasn't there yet. The things outside still ...fought... No, this changing sense was something else.

"Lizzie, look out!" Roland yelled, and she saw him reach out in a flash. Then he recoiled, red quickly spilling out from a spot on his arm. That was all the time she had to process before the talisman was on her. She fell back, struggling to keep it from climbing at her like it did Jessica.

It took her a moment to realize it wasn't trying to wrap itself around her neck. She was clawing at it while simultaneously pushing herself back on the ground where she had fallen and realized that it was trying to get to her arm. As she fought to get it off her, it fought to get back to grasp her wrist...like she was wearing it as a bracelet again.

She continued to struggle. She pulled at it, but she could feel her strength draining. It was reaching into her somehow, draining her energy out through what, her soul? She felt like it was stealing something from her and made it hard to breathe as she fought the damned thing.

Then Jessica reached them. She had to crawl, the color still drained from her face, and she could barely even whisper. It didn't matter. Lizzie swore it sounded like Jessica was yelling inside her head.

"Put on God's complete set of armor provided for us, so that you will be protected as you fight against the evil strategies of the accuser. Your hand-to-hand combat is not with human beings, but with the highest..." Jessica gasped, and for a moment, Lizzie thought she was going to pass out. Whatever she was doing, Lizzie thought it might be working. She didn't understand. Hell, she couldn't believe it, but she could feel the thing lose strength. It was staggering, wavering back and forth. Twitching as Jessica's lips began to move again.

"For they are a powerful class of demon-gods and evil spirits that hold this dark world in bondage. Because of this, you must wear all the armor that God provides, so you're protected as you confront the slanderer, for you are destined for all things and will rise victorious."

Lizzie felt something twist inside of her. She didn't believe in that stuff. Never had and didn't think she ever would. Yet, she found her lungs filling with air. Tear quickly followed. She felt like all she had the strength left to do was cry. She wanted to curl up in a ball, she wanted to...

Around them, everything had gone bright with a radiant light. Outside, the creatures hissed, and she could hear screams of pain.

"I shall fear no evil." Roland said. He had fallen back to his knees again and was next to Lizzie, reaching to pull her to him.

"For thou art with me," Lizzie said, and she collapses into his embrace, just then noticing that the talisman had dropped from her.

"Thy rod and they staff, they comfort me." Sarah said, and she joined them, her tears red, streaking down her cheeks.

"Of course, that's the only bible verse you guys remember. Didn't you ever go to church other than Sunday school?" Jessica asked as she joined the hug.

"No." Lizzie said, wiping her eyes as she looked at them all.

"We need to get out of here. We don't know how long this light, or whatever it is, will protect us," Sarah said, wiping her cheeks, but just smearing the blood across.

"Forever and always." Jessica said.

"Yeah, I don't trust that."

"How do we get you home?" Roland said, looking at Lizzie.

"Me? We're all going back."

"We're dead, remember? There's no point."

"Yeah, well, I'm not leaving you here."

"I don't think you have a choice."

"He may be right, sis," Sarah said.

"Maybe. I do have an idea, though." Lizzie said, and as she did, she started rooting around on the ground. Strange how the brightness made everything hard to see. Like with the light being foreign there, it was like an opposite of how the darkness made it so bright.

She finally found where the talisman had fallen and grabbed it.

"Help me up."

She had spoken to Roland, but they all grabbed her. They all held each other, and she held it.

"Okay, I'm going to walk back through. I'm going to hold on to this. When I do, we all hold each other. Okay?"

She looked at them. They all nodded, though they all looked grim, except for Jessica, who never stopped smiling.

"Go on. Do it."

Lizzie looked back at the barrier, gripped the talisman hard in her hand, and stepped forward.

CHAPTER 59

The breath caught in Lizzie's throat for a moment and then suddenly she was gasping for air that wasn't coming to her. Around her was dark, then bright. A color explosion swirled around her, and she thought she was going blind. There was yelling that turned to screams. None of it she could make out. She barely felt herself getting pushed around, and then...

There was nothing, and she found herself again slipping into the darkness, this time exhaustion taking over her. She had a brief thought flash through her mind, first thinking of that image she had seen, but couldn't have seen in the other place. The image of her mom as that devourer, her features distorted but the monstrosity that it was, as it tore the other creature apart. Then she remembered seeing her brother as he pushed her into the void, his face a mask of anger and pain as he did it...

Then she slipped away again, not able to grasp what was going on around her.

CHAPTER 60

Lizzie didn't need to open her eyes to know that she was awake. Why? Because there was no way she could hurt this much if she was asleep or dead.

Every single part of her ached to a degree that she wasn't sure she could even move, and there were parts of her that screamed raw like they were burning. Her head felt like a thousand hangovers all happening at once, the pounding of a million drums mingling with a legion of jet planes flying low overhead. It was a cacophony of a maelstrom that all told her one thing... She was still alive. Damn it all to hell and back. She was in pain, but she was alive.

For better or worse.

"Lizzie! Lizzie, wake up!" Roland was yelling. She could hear the worry in his voice.

"What happened to her?" Sarah, the real Sarah, Lizzie, was still so happy to hear that voice. Even if they were back in the real world, and her friend would be just a thing only Lizzie could see, it was still good to have her there. To have all of them there.

Did that mean that all of this was not over? Would this be the rest of her life?

Her brain hurt too much to think about it and she struggled to open her eyes.

The air around her was hot, and it was getting hard to breathe again. However, this air had a pungent smell. She could almost feel the acrid odor of smoke, as wood was burning somewhere.

"Don't move. We got you and your brother out of the fire, but you've been through a lot. You need to lie back." Lizzie vaguely recognized the stranger's voice. She just couldn't place it. It sounded different. Maybe her ears were affected as well. Wait, fire?

"We should get her into the house?" Jessica yelled. Was she yelling? Lizzie thought she was. She tried to open her eyes and look in the direction of the voice, but her head flopped forward, lightning bolts of pain shot in all directions from her neck. Her eyes remained closed.

She tried to speak, but it was like her mouth was sown shut and she could feel the dry sandpaper that lined her throat as she worked at creating a sound.

"Don't talk," the familiar voice said, then he must have turned to Jessica, "We can't take her in there. The cabin is gone, already burned."

"I'm not going back in there." Sarah chimed in.

"We need to get her away from them both. I've called 911. Help is on the way. We just need to get her and her brother comfortable. Here, you take one leg and you the other."

Lizzie felt herself being lifted and shuffled around. She wasn't getting used to being treated like a rag doll. It was starting to really annoy her, and she wanted to push everyone away.

"Hey big guy, think you can grab her brother."

"You're the big, strong police officer. Why don't you help her brother? I can take her."

"Hey, suit yourself. I've just about been disemboweled and currently a recovering werewolf that can barely walk, but by all means, you take the girl."

"Fuck you."

Lizzie felt herself being carried as she tried to process the words. *Wolf... werewolf? There wolf, there castle* came into her head, pulled through with a memory of some old comedy Roland had made her watch.

She felt warmth with the memory, the sense of safely being held in his arms.

She realized she was feeling safe all throughout her body as the feeling spread. Something was different. The air around her had changed. She could feel it, like a fragrance of lavender caught on the wind, the sensation wrapped around her.

As they set her down, she could begin to open an eye, though she could already feel the exhaustion was taking her again. Though in that brief glimpse, she could see the fire. The barn was quickly burning with everything inside, going with it. Everything except the old well. She could already see the outline through the burning walls. She also saw the beam of bright white light that cascaded out from the well and shone like a beam into the night sky. It made everything around them a little lighter. She also saw Roland, and she was in his hands as he was one of the ones that were carrying her. His living, strong hands, and they held her.

She saw him, and he flashed a smile, though he was obviously concerned about her. She returned the smile with her own as she slipped into the comforting dreams of peaceful slumber.

CHAPTER 61

Lizzie stood amongst the ashes of what was once the barn. The air was cool, but probably should have been colder. There was still a lot of heat from the still ground. The wood was all gone, quickly having burned away with nothing to stop it. It had burned unnaturally quick, some would say.

The surrounding clearing was still filled with the remnants of the chaos from earlier, however much of the mad energy that had been fueling the chaos earlier seemed to have dissipated the moment she had returned through the gateway with the talisman and the essence of her dead friends. Her friends that were no longer dead.

Sarah walked over to her. Her living, breathing friend who had been dead for the last month, now standing there, shoulder-to-shoulder with her.

"You know this makes no sense, right?" Sarah said as she looked from the burned down barn to the burned down cabin behind them.

"Oh, I know."

"So, you think it's over?"

"No fucking clue. I mean, something does feel different, like something had been lifted off me, but hell. I mean, hell, who am I to know about any of this? All the information I had went up to smoke in those damn books." Lizzie said as she pointed to the cabin.

"Yeah, something's different." Said a gravelly voice, and Lizzie saw the officer walking up to her. A werewolf officer. Now, how was she supposed to reconcile that one? "I wouldn't call it over, though. Evil's never gone, and the evil that tried to get through here, that was older than God."

Lizzie laughed until those dark eyes pierced through her and killed it.

"Older than God, huh?" Sarah quipped.

"Yeah, older than God. I've been around a long time. I've been feeling the pull to this place for a long time, but it grew stronger with your uncle in his last few years. I think it had something to do with that abomination that was here earlier."

"The vampire? That was a vampire?" Lizzie asked. The officer nodded at her.

"This place has been pulling evil for a long time. Something to do with that." He nodded to the well. "It's some kind of gateway to another plane of existence, I think. It's been here a long time and only gotten stronger. It was getting fed by those things. Then somehow, they found a way to break open the door. Not sure how you managed to close it again, but it's closed for now."

"So, it's over?" Lizzie asked.

"Almost." The officer said, looking off to the horizon. Lizzie followed his gaze and saw the lightening sky that would soon be the rising sun.

"Almost?"

"Think the sun will help burn away the last traces of evil here for now. Hate to say it. I don't think your friends will be sticking around. They look alive, but they have no smell."

Lizzie looked at Sarah and then over to Roland, who was walking over to them. He had been checking on Jessica, who was still bleeding from the wounds she had suffered on the other side.

"Yeah, that makes sense. I mean, could imagine me trying to explain to my parents how I'm alive?" Sarah tried to say it with a laugh, but it came out strangled and she was fully crying by the end of it.

"I don't want to lose you again," Lizzie said.

"I don't want to go, but hey, you'll be fine." Sarah said.

Roland came up behind Lizzie and put his arms around her. He didn't hear what they had been talking about and, after seeing their crying faces, dumbly said, "What?"

"Nothing." Lizzie lied. He didn't need to know. Not yet. Let them both just enjoy this moment.

"What about the Shadow thing?" Sarah said.

"It's probably still on our side, but I don't feel it anymore, and once the evil gets burned off come morning, it'll lose a lot of that strength it built up. I think you get that well taken care of; you'll never have to worry about it."

"Yeah, I'm calling in the morning. I'm going to fill that well with so much cement. Nothing will ever come from it ever again."

"Make sure to consecrate it. Put a cross down there, some holy water, all that good stuff. Never hurt, but sure may help."

"Wait, you don't believe all that religious crap, do you? You're a werewolf." Sarah said, looking incredulously at the cop.

"Didn't. Then one day I got bit. I haven't been able to step foot in a church since then. Never knew werewolves couldn't go into churches. Never saw that in any of the folklore or movies, but sure enough, step into a church and I go all wolf and start burning fur."

"Damn." Roland said.

"Yeah. Anyway, I gotta get my pack out here, then I'll call in and say I saw smoke out this way. We'll come back all official and get reports typed up. That'll give you time to say your goodbyes. We'll talk more later. Make sure you're doing okay." The officer said as he started walking away.

"Officer!" Lizzie called after him and he turned back.

"I hate to say it. I don't remember your name, but why didn't you tell me any of this earlier?"

"Well, miss, you didn't make it easy now, did you? Then later, when the kid died, I'll admit, I was upset. I liked the kid. I let my anger get the better of me. Tonight, though, I felt that shift, and knew something was coming. It was like a beacon went up, and I knew you'd need help, so I tried."

"Thank you."

"You're welcome. My name's Lowe, by the way. Roger Lowe, and I was just doing my job. I was a cop, long before I was a werewolf. I may have my demons, but at the end of the day, to protect and to serve is who I am. That's why I brought my pack here. It was a peaceful place, we thought. A place we could be and stay away from society. Damn if things just didn't get in the way."

He nodded back and then continued walking. The rest of his pack, people she had only seen in passing from around the town, walked with him until the end of the woods. Then they were wolves and were gone.

* * * *

The sun was just starting to break over the trees as Lizzie, Roland, and Sarah stood there. Jessica was on the ground, unable to stand, but they all watched as the first rays were hitting them.

The sun struck Roland and Sarah, and immediately their bodies started to fade. Within seconds, Lizzie could look through them and watch as pieces of them started to drift away.

"I love you guys." She said and reached out, trying to give them one last hug. At first, she felt them, but then they were gone. Her arms fell, as did her tears.

She looked at Jessica and lowered herself down so that she could at least hold her before she was gone.

"Do you want to know how I escaped the voodoo woman?" Jessica asked. Lizzie was watching as the sun was moving ever slowly towards them across the clearing.

"How?" Lizzie asked, her voice soft, barely a whisper as she forced out the words.

"Faith. I had faith, and you need to, too. More evil is out there. You have to have faith if you're going to survive."

"You know I won't ever go to church. Not with those hypocrites."

"Faith is not a church. It's God. Remember, Jesus loved all, and through Christ we are all saved."

"Okay." Lizzie said her face was covered in tears as she held her friend. She was crying so much she couldn't keep her eyes open, so she missed it when the sun must have reached them. She just felt it, as the weight lifted from her, and she was left holding herself.

She opened her eyes and found herself alone. For the first time since she had been pulled out of the fire, she wondered where her brother had gone, because he was gone. She was alone in the sun, and she had no clue what the hell she was now going to do.

EPILOGUE

The creature that Lizzie thought of as the shadow man or sometimes the tik-tok man remained at the edge of the clearing. The Nameless one had watched as the doorway that would bring forth its master had opened, and more troubling, had watched as it had been slammed shut. It had watched as decades of building, prying open into this reality, had finally been a success only to see the fabric of space and time ripped open, ready to release its brethren upon this infested land of light, only to have that opening collapse. It had seen glimpses of where it had come from. It had seen past this painful, torturous existence in the realm from before, the home of darkness, and then watched as all of that had been torn away.

It was left alone there again, a full creature of the dark trapped again with nothing but these mandisoons of the lighted world to occupy its presence.

It wanted to lash out and rampage through a vast amount of rage it felt. However, giving in would only be a further corruption of its being. That would make it one step closer to being like these lower forms.

So, for now, it watched. It observed as that foul abomination of a dark creation conversed with that insect.

Next to it, its rebellious creation stood. It had sent the creation to take the mandisoon's sibling and was still in the mutated body of the caretaker. The shell was long since dead, the reek of it already spreading. It was another abomination, an attempt by the shadow creature to bring darkness to this lighted world, and it had been another failure. It would be out of its misery soon; The Nameless one would not let it live much longer.

The other abomination had not made it out of the clearing before light destroyed its vessel, disintegrating the decayed corpse and the presence it had contained. Unlike the shell next to the Nameless one, it had performed its task. It had suffered for doing so, the vessel of putrid flesh being nearly torn apart, but it had gotten the mandisoon through the gateway. It had not been one to fail.

The first morning rays of sunlight touched the tops of the trees and the Nameless one looked at it with disgust.

"And it brought light, and it was good," it thought to itself. How revolting. Its existence was from before this creation and all it wanted, all it desired, was to get its kind back to where it should be, and not in some shadow realm where its brethren lived as mere reflections of their true selves.

If they were as strong or as powerful as they had once been, there would have been no stopping the rupture from being fully torn open and its master finally unleashed. The master would have come, and then darkness would have been returned, the insects of this world scorched away as an afterthought as all this existence would be gone.

Damn that creature and its otherness. The Nameless One never should have used her. The creature had made the key for it, and the key needed to be used now that the gateway had been fed so many souls.

Then there was the other one. It was old by this world's standards, but just a child to the Nameless One. Why had it been there? It had been seeing its own spawn come there from time to time, but had not realized that it was trying to feed off the essences as well. It had brought its own tokens. Why?

The Nameless One could only guess that those tokens had been part of why the gateway had slowed its growth. It must have realized the time was getting close with how it came to take away the key.

All of this was now gone. The souls having been freed, the rupture now a tiny sliver of what it had been between worlds. Everything reset back to how it had found it.

And would he start over?

It looked at the insect and the dark abomination that still stood there talking. It could continue, take its loved ones from it. It could all go back to how it had been, but something told it that the tear would not be so exposed in the future. It could hear them talk about a plan of covering up the fissure. That wouldn't work as well as they thought it would, but it would slow down its work.

And it knew it didn't need to. It had seen the darklings when it had visited the creature of the other god. It knew that there were others working to free its master. It was not alone. There were more of its kind out there, and its master was getting more influence into this existence.

No, it didn't need to do more. There were more dark things lurking in this world. It was not alone, and soon, the endless night would come. Soon...

Still, damn that creature.

* * * *

The old woman sat in her apartment, enjoying the remains around her as they still hung in decoration from her latest conquest. It had been a while since she had such a fine sacrifice, and to think that the child had thought its god would protect her.

The voodoo woman, as Lizzie had thought of her, was named Lene Dupree, and she had lived in Steven's Point for the last thirty years. She had moved there, feeling the pull of the dark place like many other creatures who hated the new god, sensing that this would be where it would meet its destruction.

She had been here and had been ready when that creature had first come to her. It had thought it had tricked her into creating the talisman that would open the gateway when she had been ready for it. She was ready.

She knew it worshipped some kind of old god and she wanted it to think she would help bring it into this world. There wasn't any way she would let that happen, but she knew her Bondye would keep it at bay when it came retribution, once it realized she had stolen its last soul. She had fed it to the key herself, and she had corrupted it.

The thing was old; she knew it came from before this new god, but it was not smart. It thought itself clever, constantly weaving different tricks and playing with its victims like it did.

The damn spiders, though. They didn't belong. They were unnatural things. She knew they weren't the tricksters. No, these came from something else that wanted into this world.

All these darklings. They all wanted to get the world back to before that foul Christian God brought light into the universe. They wanted the darkness to return. They wanted their master back. It never made sense to her. It existed in its own plane. Why come ruin this world?

She would never understand it. All these plans, webs woven by all these wishing to gain their master's favor for ending the light. None of them would ever succeed, not fully. Light was here, time was here, and it was all going to stay. It may not stay in this form, but there was no going back to before there was creation. Some things just can't be undone.

The old woman coughed. She wheezed and coughed again; the sensation causing pain throughout her body. It was a phlegm filled cough of a tired old woman, and at first, she didn't look at her hand. It wasn't until she felt the moving sensation on her hand that she looked at it.

The little black spots on the back of her hand were moving. Each of them, having eight legs as they hurried across her wrinkled skin until they forced a hole in the folds of her skin. They disappeared beneath, and she continued to watch as they quickly raced up her arm. They were joined by others, and she watched as her loose skin shifted with hundreds of them as they all raced along.

She looked back at the dark room around her, at the twinkly lights that were spider's eyes that watched her.

"No! Curse you, no!" she screamed in the empty room.

"You chose your side, witch." Came a voice in the darkness. "And you chose wrong. Now, I'm going to let my little ones take you, as our time is coming."

"Damn you and your master!" The old woman spat, spitting more of the black dots to the ground. Quickly, they dispersed to run away.

"Oh, I don't do this to serve a master. I am my own master, and I will make this world how I want to make it."

With that, she swung her cane in the direction of the voice, fighting against the growing cough that was trying to force its way from her lungs. She missed, or maybe there had never been anything there. Instead, her cane found some of her candles instead, and they were knocked over.

They fell to the floor, and she watched as the flame caught on the long shag carpeting. It raced along the floor, and at first, she feared where it would go.

Then exhaustion hit her. She could barely breathe, and she was too tired to care anymore. Bondye would care for it. Bondye would take care of them all.

THE END

More from
The EDGE OF DARKNESS universe:

Novels
Inside the Mirrors
Into Darkness
Hatched
Caught in the Web

Short Fiction:
Spiders in from the Garden
When the Demons know your name

Milton Keynes UK
Ingram Content Group UK Ltd.
UKHW040925020924
447770UK00001B/110